Trevor Miller is a British born write
wright from Manchester, England.

Mirror joked that he "is hailed by some as the voice of a generation." Since 1993 Miller has lived in Los Angeles working on screenplays and films with a diverse roster of actors including Sylvester Stallone, Billy Bob Thornton and Cara Delevingne. His directorial debut, *Riot On Redchurch Street* starring Sam Hazeldine, Jesse Birdsall and Alysson Paradis, premiered at The East London film Festival in 2012, where *Time Out* called it "gritty and epic".

Currently, Trevor Miller lives in East Hollywood and is writing/producing a number of landmark film and TV properties under his Charley Varrick production banner. Like Fight Club – right now, he can't talk about his show entitled *Lifeline*.

First published in the UK by Avernus Creative Media in 1989
This edition published by Velocity Press in 2021
velocitypress.uk

Cover design
Sophie Hardwicke
sophiehardwicke.com
Based on original concepts by Martin Jackson (The Hugo Organization)
and designs by Tony Cooper

Typesetting
Paul Baillie-Lane
pblpublishing.co.uk

ISBN: 9781913231095

TREVOR MILLER

FOREWORD

First published in 1989, just after the so-called Second Summer Of Love, *Trip City* was the first acid house novel. Other dance-floor-driven literature would follow as the 90s progressed, in the rush and aftermath of the euphoria that greeted the initial rave revolution. There was the brilliant gritty writing of randy Scottish radge Irvine Welsh, of course, and the tripped-out otherworldliness of Manchester's Jeff Noon. *Disco Biscuits*, the mid-90s collection of short stories collated by Sarah Champion, brought together the aforementioned, alongside the likes of Alan Warner, Nicholas Blincoe and Martin Millar. But Trevor Miller's Trip City was the first – the original disco text.

Trip City wasn't the first novel to feature nightclubs – by any stretch. Like most 'chemical generation' fiction writing that followed, it isn't specifically about nightclubs but rather uses them as a cultural signpost, a backdrop in places. Without giving too much away, The Tower in the book is clearly based on The Limelight, the pivotal central London emporium that was literally a church for some West End clubbing connoisseurs – before such establishments were pushed more towards the margins of cities. Round the corner from The Limelight on Shaftesbury Avenue and dipping into Soho, Wardour Street was where the Wag Club was, a slightly trendier, more boutique joint. Mambo in *Trip City* is clearly based on The Wag. Clubs such as these were pretty vibrant before acid house hit London – after ecstasy culture took over, they were off the chain.

Like the acid house photos by Dave Swindells, the music of Renegade Soundwave or Ultramagnetic MCs, and the irreverent vitality of the Boys Own fanzine, *Trip City* is important because it was there at the start. It was marking fresh snow, carving a murky neon future, blazing a trail for the segment of countercultural, post-acid house literary writing that would follow. With its plentiful London references, it self-evidently came from the keyboard of someone who'd lived the life – even though Trevor was from Manchester originally. Wherever you were for your acid house honeymoon mattered.

As Trevor says to music writer Simon Morrison in the academic book *Dancefloor-Driven Literature*: "You can't have been in and around as many discos as I was and not have it seep into you. It's like cigarette smoke, you know. I think when you go to fantastic discos that's what happens. It infects you. It gets on your clothes."

Like artists, street-real novelists write to the beat of the times. Reflecting. Extrapolating. Just as some of the 1960s beat writers emulated the musical rhythms of the era – Kerouac supposedly wrote *On The Road* to the rhythm of bebop jazz, for instance – so acid house writers would be influenced by the sounds of the dancefloor, in their myriad variations. Trevor's were clearly not all exultant lift-me-up house classics – the darker underbelly gets a good runout.

Books are generally read to a soundtrack of the reader's choice, if anything, but Trip City came with a five-track cassette tape of original material by A Guy Called Gerald, the amazing acid house pioneer (of *Voodoo Ray* fame) who went on to have such a big influence on the formation of drum & bass too. This was another first, setting a precedent for other books to come presented with attached music, such as Simon Reynolds' peerless late 90s rave snapshot *Energy Flash* and even dance music magazines as they flourished in the 1990s and beyond. A covermount CD, to contextualise what the hell those music writers were rabbiting on about, was clearly intended to counteract the old 'dancing about architecture' quote.

Written from inside a rave bubble, *Trip City* is pulp fiction – its short sentences defying most literary traditions. Writing about rave would alter music journalism, too, with some writers reviewing in a more participatory, almost gonzo way rather than passively watching and reporting on a static spectacle; ripping off – sampling – track titles or lyrical motifs for article headings, and so on. It's symbiotic.

Trip City is a cultural artefact but still stands up today. You've no need for any special FX. Enjoy the trip.

Carl Loben

TRIP CITY STATE OF MIND 2021

This is supposed to be an essay – an introduction to how a novel came about.

I think it is expected that I write about Acid House. London nightclubs. '88 and '89. Or how ecstasy changed everything. What a revelation it was.

All of that is true. I lived ALL the nights I wrote about, in one way another. Did the coke, the acid, the speed, the K and the MDMA. There was The Wag, Gold, Sullivan's, Westworld, Hedonism, Delirium, Method Air, Solaris, Cafe De Paris, Cooz, Zap, Legends, MFI, Future, Spectrum, Sunrise, RIP, Worship Street, Clink, The Brain, Love Ranch, Merry England and Limelight. Too many others to mention.

That's the tale I was telling in 1989. But 30 plus years later – it's a different world, and my world view has changed. I hope I am kinder now. I hope I have evolved. And maybe the transcendental meditation I practice – thanks to the David Lynch Graduate School of Cinematic Arts – has connected me to an ancient unified field of understanding. And it is IMPORTANT for me to understand. Or at least to find meaning in the stories, now – rather than just telling them. And the adventure that became Trip City is very much my own adventure. At least both things are connected, if not interwoven.

I can only tell this part of my story because a number of the principal characters have been gone for a while now. Nearly nine years for my brother Bernard. Mum a year after that. Dad the following year. They buried Bernard on my birthday. It didn't seem so bad at the time. Still, as the years have gone by, it feels stranger. Almost like I am a someone or something Dickensian.

My earliest memories are of vinyl records. Super-8 film. Summers spent in my father's Rocksteady and Bluebeat record shop. It was on Great Western Street, in Moss Side. Similar to Brixton's Frontline or 110th Street in Harlem. And I remember the Super-8 film because my brother, Bernard, had a camera. He would make films with me as a 'magician' or riding a bike. Stop-frame animated. Then my dad's pal, Cyril Esner, got Bernard a VHS VCR. He became obsessed with recording movies off the telly. Lots of sci-fi. The Omega Man. Soylent Green. Logan's Run. Also, Stardust with David Essex.

I don't recall how or when Bernard got sick, but everything derailed because he did. And in those days, visiting an NHS children's hospital felt off-world. Strangely frightening as if something created by Tim Burton. Lots of sick kids. Deformed kids. Abused kids. And mum would drag me round to visit Bernard in the hospital so many times it became a chilling blur. I always wondered why she couldn't spare me these Hannibal Lecter horrors. I guess she just didn't know how.

In some ways – Trip City begins because I wanted to escape mum, dad and Bernard. And in other ways, the legacy of Trip City (or at least me still being able to write) only continues because of things I learned from them. Even if that meant leaving them behind or losing them.

Telling stories started out as a daydream. I was about 11-years-old, in Firswood. In earshot of Old Trafford, Manchester United's stadium. By 1976, Bernard had been diagnosed with colitis, then Crohn's disease. But after many abortive surgeries, two comas and a particularly fractured childhood – Bernard went quite mad. Bipolar disorder. Then schizophrenia. Then other inconclusive emotional maladies. They would medicate him until the day he died – aged 54. I lived in that shadow for a long time.

Still, back to that daydream and being 11-years-old. I am sitting on my bed, looking out of the window, across the back garden and other houses beyond. The ageing window frame is rotted out. And I'm digging at it with the point of a compass. With every splinter of wood I dig from that window frame, I am focussing on escape. Thinking about how to get away from mum's tears. Bernie's madness. Dad's good-natured but quiet denial of how f#@ked-up it all was.

It took five years for me to find Saturday nights at Berlin – a nightclub on King Street, behind Kendal Milne's department store. By then, I was sneaking dad's whiskey and refilling the bottle with cold tea. I would say I was staying at my highschool friend Steven Edward's house – but head into town on the bus with my 'club clothes' hidden under a raincoat. Decades later, I realised that the kid with the flat-top I saw on the bus, who worked as 'Pot Man' in the club, was actually Ian Brown from The Stone Roses.

Saturday night at Berlin was called Private Road. They would play goth, indie and industrial – everything from the Velvet Underground through to The Cramps. I remember being drunk from barley wine in the pub but drinking canned Breaker malt liquor in the club. Even though I barely knew anyone inside the shadowy environs of 38 King Street – THIS felt like home. And those Saturday nights would lead me to Katherine and her twin sister who worked the coat-check. Those two befriended me and introduced me to the likes of Gino and Nasty – who took me to The Hacienda and Trevor Johnson, Nathan McGough and Wade Tolera – amongst others.

Around that time, Trevor Johnson was designing record covers for Factory. Nathan managed a jazz-combo called Swamp Children, who became Kalima. Wade Tolera was a male model.

We had some amazing times around venues like Cloud 9, Corbieres Wine Cavern and, of course, the 'Hac'. It was the first time I took acid. The first time I saw The Smiths play. And I remember watching Madonna perform Holiday, three feet away, for a segment on The Tube.

By the time I went to college in London, alcohol and drugs were something I used as much for maintenance as liberation. It wasn't a thing people talked about – especially me – and I often wondered if I was going to end-up equally as insane as my brother. Then again, I was studying writing at college – so I had an outlet, of sorts.

At first, London felt quite lonely. Quite isolating. The college building was only a few blocks from Oxford Circus. But it was in Soho I found a second home. Old Compton Street. Bar Italia, The Coach & Horses. For me, this was *still* the Soho of Colin MacInnes. His novels like Absolute Beginners or Mr Love & Justice. And in some ways, the venues, decor and shadowy characters hadn't changed. I would see Jeffrey Bernard drinking in The Coach. Caught a glimpse of Francis Bacon at The Colony Room. And occasionally spotted John Mortimer in The French House.

I guess Soho only REALLY became Soho for me after a particularly strange visit to Camden Market on a Sunday afternoon, late in 1984. Trevor Johnson was in town from Manchester. I'm not sure if it was for work or fun, but we ended up drinking with a group of his cronies from the market.

Trevor's guys were all loosely connected by Manchester, Liverpool or Northern Soul. There was Rick Stonell, aka Rick The Barber, because he had a barbershop in both Camden and Kensington Market. Paul Caren, aka Brookside, because he was from Liverpool and talked like the TV series. And I think a guy known as Yogi who worked in Herbert Johnson's, the hatters on Bond Street. Although I was never really told why Yogi had that nickname, beyond some vague Yogi Bear reference. And these guys were all five or six years older than me – which seemed a big difference back then.

Over the ensuing weeks, I went to Camden or Ken Market to hang out with Rick The Barber. Somehow it was Paul 'Brookside' who decided he would show me the ropes and around town. His version of it. Paul sold vintage menswear in the basement of Ken Market – but was famous for his wry wit and penchant for the two-for-one screwdrivers sold at happy hour in the bar around the corner. We would get drunk there on midweek afternoons, and Brookside would introduce me to various Northern Soul luminaries – some of whom I would buy amphetamine sulphate off to sell-on to my college pals.

My start in London clubs began in early '85 when Wiz (who would go on to direct music videos for Massive Attack and Flowered Up) asked me to emcee at a psychedelic night he was DJing in Deptford. It was in an old church crypt. The night simply being called The Crypt. Wiz and his gang (mostly from Radlett) were all riding on the mod/psychedelic revival that was sweeping across London. Scott Crolla's paisley menswear had become quite the thing, and Dr & The Medics even had a chart hit with a reworking of Hawkwind's Silver Machine.

On an unusually warm night, fueled by a surfeit of speed and blotter acid, emcee Mr. Love was born. Or at least that's what I called myself while introducing records in The Crypt as Wiz DJed them. I took the name from the Colin MacInnes novel – despite the fact Mr. Love, as depicted, had been a Soho pimp. Anyway, I just remember wearing a long wig, shades and a paisley coat I bought in some junk shop. Still, the drugs and the carnage were a taste of nights to come. Many years later, Mr. Love would emcee 'Night of a 1000 DJs' at The Limelight – which was basically a DJ Gong show... And I vaguely recall DJ Harvey (from Tonka) chasing me around the club wanting to kill me – as I had gonged him off, after only ten bars of his first record.

Mr. Love's first DJ appearances would come in Mornington Crescent later that year, in the summer of '85. Brookside had invited me and Steve King down to a Saturday night party at Barry Sullivan's wine bar opposite the old Camden Palace. It was a little boutique jewel-box of a venue with a bright upstairs and dimly lit basement, including a small dance-floor for DJs.

Saturday night at Sullivan's was called The Boiler – hosted by Dece (from My Silent War, an early Hull punk band) and Mark Wigan from i-D Magazine. And on that first night, the DJs were a particularly eclectic bunch. The most memorable alum were Baz Riley and Craig Brick playing Motown and Northern Soul. Baz was a legendary mentalist. Unique for his glass eye and self-destructive antics. Craig was the brother of Chris Brick, who had Demob in Soho. The Boiler was also where I first met Sean McLusky, with whom I would collaborate over almost three decades. But back to...

That very first night was tremendous speed-driven fun in the basement. So I asked Dece and Wigan if I could play records in the club the following week. That was how it started. And from playing records at The Boiler – next I was making videos of hair fashion shows for Ken Market cutters – Vision Industries (Dave Henley & Martin Nolan) at The Wag. I remember Chris Sullivan asking me if we could install a video set-up permanently – so he might document the various live shows and happenings. That did not happen.

It is important to consider that before the Second Summer of Love, the music had given rise to various youth culture tribes. And each tribe with its own signature sound, fashion and attitude.

Regularly at The Wag and other venues, on any given mid-week or weekend, I may have attended Rare Groove nights with Norman Jay. Acid Jazz nights with Eddie Pillar. Northern Soul at the 100 Club. Funk nights like Shake & Fingerpop, Hip Hop nights with Paul Guntrip, the Watson Brothers and Dave Dorell.

House, then Acid House and 'E' changed all that. It galvanised disparate groups of revellers into one cross-cultural 'loved-up' movement or moment.

1988 was a tsunami of drugs, alcohol and music for me. House Music. House Music all night long – drifting into maniacal calls of "acieeeed."

Shoom was never really my bag, BUT I went to ALL the others – squeaking-by by living in a squat. Earning money off occasional petty crime. Or emcee spots. Or making flyers for various promoters. Finally, I went to the O'Neill surf-wear showroom on Great Portland Street and bought an electric blue tracksuit with a day-glo motif. The tracksuit was a factory sample – so nobody else on this scene had anything like it. PLUS, I had the haircut, the beard and a steady supply of pills from a friend or acquaintance or some of the rough-neck dealers. They knew that I did the flyers, so they would probably get guest-list off me, somewhere. Maybe?

There was Hedonism on Hangar Lane. Future at the Sanctuary. Trip at The Astoria. Clink Street, south of the river. And dozens upon dozens of one-offs like Gold, Juice Box and Millennium at Cinatras. Plus, if you had a vehicle and were up for travelling – there were various events in a field or aircraft hangars like Burn It Up at Sunrise. And for the more urbane or gritty – RIP were throwing warehouse parties across the city.

Suddenly everybody knew the same tunes. Everybody had pills. And fellas like me, who fancied themselves as sophisticated club types, found themselves dancing all night with loved-up football villains who were now on the same team.

In a heart-beat, minds were expanded. Consciousness touched beyond the beyond. And adventurers like myself were pushing the boundaries. Taking every pill or powder or organic substance I could get my hands on. And there was a proliferation of designer drugs. Ice. Cake. Glass. The notorious pill known as M25 (named after the ring road). I would often talk with guys like Wildcat Wil about doing peyote. DMT or ayahuasca. But nobody had anything remotely like that. So for me, multiple pills and booze would have to do.

In the midst of this madness, I am appearing in a friend's experimental art movie for a few free dinners and some cab fares. They have loaned me this very expensive Jean Paul Gaultier suit for the film. Naturally, I was wearing it around town. The last thing I expected that night in a Fitzrovia pub was to run into Frank Hatherley. Frank was one of my old college teachers. Well, he saw the suit, thought Miller's hit the big time and offered to buy me a beer. Bingo!

Frank explained that he had set-up Avernus Creative Media – a boutique publishing imprint with his pal – an old-time sci-fi author called Brian Aldiss. As yet, I barely knew Brian's legend – beyond the fact it was legendary. And who'd believe at that point that Brian would become a fan of MINE and at some point introduce me to his inner circle, or the likes of Kurt Vonnegut, himself?

Anyway, as I regaled Frank with clubland stories of drugs, excess and Acid House – he chimed in to say "this might make a good short story for a fiction anthology that Brian and I will be putting together."

It struck me right then. A eureka moment. Boom! I mean, why be a small part of a bigger book when you could just be the whole book?

And that's when it crystallised. Almost fully formed. Like the end of The Usual Suspects. When Chazz Palminteri adds up all the pieces. All the parts of the story. Understanding in a micro-sending that Verbal Kint is in fact, Keyser Söze...

Maybe the drugs helped. But – on the fly – I assembled all the concepts into one BIG concept. A man on the run – like me, running away from mum, dad and Bernard. A life in all the clubs. Doing the doors and the flyers and promoting as a part-time emcee. It'd be Colin MacInnes. But it'd be Acid House.

But it'd be better than MacInnes with elements of Walter Tevis. The Man Who Fell to Earth. And London gangsters. But more like Fast Eddie Felson. And a good guy like Richard Hannay in The 39 Steps. But the sci-fi twist – like Omega Man. Soylent Green. Something green. Green crystals. A designer drug. A green designer drug. My drug. Green like dollar bills. Worse than ecstasy or MDMA or acid or M25. All wrapped up in a visionary experience. An endless trip, like Carlos Casteneda. Jodorowsky. David Lynch. The Holy Mountain.

I think Frank was blown away – or maybe he just thought I was mental. But he thought it actually sounded like a novel and he took a punt. If I could write up a couple of chapters of my 'epic poem' – Frank would present them to Brian – see if he might bite.

Somehow I blagged a manual typewriter. Spent bits of the weekend and Monday in the front room of my squat typing-up what became the first two chapters of Trip City. And I filled it with all my angst and pain. Thoughts just came. Words. Ideas. Characters. Little punctuation. A style. But one central idea – THIS might be the real escape I'd been dreaming of. And, truth be told, by then I was a raging alcoholic and pill head. Sure, I kept it quiet – mostly chain-smoked when I wasn't drunk or high – but it felt like my issues gave the story weight. Gravity.

On Tuesday, I went into the West End and dropped off the few dozen pages I'd typed up at Frank's office. In less than a week, Frank and Brian offered me a publishing deal to write the rest of the novel. A novel that I would call Trip City.

Rarely in life do we find a moment where all our problems and mistakes make sense. But, at the end of that summer, writing gave me purpose. I wrote in short sentences. It's how I thought. How I still think. Sometimes. But the seven weeks it took to write Trip City were also the first seven weeks I had been sober. Or off drugs. I want to tell you that writing connected the dots – kept me sober. Afraid not. But it took me 30 years to realise that the drugs and alcohol abuse was driven by my issues – my real-life family problems. Not Acid House. Not because I never really ended up where I wanted to be.

From that day on, I never took drugs or drink when I was writing. Did it a lot of other times – but not at the page or when I'm at the screen. That was how it was then. It's still the same now. And if you are interested – the drug scenes in Trip City were ALL written completely sober. Not to say that I wasn't out of my mind when I experienced the MDMA or acid madness in the clubs. Just not when I was writing about it.

So it's 2021, and what have we learned in over three decades? Or – what have I learned, more precisely?

Well, I buried my family and some of my friends. I had a bit of a career as a writer and filmmaker – but never quite sufficient to really call myself a success. There has been a global pandemic – horrifically handled by some world leaders. And I have been in my modest apartment in Los Angeles, barely going outside for a year. The corporations took over – some might say. The internet was weaponised to bring you Brexit and Donald Trump. And as we speak, some people are saying vaccines will put nano-robots in your DNA, or that devastating fires in California were actually created by Jewish Space Lasers – no less... Sounds like a book by Jon Ronson, but more so to me, it sounds like Trip City come to life. Should I say: Trip City come to life with a less interesting soundtrack.

I am proud of this book and soundtrack. Do they have immense stature? I'm not sure. But their very existence makes me smile. And I hope as you read or listen – you might find a little hope. Or consider the fact that sometimes the good guys – well, they may sort-of win, in the end. A Hollywood ending? No. But sort-of a win. Absolutely. At least a notion that escape and a better day IS truly possible. At least it was and IS for me.

The lesson? Be kinder. Be a dreamer – because even thirty years on – magic still feels conceivable to me. Play those old records. Dance around your living room. Reach out to those friends far and near – and uplift them with an affectionate word. Remind them of your shining moments together. Those nights in the club – when you STILL had everything to play for. And don't forget to say that you're sorry – even if you're just saying sorry for the angst or arrogance that kept you going through some tough times. Maybe that's just me? Maybe that's the transcendental meditation? Anyway...

If you've read this far, I salute you. If you go on to read Trip City – I applaud and thank you for wanting to connect to those halcyon days...

Just remember that being human is ALWAYS our finest hour. One love.

Trevor Miller
Los Angeles, March 2, 2021

ACKNOWLEDGEMENTS

There are a few people who have been there since the beginning of this journey and others who climbed aboard along the way. These are the brave souls who had the courage and tenacity to stick with me through the rough and the smooth. Their names need to be mentioned and celebrated, and I want to thank them, personally:

Rick 'The Barber' Stonell and Paul 'Brookside' Caren – gone but never forgotten
Karl Augustus Hunter – MIA
Steve Keeney, Fabian Friedland & Maurice Bernstein
Jessica Montanez Prince and David Seagull
Dr Disco Simon Morrison, Sarah Champion, Nicholas Blincoe and Louder Than Words
Martin Jackson, Tony Cooper and The Hugo Organization
Nadia Gabbie
Harry 'The Dog' Bridgen
Simon Lovejoy Fisher
Carl Loben and DJ Magazine
Frank Hatherley and his wonderful daughters
A Guy Called Gerald and his crew
Matt Holt and Wayne Kelly
Sean McLusky, Katie and The Brain Club Massive
James White
Michael Holden
Colin Steven and Velocity Press
Mum, Dad and Bernard
And, of course, Daniella

CHAPTER ONE

It was a blue Monday. Grey light split the blinds. Traversed the wooden floor. Then it hit the bed. Cold and piercing and harsh. There was no gentleness left.

It swathed Valentine's half-naked body. Picked out stains on his shirt. Painted the pistol. Matt black.

There were few signs of the struggle.

Bitten fingers grasped the pillow. Saliva dribbled from his mouth. Then Valentine woke up.

He felt cold. Muscular pain gripped his spine. There was the rumble of a tube train.

Valentine stood up. He rubbed his eyes. Things felt no different.

The classy studio still seemed elegant as a sushi restaurant. Black lacquer and sumi painting.

His boxer shorts were sticky. Yesterday's memories were vague.

He tried to think clearly. Notions were jumbled. Each pace stiffer than the last. He walked towards the window. Prised the louvre with his fingers. The City's machinery ticked over. People going to work. Cars jammed onto the bridge. Only the dock basin was silent.

He remembered the girl. Face down on the bed. Virginia was good at sex. He was confused. Their violent confrontation made no sense. Their plan would never seem real. But he had woken up alone. She was gone. And the game had begun.

A half-smoked cigarette poked from the ashtray. The filter was tarnished with lipstick. Red. He turned on the TV set. Picked up the dimp. He was dying for a smoke, craving for a whiff of sanity. The bookmatch flared. The tip was perfumed. He remembered how she tasted.

The newscaster's tie was purple. He was bald. "Good morning, Britain."

A cargo ship had sunk in the Channel. Containers were washing ashore. Toxic waste. Washing up on Brighton Beach. They were cordoning off the area, protecting the nudists. Greenpeace had been alerted. The first container had been full of biscuits.

Valentine tried to switch off. Another drug scandal from the Olympics. Everyone was doing it. Going for gold. Valentine crunched out the cigarette on a silver ashtray. Green flashed through his head. It was anger. It was envy. It was something else.

He bent down to slip on his shoes. There were no socks. He pulled on the left. Lurched for the right. A blister bulged from his right foot. Then he saw the gun.

Valentine slumped into a chair. He held his breath. Grinding reality began again. Unclean. Uncaring. Valentine had to stop the machine. That was all that was left.

The Luger grip chilled his palm. He wanted to piss.

He slid out the magazine. One bullet was missing. There was still enough.

The clock on the screen was ticking over. Later than he expected. It all had to be finished by 12.30. Valentine slapped the clip shut.

He put on his jacket. Stepped awkwardly into his trousers. The pistol bulged in his pocket. He checked the address. The yellow security pass. One final tarnished paper wrap. What if they caught him? Nobody would believe.

He shivered. Buttoned up his jacket. There was a tune in his head. 'High Noon'? No. It was the Shake n' Vac commercial.

Powder fluttering from the carton. On the carpet. Useless. He turned off the set.

Valentine had enough for a cab. Six pound coins and some silver. He was not sure how far it would take him. There was never enough.

He padded to the door. One last look. This could have been everything. The time. The place. It was all wrong now. Meaningless.

There was no love. No hate. Only a sense of loss.

He tried to rewrite the end. But there was no other way. Valentine closed the door.

He walked across the grey courtyard. Down Jamaica Road towards London Bridge. Blue light painted the warehouses. He could have thrown a great party here.

Tooley Street was busy. The shopping Galleria looked like a greenhouse. Plants in the atrium were triffids, spitting poison at passers-by, gobbling up accountants like grey Twiglets. He shook his head.

Southwark Cathedral dripped birdshit.

He stepped onto the road, almost wanting to be run over. A dispatch rider jockeyed past. The taxi wheels wailed. Juddered. A foot slammed on the brake. The driver grimaced. Stopped. The bonnet was two feet from Valentine. He sidestepped, then climbed inside. "Paddington Station." There was no bravado in his voice. No boldness in his action. He was a frightened little man.

His eyes fixed firmly on the meter. He wrestled the coins from his pocket. Played with the change. There had to be enough. Time seemed to be floating. Life had become the end of a cab ride.

Valentine was oblivious of the journey. He was in a large black goldfish bowl. London landmarks looked in at him. Along the Embankment. Grey battleships. Forgotten tarnished breeze-blocks. Inns of Court like the set of The Prisoner.

The meter ticked over. Nearly four quid. Valentine slipped lower in the seat. He was losing concentration. He felt sick. The numbers were becoming a blur.

The cabbie glanced back in the mirror. He reassured himself. This fare was in no state to do a 'runner'. He turned into Euston Road.

Valentine tried to find the sun. It was behind thick cloud. His reflection bounced from the glass. He pushed the hair from his eyes. It plastered against his forehead. The flesh was lined. Eyes black and empty. A bump rattled the gun. He clasped his lapels shut. No-one must see.

They were on the Westway. The meter blinked six quid. Cars skimmed over the flyover.

"Here." Valentine's voice was shaky.

The driver looked incredulous. "Not on the dual carriageway, chief."

Six pounds twenty. "Here!" Valentine insisted. The driver veered into Warwick Avenue. He pulled up at the lights, leant on the clutch.

Valentine fumbled with his change. There was not enough for a tip. He placed it all in the driver's hand. Shrugged his shoulders. Felt no shame.

He stumbled onto the pavement, slammed the door. The lights changed. Everyone moved on. The cab shot away. He was on his own again. The suit was small protection against the cold.

He approached the depot. Mottled by graffiti. All West London steamer gangs he had never heard of. One of the barn doors gaped open. The shadows mutated into black sodden faces. A taut stomach below a cropped top. She was from the plastic population.

The 'Friday Nite Funksters' had thrown parties here. A large red skull was plastered across a pillar. It looked angry.

A wooden sign lay under girders. 'FUNKTION THIS WAY'. Valentine stepped over it. He faltered on the large truck tyres.

The round building was empty. It smelled of stale sex.

Two dead pigeons had been crushed. Smashed under the wheels. Fly and Niki?

The party had moved on. Valentine roamed through the carnage. Still.

He climbed the wall and dropped into the shunting yard. It had been laid to waste. Large mounds of hardcore flanked him. The developer's vans were empty. Gypsies were moving in. Mongrel dogs were running wild. He could hear a baby crying. Maybe just in his head.

The blister began to hurt. His reject loafers splayed. Mud spattered the bare ankles. A train hurtled by. It didn't seem real. Then it was gone.

He neared the arches. He would soon be in Paddington, surroundings he could comprehend. The mutating decay was frightening. The off-worldness shook his motives. There was always the gun.

Through the arches and up the concourse Valentine passed. Brickwork shook like an earthquake. It was not happening. The buildings were solid. He focused on the pavement. The sky blackened.

He stopped to look in a shop window. Its sign boasted designer porn. 'SNUFF MOVIES, ON REQUEST'. He felt sick. There was a picture of a hand being crushed. Blood spurted out. He lit another filter. The nude men and women looked on. He coughed heartily.

He progressed up Paddington Street. Nobody knew him. He knew nobody. He cowered past two uniformed officers. As he got nearer to Praed Street the sinews tensed in his neck. He ached.

Valentine saw his destination in the distance. It stood out above the rest. The building was tall and transatlantic. Three shiny black towers. The windows were all black mirror-glass. Stillness surrounded it.

The towers bore down on him, each one bigger than the other. They encroached on his space. The more he tried to relax the more fear tore at him. He wanted the way out. This was the only way.

He progressed up the steps. He swung through the revolving door and paused in the foyer. He clutched at his palmed security pass. A guard approached him. He mumbled "Clearance A" and held up the yellow card. The guard was still. His glare remained fixed.

Valentine said it again. He had to get through. If he grew any tenser he would snap. The guard sidestepped. Valentine walked on.

He pressed the lift call and waited. It had been too easy. Something was wrong. The guard was probably raising the alarm. Any minute now, he would be surrounded. He wished the lift would hurry. Why was it taking so long? They may have turned it off. The door opened. He strode in and it shut behind him.

His head swam. It was a mixture of fear and the kind of tiredness that comes from lack of money or peace of mind. Madness.

Valentine's chest tightened as the lift door slid open. He squared up and walked through the door with spiralling apprehensions. The corridors were imposing, all black shellac and pure marble. The pillars strained under basalt headpieces. Everywhere shone and stank of polish.

He looked around and swallowed. His throat dried. Cigarette, must have one. No. His head hurt. Thoughts jangled about in emptiness. Confident movement was difficult. Inches seemed like yards, yards like miles, miles from home.

They had him. Gobbled up and spat out, but nevertheless, they had him. A piece of meat. He followed the signposts.

The light strained his eyes. He tried to rehearse his speech, with no memory. He tried to feel sad. He tried to cry. But nothing. Blankness. Passers-by ignored him.

He approached the door and stood still, looking at the shadow. His shadow. No Adonis. No wit. Only Valentine. He strained a smile. Looking into the woodgrain he lifted his head and knocked. Twice.

The door registered two dull thuds. Ebony. Expensive.

There was silence. Perhaps no-one was in. Good. Five seconds, ten seconds, fifteen seconds. A low authoritative voice rippled the calm. "Come".

Valentine paused, turned the handle and entered.

The office layout pushed him back. It was power. The kind of confident calm that puts whole nations through the mill. The black desk was at least fifteen feet across, lit only by an Italian cantilever table lamp. The wall behind the desk was glass. The London skyline shone beyond all this black magnificence.

Richard Domaine surveyed the situation. He was in control. Like a game of chess. He threw a knowing glance at Valentine.

Valentine was in no position to throw it back. His mind raced ahead. He could not go through with it. It would be easier to just walk away. No. There was no turning back. He closed the door behind him.

Valentine walked and sat down. The sumptuous black leather clung to him. He tried to relax. It was impossible. He was sitting in front of God. This was not the time for an act. It had to be real. There was nothing else it could be.

Domaine pushed over a gilt cigarette box to the corner of the table. He flicked the lid open. "Smoke?" Valentine shook his head. He was desperate for one but he didn't want to give a corner. Domaine pushed the box closer. "It's only a smoke." He smiled.

Casually Domaine reached over and took one white filter tip. He lit up and drew a long breath. Smoke cascaded from his lips. He stood up, walked to the window and surveyed the vista. There was something sexual about his relaxed way.

"All of this is mine." He knew exactly how it was. No illusion. He was not cold, just disinterested. Domaine knew everybody's price.

Valentine was getting sucked in. His only weapon, apart from the snug gun, was his tension, his illogical thought. Domaine's tranquility almost engulfed him. He would have to make a move. Feverishly he took a cigarette. Lighting it with a book match from his top pocket, he slammed the gilt box shut.

Domaine did not recoil. He blew a smoke ring. "Don't mind if I call you Valentine?"

Valentine winced as Domaine said his name. If he knew who he was, he knew why he was there. Then how could he be so relaxed? Count to ten then begin. Eight, nine, ten.

Valentine fumbled with his mock-croc wallet and withdrew a passport picture. He placed it on the desk. Domaine padded over and sat down. Lifting the photograph, he shook his head. "Pretty girl." He looked closer. He rested his head on his interlocked fingers. "Not for sale, I presume."

Valentine's hands tensed. The more annoyed he got, the more he could take control.

Domaine asked if he liked women. Valentine said she was dead. Visions of her broken body jarred him. He tried to explain. The crushed limbs. The scarred face. The splayed frame, lifeless like a rag doll.

Domaine tried to align the picture to Valentine's words. It did not fit. Her slightly oriental eyes shone out of the photograph. Valentine's eyes burned. Domaine looked through both of them. "Where do I come in?"

Valentine played his ace. He reached into his pocket and took out the paper wrap. He opened it. Hands trembling, he shook the contents onto the black desk.

The green phosphorescent powder glinted under the light. The holy grail one last time. FX. The sweetener, the turkey at Christmas, the perk of all perks.

It was free. It was good, the best, like death.

Domaine knew. Valentine knew. The seller and the sold.

"Want some?" said Domaine and sat back.

CHAPTER TWO

Valentine strained. He pushed his flight bag in the rack. The zips bulged. He could barely reach. Coach travel was cheap and nasty. He slumped into the seat.

For the first time in months, he was scared. Anonymity had been easy. People he hardly knew. The welcoming arms of the 'North'.

He lit a cigarette. It made no difference.

The bus station was tiled brown, bathed in electric light. The cafe sign was smothered in grease. An Albert Tatlock dished up barm cakes. Perhaps they sent you barmy.

Valentine had no friends. He had left all that behind four years ago. Four years from London. All that remained was his invented name. And the debts of course.

It had been like the Wall Street Crash. Many got ruined that night, the last night of the Underground. Courtney got busted. Maybe Fly, too. Valentine wasn't sure. He hadn't stopped to ask. Just ran.

He had never wanted to go back. Until now.

Valentine reached for his carrier bag and the two cans of Super Tennent's, the last vice he could afford.

"Is that seat free?" The woman wore glasses. Valentine stood up. She squeezed by. Passed him the crinkly carrier bag. They both sat down. "Always like a window seat."

Valentine nodded. He was slightly embarrassed. The beer cans and the woman. Coaches were not too intimate, everyone facing the same way. He put the cans on the floor.

The coach swung out of the terminus ten minutes late. Valentine had no appointment to be late for.

Things were changing, even here. King Street looked like an Olympic Village. Dirty granite had been freshly sand-blasted. Showrooms full of radiophones. It was not a backwater anymore. Everyone was listening to Acid House. Doing fashion shows in Japan. It was definitely time to head South.

Valentine cracked open a can. The beer was too sweet. He never liked the medicine. Just its effect.

The book cover was half folded. Valentine could just make out the title. She was reading *On the Road*. It was appropriate. They were on a voyage of discovery. Boldly going where everyone else had gone before. Strange new worlds off Tottenham Court Road. Alien civilizations in Soho dives. Galaxies beyond the West One Nebula. Up Uranus.

What kind of traveller was this buxom woman? An outcast of the white slave trade? A lady of letters? Probably a student. Who else travelled by tacky coach?

She asked Valentine for a light. A Scottish accent. Gordon Jackson's daughter?

He lit his England's Glory. She inhaled. Then returned to her book.

Valentine supped more beer. He was bored. Nothing to read but the matchbox.

"Like the book?" he asked. The woman smiled. There was a long pause. She forced two antihistamines down her throat and placed the bottle in her pocket. "Just research."

Valentine didn't know what she was talking about. He didn't care. It was like pub talk. Chatting with the local loony. Smiling and nodding usually worked. At least it passed the time.

He offered a swig of beer. Strangely, she accepted. Valentine passed the can, bemused. Two big gulps. Definitely the local loony. Then it started. The preliminaries. Who was he? What did he do?

Valentine did not like questions, especially from strangers and wackos. This woman was both.

He wanted to tell her the truth. Say he had been a club promoter. One of the biggest in London. He had set up the *Underground*. Ran the most successful warehouse parties ever. But it was a long time back. Nobody remembered. Nobody believed him anymore. He was travelling by coach. Drinking in the afternoon. A has-been. It would be easier to lie.

He answered obtusely. Said he had done lots of things.

She would not let go. It was like twenty questions. Was he a student of philosophy? An art student? Valentine was indignant. A student? She was the student, not him.

One last try. What was his name?

Valentine took the ticket counterfoil from his pocket. Held it in front of her face. She read the block capitals. Raised an eyebrow. "Valentine."

He had to be an actor with a name like that. Think of Valentine Dyall. Billy Ray Valentine. But he wasn't.

She considered herself a good judge of character. This man was unclassifiable, like a cheap wine. Maybe he was on the dole. Maybe he was lying. Perhaps even both.

She looked out of the window, watched the road. She announced that she was a journalist. Valentine said "Oh".

The arrogant bastard. Her profession normally provoked some interest. He looked too old to be a dole boy. Maybe twenty-five or thirty, it was hard to tell. The denim looked very worn, perfectly matched with the stubbly beard.

He was more than well built. Fat.

Valentine ignored her roving glare. He grinned. It was his turn to play. He checked her rucksack. He looked at her shoes. They were DMs, probably from *Red or Dead* in Camden. She was wearing a Bomb the Bass T-shirt with a yellow smiley face. Valentine said she was a music journalist, either living or working in Camden, and her name was Anna. Then he finished the last of his can.

The woman looked sideways, puzzled, annoyed. How did he know? This knowledge seemed a violation, intrusive. She tried to convince herself they must have met before.

Valentine opened his second can. A well-bitten finger pointed at the rucksack. The woman looked down. Her luggage label had her name and address typewritten. A few backstage passes were plastered on the pocket.

Anna acknowledged his observation. Victory fired his ego. Another vice he had not forgotten. He started to tell her who he was, hoping to make 'running' sound like a quest. He said he had been travelling, trying to find himself.

It was not like that. He had been avoiding debts, retribution. Little spirituality was involved. Sure he had been wacko, but not from a troubled soul. Valentine had been a speed-freak. Coke as well, when he could afford it. Of course, he would not admit such transgressions to a stranger. Speed was unfashionable now.

Valentine drank more beer. He had once been a journalist. A writer. That sounded better. He squirmed a little, feeling like a compulsive liar. Anna was becoming more interested, animated. Writing would be common ground.

Neither really knew about writing. Valentine had had two articles published. Two in four years. He had applied for an editorial job, subbing short stories for a soft porn mag. He'd failed the interview.

For the rest of the time, he had signed on. Worked cash in hand. Shit jobs. DJ at tenth-rate clubs. MC at cabaret pubs. Bartender. Signwriter. Landscape gardener. Anything and nothing. He had hung out at student bars where the beer was cheap, the company gullible. Valentine had lived on past glories for years. Young guys were impressed. Girls fresh from home, blagged by stories about cocaine and kisses from popstars. Every reminiscence had become so convoluted. Valentine didn't want that anymore. No more running.

The conversation came to a halt. The air was full of bullshit.

"Where are you coming from?" Anna's words came slow. Valentine pursed his lips and tried not to laugh. It was one of those phrases, like 'go for it'. Modern. Incisive. Meaningless.

Valentine really wanted to make sense. He raised himself in the seat. Poised demonstratively, he said he moved ideas. Once he had sold dreams, entertainment in its purest form. Dreams could be real. Reality was only an adult dream.

Anna shook her head. "Bullshit."

Valentine shrugged it off. It was hard to be serious, especially here.

She was losing interest in him. He was ceasing to be different.

Anna said she needed 'the loo'. He got up. She pushed into the aisle.

Valentine felt a bit merrier. He had not told her anything. Not about himself. It was usually better this way. He pushed the empties under the seat. He was not sorry to see her go.

A head popped up and rested on the head restraint. The small girl was staring at Valentine. Her Afro hair was in braids. Valentine smiled, ran his hands through his hair. His slightly receding hair made him self-conscious, uneasy. The little girl pointed at him. It was alright. He liked children. "It's all standing up." Valentine saw his reflection in the window.

The stubble was black. A heavy growth. Eyes were heavily ringed. Anna was right. He looked too old to be a dole boy. Still only twenty-four. Valentine was always looking at his reflection. Perhaps because the ageing processes were working overtime. More likely because of his unshakable vanity.

He pushed his wavy hair flat and turned to talk to the child. But she had disappeared. Back watching with mother.

The bus was in midflight. They had been travelling for an hour, maybe more. There was no way of telling. Valentine had no watch.

He glanced at the road signs. Tried to gauge the distance. Each Little Chef made London feel closer.

Thoughts of reprisals filled his head. Miki, the girlfriend he had run out on. Courtney, his stitched-up partner. All the favours that people would have forgotten. What if nobody remembered? What if they all snubbed him?

In '84 the Metropolitan Police busted most of the Warehouse crews. Valentine insisted they should carry on. It was a fatal mistake. Everyone sank the last of their time and money. That amount of gear was a dealing offence. Valentine could have warned them. Should have warned them. There was no time. So he ran. Into the station. Onto the train. Back where he came from.

Of course, the money ran out. He thought he could never go back.

But here he was.

Sunlight was breaking through the cloud, bright and blinding. It strained his eyes. He put on his pilot glasses, gilt-edged Ray-Bans. They were bent, but the only expensive souvenir left.

His rakish pose was short-lived. The stewardess told him to draw the curtains. He took off his glasses, pulled the orange fabric. The speakers crackled. Something about the TV screen distracting other drivers. The sound was distorted. He peered at the fourteen-inch monitor.

Anna tapped his shoulder. He slid his knees across. She edged past, then sat down. She had been a long time. Probably talking to someone else.

A filled barm cake sat in her palm, encased in clingfilm. Valentine had no money for 'luxuries'. It was ham salad, at least something pink and curly. "Cordon Bleu?"

She snorted. Just looked at him. Anna began to unpeel the film. Then the film began.

A roll of drums. A horny fanfare. It was Wrekka, a F production. An ad agency had bought a film company. The content of their pictures was irrelevant. Each feature-length commercial starred Ranee Hubbly; an American footballer turned porn star turned serious actor. He was working-class and right-wing, a winning formula for the late-80s. The story began to unfold.

In the first five minutes Wrekka killed thirty Vietcong. Blood poured like rain. Disembowelled corpses on bayonets. The violence was bizarre. So were the product placements. This company made films to sell consumer disposables. Wrekka dressed in Lacoste, drove a Ferrari and smoked forty Marlboro a day. Every street punk guzzled Coca Cola. The Vietnamese general took the Pepsi challenge, then Wrekka blew his head off. The small child in the seat ahead squealed, not with fear but delight. Justice had been done.

By the end, Charlie Wrekkowski had used a million dollars worth of consumer product. Difficult on an army pension. Sex and violence were incidental. What mattered was shifting units. 'Underline selling' affected everyone. Valentine thought he would sell his soul for the Ferrari. Who wouldn't? He lit a cigarette.

Anna had fallen asleep, curled up, hands still clutching the book. It was safe to open the curtain now. Valentine dragged the drape. Yellow light washed the seats, painted her face. She was not bad looking. Needed a decent haircut.

Valentine was bored again. He clawed at his teeth. Looked up and down the aisle. Watched the fields passing.

Then he was asleep. Valentine had strange dreams. Running. Always running. Getting nowhere. Always further to run.

When Valentine woke up he was sweating. The seat was very uncomfortable. The stewardess was offering 'fresh' sandwiches, curly and stale. He shook his head. Besides, he could not spare the cash.

Valentine lit another cigarette. He smoked habitually, especially when travelling. Usually out of boredom. He watched the smoke curl. They had travelled a fair distance.

Passing cars seemed more executively styled. Londoners on the coach started speaking cockney.

A familiar voice boomed from the speakers. The stewardess had switched on the sound of the city, 'Mainline' London Radio. A smoochie soul sound for redundant soul boys. Barry Whitman broadcasting live. "You know it makes sense." Barry had been fired by the network. Too many tales in The Sun. But the ILR primates loved it. Barry's benefits grew larger, the programmes more salacious. Ratings soared.

"This one's for all you ladies still in bed. Here I come." Marvin Gaye eased in with 'Sexual Healing'. Valentine's libido was frustrated. The song triggered memories. It was embarrassing. Anna was awake now. She was facing Valentine, smiling. He was going to grin, show his pearly whites. It was a bad idea. He had not cleaned his teeth yet. Valentine buttoned up his jacket.

Anna's pose was threatening. She would not look away. There was uneasy silence. She leaned nearer. Valentine had become interesting again. "I know who you are."

His palms went clammy. There was a vague chance. Her voice drifted into a whisper. "Your real name's not Valentine." He nodded his head. Tried to speak.

She had seen him in '84 at the Hammersmith Odeon. A Kid Creole gig. He was the percussion player for Sonido D 'Espresso. They had been the support band.

Valentine sat back. He could continue being what she wanted him to be. She started calling him 'Val'. That was always a good sign. He called her Anna. Perhaps she had a penchant for musicians.

Valentine was along for the ride. He played blag for blag's sake. In a club, on the street, on a coach. It was all the same. The thrill of deception. Adventures in your head. It was self-expression. It was Valentine's drug. Addictive. Destructive, like all the best drugs.

Anna said she liked jazz. Valentine said he liked jazz, played jazz, lived jazz. It was bullshit, but musicians can say that kind of thing. He had seen 'The Man with the Golden Arm'.

The bus spiralled off the motorway. Past Scatchwood. Round the flyover. There they were. Going into London. Brent Cross was the usual suburban wasteland. Mr 'Mud' Club lived in a house behind the shopping mall. Scally had thrown parties in Golders Green. Soul allnighters were held above The Alexandra down Finchley Road. He saw the car breaker's yard where they had dragged in their first sound system. The crusher was inert. It was a long time ago. The yard was derelict again.

Valentine hunched his shoulders. There was a traffic jam in Camden. Drivers were honking horns. Fists turning purple. Drumming fingers. The motor hummed, waiting to pull away. Anna pointed at the Lock Tavern. Her flat was down the side, at the bottom of Harmood Street. It was a council flat, acquired from an old boyfriend. Maybe she was fishing. "Have you got a new boyfriend?"

Anna shrugged her shoulders. Not today.

It surprised him. She had everything else.

She asked where he was staying. Valentine thought up an answer. There was his old friend on Charlotte Street. It was fashionable. Very hollow.

Anna said she had a spare room. It was empty.

Valentine wanted to accept but he was too proud. Accepting would make him a nobody. He tried to forget the offer. It felt better. Human contacts spread disease.

"Thank you." He smiled. Anna smiled. It was an awkward moment. Both had reacted foolishly.

Traffic jostled on rush hour Euston Road. Anna took out a black filofax. It bulged with papers. She asked Valentine for a pen. He didn't have one, not even a bic. She struggled with her pockets and produced an anodised Mont Blanc.

The Telecom Tower hung from the skyline. Valentine looked up. Just like the commercials. The tower was power. Money. Valentine had neither. There was no turning back. He could win it all back. There was nothing left to lose. Except his sanity.

The paper tore from the binder. Anna had written her phone number on a single green sheet. She handed it over. Then there was silence. Valentine was not sure what to say.

"Call me," Anna insisted. They could go for a drink or something. Something? He took out his mock-croc fax, and tucked the paper inside. Anna raised an eyebrow. There was no need to worry. The skin was fake.

The bus juddered to rest in the Metropole car park, facing Russell Square. The stewardess bid the punters a safe journey. "Thank you for travelling with Skyliner."

The grip strained on Anna's rucksack. She pulled it free. Valentine stood up. She was three inches taller than him. They moved down the aisle. Anna was rushing. She was late for something. Down the steps onto the street. The stewardess smiled. They made a 'nice' couple.

The hold was half empty. Valentine had his bag in his hand, travelling light. He followed Anna by the bus. The driver panted pulling out the luggage. He was having trouble. The overstuffed Louis Vuitton was jammed. One last tug. It grazed free. It was Anna's bag. She hoisted it onto her shoulder. Valentine was about to walk away. "No goodbye?" she said.

Goodbye was forever. Valentine did not like forever. She stepped towards him. Valentine said "See ya." Then she kissed him on the cheek.

She felt warm. He tried to smile, shrug it off. His movements were self-conscious. He was screaming inside his head. Why was human touch so unnerving?

Besides, she was kissing some percussion player. Not Valentine.

Anna walked off toward the tube station and waved. Valentine watched her DMs disappear round the comer. He could always call her up. Maybe.

Other travelers hustled away. The sun was shining. Valentine was just another face in the crowd. No bells were ringing. There was nobody there to meet him. He put on his dark glasses, slung the bag on his shoulder.

One deep breath. It was London air alright.

His heels clicked. "There's no place like home."

Only one fiver in his pocket. He needed a drink.

Valentine walked down Woburn Place.

CHAPTER THREE

Russell Square bragged money. 7.95 for meat and two veg. Foreign students roamed in packs. American girls wore dental braces. Hair was permed and yellow. Cropped jeans rose toward large Germanic buttocks. These young women were too clean. Not exotic at all.

Valentine ran across the zebra crossing-. Passing the School of Eastern and Slavonic Studies. The vodka was cheap in the student bar. His ex-girlfriend had looked like a pretty boy.

Each step forward was a step back. It was like a conversation with an old friend for sentiment's sake. No common ground anymore.

The U.C.L. campus was a short cut. It joined the square with Malet Street, Tottenham Court Road beyond. Haircuts had got short again. Here was the spirit of the age, private incomes buying education, a passport to City brokerage firms. Valentine had venom for these 'haves'.

Off the campus at a rapid pace. He glanced in the bookshop window. The first 'Aids Novel' didn't worry many people. Tabs of ecstasy had made sex fashionable again.

He had not had sex for months. This posed no problem.

New clothes shops had sprung up. Anonymous and Next. The names were appropriate. All the dummies wore bandanas. Androgyne had become unisex again. Valentine had kept up on trends. He read the Sunday newspapers.

On Tottenham Court Road first-time buyers flooded out of Heals. Sunshine bounced off his glasses. He had a problem. His cigarette packet was empty. A fresh packet was an unaffordable extravagance. The Charing Cross kiosk sold single Hamlets. He bought one. Valentine lit up outside the Dominion. At least Time had finished. Kylie Minogue was on tonight.

He looked along Oxford Street. This had been his 'manor', loud and grimy. The lights changed. Traffic halted. He crossed over the road. Buses reflected off Centrepoint. Kentucky Fried smelled worse than his cigar.

Fried chicken had been a late night feast. Kebabs tasted good at three a.m. as well. They were pissed by then. Going home to cold flats, sleeping through the next day. Still speeding in the cab. "Another line of sulphate?" It was all a bad smell now.

The Astoria was not a theatre anymore. Not even a club. Promoters rose and fell. Valentine had fallen. He wondered if anyone would remember. What if Courtney wanted to do him still? Courtney was famous for doing people.

Valentine skirted 'Private Shop' browsers on his way into Soho, a danger spot. Creditors might see him. His stomach gurgled. Only one acquaintance had to see him, then the world would know.

He pulled on the cigar. No smoke without fire. The excitement felt new again. Running the gauntlet. 'Rather a king today than a schmuck for a lifetime' – Rupert Pupkin.

Something caught his eye. He stopped. Two battlemented towers jutted from the comer. It was a Gothic horror, castellations peppered with mirror glass. Crimson banners billowed in the wind. A thirty foot arch framed the doorway.

The Miramar Hotel had closed in the seventies. Now six nights a week it was the Tower of Babel, with the biggest sound system in London.

Its shadow engulfed the pavement. This was where the scene

had been heading. Predictable legality and contrived wildness. It stank. The new promoters were businessmen. DJs had mortgages. Suburbia in the West End heart. The journey had been worthless.

Car engines revved, waiting to enter the all-night car park. He pushed between two bumpers. Gerrard Street had been paved for pedestrians. Chinese arches looked like the set for a cheap remake of 'The Last Emperor'.

Around the corner was the Mambo. It was an institution. Punters could mix with 'faces' and has-beens alike. He was surprised it was still going. Sufficient new faces must have usurped the old. At twenty-four Valentine was young. At the Mambo that was old. The thought irritated him.

The Cellar bar was under a pub. Through the swing door, the decor remained mid-fifties, a kitsch vision of hell. Everything was dark red. The location for many an interview.

Valentine sat down. "Barley wine, a pint." There was not enough change for another.

The Cellar had been a gay bar, colonised by the young and trendy. In the evenings the club cognoscenti had poured in. Four years later it was still staggering on. A few gay clones remained regulars. As had the barman. He was dressed in pale yellow, an avuncular Jimmy Saville under the drag. He poured out two bottles of Gold Label. Valentine took the top off his golden pint.

In truth the Cellar had been a compromise, really on the borders of Soho. Far enough to avoid danger spots of recognition. Near enough for angry acquaintances to appear at any moment.

Two figures walked through the door. He turned round. The bar lights lit his face. There was a moment of eye contact. Neither side wanted any trouble. Valentine backed off. He moved the stool further away. The legs grated.

The newcomers ordered 'screwdrivers'. Doubles.

The smaller man was blonde. Maybe highlighted hair. His Scottish brogue was affected. Valentine was earwigging their discussion. The fat man was a publisher. He bulged from his Hamnett suit. The Scot was a writer. His new book was out that day.

They were talking about drugs. One drug in particular. A particular kind of person. Success. Bits were missing. Valentine didn't quite understand. The publisher looked round. Someone might be listening.

Valentine's attention roamed elsewhere. Somebody else was watching him. The man was black, with broad shoulders. A Muslim cap covered his shaved head. Valentine reached for his drink. The black man was striding over.

"Aren't you Valentine?" he smiled.

Valentine shook his head.

"You fronted the Underground."

Valentine was pleased the man remembered, but it was safer to be forgotten. This man may have worked for Courtney. Valentine said he was a percussion player. London was a big place. Lots of people looked similar.

The man said nothing, sipped his pineapple juice. Valentine's face was unmistakable.

"I just want a quiet drink." Valentine's hand shook perceptibly. If he denied himself he was still running. If not he might get slapped, or much worse.

The black man took out a fiver. "Tell me the truth. I'll buy you a beer." The offer was tempting.

Valentine could not afford more beer. Even if Courtney was in the alley he had to face it. Cards face up. Now.

Valentine stared into space. "I'm Valentine. Who wants to know?"

"Another pint?"

"Gold Label."

The stranger smiled. Then introduced himself as A1 Jay. The name was as unfamiliar as the face. He gave Valentine a cigarette. It was a poor man's peace pipe.

Valentine was still furtive. Fear had chewed up his brain, had become part of him. He had believed his paranoia was gone. It was still there. Festering over the years. Valentine downed his second pint.

A1 had won a bet with himself. This was the Valentine people still talked about, the man who had disappeared. They reminisced about old raves. The best clubs of their youth. Previously A1 had been the punter and Valentine the promoter. Now roles were reversed.

A1 had hooked Valentine. Now he was pulling him in. They talked about the original Underground, Valentine's first warehouse party. Some of the 'old guard' still remembered it. A1 had been there. Red Stripe had run like piss. Enough sulphate to sink the Middlesex Hospital.

The words now seemed larger than the reality. Valentine had created his own folklore, just like his made-up name. He had created himself and it was difficult to tell who he had once been. Word of mouth had taken over. Lip service. The two dozen successful nights had become hundreds. A thousand punters had become millions. It was bullshit.

Valentine was on his fourth drink. The chip on his shoulder had become a large portion of chips with salt and vinegar. Articles in The Face and i-D. Big money taken on the door. Then it crashed. People got arrested. Rivals broke each others' legs. They had all screwed him.

Despite this verbal barrage, A1 remained calm. Beer couldn't loosen his jaw. He was on the soft stuff. He was a good listener. Valentine was backing into a comer. Blagging himself. His words drowned in despair. Then he stopped to think.

"What do you do, A1 Jay?"

This question had never arisen before. A1 seemed strangely embarrassed, vague. He was starting a jazz club soon.

Valentine grew wary. Why had this man got him pissed? Who

was he working for? The beer made him braver. He grabbed A1's arm.

"Don't blag a blagger."

A1 balked at the threatened violence. Valentine's brewing anger was unpredictable.

"I run the scams at the Tower of Babel."

The big tacky club on the comer? This man was a fellow promoter. Why was he so embarrassed about it? Valentine was intrigued. He sat down again.

"Buy me another drink?" He tried to be gracious. A1 may be picking his brain. He was pissed enough to be flattered. More drinks.

A1 attempted an explanation. He had worked the Tower for a year. Now he wanted to leave, go back to doing jazz clubs. The West End vibe had changed. House and a provincial mentality had taken over. So why had Valentine come back?

Valentine reeled on the stool, embarrassed now. He had no new scam. His name was probably shit. No one would trust him. Maybe he could do it again. Maybe. He looked at his shoes. Even they were cheap imitations. Then he looked at A1. There was no sympathy in the eyes.

Sweat edged on his brow. A1 had walked in the pub broken. Now the answer sat in front of him. He had manoeuvred Valentine. It was working. In for the kill.

He had an idea for a last scam. He could leave the Tower a winner, not like a whipped dog. Valentine understood the notion.

He even had the name. West. It would run every Friday night.

He wanted to recreate the warehouse vibe. Put it in a regular, legal venue. The punters would love it. West every Friday at the Tower.

Valentine was sceptical. Punters wanted different times now. A permanent legal warehouse? No. It wouldn't work. A warehouse party belonged in a warehouse. The ticket would have to be right. The DJ would have to be right. Even the front man would have to be right. But there was nobody left. Nobody who knew how it should be.

A1 spoke softly. He needed a diplomat. Somebody to work the scam. He waited.

Valentine's brain was all played out. His thoughts were sluggish. He should have stayed home. All pissed up and nowhere to go.

Then A1's finger was pointing. "What about you?"

Valentine frowned. He thought he had missed something. The finger still pointed. "I'll pay you a ton and a half." A hundred and fifty quid each week.

Valentine felt sick. Too much beer. Too good a chance to miss. But Courtney would be able to find him. And the rest. Besides he was persona non grata. He knew no fashionable DJs.

He floundered for excuses. A1 had all the answers. Valentine could use the old Underground DJs.

West.... Raising the Underground. It had a good ring to it.

Still Valentine shook his head. How would he ever find Fly and Big Jack? They had moved on. Only God knew where. It was all too late.

A1 kept up the pressure. They would get a hundred and fifty, too. A hundred and fifty each. It wasn't the money. Justice. Honour. Everything was at stake. He played all his cards.

Now Valentine was silent. The man with the big words was bottling. He hunched his shoulders. The last four years he was nobody. Different places. Different names. He had nothing. Only hopes of a second chance. He'd lived it a thousand times. Now here it was.

Valentine stretched out his hand. "I trust you," he said.

A1 nodded. They shook hands.

A tequila each to seal the bargain. A1 drank it in one, a double. A1 had not 'drunk' all evening and now there was no reason to hold back. West had a frontman. Or fall guy. Either way it was Valentine.

The clock read ten thirty. A1 was late. He had meant to leave hours before. Chrissie would be waiting. They agreed to meet the next day, three o'clock in A1's office. Despite Valentine's pleas, A1 left quickly.

Valentine sat on his own. The pub had filled up. No more cigarettes. No more free beer. Nobody to talk to. The women didn't seem worth blagging. He would not get far on two quid odd. He ordered another short. Downed it rapidly. Then off up the stairs.

Valentine tottered into the cool evening. He could taste tequila in his mouth. Wind chilled through the denim jacket. He was sobering up rapidly. His mind began to race. Crowds hustled down Gerrard Street, fresh from theatreland. All going opposite ways. Trying to get to the tube. Dashing into Chinese restaurants. Trying to get a table.

He was not sure what he had done. Made a commitment with a stranger. Agreed to work a club he had never seen the inside of. Signed up for a hundred and fifty quid. It was a no-win scenario. He staggered about, trying to get his bearings.

There was a more pressing problem. Valentine had nowhere to stay. He had walked all night before. But now it was too cold. He thought about Euston station. It had been warm in the past. Valentine had no stomach for it, not any more. He slung his bag on his shoulder. This was all he had, everything. It would be a lot to lose while dossing on a form. No.

The phone boxes on Gerrard Street were like pagodas off The Last Emperor. Valentine stepped inside. He played with the last of his change, a few silver coins. It was easy to feel shiftless, a drifter. Drifting never got easier, not in London. It created a vacuum in his head. Sucking everything in.

He unzipped the bag. The clothes were creased. He opened the fax to the page marked 'C'. Change slipped into the slot. Twenty pence flicked up on the screen. Tiny grey numbers. The dial tone. He pressed seven digits. There was no reply.

Onto the "S' page. That line was dead. The numbers were years out of date. He was running out of favours owed.

Try Derek. Derek could be relied upon. He wouldn't have moved. He lived in a council flat. He would understand. It was good timing. Derek never went out before twelve. He might even be staying in tonight. Maybe wrecked already. The logic was flawed. Phoning up after years, asking to stay, it was like Lord Lucan calling the Palace. People would prefer him to be dead. He could hear himself breathing.

Valentine dialled the number. He watched his finger tap the fax. "Come on. Come on." The phone was ringing. He waited. Ten seconds. Nearly thirty seconds. Somebody picked up the receiver. He held his breath.

"Hello." A woman's voice with an American accent. He was intruding.

He asked if Derek was in. "No."

He asked when Derek was due in. Derek was modelling in Japan. No. He didn't want to leave a message.

Valentine hung up. Ten pence jangled out of the box. He watched a vagrant through the glass. He could walk a while. He felt old. He wanted to throw his book away, the numbers were useless. Nobody else to call. He pulled out a torn sheet of green paper. There was a phone number and a name.

Camden was not far. She might not be in. She might tell him to "fuck off." He tingled.

Valentine put the ten back in the box. He read the number. Tapped out the seven digits. The telephone rang. Selling his soul was easier than vagrancy. Still ringing. No way of knowing the outcome. Someone picked up the phone.

A woman's voice answered.

CHAPTER FOUR

Domaine said "No calls." He replaced the receiver. They were alone now, staring at each other. Valentine felt for the gun.

Domaine fingered the green crystals. "Pretty, isn't it?" he smiled. "I suppose you want answers?"

Valentine nodded clumsily. He clicked off the safety catch.

Domaine paused and stubbed out his cigarette. He swivelled round in his chair.

Valentine watched the back of his head. One bullet. That was all it would take.

Domaine pointed to the window, through the glass, into the heart of the city. "There is your answer, Valentine."

FX. The city. The dead girl. Valentine wanted it all to fit together. It would not.

Domaine stood up. "Connections. Connections. Add it up." He was getting impatient with Valentine. He scooped up a handful of green powder. This was power. This was product. Everything was product today. Even people.

Domaine's voice was broad and powerful. He could have been addressing a crowd. Grains fell from his palm. He sold dreams, lifestyles. FX was to be the catalyst for the ultimate leisure society. But it was strictly for high rollers, people who dealt with ideas. It could make a day's rest like a long holiday. Send the mind out to lunch. High pressured minds can crack, but not with this. FX evened out the strain.

He threw out his arms. The people wanted it. Just like two weeks paid holiday. Just like low calorie cola. In small doses it was harmless. The right people got happy. Unfortunately the wrong people abused it.

Who were the "right people"? Valentine didn't know. The rich people? The successful people? The people who could walk away? He watched Domaine's face, the lips curled into a smile. But the eyes looked uncertain, as if he was waiting for Valentine to speak, gauging every reaction.

FX was harmless. Perhaps Valentine was crazy. Perhaps no-one had really died.

Valentine would do one more line. His arm began to shake. Then his shoulder. Then his entire body. One more line. Straighten himself out. No. Valentine's words were stuttered. "W-w-why don't you try some?"

Domaine shook his head. He dealt with a major soft drink account. He didn't try that either. In the right hands FX was totally harmless.

He walked over to the drinks cabinet and poured out two scotches. He sat one in front of Valentine. The tumbler was heavy crystal, half-filled with golden liquid. Domaine held his glass in the light. "People like nice colours." He took a sip.

Domaine tried to clarify his position. He also dealt with display ads for distilleries. Translated into thirty languages, in Sunday papers all over the world. Scotch whisky was a unique product. It provided smooth intoxication. Just like FX.

Watching the pile. Watching Valentine. Hoping for the right reaction.

Scotch had its minus points, of course. It made some men wife beaters. It made others drunk drivers. Hundreds had been killed by drunk drivers. Who was to blame? The consumer? The producer? The product? Domaine only did the advertising and

31

conducted the market research.

Scotch was meant for everybody, sold as part of a proletarian lifestyle. FX however was hooked into 'high speed'. Because it was free it had become priceless, the key to an exclusive members-only club. Valentine had been incorrectly 'signed in'. That was why things were going wrong.

Domaine finished his drink. "Confidentially, I do own a distillery. This is my brand." He tilted the empty glass.

Valentine gazed at his full glass. Why was Domaine involved? Maybe he had a new client. A drug baron. "Where does it come from?"

Domaine offered a simple answer. "Me."

Valentine wanted him to break down, offer some provocation. Valentine could not kill him in cold blood, even if Miki and Fly were dead. He would not play Domaine's relaxed game. It had to be over by 12.30.

He was in the desert. There was no water to be found. Only scorched earth. There seemed no way of winning. He was about to pull the gun out. Finish it.

Then Domaine took out a key. It was tiny, silver. He unlocked a desk drawer, one of five that ran the breadth of the table. It slid on the runner.

Here was Valentine. A number. A piece of paper. His file was very thin. He wouldn't bother taking it out. He knew everything. Valentine's moods, movements, even his real name.

Domaine was not Big Brother, not the Prince of Darkness. Valentine had merely cropped up on his market research files. There was only one thing that interested him now. How Valentine's file could be closed. The drawer slid shut again.

Valentine wasn't listening anymore. It seemed futile. He looked out of the window at the city a long way down. He wondered what Fly had thought when he was falling. There must be a sense of freedom. One second of truth before you hit the ground. Back down to earth.

Domaine was still speaking. Valentine watched his jaw move. Words made strange shapes. Then he knew he had to do it.

It was a cat and mouse game. Who was chasing who? Domaine didn't know how much FX Valentine had taken. He was pushing him towards the edge.

He trailed his letter opener in the powder. The gilt blade drew a green line. He produced a glass tube from his top pocket. "Try another line."

Would Valentine take the Pepsi Challenge?

Domaine was acting like a bizarre commercial. He wanted to know how much was needed. What was the noxious dose? Valentine seemed an ample guinea pig. Here was first-hand market research in action. Would the stains come out in the wash? Valentine was certainly tainted. Stale sweat under the armpit. Touches of tomato on the shirt. Could FX clean straight through to the heart of the man?

"Just one more line. You know it makes sense." Domaine grinned insincerity. He owned game shows as well.

It was taking too long, thirty seconds, almost out of the commercial break. He had not planned on resistance. Why wouldn't Valentine take the chance? Lowlife never had any resolve. They ate cornflakes instead of muesli. They thrived on E numbers.

"What have you got to lose?"

Valentine knew he had nothing to lose. He took a deep breath. One more flight of insanity? It was not a bad idea. Perhaps when he came down everything would be alright.

He couldn't get Miki's face out of his mind, bashed into oblivion. Fly had looked lost. There had been two wraps of FX on the floor. They had killed each other fighting over a line.

He stood up. "Why?"

Domaine squinted down the diameter of the glass tube. FX was not meant for the likes of Valentine. Art Directors got it. Ad Managers. Designers. Muso Execs. They had the money to deal with it. Success had exorcised their doubts. Money had liberated their petty paranoias. They could have beautiful dreams.

Then there was Valentine and his friends. They had no money. Their vision was narrow. Poverty made their nightmares real, etching minds with the spectres of fear and loathing. FX was too good for them. Taking too much was easy. It was poor man's greed.

The green crystals remained in a line. On the table. In Valentine's head. The pressure was relentless. But he walked straight past and spun Domaine's chair round till it faced the window. If the answers were not in Domaine's words they might be in the barrel of his Luger.

Sun blared through the windows. Valentine stood next to the glass. He reached out and touched it. There was the city. There was beyond.

He half understood. Perhaps that was what successful people wanted. Luxuriance. Product. A life in the fast lane. Another line of FX. That bitter-sweet moment. A portal to dream-sleep that energised thought.

There was nothing for those like Valentine. Excess FX caused madness. Flashbacks that could see night and day. That never seemed to stop.

Valentine opened the window. Cold air chilled his face. People wanted illusion. A commercial that could become a soap opera or a game show. The price is right. Big breasted girls quaffing Martinis. Anytime, anyplace, anywhere. Lives had become slogans. Not lives anymore, lifestyles.

He could hear Domaine walking over. Valentine didn't turn round. "One more line." Another slogan. They could put it on the packet.

He raised his foot onto the window sill. It was a long way down. Maybe the only truth was death. He saw the cars passing by, small coloured specks. Exhaust fumes singed his breath. At least he'd be on the news.

Highrise towers were cameras, St. Pauls a suited newsreader.

What was real? Three Deaths on the Rock. The CIA assassination of Zia. No. The only thing that was real were the ads. More big prizes for the masses. And there was FX. The biggest prize of all.

"Take the money."

"Open the box."

"Higher, higher."

"One more line."

The audience were chanting. The whole world was watching.

"Freedom."

He grabbed the glass. Leant forward.

He could feel Domaine's breath on his neck. He was ready to go. It would be over.

He tilted his head round. Looked at Domaine's eyes. Looked deeply. There was nothing there. No regret. No fear. Only certainty.

"Finish it," Domaine whispered. He wanted to close the file. Tie up the loose end.

Valentine took a deep breath.

Yuppie, Yippie, Yardie. Lifestyle, loveplay, foreplay. Safe-sex, Tex Mex, twin-bed duplex.

Domaine stretched out his arm. He was close enough to push. Judge, jury and executioner. Words tumbled from his mouth, slow motion in Valentine's head.

"The whole world has died and gone to hell. There are only two things left. Business and FX. Now I'm closing the file on FX. The rest is just business."

Valentine's friends had died for nothing. Valentine had gone crazy for nothing. "Just business."

It was like a body blow. Thoughts of impotence and futility flashed through Valentine's mind. There were his dead friends' faces. His rage exploded like a volcano. He would not die just for bullshit.

His free hand flew into his pocket. Domaine thought he was jumping.

The Luger was a blur. It whipped across Domaine's face. The flesh contorted. Sinews snapped backwards. Domaine flew like a crumpled paper plane.

There was a dull thud. The body landed on the table. Arms dangled spreadeagle. He rolled sideways. Blood ran from his mouth. A trickle of red.

No more words.

CHAPTER FIVE

Valentine counted the change into the bus conductor's hand. It was one penny short.

He tried to smile winningly at the grey-clad Asian man. The man looked back blankly. It had been a long day and he had no stomach for argument. The ticket whizzed from the machine.

Valentine tried to remember the conversation from the coach. He took out his fax. What was her name? It would look bad if he called her the wrong name.

It was Amanda, no, it was Hannah. Valentine unscrambled the green paper. He held it up in the yellow light. The handwriting was nice. He read 'Anna'.

The 253 cruised down towards Camden High Street. He was surprised she had asked him round. She sounded drunk. He wondered how a percussion player would act.

Irish rowdies poured out of the boozer at Camden Lock. Le Bistroquet loomed up on the left. He had often eaten there with Susan, the Irish girl. Somebody had told him she was working in advertising now. Perhaps he could send her flowers. She might see him at the Tower.

Valentine careered down the stairs. The bus pulled up. His muscles strained, then he jumped off, intact. His confidence flagged. What if she was a man eater? He had visions of Ruth Ellis.

The Lock Tavern was straight opposite. He crossed at the zebra. His reflection leered from the silvered pub window. He bobbed between the letters. Valentine did not look young anymore. He had lost weight. Stress etched rings around his eyes.

He walked along Harmood Street gauging the numbers. 9b was a red door next to a pub, almost the first house on the street. He looked at the illuminated bell. The name 'Anna Douglas' was typewritten on white card.

He pushed the bell. There was no sound. Then he noticed the scribbled note. 'Bell not working. Please knock.'

He banged on the door.

Valentine could hear heavy feet running down the stairs inside. The door was flung open.

Anna wore a white T-shirt with '501' written across it in huge black letters. It was Paul Smith from last season. The jeans were old and patched.

She held a lipstick-smeared glass. In the other hand she swung a half-empty bottle of golden tequila.

She grabbed Valentine's arm and pulled him inside. "Race you upstairs," she shouted, already running.

He paused, then unsteadily chased after her. They dashed into a small square room. She knocked him backwards into an armchair.

Valentine scanned the room warily. The walls were marbled, grey and khaki. The floor was strewn with thumbed magazines and unsheathed white labels. She hoped he didn't mind.

Anna sat on the settee. "Want a drink?" she slurred.

Valentine nodded. She pulled out a half-pint glass from behind her seat. Reeling slightly, she filled it with tequila. The bottle was almost empty. She had drunk the best part of it already.

Valentine took the greasy glass in his hand. The booze lent neither of them more charm.

Where had he been all day? Who had he seen? Did he like Danny DeVito?

Maybe he reminded her of Danny DeVito.

Valentine didn't answer. He took another large gulp. Tequila stung the back of his throat but didn't make his situation feel right. She still seemed like a bad drunk.

Anna slid over to the video recorder and pressed the play button. White noise fizzed from the screen, then the title scrolled up. Tin Men. Valentine had seen it before.

The flickering glow painted her face. Frown lines oozed fatigue. She looked much older than in daylight. There was something unhappy about her.

* * *

Valentine noticed the picture collection around the walls. Facing the front was William Holden, on his right, Errol Flynn. Tony Hancock hung by Truman Capote. All in black and white, all eyes mocking. Valentine had to turn away. It was freaking him out.

"I wonder why you are here," Anna murmured.

Valentine thought of all sorts of answers. He was after sex. He was after a drink. Actually, he was just after a place to stay.

"You're putting the band back together." The rumours had to be true.

Valentine slumped back from the edge of his seat. He feigned surprise, nodded his head. He was back on the road with Sonido D 'Espresso.

Maybe he and the drummer really did look similar. They were both too pissed to bother.

Anna told him she wouldn't tell the others at Sound-Express. But she always found it difficult not to mix business and pleasure. Something was playing on her mind. She sounded more and more strung out.

Danny DeVito's wife was leaving him.

39

Anna had started to watch the film again. She took two cigarettes from the packet, placed both in her mouth, struggled with the table lighter. The dual cigarette trick had worked better for Paul Henreid.

As she replaced the lighter Valentine noticed the picture on the table. A man's face filled the frame, a sunny holiday snap. He had dark curly hair. He was smiling but the expression seemed pathetic. Valentine had seen exactly the same look somewhere before. As he leaned back she gave him the already lit cigarette.

Then he made the connection. It was the same as the other men hung on the wall. He looked at the faces again. Each one seemed more chewed up than the last.

They had all drunk themselves to death.

Valentine puffed at the filter and asked who the man was.

Anna drank more spirits. His name was Billy. He had been the leaseholder of the flat. Billy had run off to the States. She tried to stop herself from crying.

Valentine looked at the photo again. It was not difficult to imagine Billy as a bad drunk. He had the face for it.

Anna went cold. "I stitched him up in print." He had been a guitarist with 'Roar'. Valentine remembered that they had split up over some drugs scandal.

Anna slid into a heap on the floor. It was all getting out of control. She fumbled for the bottle and knocked it over. Valentine managed to rescue the dregs.

There was now an unsightly wet patch amongst the debris. Several of the magazines were sodden. Anna was drowning in a sea of self pity.

Valentine didn't want to watch. But the carnage seemed strangely compelling. He joined Anna on the floor and gazed at the photograph.

"Why did Billy run?"

She didn't know. Maybe he had been running from her, maybe from himself.

Being drunk and oblivious was never the answer. Surely she realised that?

Anna grabbed the bottle back. "You're the alcoholic, mate, not me."

Billy used to beat her. She hadn't minded at first. He had broken her arm once. She told the boss she had fallen down some stairs.

Billy was always apologetic but nothing really changed. He started threatening her with kitchen knives.

One night he came in screaming. He'd seen what she'd written in Sound-Express. The boys in the band egged him on. They always did.

Anna met him at the top of the stairs. He hit her hard in the face. Her flailing body sailed into the sitting room. Her face was bloody. She reached for the phone. But he kicked her.

She kept trying to call the police. Each time she tried to fight back he kicked her again. She felt her ribs crumple.

She screamed, how she screamed, but the neighbours were used to it.

When the lights came back on again, Billy was gone. She remembered looking at her face in the mirror. It was bloody and ravaged, a war zone. She locked the door in case he came back.

All his things were gone. There was not even a note. He phoned her office to say he had gone to America.

Anna sobbed, leaning her head on Valentine's shoulder. She told him she felt sick.

Valentine looked at her. He didn't need this. He felt the mocking smiles on the walls were directed at him. He couldn't leave. There was nowhere to go.

She tried to kiss his lips but missed. She hit his cheek instead. It had been a mistake to call. No amount of dirty talk could make this scenario appealing. She kissed him again. Her breath smelt of stale tobacco and tequila.

She was definitely up for it. The whole idea was making his stomach churn. The cocktail of barley wine and tequila felt noxious. He was pissed. This woman was more freaked-out than he was. And she was going to be sick.

"Where's the bathroom?"

She mumbled incoherently, pointing down the hallway.

He had to do something. He stood up. His arms flailed for balance. He steadied himself. The rag-rolled wall looked vomitous through drunken eyes. Bending forward he hoisted her onto the sofa. She lolled spineless like a marionette.

He put his right arm under her feet, his left under her head. With concerted effort he hoisted her into the air. Now came the difficult part. He proceeded to carry her down the corridor. His legs were unsteady.

Valentine pitched and yawed. The floor wouldn't stop moving. He kicked a door open.

This was the bedroom. She laughed.

Valentine stumbled down steps, finding the bathroom. He might have commented on the decor but he was too pissed. He sat her down on a stool, propped up by the wall. He flicked the light switch. The neon blinked, eventually flashing on. The yellow light made him feel worse.

Bending uneasily over the bath, he jammed the plug in and turned on the cold tap. This was the only way he knew of getting sober fast, avoiding the interim stage of vomiting.

He kicked off his shoes, then took off his jacket. Anna attempted to ask what he was doing. He wasn't sober enough to answer.

He pulled off his jeans, then his shirt. He staggered about in this stranger's bathroom in his boxer shorts and Argyle socks.

Anna giggled.

He made sure his dick had not popped out.

Now it was her turn. He tottered over and pulled off her T-shirt. Her tits had a sun-tan line where she had not gone topless. He pulled off her jeans. She wriggled about.

He wasn't going to take her pants off. Not through embarrassment, it was just not the sort of thing he wanted to do.

She remarked on his hairy shoulders. He had never liked them either.

The bath was now beginning to brim. He swished his hand in it. My God, it was cold. He tried the acid test and dipped his head in it. It was just about ready.

Grabbing her arms, he lifted her up. He walked her over to the bath and stepped in the water. She followed. They both sat down.

There was a delayed reaction.

They screamed simultaneously. It was hellishly cold.

He asked her how she felt.

"Sick and cold."

He reached over and picked up a pink shaving mug. Filling it with water he doused her semi-conscious head. She screamed with discomfort.

There was more where that came from. Valentine bent her neck forward and started pouring cold water over her. She began to squeal instead of screaming.

She gasped that she felt better. Valentine would only stop when she could guarantee not to be sick. They sat in the bath of cold water until both could safely say they were more sober, if not completely straight.

He stepped out of the water and exchanged his wet boxers and socks for a white towel hanging from the door.

He threw his wet things into the sink and tied the towel around his waist. It had Property of Camden Council written on it. He handed Anna a blue viscose robe.

Stepping out of her wet knickers, she pulled out the plug.

She shook the water from her hair and dressed in the robe. It clung to her.

Valentine walked through to the sitting room, heading for the couch. Anna followed him. She asked whether he was coming to bed.

He pointed to the sofa.

She said the bedroom was much warmer. Besides she had no spare blankets.

Valentine said he did not mind.

She told him all the sheets were in the wash. Even the duvet cover.

He didn't mind that either. He only wanted to go to sleep.

Anna was not taking no for an answer. She grasped Valentine's arm and led him towards the door.

The bedroom was definitely much warmer. There were no sheets on the bed or even a duvet cover. He didn't mind.

"You are a nice man." She undid the robe, slipped it off and threw it over a chair.

Light glinted through the roller blind. It painted her body golden like a Matisse. She stood motionless. Valentine just looked at her. His head hurt. He was tired. He had a meeting to get to tomorrow.

She did look sexy, in a sleazy sort of way. Her skin had felt smooth in the bath. Valentine dropped the towel from his waist. She slipped into bed.

The LED clock glowed red and 2:30 a.m. He slid under the duvet. He kissed her on the cheek.

Valentine said, "I'm going to sleep."

He pulled up the duvet and turned over.

CHAPTER SIX

Valentine stepped aboard the 253. He jostled past the two Eric B clones. Their jewellery jangled as the bus moved off. The Camden streets were bustling with activity.

He strode up the stairs and sat down. A few quid of Anna's money in his pocket. A smooth jaw, thanks to her lady-shave. He remembered his reflection, naked in a stranger's bathroom, hairy shoulders and all.

She had worn Shalamar perfume. The smell hung in his nostrils. Valentine had doused himself with it. It made a change to smell good.

He lifted the fax out of his bag, then transferred her name and address into his book. Signed, sealed and delivered, he put the book inside the flight bag, zipped it up carefully and repositioned the safety pin.

This was how it should have always been. Deals to make and people to see. Rent-free accommodation. It was perfect.

He took a bent filter from behind his ear and lit up. The Tower bookmatch glinted purple and gold. Anna must have gone there at some time.

He wondered about A1. He had made a very big commitment. Valentine took the half-empty bookmatch and flicked it out of the open window.

The bus hurtled through the hospital campus. It was coming

up to three o'clock. The suited fraternities were running back from late lunches.

Valentine had the luxury of being on time. He could take a leisurely stroll via Soho.

He cut through Charlotte Street. Down Rathbone Place. Then onto Oxford Street. The pavements were full. Valentine's thoughts marked time.

He couldn't possibly find Fly. Jack would tell him the whole thing was a bad idea. No regular venue could work for their irregular crowd. It would be like forcing square pegs. Why was Valentine doing it?

Warily he crossed Oxford Street, traversing into Soho Square. He stood on the corner looking into the meagre park. The gardens were veiled in mist from the sprinklers. The benches were full. A small group of women caught his eye, sexy and fashionable. He walked through the park and passed up close to them. They were smoking a joint. One of them looked up towards Valentine, pulled on the joint and licked her lips.

Valentine's nerve went. He hurried towards Old Compton Street.

Around a corner the view of the Tower of Babel hit him more powerfully than before. It exuded a lifestyle, high spend. Valentine drew nearer. All his better judgment was slipping away. This was the key to everything he wanted. No score would be left unsettled, no debt would not be paid in full. Nothing would be out of his reach.

He walked up the stone steps. This was all wrong. He looked up at the banners. They were gross. The whole thing stank. He couldn't fathom the drive that pushed him further.

Valentine rang on the entryphone. The reply squawked distorted. "Reception. Can I help you?" Valentine said he had an appointment with A1 Jay. There was a buzz. Then the lock clunked open.

You could tell it had once been a hotel, though the walls were now covered in graffiti-art. The chandeliers remained. A staircase rose up from the centre of the hall, split into two and met large landings up above. The marble-topped reception desk snaked around the far wall. Despite the expensive fixtures, the place looked dusty in the natural light.

His heels clipped across the parquet floor. Large video screens stood blank.

There were two men at reception. One was short and black. The other tall and white, dressed in black.

Valentine placed his bag between them. He was about to state his business. The phone rang. The black clad individual picked up the phone.

"Hello? Tower of Babel, can I help you? No, A1 is not in today. I'll tell him you called." He replaced the receiver. Obviously A1 was only in when he wanted to be.

Valentine wondered why he was there.

There was a glimmer of recognition in the black man's face. The white boy said he would see if A1 was in. He buzzed upstairs.

The black guy chuckled. "You used to be fatter, Val." He remembered the Rumble, one of Valentine's latter one-offs. His hat was turned back to front. He wore expensive English officer's boots. His name was Flashman. One gold tooth sparkled in his grin.

They exchanged an intricate handshake. Laughter subsided.

A1 Jay jogged down the stairs. His style was different to the night before, though equally impeccable. Valentine began to feel underdressed. His clothes were shabby.

A1 greeted Flashman with a surprised hello. He asked Zeke if there had been any messages. The young man handed him a sheet of A4.

Motioning to Valentine, A1 moved off. They could talk over coffee. Zeke buzzed the door open. They both stepped out into the daylight.

A1's manner was easy. He glided rather than walked. Valentine trotted along beside him. The Polo Bar was A1's favourite. Not too busy at this time of day. It was smack in the heart of Old Compton Street.

They hustled up Greek Street. Porn shops had been replaced by accessory shops. The people were different too. Seedy film makers had exchanged their glad rags for Armani. The ropey tarts were gone. Design company secretaries marched on their pitches. It was worse than Valentine had imagined. Sex for sale had become sex for corporate acquisition. Women wafted by, reeking of power and position.

He turned his head to root out would-be pursuers, angry debtors or cheated friends. Strangely, the thought of detection turned him on. He must be going crazy.

They reached the Polo Bar and sat in a booth by the door. The old Italian waitress must have come with the property. She placed two menus on the table then disappeared in a kitchenly direction.

A1 had been trying to calm Valentine. He could sense the tension. Every moment they sat wound Valentine tighter and tighter. It was no longer the spectre of lurking creditors. This was the glorious realm of possibility.

The cafe was filled with the 'beautiful people'. Bohos in Brookes Bros shirts, sweating beneath purple pinstripe. Magazine PRs with large breasts. Valentine had missed them.

The waitress returned. A1 ordered two cappuccinos and two pieces of cheesecake. Valentine nodded agreement. They each took a Chesterfield then began talking business.

A1 wanted West to be an 'attitude' club, the attitude that had previously predominated 'up west'. That was why he wanted Valentine as the host, Majordomo, whatever he wanted to call it. It made sense in PR or press terms. An old hero of clubsters relaunched in a West End venue, emerging with his old team intact. It would be a riot, a roadblock even.

Then the coffee arrived. A1 munched on the cheesecake.

Valentine wasn't sure if the deal was worth it. The whole thing sounded very phony. The chance of Big Jack and Fly working again was slim. They certainly wouldn't want to work in that kind of venue.

Valentine could have carte blanche. The tickets and everything. A1's bosses would pour money into promotion. Valentine could have his own PR agent. Surely he wouldn't pull out now. The bosses were already sold on the idea. This was Valentine's chance.

A1 certainly sounded as if he believed. A believer could make the difference. Valentine was sober. There was no excuse if he made the wrong move.

The jangle of car keys took his attention. A woman in a white duster coat glided by. He noticed her easy manner as she reeled off a twenty pound note from a roll to pay the bill.

He basked in her generous smile. She left all the change. That was exactly what Valentine had always wanted. Not recognition so much as the easy power that was recognisable. Money, as plentiful and sweet as honey.

One-fifty for a night's work was no million, but it beat the shit out of nothing at all. If West took off he could be in gravy. Worlds had turned on less.

Valentine took another of A1's Chesterfields and lit it. He wanted to savour the moment. He would conditionally accept. The details seemed a secondary concern. When was he supposed to start work?

A1 took out his diary and flicked it open. Their starting date was going to be the thirteenth. Friday the thirteenth. Only two weeks to find Fly and Jack.

Valentine needed an advance to work with.

"Will fifty quid be sufficient?" A1 withdrew an envelope and passed it over. Valentine nodded, finishing his cheesecake. It would do for now anyway.

A1 had boxed him in well, more professionally than he had expected. There was no contract, just a handshake. It seemed firm enough. Neither man knew how much he could trust the other. Wariness made for a good bond.

Valentine perceived a change within himself as he leafed through the fivers. He could even buy Anna a drink. React a little less mercenary. Should he go back there tonight? He was not sure.

Business was done but A1 did not dash back to the Tower. He seemed content just to talk.

A1 had begun in PR. He was living in the East End now. Valentine's present accommodation raised a smile. Was Valentine screwing a complete stranger?

This was the blag. It permeated their entire existence. The two men hardly knew each other but they talked like old friends.

Valentine felt easiest with strangers. They could never really catch him.

A1 had to get back to the office. He handed Valentine a white cardboard ticket, an entrance to the Mambo eighth anniversary. Such parties were legendary. There was free booze all night, and women were packed tighter than sardines. Valentine remembered the fourth anniversary. Most of the faces would not have changed.

They stood up, shook hands again. A1 nodded. "Urgent business." They left in separate directions. They both had time on their hands. This was the nature of the game.

Fear of detection was evaporating. Valentine had fifty notes in his pocket. If anyone caught up with him at least he could buy them a beer.

He waded headlong into Le Routier. Valentine's oldest haunt was packed. It was a French style bar with small jugs of water to dilute the Pernod. Most of the bar staff were French nationals. He pushed his way to the front and asked the short dark barmaid for a number one barley wine.

Valentine felt edgy in the midst of the crowd, each clique vastly different from the other. Old soak journos rubbed shoulders with rag trade boys. Modern ballet dancers with out-of-work photographers. Crimpers with waitresses from The Medici.

Valentine peeled out a crisp blue note. This was the style he liked, not having to count the change. He looked round for a seat. There was not even standing room. It was traditional for many of the regulars to stand outside. He made a beeline for the door.

Valentine posed outside, his glass balanced on the window sill. The winos cavorted in the car park opposite. A BMW and a Merc attempted to double park. It was summer in the city.

He was about to finish his first when terror struck. A large besuited man was approaching round the comer, his crop more severe than ever. If Valentine's luck was in the man would sail by. His hands tensed around the glass.

Scally let out a familiar greeting. "Yo, crazy?"

Valentine faked a hearty greeting and offered to buy him a beer. Scally halfheartedly accepted and Valentine slunk inside.

The cockneys had called him Scally because he came from Liverpool. He was older than the rest. His sense of humour stemmed from doctrinaire socialism, views unshakable as rock.

He had despised what Valentine had become, even years ago. Scally had launched Valentine on the scene but Valentine had become more of a name than Scally and had shafted many of their mutual friends.

When he returned with two pints Scally had taken up his usual slouch, puffing maniacally on a Benson. Grudgingly he took the drink. His rule of thumb was to take nothing from nobody. Every comrade deserved a fair deal.

He thought Valentine had done a runner. Some even presumed he was dead. A lot of people had been after him. His name was mud on the scene. If Valentine had only explained the score, people would have waited for their money. Running made people assume they had been ripped off. Some had wanted to put out a contract.

He asked Scally what the score was now.

Scally wanted Valentine to make it right between their friends. He had wronged them. He had to settle up. None of them would whack him.

Scally wanted him just to be the little crazy guy like when they first met. In '83 they shared a flat. They had no TV. Valentine provided the entertainment, jokes, stories, impossible dreams. This was how Scally wanted it to be still, no malice or double dealing.

Valentine had changed. It was not enough to be a crazy man. They had thrived on his energy. How many had hired him only to haggle over money? They had ripped him off. The sharp dollar ruled.

In the beginning Scally had imparted his notions of honour to Valentine. The rules had to be fair. They were not. Valentine had played the only way he could. All or nothing. The scene was hard and two-faced. Nobody could afford to play straight. It galled Scally. He saw his friend help their enemies if the price was right.

Valentine smiled. Everyone would get a fair shake this time. He would pay off all his old debts. This was going to be the one. He had secured a regular spot at the Tower.

Scally laughed. "It was never any good when it started. Nobody wants to go there now."

God, how Scally annoyed him sometimes. He could never see possibilities. He was still worrying about the same fifteen quid deals. How many new rucksacks he could fit in his shop. How much he could make on a gram of charlie. It was old news.

This was not what Valentine needed. They were finishing their beers. Valentine wanted to get away.

Fortunately Scally said he would have to be going home. He had not been there for two days. This was nothing new. He pushed a card into Valentine's top pocket. Moving off, he asked

Valentine to call him when he started his new spot. He bounded off en route to the Central Line station.

Valentine picked the card out of his pocket. It had the word Prole written in fake cyrillic. Men's Clothes and Accessories underneath. There was a phone number. Valentine felt a little sad. He placed it back in his pocket.

All he had wanted was recognition from his friend. Surely he deserved that much?

CHAPTER SEVEN

Empty glass in hand he ventured inside for another drink. Le Routier was now full of the pundits its reputation bragged of. Valentine stood in the corner and sipped from a fresh glass.

"Hello, Val, surprised to see your face again."

Small and wizened, Bryce was lowlife on any scale. If there was a grafter to be blagged, Bryce would be there. He was a lonely man. Lonely in his addiction. The dragon had etched itself deep on Bryce's face. He dealt heroin and cocaine to support his own habit. He was wired most of the time. By Valentine's calculation he must have been nearly forty.

Bryce was angling for a drink. Valentine saw his glass of Pernod was almost empty. He ordered another. With a fresh drink Bryce might go away.

But Bryce wanted to talk. He was now working as a 'concept visualiser' for an ad company. He had been a photographer and a designer. His unsavoury sidelines had opened many doors for him. He had furnished the cravings of many a media type.

Bryce's verbal barrage dwindled to a trickle. Valentine announced that he was relaunching the Underground. He intended to put Big Jack and Fly back on the decks. The Tower of Babel had made an offer he could not refuse.

Bryce looked incredulous. Surely Valentine knew that Fly was in no condition to work again.

Valentine wondered if Bryce was Fly's current dealer.

Bryce fumed at the suggestion. "Look, I don't deal in anything anymore. You've got the wrong man."

Bryce was on the run. Valentine pushed him forward to buy another round. Bryce recoiled.

"I know where there's plenty of free drink. Want to come?"

Valentine did not trust him. But he followed Bryce into the street.

* * *

Before the door swung shut Bryce was on his toes. Valentine hurriedly followed. His quarry darted down side roads like a rabbit. Then they were back up Frith Mews.

There was a crowd gathered up on the right. The throng looked rich and sexy. They oozed affluence as ripe as a tomato. This couldn't be where Bryce was heading. But Bryce gave a theatrical wave to a tall man, then waited for Valentine to catch up.

The building had a white shop front with a modern sculpture in the window. Its sign was plain yet appealing, Loach and Grierson Gallery. There was a launch party going on. Some of the revellers had spilled out into the evening.

With a facile gesture, Bryce introduced Valentine to the tall man. His name was 'Nev' and he worked in publishing. Nev felt the name 'Valentine' was 'very street'. Valentine was not sure whether this was Bryce's friend, foe or client.

Bryce ushered Valentine inside. Laurence Walker was an 'interesting' new artist and sculptor. His main piece sat in the middle of the room. It was a motorbike made of cannibalised washing machine parts. The rider had been constructed from inflated condoms.

Elsewhere, a pink rubber vibrator pertly oscillated on a revolving bentwood chair. A slow trickle of sticky white fluid oozed from the crudely automated face of the 'Laughing Man'.

The assembly proved an even greater delight to Valentine. Each woman seemed burgeoning for sexual conquest, yet each man seemed more camp than the last. Valentine felt estranged.

Bryce nudged that they should make use of the free bar. He seemed much at home in these circumstances. He jostled Valentine to a large table crammed with red and white house wine. People aggregated round it, magnetised. Bryce picked up two fluted glasses and handed them to the steward. He asked for white.

The steward looked warily at the two men. It was clear they were not regular browsers or critics. But they looked no more on the take than any of the others. He returned the glasses full.

For the second time that day Valentine felt badly turned out. His uncertainty shone through his stance and he constantly seemed to be stepping out of people's way.

Bryce put his arm on Valentine's shoulder. "You should learn to relax more."

This was an ironic comment from a man like Bryce.

Glass in hand, he led Valentine deeper into the crowd. Soon they stood under a large red exhibit. The Polaroid collage featured a photograph of a pair of androgynous buttocks. The word 'Fuck' was written in lipstick. The whole thing was stapled together. It hung from the wall at an angle. Valentine raised an eyebrow.

A greeting cut across the laughter. "Philip, Philip, you scumbag."

A man and a woman waded in their direction. She threw her arms around Bryce who kissed the woman sloppily. She had a short green dress with a leather-studded wrap.

Bryce asked Eleanor how she was. It had been a few months since they had seen each other. She and Franco had been to L.A.

Valentine attempted to look at the painting but Bryce swivelled him about, presenting him to the odd couple.

"This is Valentine. He's going to be a big noise in the clubs again." Bryce pushed Valentine's hand into Eleanor's. She looked him up and down. Bryce explained she was a 'performance artist'. Franco was her manager, a New Yorker.

It took almost a minute before Valentine could break free from the woman's grip. Franco told her to calm down and she dug him hard in the ribs. He coughed, pained. Valentine wondered who was managing who.

Again Bryce was waxing loquacious about his new consultancy position. Valentine could still not place the name of the agency. Eleanor and Franco looked on with disinterest. It was becoming increasingly obvious what their relationship with Bryce was.

Franco mentioned the heavenly 'Bolivian Flake' they had acquired while touring the West Coast. Much better than Philip could ever sell them. Bryce looked annoyed. He told Franco to lower his voice. Valentine was not sure how such matters sat in this circle. Eleanor agreed Francisco should watch what he was saying.

Bryce lowered his head and muttered something to the floor. When he looked up a wide grin stretched coldly across his face. He scanned Franco, then the woman, finally Valentine.

"Let's see if the children can take the pace." Like a crazed pied piper he beckoned them to follow. Franco moved off, Eleanor next. Valentine hung back. It was a bad move to get involved with Bryce. Especially on this level.

Eleanor looked back at Valentine. She mouthed "come on". A come-on in the purest sense of the word. Valentine couldn't bottle out now. He only needed to follow. No need to partake in anything. Besides, this road might lead to Fly.

They snaked to the back of the hall, round the back of a large canvas and through to a black corridor.

Valentine caught up with the three as they hovered in a doorway. He could just about make out the white perspex shape of a man. This was the men's toilet. Bryce swung through the door.

Valentine entered behind Franco. He saw Eleanor poised beside one of the gallery voyeurs who was pissing in a stall. Eleanor stood motionless looking down at his leaking dick. She smiled. He suddenly felt her presence. Then flinched. Then boiling embarrassment. Franco looked peeved as the man clumsily put it away. Eleanor creased up. Nervously the man shambled through the door.

Eleanor stared at Valentine. She clasped her hands together. Franco swore at her.

Bryce's head poked out from one of the cubicles. Were they going to step inside or not?

They quietly moved inside. Valentine dragged his heels and was last in. Wedged against the door. Eleanor was in front of him. She stepped back pressing her body against his. Slowly she moved her hips, rubbing her arse against his crotch. Franco and Bryce were preoccupied. Valentine began to sweat. Eleanor looked over her shoulder and winked.

Bryce took out a plastic 'seal-easy' pouch. He shook it under the dim light.

The four of them were crushed into a single cubicle. It was very warm. Bryce was obviously used to it. Valentine was not. Eleanor's hand moved down his leg.

Bryce had several grammes in the pouch. Meticulously he clicked open a Swiss army knife. He spooned a fair amount onto the porcelain cistern top. He replaced the sealed bag in his pocket. Then proceeded. Chopping out four lines.

Her fingernails scraped Valentine's legs repeatedly. He could feel veins in his neck popping. Franco was licking his lips. Bryce mumbled. This batch was not for the squeamish. Eleanor breathed heavily. Valentine's heart pumped faster. Franco gave Bryce a new twenty pound note. The sinews stood out from his wrist.

Bryce rolled the bill into a tight tube. His eyes flickered in the light. Eleanor was feverishly groping for Valentine's hard-on.

The air grew very sticky. Bryce took the tube. He wedged the end firmly in his nostril. He devoured the first sparkling line of charlie. He snorted. Dabbed the remains on his finger. Rubbed it on his gums. He gave Franco the tube.

Franco snorted greedily. His eyes bulged. He reeled, passing it on to Eleanor. She tensed with excitement. Bending forward she began to inhale. Halfway through her share, her pelvic activity heightened. Valentine felt primed like a time bomb. His self control was battered. Tight as a drum. Bryce was sniggering. Franco was almost glued to the wall. Eleanor paused, handing over the twenty. It was Valentine's turn.

She was bent double. Ready for anything. Each pose like something from the Kama Sutra. He had to take a chance. She was wanton, primeval. Her lust permeated his every thought. She grabbed his hips. He swung forward knocking Bryce and Franco out of the way. The note embedded. He chased the remaining line relentlessly. Every last crystal shot inward.

Valentine's head swam. His entire system juddered. Nerve ends fried. Neurons pulsed. Blood careered torrentially through every vein. He felt an exquisite nothingness fill him with power.

Eleanor squirmed round. She stood to face him, flinging him against the door. She kissed him. Her tongue reached deeply, feeding.

Her embrace was like a vice. She pushed him harder and harder. Her hands were all over. She moaned. She needed every last drop that could be extracted.

Valentine was finding it hard to breathe. Her mouth was suffocating him. Her nails clawed his spine. There was no air. He was floundering.

Pleasure was turning into pain. Lust into distress.

He tried to fight her off. He pulled her hair. She was too strong. Her muscles snapped taught. The mouth gaped then sucked. Valentine was drowning in saliva. His free hand rattled the door, felt for the bolt. Fingers slipped on the cold metal. Valentine gasped. The bolt slid open. Their bodies flailed. The door flew open.

Eleanor grabbed Valentine's shoulders. They tottered, then crashed onto the tiles.

Valentine's head hurt. Eleanor lay on top of him. Her body still heaved. There was nothing more to be had. Her expression rested, disapproving. She rolled off.

Franco extended his arm. She hoisted herself up. The heels rocked steady. Eleanor straightened her dress, repositioning her left tit back inside. Valentine bent double. Eleanor cradled his elbow then lifted him up.

Franco seemed unperturbed. He buttoned his Gaultier Junior, straightened his collar in the mirror. Eleanor stroked Valentine's cheek. She seemed to be about to bite his neck. Valentine winced. She stopped. A switch had flicked in her head. Her mind was suddenly somewhere else.

She ran her hands through her hair. She was laughing at nothing. Her eyes scanned the room. It was the men's toilet. Was it? Then there was Valentine, visibly quaking. She thought he had been taller. Maybe it was somebody else.

She thanked Bryce for the line then motioned to Franco. He said the plane was waiting. This seemed a strange comment. Neither reacted. They walked out of the door.

Valentine rebuttoned his shirt.

"I think she likes you," Bryce said.

Valentine's face was smeared with lipstick. Bryce unrolled some bog paper and Valentine wiped himself clean.

It made no sense. Eleanor was very attractive. She could shag most men if she wanted. Why pick on Valentine? Her brain must be fried. It was surely not the coke. Maybe an earlier tab. Maybe ecstasy. What was she on?

Bryce's headrush was levelling out. He looked straight. Except for the eyes.

Now Valentine surfaced into the hit. He was high, looking down from a peak. The sexual paranoia dissipated.

"Come on. Let's go." Bryce slipped through the door. Valentine followed.

They stood in the gallery once again. Valentine felt calm, his shame all gone. He couldn't remember when he had last had charlie. It was a long time ago. He wouldn't get hooked again. It was only one line.

Valentine no longer dodged inquisitive glances. He stared back. There was no more fear. No more self-consciousness. It was a big crowd. They might all be Bryce's clients.

Bryce headed off for more wine. Valentine placed his hand on his hip. They all posed with affectation. It seemed de rigeur. Valentine swaggered across to a small crowd huddled around a painting. Their voices seemed unusually quiet. The man wore a Conran coat. Wine splashed his heavy brogues. He was handing over a small package, encased in plastic. The trim blonde grasped it. She slid it into her pocket.

The fat executive woman was confused. "It's free!" Parachute silk sagged from her girth.

The pretty blonde lit a cigarette. "I've always wondered. Why is it called FX..."

She stopped in mid-sentence. A stranger was watching. Listening. The crowd turned away. But the blonde couldn't. She wondered how much he had heard.

Valentine stared straight at her. "Like it, do you?"

She felt cornered. How much did he know? She tried to smile.

Valentine tried again. "Do you like it? The painting?"

Her expression changed. There was relief in her eyes. Valentine did not understand. She put on her glasses and looked at the canvas. This one was called 'Street Perversion'.

She wrinkled her forehead and began to answer. Valentine watched the way she moved. Focussed on her red lips. The cropped jacket exaggerated her hips. She had long legs. He wanted to touch her. A warning light went off in his head. Things were moving too fast.

Then he felt a warm breath on his neck. Valentine spun round. Eleanor grabbed his wrist, pulled him close. The two women obviously knew each other. There was a brief greeting. Something about a new 'treatment'.

"Have you tried it?" Eleanor asked.

"Not here." The blonde pointed to Valentine.

There was an uneasy silence. It sailed over Valentine's head. All of it.

Eleanor just giggled. Then she whispered into Valentine's ear. "We could try it in Franco's car." She took three steps backward.

Try what? It was out of control. Something pulled Valentine to follow. She waded out into the street.

He couldn't smell Chanel, only sex. She wanted him. Why not there and then? Another exhibit for the liggers to watch. That would draw a big crowd. 'Live from a gallery floor in Soho'. She was a performance artist, wasn't she?

Valentine waited for her to return. His bottle was going. Then he could wait no longer. He dashed through the crowd and into the street. They could screw all night. Starting in Franco's car.

He looked to his right. He couldn't see her. Jogged down the alleyway. She wasn't there. He jostled back through the crowd and bumped into Bryce, spilling his wine.

Valentine panted. "Which way did Eleanor go?"

Bryce shrugged his shoulders. "Has she offered you a fuck yet?"

Valentine said nothing. Bryce was wiggling his hips mockingly.

"She'll have gone by now."

He offered Valentine his part-filled glass. Eleanor was a tease, pure and simple. Men? Women? A line or two? The car was as good a place as any. Valentine was surprised he had fallen for it.

The breeze got under his collar. He took the glass. One swig and it was gone. His ego was bruised. He felt impotent, helpless. The gallery was a bore, like a bad joke everyone else laughed at. Maybe Valentine had missed the punchline. He felt half-cut and the worse for the charlie. His neck was stiff. So was his dick. Something was wrong. These people all seemed crazy. Especially Bryce. He placed his glass on the pavement.

Bryce dropped his glass. A few people looked round.

"Want to go to a better party?"

CHAPTER EIGHT

Philip Bryce lived in Whitechapel, at the end of Romford Road. The cab driver pulled up to the pavement. Bryce leapt out and tendered a tenner. Valentine sighed and stretched.

Chez Bryce was singularly unremarkable. The bronze brick tenements sprawled for three hundred yards, swathed in squalor.

They marched through the car park. The central stairway stank of piss. The gangways sported soulless graffiti. There were a lot of stairs to climb. Bryce's flat was Number 51, on the next but top floor.

A large bunch of keys rattled in Bryce's grasp. There were three locks on the battered yellow door. A padlock top and bottom, a Yale in the middle. Security was clearly a priority.

He undid the final padlock then eased the door open. Bryce removed the 'gone to the shops' note and pasted it with the others on the hall wall. He slid the table away then stepped inside. Valentine followed and closed the door. Bryce wedged the table back against it.

This was a mixture of paranoia, habit and a strange form of common sense. Nobody could manhandle his way inside now.

Bryce crossed the narrow hallway into the main room. He kicked a pile of books. Valentine waited in the doorway. Bryce offered a bentwood chair. Valentine slowly sat down.

The room was jumbled with debris. Cliched despair hung on

each wall. A rake of bad cubist paintings. There were half-broken acoustic guitars in one corner. Jimi Hendrix shaped coathangers stained brown. Bryce was rumoured to have made a lot of money. He had not spent it here.

It was not difficult to imagine where it had gone. He had shot, chased or snorted every penny.

He turned on the portable TV. The picture strobed. He twisted the aerial. The movement hiccoughed then slowed. Bryce reclined back on to a mattress. The floorboards creaked. They would have some food, then he'd try to dig out Fly's address. After that they'd head for Debbie's party. There was tea in the kitchen if Valentine wanted.

Valentine walked through to the kitchen. All the appliances were crushed against one wall. The sink was full of blackened pans. He opened the cupboard to find a solitary tea caddy with only two bags left. He filled the kettle, placed it on the gas ring, lit a match and ignited the flame. He rattled through the dirty dishes to find some cups. Only one had a handle.

The milk was on the turn when he poured it on the stewing tea. It partially coagulated on top. Valentine grabbed the cups and went back inside.

Bryce sat cross-legged. Valentine placed a mug of tea in front of him.

On his right Bryce had a large pile of notes. It looked like several hundred quid in various denominations. On his left, a roll of kitchen foil. There was a large square of oil in front of him. A trace of brown powder snaked across it. This was the 'food' he spoke of. A lighted filter tip smouldered in the ashtray.

Bryce put a silver paper tube in his mouth. He lifted the foil square and ran a lighter underneath. The powder caught, letting off a trail of grey smoke. He sucked hard on the tube. The smoke followed. Brown powder ran away from the flame. It left an oily black trail. Tiny grains darted from side to side, always just ahead. The smoke curled. He moved the light faster. The last puff rammed home further than the one before.

This was his Jerusalem. His eyes glazed, consciousness raised, evaporating like the smoke. He alternated his half-burned cigarette from hand to hand. Then his mouth. He was beyond void. Only his physicality kept him earthbound. He trailed out a fresh line. Leisurely he handed it to Valentine.

Bryce was not corrupting the innocent, just looking for a way to share the moment.

Valentine remembered what it had been like. The dragon helped internalise emotion. Worlds were turning inside Bryce's head. The holocausts of war. Man's inhumanity to man. The frailty of his own existence.

Valentine did not want it. The price was too high. It had almost destroyed him before. The squalor. The cliche of the hard-living man. Here was a loser. Valentine wanted so much to be a winner.

The smell of death gripped him. He gazed at Bryce's cadaverous face, eyes like bottomless pits. This was the powerful dealer in his lair. It was a bad joke.

Bryce smiled an apology. He took the line back. He would have to eat it alone. He lit the flame and began to chase the second line. It was like throwing a drowning man lead weights.

The second dragon was cutting Bryce. His movements grew lethargic. The last whiff of smoke trailed into his mouth. He removed the tube and placed it in his top pocket. He screwed up the etched silver and tossed it into the bin. Then lit another cigarette. At last he sipped on his tea.

Valentine wanted to go. He asked for Fly's latest address. Bryce lumbered to his feet. He searched through a mass of paper and empty cigarette packets. Eventually he produced a gilt-edged address book, weighty like a bible. He scanned the pages clerically.

It was difficult to assess how far gone he was. He moved his fingers with astonishing acuity. The first line had sent him to outer space. The second steadied him in orbit.

He was not sure whether Fly was back in the country. Sources told him that he might still be in Paris. Scoring acid, by all accounts.

Taking out a pen, he scribbled an address on the back of somebody's calling card. Bryce was about to hand it to Valentine.

There was a knock on the door. They both stopped still.

Valentine wondered who it was. Bryce knew.

He looked at the deco wall clock. Then shook his head. He should have been out by this time. It was a gross error. His habit had got the better of him again.

A voice rang out from the other side. "Open the door, Philip."

This was not a suggestion, more of a demand. Bryce was flummoxed. He bundled the money into his pocket and clumsily stumbled to the door. He shouted for the stranger to identify himself.

The voice replied, "Open the door."

By now Valentine was interested to see who it was. The stranger was certainly having an affect. Bryce removed the table and turned the lock. The look on his face screamed panic.

A man stepped inside. Bryce crept behind. The tall man acknowledged Valentine with a whimsical "hello". There was something brutal about him. Nothing he said. Not even his manner.

He looked around the debris, told Bryce he should get a cleaner. Bryce tried to laugh.

He asked Bryce for the money Bryce tried to explain.

The man sighed. Without another word he threw Bryce against the wall. There was a dull thud.

His face remained expressionless. He grabbed Bryce's hair. Then wielded a shiny metal corkscrew. He lunged towards Bryce's head. Valentine's guts were all twisted. The man seemed unconscious of his presence. He drew the corkscrew down Bryce's face. An eighth of an inch from the skin.

"Look, Philip, I could drill right through your face. You don't want that, do you?"

Bryce swallowed. He said he could have the money by midnight.

The man remained poised. He pulled tighter on the hair.

Bryce screamed. He tried to wriggle away. The man was powerful.

Valentine could not look. This was too gruesome. Clearly Bryce had pushed his luck too far. The man was going to take his pound of flesh. Valentine wanted to stop it. But he could not overpower this man. He didn't want to get involved.

Just by being there he was involved. It might be his turn next.

Why the hell wouldn't Bryce pay?

The man raised his hand. Seconds passed like hours. He was ready to strike.

Then as quickly as he had grabbed Bryce, he released him. The corkscrew disappeared back into his pocket. He walked towards the door. He looked back at Valentine, paused.

Sweat poured down Valentine's face. His complexion had turned grey. He knew he had seen too much.

The man just winked. "See you at twelve, Phil."

He skirted by the table and closed the door behind him.

Valentine imagined the corkscrew being wound into Bryce's head. He shivered. Bryce lay crumpled on the floor. The man might easily have fixed them both. It was not hard to imagine that he had enjoyed his work. There must be a certain charge involved in this kind of terrorism. The whole idea was too perverse. There was sexual energy in that kind of penetration. Valentine stopped thinking about it. His flesh felt sticky.

Bryce explained that he did not have the money. The four-fifty stuffed in his pockets was somebody else's. They would not give him a chance. Hunt would do more than threaten next time. He had to avoid the flat until tomorrow. He could get the money by then.

But Hunt was coming back at midnight.

Bryce trembled slightly. The corkscrew had torn at the effect of the skag.

Valentine wanted to go back to Anna. He could handle a freaked out drunk. Not this. Around every corner there was some pervert. They all seemed friends of Bryce.

He took the address from Bryce's book. No matter how fucked Fly was, it could be no worse than this. He needed to get out before the man with the corkscrew returned.

By now Bryce had collected himself. Shakily he lit a cigarette. It would be best if they left quickly. Whitechapel tube station was just up the road. They would be late for Debbie's party, but it was not far.

Valentine was being manipulated. He did not want to go to this party with Bryce. He had his information. There was no need to carry on.

Bryce clamped the locks shut. He transferred a note from the wall to the door. Will be back at Twelve.

Valentine sped down the stairs. He was thinking about going to Camden. Maybe a late supper with Anna. He had enough money. She was alright if she kept sober. There was something between them. Her pathological mistrust of men, his hatred of drunks. He did not care how he would have to perform. It was a safe place to stay. He gave survival number one priority.

The tube station was very close. Valentine could see the familiar circular sign. Ten yards ahead Bryce slipped into the 7-Eleven shop. He returned with two cans of lager, The Sun newspaper and a packet of Twiglets. He gave a can to Valentine. They popped open the tops and drank.

"Fancy a Twiglet?"

Bryce had been very fair. He had shared all with Valentine. Even the violence. He had not attempted to involve Valentine in the conflict. Nobody had actually been hurt. They had both walked away.

The beer tasted sweet. It was a welcome rest on an eventful evening. Valentine looked at Bryce. He was a funny little guy. They were building up an understanding. Valentine agreed to differ only where the skag was concerned. Perhaps he was just lonely.

Valentine asked where the party was. Bryce pointed at Ladbroke Grove on the tube map. Some friends from work were having a get together.

Valentine had never liked advertising types. Especially the ones that would invite Bryce to a party.

He should phone Anna. She would be expecting him. What if she had gone out? What if she had had second thoughts about the whole thing? This would not be completely unheard of. If he got to Camden and she was out he would certainly be worse off. He had to hedge his bets.

He knew that Bryce would not be heading home after the party. Hunt might be waiting. No. No. No. It would be abject lunacy to spend any more time with him.

Valentine was trying to be honest with himself. He was lying badly. He wanted some excitement. He wanted to meet more women like Eleanor. If the party was no good he could go back to Anna's in a cab. Who knows, he might even get another line or two.

He didn't really give a fuck about Bryce. If he wanted to get his face corkscrewed that was his problem. None of Bryce's friends would know who he was. They would never see him again. Anyway, Valentine wanted to get screwed.

He liked thinking like this. It was hard, brutal. It gave him an erection. Valentine wanted his mind and body to get fucked.

They had both been very close to a serious kicking. They were still intact.

The train rolled into the station. Valentine asked whether he was still welcome. Bryce stepped onto the train and stood between the doors. As they were about to close, he grunted "yes". Valentine leapt onto the train. The doors clipped his shoulders as they shut.

Bryce cheered up a lot. He believed he had a friend. He lit up on the tube. This was illegal. Valentine had no respect for authority but trivial illegality worried him. They would have to change to the Met at Kings Cross. It was not a good idea to arrive there smoking.

Besides, Bryce had a lot of gear on him. But his mind was elsewhere, glazed over. He browsed through his paper. Then offered Valentine some Twiglets.

He chuckled at the Page 3 girl. Fingers flicked to the TV page. "Midnight Express is on again." Valentine tried to look at the 'Tyson Exclusive' on the back page. The tube rattled too much. It was impossible to focus.

He looked up the carriage. It was a strange time. Not many people were travelling through the West End. He was more tired than he wanted to admit.

Bryce mentioned that it was Debbie's birthday party. He rambled that he and Debbie once had an affair. Valentine looked incredulously at Bryce's physique, puny and wasted. Hardly the pulsating bulk affairs were made of. Debbie was an American set designer that Bryce had met at the Mambo. She was on the rebound from her first husband. The divorce was going through. She had two kids. Bryce was hardly expert at playing daddy.

The more he explained, the more unlikely it sounded. Maybe the woman had a thing about casualties. Valentine did not care whether it was true. It made Bryce happy to see things that way. He was crying out for normality in a sea of self-destruction. It was not hard for Valentine to respond.

The train jerked into Kings Cross. The escalator arches were charred from the recent blaze. The place still seemed like a death-trap. Valentine felt relieved that Bryce had extinguished his filter. It was not right to taunt the dead.

They marched through the barrier ticketless, mumbling that they were changing lines. It was a question of the right attitude. The inspector paid no real attention.

They passed onto the Met platform. A Hammersmith train flashed up on the indicator. It was only going to take another fifteen minutes. Bryce whinged, suddenly worried about their lateness.

Within seconds the train arrived and they were rolling towards Paddington. Bryce was growing increasingly impatient. He searched through his pocket, eventually pulling out a small hinged box. Silently he opened it. Valentine gazed at the contents, a single marcasite clip. It flashed silver under the yellow light. Valentine could not imagine Bryce presenting a gift, unless there was a price to be paid.

Bryce nodded. It was for Debbie. This was to be their secret.

Ladbroke Grove station was the same as ever. Plasterwork crumbling. Poster faces tagged with magic marker moustaches. Subway graffiti transplanted from New York. Valentine jogged up the worn wooden stairs, his companion four steps in front.

Bryce ran straight past the ticket inspector. The guard shouted. Bryce did not turn round. Valentine walked up and paid his fifty pence, the fare from Paddington. There was no need to skank through. He knew Bryce could have paid.

Bryce stood outside panting. Valentine approached him relaxed. He had no business running. Valentine made time to light a filter. Bryce refused the offer. He paced off maniacally.

Apparently their destination was a fair distance from the station. Lateness was a problem. Bryce wanted Valentine to move faster. Mounting excitement was enough to heighten his pace. Valentine felt obliged not to be a millstone.

The Grove was busy. Cruisers abounded. Bryce hailed a black cab in front of the off-licence. Valentine asked whether they should take a bottle. Bryce pulled him inside the taxi.

There had been something relentless about this journey and Bryce's need to put miles between himself and his flat. Maybe he genuinely wanted to arrive on time. Still, they had cut a dash.

He told the driver "Cardew Villas". The cab swung a U-turn. When they hit the straight they motored at fifty. Bryce was pleased with this recklessness.

Most of the houses looked similar, tall and white, some more well-kept than others. The driver was smoking what looked like a Castella. Suitable enough a distraction, Bryce thought. The driver hung a sharp right.

Bryce steadied himself. He removed a foil wrap from his pocket. Then stuck the tube in his mouth. Unfolding the paper, he shook the brown powder into line. He flicked on his lighter. A blue flame lit under the 'brown sugar'.

Valentine watched incredulously. Smoke spiralled. Bryce sucked harder. The driver did not look round.

Valentine felt his palms beginning to sweat. This performance was dangerous. What would the driver say? What if anyone driving by noticed? Valentine was his friend. More like 'accessory after the fact'.

Valentine must remain calm. He could not afford to draw attention. Time ticked slow, frame by frame. The only sound Valentine could hear was the low crackle of the silver paper. The skag fizzled and fused, dancing. Bryce sat mesmerised by the movement.

Valentine sat as powerless as Bryce. He could not move. Visions of arrest and imprisonment flickered in the light from the meter. Each eye that drove by flashed accusations.

Bryce took forever to finish, squeezing every last grain, black with the flame. Extracting the last trail, he coughed then folded the paper back into his pocket.

Time jumped back into place. Cars began to rumble outside again.

A garage came into view. Bryce asked the driver to pull in. "More cigarettes." He was oblivious to any sense of alarm. He had done nothing wrong in his terms. It was as if he had just finished a can of lager in the cab. He could not arrive at Debbie's party without a stiffener.

The taxi parked by a petrol pump. Bryce fumbled with the door and rolled out. He staggered to the cash window and asked for his favourite brand. He wondered why Valentine was breathing so heavily. The cabbie had obviously seen nothing.

Valentine raised his head, trying to look calm. A nerve above his eyeball twitched. He had been very scared. Maybe that was the reaction Bryce wanted.

CHAPTER NINE

101 Cardew Villas looked pristine even under electric light. There was a single coach lamp by the door. The path was blocked by a '68 Karmann Ghia and a low slung old Cadillac. Bryce and Valentine squeezed between the cars and climbed the steps.

Bryce rang the bell. They waited. Lights went on. Footsteps clattered. A wail of music drifted louder. The door opened. Valentine tried to look sexy.

A tanned face offered a formal "hello", then held out his right hand. "How are you, Philip?" Bryce shook his hand. He introduced Valentine to Michael. Michael's shirt was crisp, his trousers plain black. His hands felt soft, manicured. He exuded the ease of wealth, his bearing devoid of fear or repression.

The hallway was beige and mauve. Pictures looked stylishly isolated. Someone had spent a lot of money to create this calm.

Michael wafted them through, then down a winding staircase. The three stood in the entrance to the kitchen. Valentine had never seen the like. It must have run the length of the house, about eighty foot square. It might have been ripped straight from a magazine. The fittings were white and half-surrounded the room. The rest was a dining area.

There were no naked revellers. No grinding music. A group of about fifteen people stood talking. A compact disc burbled in the comer, something Latin in flavour. Valentine did not know how to react or stand. This was no house party. It was a dinner party. A classy one at that.

Michael handed them glasses. He filled each with champagne, French and expensive. Bryce made his excuses, and drifted across the room. He must talk to Deborah.

Valentine stood isolated. A spare part, an illegal alien. Michael was waxing lyrical about Philip bringing his friend. It was all very cosy, but Valentine wriggled nervously. Michael explained he was an Art Director at 'Patrick's'. He laughed easily. Philip worked for their competitors.

Valentine asked if all Deborah's friends worked for ad agencies.

"Most do." He pointed them out.

The tall thin man was Jobere. He worked at Langton-Black. The guy with the ponytail was Max, over from the States on an exchange for the McTeel Corporation. Then the rather attractive woman was Virginia Nixon. She was one of the bosses at Reaction, where Philip was working. It was a small agency that did commercials and conferences.

So the list went on, until there were only a few unknown faces left, either boyfriends or wives.

It made no difference. Valentine was still very alienated. Here was all the power and wealth he had fantasised about. It was not wild. It was ordinary. There was a sense of family to the group. You could not fake this calm. Their security came from high lifestyle, power. They all knew the secret.

Valentine had nothing to say to them. He was impotent. A nonevent. He should go now. But still he wanted to understand. All faculties hung in suspended animation.

Michael asked what he did for a living. Valentine tried to think of a smart answer. All he could come up with was the truth.

"I promote clubs. I dabble a bit in new music. I used to DJ." Michael glowed with interest. "Ginny would love to meet you."

She was always on the lookout for new ideas. Michael would bring her over. Then he was gone.

Valentine looked at his worthless carcass. There he was with forty quid in his pocket. They might earn forty grand. He felt sorry for himself, sorry and isolated. Anna was waiting. Why couldn't he be satisfied with that?

A top man in clubs? This was nothing, a bagatelle these people might find in their cornflake packets. Why could he never be satisfied? Why should his greed drive him to despair?

These were the kind of people who told the nation what to wipe their arses with. What kind of shit to eat. The way to think. They were the future.

He had no future. The only thing to do was get drunk. Valentine took the champagne bottle from the worktop, headed for an armchair and sat in the comer.

Bryce was talking to a small dark-haired woman. She laughed loudly as he cut up a French stick. Bryce glowed in her light.

More champagne? He watched the bubbles rise to the surface. They hit the top and joined the foam. A bath oil for the rich. As he looked into the froth a voice broke his concentration. A young man was asking for a light, holding up a filter tip.

Valentine withdrew his matches then struck up a flame. The man puffed and drew back, now on the level with the woman beside. She was young, her clothes almost identical to her man's.

He had not seen Valentine's face before. His name was Greg. He pointed to his girlfriend, Roz.

Valentine was not pleased someone had spoken to him. He really just wanted to finish his drink and go. He told Greg he had come with Philip Bryce. Valentine didn't want to give any more away.

Greg launched into a tirade about work. Pressure. Moving units. Moving ideas.

Valentine detected a note of derision in the man's voice.

Because he had come with Bryce, Valentine was being written off as the lowlife associate of their lowlife friend.

Greg was talking about generating needs in the public mind. Valentine cut in. There could be no such thing as creating false needs. Everybody by nature wanted everything. Actually, everyone wanted more than they could have. Greed flowed freely through most people's veins. It made bank robbers, adulterers. The lucky ones ended up rich. There were no rules in that kind of game. Purely failure and success.

Greg looked miffed. Who was this man, bordering on the burnt out, telling him what worked? He earned a lot of money. The stranger looked as if he hardly had the bus fare.

Somebody had turned the compact disc louder. It started to cut through the chatter. Greg presumed that "Mr. Valentine" might have equally strong opinions on music. Greg bragged. He had seen Caliente and her band when he was last in Barcelona. She was smooth and sexy. They had recorded their new album there.

Valentine waited for Greg's trump card to fold. He too appreciated her vocal purity. More so her marketplace success. He had put Caliente on in the Underground in '82. She didn't even have a record deal then.

Greg did not believe it. "What exactly is your line of work?"

Valentine smirked. He created the ideas this year that people like Greg would move into advertising and marketing next year.

Greg searched for a suitable put-down but at this moment Debbie called out for everyone to sit down to dinner.

Valentine finished him off. "I'm sorry I've not dressed for dinner. I prefer to travel incognito." Greg floundered and Roz dragged him off to the table, mumbling his anger all the way.

Finishing the last of his champagne, Valentine took his position at the table, next to Bryce. He made sure he was a safe distance from Greg.

Debbie was still darting about placing the last of the serving dishes on the table. The crowd was now firmly installed. Each had a large oval plate in front of them. Every inch of the long table was crammed with Greek food. If it swam, grew or crawled in Greece it was there, garnished with dark vine leaves. They scrambled for the food.

Valentine piled his plate high. It tasted excellent. Bryce struggled hopelessly with small pieces of fried squid. Michael circled, refilling glasses with champagne. There was no great table talk. People were keeping to themselves.

"Not as you expected?" said Bryce. Valentine nodded, his mouth stuffed. The only thing that caught his eye was the Nixon woman.

She was not so pretty, but there was something about her way. She had very little food on her plate, but glugged the champagne like it was water. It seemed to have no effect on her. She lit up a long white cigarette much to the disapproval of her fellow diners. The man next to her nudged her elbow. She blew smoke into his food.

She had been bold, impressive. The others ignored her. This was Ginny's normal behaviour. She pushed the plate back from the table and adopted a mannish pose.

Most of the dishes were empty. Valentine finished the remains of his food. He buried a stick of celery into the last of the taramasalata. Michael topped up his empty glass.

They had gorged, elemental. This was the way of their everyday lives. Always enough food. A river of champagne. Constant, intravenous. Never that feeling of bloatedness. They were used to cornucopia. None would have to slacken their belts.

Now the champagne was flowing they could relax. The policemen of the psyche were signing off for the evening. Sanity was about to take its leave. The wildness they had harnessed could roam free. The real party could begin.

Michael announced it was time to go upstairs. People slid their chairs from under the table. Bryce flew off to speak to Deborah standing by the fridge. She hung back conspicuously. It was obvious they wanted to be alone. The guests trudged up the stairs. Valentine tagged along, not wanting to be a spare part in the kitchen.

Up the snaking stairwell onto the landing, growing unruly as they went. Valentine followed behind Max, Virginia Nixon behind him. He looked back as they entered the large room. She glanced disapprovingly. She was deceptively short. Her shoulders hunched as she pushed by.

The main room was as grand as the basement. Its style was vaguely Eastern. There was a large Persian rug in front of the fireplace. Michael flicked a switch and the fake log fire ignited. Flames leapt and curled.

The sofa was full, as were the armchairs. Those left standing pulled up square foam seats. Valentine sat next to a swarthy man. There was a particular ambience as this individual pulled out a brown leather pouch. The noise drifted to its minimum. The man called Jobere lit a joint. Michael turned on the hi-fi. A mixed beat hit out. The bass thudded through the floor. A few tapped their feet. Others nodded in time. The swarthy man opened his pouch methodically.

The Nixon woman stood by the fireplace. "Stop fucking around, Dino," she murmured. The swarthy man paid no attention. He lifted a six inch square mirror tile onto his lap. His hidden tackle spilled out onto the slate: razor blade, perforated crushing plate, and a large plastic bag full of cocaine. Valentine estimated four hundred quid's worth. Deftly the man emptied a large pile onto the glass. It sparkled like sugar as he chopped out a line. He put a silver straw in his right nostril.

Without a pause, he sucked up the trail. He removed the tube, sprinkled the remains back onto the tile. Arching to one side he gave the tile to Valentine.

"Your turn," he said curtly.

Many eyes were turned on him. It was like an initiation to a boys' club, only girls were allowed in too, if they paid their dues.

Valentine chopped one out. He had done it a thousand times on the street. Not in this kind of scenario. He was not going to be bested by a group of desk jockeys. If they wanted to play space cadets, so be it.

Taking the blade he metered out a fair amount. He chopped it, fanning out a line. The tube was solid silver. Up the nostril and down with the line.

He snorted. God, how he snorted. The charlie spilled down his nasal passages. He could feel it in the back of his throat. He sniffed as it tore into the membranes, some sticking on the hairs in his nose, the rest passing mercilessly into his blood.

How good it was. Pennies from heaven. Pandora's box. A whole microcosm exploding inside his head. His body throbbed with the music, alive with verve and wit. He liked this. It affected him the same as when he and Fly used to do 'white-light-white-heat'.

This crowd was no longer a match for the mighty Valentine. He felt invincible. Every sinew standing to attention. A bristling army ready to repel boarders. He straightened his back, swaggering at their faces. But he saw no animosity. Only concurrence, approval. He passed the tile along to the next taker.

Dino explained that it was very special. "Bolivian Rake". Incredibly difficult to acquire in this country. "It's a good hit." He prodded Valentine.

There was no reply. Simply a contented sigh. Valentine hoped it would be his turn again. Soon.

By the time Bryce and Debbie entered with a birthday cake, the plate of charlie had been round twelve people and was on its way back in Valentine's direction. He had lost track of time. The music was growing perceptively more powerful, the conversation ebbing and flowing. In and out of phase. He was losing control.

The poison and the antidote were the same. How long was it going to take them? Were they so blind? His need was greater than theirs. Surely Dino realised.

Tottering through, Bryce placed the cake on the table. He insisted they all sang 'Happy Birthday'. He cajoled repeatedly, finally getting a reaction.

Michael turned down the hi-fi. Grudgingly they began to sing. First one, then five, then fifteen.

"Happy birthday to you, happy birthday to you..."

The words grew louder. More garbled, less caring.

Debbie leant and blew out the candles. Bryce proceeded clumsily to cut the cake with the Sabatier knife. Nobody seemed to want any.

Dino took the first piece. It was pink and smothered in cream. He forced a bite into his mouth. It stuck, smothered on his moustache.

It was quite amusing. Valentine laughed. Soon everybody was laughing. Relentlessly, Dino gorged. Bite after bite, layer after layer. Valentine felt queasy. Dino continued. More, more, in time with the music. His face was painted with cream. He took a second slice.

They followed his lead. One piece after another. Each person trying to consume it faster than the next. That was it. A race. A cake agility test. Forcing cake into each other's mouths. Cream fell onto the carpet. Their faces were awash with cream and icing.

Valentine had held himself back. He did not like cake. One woman fed a piece to her boyfriend. He half chewed it. Then she stuck her tongue in his mouth, licking out the squelch.

Dino wiped his mouth on his sleeve. There was no cake left. Only an empty plate. The hilarity was waning. The last ones moving were Greg and Roz. The rest had no more cream.

Valentine felt that they would have gorged on each other's shit if that was the order of the day.

Debbie had watched demurely, as if she was not at home. Dino reclined, spent like an aging Don Juan. Michael poured the remains of his bottle of champagne into a glass. There was plenty more downstairs.

At the mention of more champers, four or five made a beeline for the stairs. Others split off into the back room. Taking a dab of coke off the tile Bryce sat down next to Valentine. Dino sat up and gave a hearty "Hello, Philip."

Bryce tittered. The birthday cake had been riddled with hash. Dino should know. He had made it. He snorted a last line of chas, leaving the rest for Valentine.

The tile was almost empty. While Valentine gazed forlorn, Dino offered him the pouch. "Help yourself." Dino was beginning to grow on Valentine.

He opened the easi-seal bag, then poured enough for two large lines on the tile. Vigorously he chopped, until all that remained were two perfect trails. He lined up the straw and did them one after the other.

It was a smooth hit, a racing sensation that built into a surge, then a soaring flight. He was certainly ready for action now. All he had to do was choose the stakes. The only problem was his powerful thirst. The champagne was downstairs.

Wired, Bryce asked if either of them wanted a drink. They nodded in unison. He produced an unopened bottle from behind his back, then took three dirty champagne glasses from the table. He filled them with vodka. This was more like it.

Valentine drank and felt soothed. Bryce spilled half of his. Dino finished his glass in one and took some more. He said he had heard Bryce was leaving Reaction. Bryce could not afford to. There were too many expenses he could not otherwise meet.

Dino announced that he was going to retire. He did not look more than thirty-five, but that was old in his business. He had left college as a radical in the seventies. For years he drifted. Then an old friend asked him to proof some copy. He was a graduate in English so he rewrote it. Brightman, Bull and Cole gave him a job. He moved on rapidly. Dino wrote a jingle for a beer commercial. The campaign went worldwide. They wanted to make him a partner. He preferred to remain an employee. That was a few years ago. He now pulled over a grand a week.

But something was going wrong. There were no ideas left in his head. He felt burnt out. And there was something else. Too many art directors were doing The Drug. They had no ideas left. The Drug was taking over. Dino had only tried it once. It was a bad trip. His friends were playing a dangerous game. There was no way of stopping it. The whole thing was too big. It was sending people wacko.

Valentine did not understand. Dino was speaking in riddles. He finished the vodka. Bryce was obviously too wrecked to join in.

Dino had bought a house in Barbados. The weather was much nicer. He hoped it was far enough away. But perhaps they were dishing it out there, too. The Drug was dynamite. You only needed one line.

Valentine was confused. One line? "What are they taking?" he asked.

Dino looked startled. He remembered Valentine was a stranger. He wasn't in the business. Perhaps he had said too much, certainly too much in front of Bryce. Dino needed a piss. He didn't excuse himself, just stood up and walked away.

The whole thing seemed very curious. "Only one line." It stuck in Valentine's head. He was too wired to think straight. Shakily, Valentine poured another vodka.

Virginia Nixon appeared from nowhere, leaning against the fireplace. Her eyes tore into Valentine. "What have you taken?" she purred.

Valentine replied sharply. He had taken no more than anyone

else. It was no business of hers. But Virginia would not leave it at that. She wanted to know who "this man" was.

Bryce sniggered. "Nobody knows who he is."

Virginia sat down in front of them. She ruffled her hands through her hair and gazed inquisitively. "You look as if you're on purple hearts. I used to take them when I was sixteen."

Valentine was not going to take this. How dare she project her inadequacies onto him. She had written him off in ten syllables. But that was her problem, not his. Why didn't she just "Fuck off"?

Virginia coiled. Few men rose to the bait so quickly. She smiled diplomatically.

Perhaps he had some FX?

Valentine didn't know what she was talking about.

Bryce looked on. The Boss Lady was blabbing.

Then she realised she had said too much. She apologised to Valentine for being rude. It had been a hard day at the office. Hers was a high-pressure business.

"Just like selling second-hand cars," Valentine said.

She paused, then laughed. There was still the question of FX. Virginia wanted some badly. And she wanted it now. Valentine was her new face. It was hard to tell if he was lying. Most of Bryce's friends were liars. Pleading ignorance was their simplest form of evasion.

Virginia Nixon asked Bryce who his friend was.

Valentine offered his name and a handshake. She enquired if it was 'Mister' Valentine. It was just 'Valentine', plain and simple.

Virginia skinned up a joint. She then described a cook's tour of her current life. There were the bigger accounts, the parties, the commercials, the product launches, Christmas with the family, the trail of inadequate men, the prissy PAs, the art school cameramen, the coke, the late nights, the dukes, the mooks, the dykes.

Valentine scanned her body. This trip was more interesting. She looked as if she had just turned thirty. Her hair was blonde, tousled. The face was pale and animated. Her lips shone a pale pink. The black rubberised jacket clung to her shoulders. There was no excess flesh. Her breasts bobbed as she spoke. No sign of a bra.

The joint burned freely in her mouth. Smoke spiralled. She extended a heavily jewelled finger. Lots of rings. There was no break in her speech. It was Valentine's turn.

He tasted the joint's cloudy emission. It brought him down to earth.

She had mixed a cocktail of black and grass. It was perfect, slim and tight like a regular filter. She had done it before. He took a third drag and began to listen.

Virginia spoke about drugs and creativity. It was a bad cliche. Great artists required great compulsions. Janis Joplin and her skag habit. Bukowski and his alcoholism. Joe Orton and his rampant homosexuality. The end justifies the means. Even in death. It was the same in her business. The creative ideas had to flow no matter what the price was.

And what about the losers? Valentine had seen such compulsions crush himself and his friends.

Virginia didn't understand the sentiment. It was difficult to lose on 75k a year.

Her ruthlessness seemed very attractive. It was life for the living, not for tomorrow. Was it all just rhetoric? She simply named her price, and never played when the stakes got too high. There was no way to lose.

This woman could never understand the Blag. It embraced everything. It was the losable gamble. That sharp edge. Valentine's honour stemmed from it. Honour? He surprised himself.

Bryce got up and stumbled towards the door. She sat down next to him. "Come on, Valentine, let's get it on."

Virginia got closer and closer. She asked for a couple of lines. He didn't know what she was talking about. There was no coke left and Valentine certainly had no money to buy any. He told her. But she shook her head. Money? FX was free. He had to give her some.

"FX?" He had never heard of it. Perhaps it was a new name for ecstasy. A crack substitute. Maybe fresh angel dust. She grabbed his arm. Dug her nails in.

"Stop playing games." She didn't whine like a junkie. Her demand was for stimulation, not release. She needed something more potent than a coke rush. The grip got tighter. Her hand tore at his sleeve.

Finally Valentine shook free. He was confused. He rubbed his arm.

"What the hell is FX?"

Virginia sat up straight. She floundered. What if he was telling the truth? What if he really had no FX? Valentine seemed an implausible character, especially where drugs were concerned. She was no longer sure.

He thought for a moment. Seventy-five grand would buy a lot of drugs, the possibilities were frightening. But she had said *"It was free."* Nothing good was free. It made no sense.

"I suppose they give it away," he said.

Virginia's face remained expressionless.

She was taking the piss, seeing if he would rise to the bait. She had made the whole thing up. There was no such thing as FX. It was all an elaborate game.

Was it?

Virginia was scared. She had spoken too freely. What if every user passed the story on? There would be a scandal that none of them could afford. Careers would be ruined.

It had to be a closed club, a new religion. Valentine was an outsider. Was he? She had to know for sure. There was only a little left at the flat, only enough for a couple of lines. She had to work on the premise that he had some. Nothing else mattered.

She didn't find Valentine particularly appealing. But as a dupe he would suffice. "Alright, Valentine, you win."

Valentine congratulated himself. She was becoming quite cosy now. Talking became easier. He told her about the Underground. He talked about the big promotional scams, all the new fashions he had set. But they were all 'nickel and dime' ventures.

Virginia could see that. She enjoyed going to clubs but there was no mileage in them. No money. Perhaps he would make a good account director. Virginia was always on the lookout. She wanted to see him burn.

Valentine saw admiration in her face. He completely missed the brutal calculation. Her life seemed to revolve around power, wealth and excitement. She had it all. But wanted more. He understood that greed. It made his stomach churn. He wanted more. He wanted her.

They were now completely alone in the room. This was the end game. Valentine had played all his cards. He had nowhere to invite her to. No ritzy pied-à-terre. He knew it was over. They lived in different worlds.

Virginia smiled. She zipped up her jacket. It was late.

She stood up and walked towards the door. Her hand rested against the frame. She looked back at Valentine. He looked at her.

There was nothing to say but goodbye. So he said nothing.

Virginia sighed. "Aren't you coming?"

CHAPTER TEN

She slammed the door of the Karmann Ghia. There was a dampness in the early morning air. Driving would be treacherous.

They clicked the seatbelts taut. She adjusted the mirror. With
one turn of the key the engine roared. It ticked over like a big cat.

First into reverse. The car rolled back out of the driveway. On
the street there was no other movement. They turned at forty
five degrees. Another gear change. The clutch was still depressed.
The motor raced. Power building up. She turned to Valentine,
narrowing her eyes. Not one word. The revs continued to swell.
Harder and harder. The drive pulling against itself. She slid her
heel from the clutch. With a loud whirl of rubber the car shot forward. They were catapulted simultaneously back into their seats.

The notion inside Valentine's head was a mixture of tension
and excitement. He believed he had scored in a big way. It had
not crossed his mind that she had made the move, that she might
be pulling the strings.

Virginia felt for the gear shift, her hand brushing his thigh.
There was no room to recoil, no possibility for second thoughts.
He was strapped in for the duration. His body tingled. Her touch
was strong. She gloated, teasing. The car grunted into second
gear. The vibrating gear shift slid into third.

The view blurred. It was barely possible to make out terraced
Maida Vale. Such paleness seemed alien against the black. Street

lamps shot off at angles. Cats' eyes no longer operated in terms of distance. There were no reference points. Only a relentless pace that gave no respect to the eye.

Valentine gripped the seat, the remains of the coke and booze spinning inside. This was not a clever way to travel. He noticed the speedo clocking against sixty. It fluttered, only to push past the fluorescent marking. Steady at 65. He looked for signs of respite on Virginia Nixon's body. There were none. She gripped the wheel rigid, showing no signs of worry.

Images of a write-off oozed into his psyche. A ball of fire engulfing the car. The motion of a rolling wreck. A face through the windscreen. Cuts. Gouged flesh. Blood splattering like rain on the street. Rivers of red.

A stop light was approaching. Less than a hundred yards. Less than fifty. Seconds away. She was not slowing down. Her foot hovered above the brake.

The car screeched to a halt. Valentine's chest was buffeted on the seat belt. Sweat was pouring from his brow. His breathing was rapid. Nervously he rubbed the perspiration from his face. Virginia was still staring at the road.

"Don't worry. I'm a perfectly safe driver."

She had been testing him. Why had he let his paranoia take over? Why didn't he revel in the danger she fed him? He felt he had failed. The woman had him exactly where she wanted. At least he had not cried out. That was one consolation. The lights changed and they rolled into action once again.

Virginia took a filter tip from the half-full box on the dashboard. She felt for Valentine's breast pocket. Unhooking the button, she pulled out matches. Striking the box and match with one hand, she lit up.

She still didn't know if he had any FX.

She held the flame aloft and told Valentine to help himself. Quickly he took one and drew through the flame.

She apologised for racing.

Valentine asked "What do you want?"

There was no reply. He could get nothing out of her.

They were now motoring down Park Lane. Each building was set back further than the next. Grandiose hotels. Rolls Royce dealers. The trappings of wealth, greed.

"Nice work if you can get it," she said.

It started to rain when they crossed Vauxhall Bridge. The stench of the Thames blew through the air ducts. Valentine felt rough.

He asked her again. What did she want? She wanted a man, was that not answer enough? No, it was not. There had to be something more. Companionship was no high priority. Surely it was not the sexual encounter? Conquest. Supremacy. The knowledge that you can meet any challenge.

Valentine wondered what she was like in bed. He noticed how her hands gripped the wheel, veins protruding with tension. She might make a frightening partner. Vampiric. Ready to draw his life's blood.

God, how she wanted that FX. So bad she could taste the thrill. It would not be long now. They would be home soon. Then the real party could begin.

Valentine was a funny little man, more bravado than brave. Like all men, he could serve a purpose. Before too long he would be doing her bidding. All she had to do was box him in. Close the lid.

They hit the Oval. This time Valentine did not balk at the speed. He sat back and collected himself. If she wanted to play, why not? He unclipped the seat belt. Tenements bobbed past the rear-view. Raising himself up on one hand Valentine landed a sloppy kiss, a direct hit on her mouth. With all the strength he could muster he held himself in place.

His face was blocking her view. She could not see the road.

A fight to keep the wheel straight. She tussled with him. A second longer, she would lose control. She knew there was a sharp left coming up.

She raised her hand across his face. Her fingernails ripped and broke. Blood spurted and he fell back. The car skidded towards the corner. She lunged, spinning the wheel manically.

The car avoided the kerb by a matter of inches. In her fury she was not going to slow down. She smeared the remains of the lipstick from her mouth.

Three ruby grooves were opening just above Valentine's cheek. They were painful, although not deep. He panted like a wounded animal. He had not expected her to hit him. He thought she would slow down. Stop, even.

She guided one finger across his cuts. Raising the finger to her mouth, she licked the blood away. She had regained control.

Turning down Jamaica Road, she breathed relief. They would be on home ground in minutes. Now she had some leverage, this man's guilt.

Valentine rubbed his bloody face. He felt cheap and worthless. A rapist. No amount of explanation would excuse his action. He was lowlife.

Maybe she got off on violence. He tried to tell himself he did not, but the whole thing had turned him on in some perverse sort of way.

She slowed down. He felt sure that Virginia was going to kick him out of the car. But they turned through a large portico. The car drew to a halt.

They sat motionless. She turned the key. Silence. She unclipped her seatbelt. He began with a "Look, I'm ..." but before he could finish his sentence she had reached over. She smothered his lips with kisses. He opened his mouth. Deftly her tongue entered, entwining with his. She swooned and probed.

Then, as mysteriously as she began, she stopped. Opening the door she stepped outside. Valentine followed suit. They stood facing each other, the car in between. He still wanted to explain himself.

"No words. I don't want to know." She beckoned him to come inside.

When she flicked on the lights Valentine felt he was in the wrong place. This was a warehouse conversion. Just like the ones he had seen in TV commercials, or that play about the stock exchange. The room seemed to stretch for miles. It was sectioned off with rice paper screens. The windows were covered with black rubber blinds. Although there was no carpet, the room exuded a peculiar heat.

He was about to step inside. She shouted, "Stop. Take your shoes off."

He slipped off his tatty footwear and walked in. Virginia slid a screen out of the way to reveal a crisp white futon. His heart rate increased.

He smeared more blood from his face and gazed at the redness on his fingertips. It was unclean, his 'curse'. He could not screw her. Not now. The tears welled up in his eyes.

Virginia slid the jacket from her shoulders. Untying her crossover top, she stretched her arms forward. It fell to the floor.

Her tits heaved. He watched, riveted. She circled her fingers around one nipple. Licking her lips she urged him to come over. He moved unsteadily on the polished floor. Tears streamed down his cheeks, each droplet mixing with the blood.

She wrapped her arms round him and kissed him passionately. Her hands felt down his back. They reached for his waist.

He caressed her naked shoulders, gripping the warm softness. His heart pumped. She writhed. He touched her breast and squeezed. She pulled her mouth away. He fell to his knees and buried his tongue in her navel.

Who the hell was this guy? Not Casanova, that was for sure. Grabbing his jacket she wrenched him back.

Valentine looked up. Powerless. She crouched down and wiped her mouth across his scars. Her face was painted with his blood. He cowered impotent. He was going to be the hors d'oeuvre.

She stepped back. "I'll show you mine if you show me yours."

"You show me yours first."

There was a quaver in his voice. An anticipation. She had not gone through all that just to see his cock. She must be into pain. Humiliation. Wounds. Injury. He felt his cheek. What did she have in mind next?

Unbuckling her belt, she pouted. "OK, I'll show you mine."

She walked over to the bed and unlocked a bedside drawer. It clicked free. Valentine expected her to produce a whip, a vibrator, maybe even a knife. The object was in a velvet bag. It looked angular and sharp. She knelt in front of him and lifted it out. Valentine's whole body tensed.

There was a mirror tile and a small plastic bag full of green crystals. It looked like charlie dyed green. She dug her nails into his shoulder. "It's your turn."

What was he supposed to do? What was there for him to offer?

She snarled. "Where's yours then?"

Valentine shook his head, mystified. She pushed him back onto the floor. She arched, poised, ready to strike.

Then she was back on her feet again. Virginia had been wrong. He had nothing. No FX. He didn't even know what it was. There was no more. Only what was in her bag.

She stalked over. Threw her jacket on. Her eyes raged. She had told him too much. He had seen it with his own eyes. He could tell anyone.

She walked over to the table where spirit bottles stood clustered and poured two glasses of wine. She gave one to Valentine. He gulped hard. She sat on the bed in front of him.

He attempted a calm cross-legged position. It was difficult.

She had gored him, pushed him, scared him to death. Then nothing. Now she was pouring wine. It made no sense.

The green powder still lay between them. A bag of dust. It looked harmless enough. Bright sherbet. It must be valuable. He asked what it was.

"It's known as FX."

This was the drug she had wanted earlier, the stimulation Valentine could not provide. He knew it must be expensive. Yet he remembered that she said it was free. This was beyond comprehension. He glugged the remains of the wine. The questions bubbled in his head.

"What's it like?"

Virginia breathed heavily. The hit was inside and outside. It was the world. A surging passion. It flowed white hot. Tearing as it raged. It made you feel you were God. No crappy coke rush. No boozy skaghead downer. It was purity. Control beyond control. Situations melted into one. One big orgasm. Unstoppable. Unsurpassable. There was nothing to equal it. Even the comedown was good. Like landing in Concorde. There was a surge. Then a floating. A few short bumps. Then solid ground. Time snapped back into place.

What a hit. Then no downer? Valentine understood why she fought. A form of relaxation that instantly rectified the conflicts of existence? Strong medicine. This could make shit palatable.

He felt his heart pound in his chest. The pounding travelled to his ears, then to his head. A jackhammer. His face tightened.

There was no longer shock between them. Instead, a glimmer of recognition. Their eyes met in mutual need. There was lust for the drug. Not each other.

Virginia felt like a high priestess. She held the secret that this supplicant wanted to know. She had never told a stranger before. It might be too much for him. He would have to gamble.

She opened the small plastic bag. There was a sheen on the green powder as the contents spilled onto the mirror. She split the pile in two, drew two lines with her fingernail both about five inches long. She tapped the residue from her finger. Virginia withdrew a glass tube from the velvet bag, then placed it by the mirror.

She sat back. Waiting.

Valentine wanted to remember this moment. A crazy beautiful woman. A wonder drug never tasted before. A new dawn about to break.

He picked up the mirror in his right hand, the tube in his left. He saw his bloody reflection in the glass refracted sharply. He swallowed. One last breath of normality. The tube slid in his nostril. It was cold. He raised the tile higher. The tube touched the glass at once. There was no time for reason. With one snort he devoured the line. He placed the equipment back on the floor.

It was her turn. He sat and waited, unaffected.

She picked up the glass impatiently and tapped the line straight. The tube went in her nose. It screeched along the mirror. She snorted again. The second line was gone. She swayed back on the bed.

They both sat silent. Anticipating. Trying to judge any switch.

Consciousness remained unmoved. He felt cheated. It was one big wind-up. There was no wonder drug. Just another amphetamine derivative. If that.

He rose to his feet. Another drink? That was a hit he could be certain of.

He padded towards the bottles. The vodka was unopened. He snapped the seal. Virginia's gaze cut into his back.

The vodka tasted smooth. It tingled as he drank.

He turned to face her.

He focussed on her chest. Rising. Falling. The movement speeded up.

The glass was cold. He sipped once more.

It was as if the glass no longer existed. He could see through it. He tightened the muscles. There was a loud crunch. He did not hear. Shards of glass cut his skin. He saw no blood.

A notion was surfacing in his mind. He could pass through. Stand above time. Think reality into oblivion. Nothingness. He was unscathed.

Valentine felt himself drifting back. He had never left her side. The mirror lay below. There were no marks on his face.

He had a warm glow. He had never noticed it before. There was the hint of a suntan. A natural bronzed complexion. His skin felt smooth to the touch. There was a heat. He circled his finger on his cheek. There was happiness. No empty laughter. Fulfilment.

He looked at Virginia Nixon. There was no smudged make-up, no rings around her eyes. She shone. Light danced in her eyes. Beckoning flames. He loved her. He had known her forever. They had gone to school together.

He remembered what she had looked like as a small girl. Her hair was in braids. He was going to marry her. This would be their home. Spacious for children. He would have to fit a burglar alarm. Nobody must get in. Nobody. Only her.

The bed was spacious. Inviting. She lay down beside her Arabian Knight. The gold sheets glistened. There were twelve cushions. She had bought them specially.

Mr. Valentine had flown a long way. His divorce must have come through. He could buy that kind of thing. Nothing was beyond his grasp. He could own anyone. He had acquired most of London.

She remembered the conference. It had been a success. The dinner was exquisite. She had never believed he would come back.

He had been good in bed. Not like most of them. "All night long." He was Lionel Richie. Better looking. He had a good voice. Strong. Demonstrative. She wished they had met earlier.

It was getting late. Was that the time? He had to leave in the morning.

Not so soon.

He had commitments.

The gift sparkled. A pearl necklace encrusted with diamonds. It shone on the floor. He had placed it between them. She could not accept it. He made her feel nineteen again.

His apartment was so stylish. It had been in Home and Garden. Another gift? So soon. She had not worn the last one yet. It was a platinum dagger. He insisted. She accepted. There must be a thank you kiss. She touched his forehead. Their lips brushed. He tasted of Gucci aftershave. He was older. A father figure.

Valentine did not expect to be kissing David. He was sad and excited. He had never kissed another man. He and David only met this evening. A chance encounter. David was gentle. Valentine yielded to his touch. They kissed deeply. It was dark in the Sombrero. Odd it was still open.

He was a regular. The wine was sweet, in tumblers decorated with nude men. Amyl nitrate hurt his nose. His blood pumped faster. Veins opening wide. The man's hair was soft. Tousled. They rolled on the couch. The sensations were new. He felt degraded. There was no stopping now. He peeled the jacket from the man's shoulders. The embrace grew stronger. Valentine felt for Anthony's shoulders. They burned with heat. He could not stop. The jacket fell to the floor.

The evening dress lay crumpled. Valentine had torn it off. She egged him on. They were very drunk. It was only an office party. She turned the video camera on.

It was not blackmail. She wanted to see herself screwing with an employee. It was thrilling. Anyone might walk into the studio. They could join in. The lights were bright. The picture flickered. It was sordid. Disgusting. He was unclean. His breath stank of puke. She bit into his neck.

The doctor had come late. She wanted him to stay. His flesh was black. Inviting. She ripped off his shirt. He was a married man. That made it more interesting. How she hated his wife.

The surgery was small. The couch red leather. He pulled off her pants. There was no unborn child to scan for. The film was pornographic.

Virginia could not resist Larry's advances. He sucked on her tits. His boxer shorts were wet. It was no time to go swimming. He should be dry. She could put them in front of the fire. She eased them away.

The prostitute was rough. She manhandled his trunks off. It was only fifty guilders, the going rate. She sucked his cock. He did not want a blow job. He wanted to fuck her. That was the deal. He was not scared of AIDS. That was her problem.

James Brown belted the speakers. The sun lit the bottom of the curtains. He had told his girlfriend it would take ten minutes. He had to hurry. Her hair was peroxided. He pulled. The wig fell off. She must be forty. She had fucked hundreds of men. Her nails were crimson. They tore at his buttocks. She gobbled harder. He was going to come.

Not yet. Not yet.

He was on the screen. His old man's face was wrinkled. His nakedness was ugly. He fumbled Yvette's knickers off. He had to fuck her. There could be no second honeymoon. He was one hundred years old.

Her father lay there naked. His cock had slipped from her mouth. She did not know how to feel. She felt used. She wanted it so badly. He eased inside. He was too big. She squealed with pain. He jerked in and out.

It was a violation. She had opened the door to the stranger. He raged with anger. There was no reason to fight it. She was coming.

The cab driver was a kind man. She loathed him. It had to stop. Harder. Harder. Harder.

The gun went off. Shot inside her. Her stomach wrenched. The bullet tore. She gaped. Blood poured. Red rivers. Hot with pain.

She threw him off. He crumpled. He was dead. Spent.

She embraced his rotten carcass. It stank of death. There was no life left. His cock hung limp. His frame was broken. She kissed him one last time.

They poured earth onto his coffin. He was at peace. She closed the lid over herself. There could be no more pain. She wiped the dirt from his cheek.

It was warm by the fireplace. They had been married forty years. Her face was old. The children had gone. The house was quiet. He had loved her. It was forever and a day. He kissed her. There was ancient passion.

She said good night. They curled up on the rug. He turned the lights out. Then there was sleep.

CHAPTER ELEVEN

Valentine stepped from the shadow of the bridge. He was dazed, tired.

Latimer Road was empty. There was a concrete pub on the corner. A man browsed through vegetables. The shop was poorly stocked.

The address was crumpled. It had resided too long in his sweaty pocket. The ink had run. He pressed it flat. The message was marginally decipherable. This was the place alright. Freston Road was opposite.

There were several rows of prefab council houses, each one identical to the next. Only the doors were different colours.

He walked through the estate. His muscles twinged from over-use. The stillness seemed bizarre. It was unimaginable that the city was so close. This was not a place many visitors ventured to. He checked the names of the buildings. Millfield Court. Spencer Walk.

He noticed his hand was bandaged. It was slightly numb. He did not remember how it happened.

He was on Wll Bombers turf. That was apparent from the graffiti. There was a burnt-out Cortina in the street, its green metallic paint charred. Broken glass was strewn across the pavement. The brittle shards crunching beneath his feet struck a chord. His palm throbbed. He had cut himself last night. He was not sure how. The woman must have bandaged it. She was gone in the morning. He envisaged a prostitute. An old woman. There were no links. That was unsettling. Clarity evaded him.

He was here to find Fly. That was simple enough.

Valentine tried not to worry. The time gap remained a problem. It grated and gnawed. He tried to convince himself there must be a logical explanation. He was phasing in and out.

Fly was the key. Commitments had to be met.

He wondered where Anna was. Whether Fly really resided at this bleak address. Bryce had been unsure if Fly was even in England. The female executive wedged in his brain. A face. The colour green. A big payoff. Then nothing.

A breeze whistled through the courtyard. Then through his head. The pathway forked. On the right, green derelict garages. A YMCA hall blocked the horizon. The Y hung down.

The tower block stretched isolated fifty yards beyond. Each floor had a balcony. He counted to the lop. Twenty-six in total. Frinstead House. The sign had square lettering. His piece of paper read Fronstead.

Valentine walked into the entrance hall. The doors squeaked on their hinges. Neither was intact. The windows had been kicked out. He glanced between the lifts. One gave access to the even numbers, the other to the odds. Fly lived at number 42.

Valentine pressed the lift call. There was a pinging sound. The green arrow lit up. Green powder on a mirror. Images crystallised. Like a poignant film with no soundtrack. He could not lip-read. The narrative was unclear. He leant against the wall.

The lift doors opened. He wanted the twelfth floor.

Uncluttered thought was a problem. This was the only chance to get Fly. He had to convince him. He had to convince himself. Working at the Tower was a fresh start. Valentine needed to be on top form. Fly was usually maudlin. His habit used to be worse than Bryce's.

The lift pinged once again. Valentine juddered to a halt. The landing smelt of piss. The sides of the building were open. Air streamed through. He looked for 42. All the numbers were missing.

One door stood out from the rest. It was painted with a psychedelic portrait of George Clinton. He rapped on the letter box. The metal clanked.

If Fly didn't answer at least the inhabitant may hold information. He thought of how tired he felt. Without Fly there would be no work. No escape. No vengeance. His head still flooded green. Incoherent.

Someone shouted "hello" through the door, a man's voice. It rattled, clouded through coughing. "Who is it? What do you want?"

Valentine grappled with momentary incoherence. "It's Valentine. Is Fly there?"

There was no reply. Silence. A sense that nobody knew what to say next. It had been a long time.

The lock clicked. There was a strange anticipation. Valentine flinched. Then the door was open.

Fly was over six feet tall. His body was thin. He looked a very sad man.

The two said nothing. There was a silent understanding. They had known this moment would come. It was inevitable. There was no room for apology. Fly ushered Valentine inside.

The flat was beyond untidy. No explanation could excuse such clutter. Valentine balked at the smell of rancid cat shit. They stepped over cardboard boxes to stand together in the front room.

It was very dark. The only source of illumination was a car inspection lamp hung on the electric fire.

Fly crumpled into a worn armchair. His complexion was pallid. The walk to the door had made him sweat. He held out a wiry arm. His hand trembled as he brushed newspapers from the sofa. Valentine sat down. The stench was hard to manage.

Valentine lit a filter and gave one to Fly. He wanted to offer good counsel. It was unlikely he would notice. Straight down to business.

He explained that he had been offered Fridays at the Tower. The money was good. All he needed was Fly to DJ for him, then he could close the deal. It was no problem either way.

He knew Fly needed money but pressure could scare him off. Push too hard, Fly would say no. He dare not tell Fly how crucial his answer would be.

Lure him slowly, that was the way. "Just your name on the ticket."

The words sounded insincere, the sentiment dishonest.

Fly had said nothing, only coughed between puffs on the filter. He was sinking smaller and smaller into his seat. The light made patterns of the smoke. There was a pink glow.

Valentine saw smudged lipstick. A woman's nakedness. Nipples that were firm to the touch. There was a moaning. "No, no, no." It was a female voice. The words came from Fly's mouth. They took on a bass rumble.

Fly had said 'no'. He did not want any part of it. Valentine could not understand the distortion. His senses were playing tricks. Cigarette ash fell onto his lap. Time became real again. He was back on the sofa.

He strained with his thoughts. He must stay in reality. 'No' was not an acceptable reply. He told Fly he did not need him. There were plenty of others. A junkie was bad for business. It was just that Fly was his friend. He wanted to give him a break.

Fly stubbed the cigarette out. He looked disdainfully at Valentine. He tried to laugh. It came out as a wheeze. This was a joke. Valentine did nobody any favours. Fly remembered how many times Valentine had ripped him off. He did not want to play anymore. He rubbed his wrists. He needed another fix. Just one more. Then it would be okay. Fuck this bullshit. He wanted some brown sugar.

He stood up. There was a cracking from his joints. Fly hobbled, then rested against the fireplace. The car lamp threw a tall shadow. He told Valentine to shut the door when he left.

Valentine saw an old couple knelt in front of the fire. The old woman looked familiar. The man was Valentine, his skin wrinkled. The woman kissed him. Her breath smelled used. He looked at his own reflection. The eyes were cold.

Then it was Fly's face. Fly was standing over him, puzzled. He could see Valentine's fear. He went to touch Valentine's shoulder.

The hand grew red fingernails. Valentine felt his cheek bleeding. The nails tore deeply. He reached for his face. There was a large plaster stuck on it. She had dressed his wounds.

"Are you alright?" Fly was by the tape deck. There was a long hissing noise. The room reverberated. Fly could see he was slipping away. He understood that feeling, the notion of madness in a sane body. Perhaps the music would stabilise reality. Sometimes it worked. The power of the bass could root you to the floor. It was the only safe stimulant he possessed.

The bass hit out. The snare filled in. Melle Mel emcee'd. *"It's like a jungle sometimes, it makes me wonder how I keep from going under."* Valentine watched the speaker frontage pulse.

He begged Fly to do the Tower. He was off his head. Fly had to DJ. There was no deal without him. Fly was not listening. He swayed his head to the music, back and forth. The answer was still "no".

Movements were merging, colours blended. A picture loomed. It was a polaroid of a woman. It was Virginia Nixon.

At last. Valentine put the name to the face.

The frame was in a man's hand. Then it was Fly's hand. The picture was Fly's old girlfriend Sarah. She had left him. He still wanted to destroy himself.

Valentine knew her face. If Fly played the Tower he might get Sarah back.

Fly shook his head. Besides he had no records left. Fly pointed to a box. It was filled with broken vinyl. He lifted a ball-pane hammer and brought it down through an already damaged twelve inch. Sarah had said he loved the music more than her. Then she left. At first he thought she was right. So he smashed the records.

He had no tunes. His hands shook too much. He had no will to work anymore. It was a no-win scenario.

So Valentine changed the rules. He put a silver wrap on the table. It looked clean among the rest of the shit. He peeled the package open. There was a large deal of skag, brown and lumpy. "I'll pay you in gear every week."

A coldness took the moment. This was brass tacks. Fly wanted it. Valentine had it. Simple. Fly looked for sympathy. There was none. Only a calculating stare. Remorseless.

Valentine felt sick. He knew what he was doing. He wanted to stop. He could not. The Tower was all important. Fly was crucial. The deal must continue. Valentine was charged.

Fly's compulsion drew him forward. He fingered the crystals. He held the silver under the light. This would be the last time. The final scene for the Underground. It had come to this. Friends killing each other for greed. A bond that cut deep, clean to the bone.

He nodded his head. He wanted the same deal every week. This amount. No bullshit. He did not care if they fucked Valentine as long as he went free.

Valentine had begun a new kind of game. This was no blag. It was all real. The table stakes were high, life or death.

Fly swooned above the brown mixture. Valentine could see the face reflected in the foil, swollen, angular. It was not Fly's face. It was his face. He had a tube up his nose. It was cold. It hurt. He was snorting green. It was free. It was priceless. Beyond imagination. Beyond existence. Up his nose. Inside his head. Swirling.

Mutating. It was out of his hands. The crowds gorged on it. A hundred thousand Valentines. Each one chanting. Screaming. Wailing.

FX. FX. FX. FX.

The wail grew to a rumble, then to a roar. Jet engines. It was Concorde. He held his ears. He rolled his head. He screamed, his head exploding. Pieces of brain flying like shrapnel. Then nothing. Blackness. He jumped to his feet, grabbed for the blackout. The curtains fell to the floor. The room was awash with light. Cars shot over the Westway. The breaker's yard scattered with debris. The gantry cranes swung relentlessly.

He was going mad. He spun towards Fly shielding his eyes from the unexpected glare.

That was it. The green light. It was FX. Virginia Nixon had given him some. It was running riot inside his head.

But it had been the final crescendo. The Concorde. The landing. Now it was gone. Could he trust his senses? He felt his face. It was normal.

He asked Fly what he knew of FX. There was no reply.

He told Fly to imagine the wildest hit in the world. Then multiply it a thousand times. That was FX.

There was no recognition on Fly's face. He did not understand. Valentine was bursting with his secret. Then he noticed the wrap in Fly's grasp.

He had passed it on. Half an ounce of slow death. Surely not. He was off his head. How could he give this to an associate? Let alone a friend.

He snatched it back. Fly recoiled. He would not work without it.

Alright, Valentine would pay up when the job was done. Fly would not get one grain until he was in the Tower.

Valentine held the wrap in his palm. He could not finish the deal. Fly wanted a taster.

Fly needed the gear. He could taste its sweet oblivion. He was not sure what had been going on in Valentine's head. But neither, it seemed, was Valentine. The payoff was all that concerned him.

Valentine held out his other hand. "Shake on it?"

Fly looked away. The curtains needed closing.

CHAPTER TWELVE

Changes were occurring. Valentine felt different.

He was pleased with his new worn Levis. The denim brushed crisply against his skin. There was not much of the fifty left. He had pissed it away. So what? The drinks would be free tonight. The bar would be packed by eleven-thirty. He didn't know if he was late. He never wore a watch.

He walked up Wardour Street.

FX was strange, nothing like tripping. It had turned him inside out. He had to have some more.

There was no knowing the source, the river where FX sprang from. It seemed to be a closely guarded secret. An exclusive club that he could not join.

The Tower was the key, a leap to her level. The lion's den was inviting. Few had recognised him. That would change. He would be a success again if only Big Jack could be found.

The street was crowded. He dodged the mounds of garbage. A drunk dived into some boxes. Rockers huddled in comers. Punks spilled out of the Fox. They were pissed. He wanted some Special. Valentine did not like meeting strangers straight.

Valentine was not used to walking a long way. His ankles rubbed. The ligaments stretched. He raised the tempo. The blisters burst.

Anna had been marginally receptive. The call was a short one. A sucker for punishment, she invited him back again. He could turn up later. She would be awake, probably drunk. A cab fare was affordable.

Shop windows threw long shadows. Brasserie neons reflected. His shoes looked blue-black. He lit up a cigarette, his only steadier. His mouth was dry, the taste foul. He licked his lips.

The Blue Posts looked full. He scanned through the crowd but there was no sign of A1. He had to go inside. Perhaps A1 was late. Perhaps he had missed him. He fumbled for the Mambo invite in his croc-skin fax. 'Admit One'. He could go alone but it was safer in twos. Besides he wanted the company.

That was a lie. It was business.

Valentine slunk into the boozer. The tension made him self-conscious. He hunched his shoulders. The bar was eight bodies away, the crowd unfriendly. They were very fashionable, overdressed. They would not budge. Their eyes mocked his build, his clothes, his uncertainty.

No way of getting a drink. None of the black faces belonged to A1 Jay.

Salvation was at hand. There was a staircase, an upstairs bar.

The aggression swelled. Valentine jostled with elbows, fought his way across. An umbrella scraped his ribs. Stray slops of beer splashed his jacket. It was claustrophobic, a sea of bodies. One last jerk and he was through. The channel closed behind.

He caught his breath. Discordant jazz dripped down the stairwell, uneasy bop. He grabbed the balustrade. One foot carefully between the couple on the step, he launched himself up. The rest was easy. The music got louder. He jogged up the stairs.

He opened the panelled door. This bar was for the regulars. Its pace was slower. The air was warm. Smoke hung. The music lifted his imagination. Things began to make sense.

Valentine ordered Special Brew. The Eurasian barman poured it into a balloon-shaped glass. There was little head on the mixture. Valentine took a big glug. The clock read ten forty-five. He was only a few minutes late. He drank heartily. Then ordered another.

He tapped his hand in time with the music. It was still bandaged, the dressing now grubby. All traces of pain had evaporated. The second glass tasted smooth. It was no longer a question of how to blag A1 Jay. But when. He had boxed up Fly. Next he needed to get a line on Jack. Then the game could begin.

Time was short. Only a week or so. The guys at the Mambo Anniversary might have the answers. Some would be gunning for Valentine.

Bryce would be there. It was not safe to associate with him. He had fresh fights.

Bryce might have some FX. Anyway he would know the story.

It was no problem. He could live without it. A large dose might be lethal.

One more hit would be enough.

Then there was a "Hello."

A1's mackintosh was spotless. He shouted up another drink. "In the wars, Valentine?" A1 looked warily at the bandages. It was none of his business. Valentine agreed.

They drank to each other's health. It seemed appropriate.

A1 glanced about the room. There were a few familiar faces. He did not want to see the Groove Boys. The Tower owed them money.

The bar got busier. Valentine tried to explain his adventure. A1 was a safe confidant. He oozed calm. Another wild story was no concern of his. He liked Valentine. That was the only reason he listened. Somehow he brought every subject of conversation back to the Tower.

He had to get out of clubs. The corruption was insidious. It flowed from every pore. He wanted life to be slow but the fuckups fell like rain.

Valentine said he had found Fly.

A1 did not look too pleased. He had heard rumours. It was common knowledge that Fly was off his cake, a leper.

Valentine looked at his wounds. It was true. He remembered the wreck of a man. That gaunt face. All they needed was Fly's name on the ticket. The ghost would not matter.

A1 did not like junkies. It was bad press.

Valentine saw his reflection. His face looked old, unshaven. He was paying his friend with skag. He tried to feel remorse. There was little left. Money had not been enough. Money was never enough.

It was last orders. Another drink was the only poison available. The Mambo party loomed closer. The gathering of the clans. All the unsettled scores rising to the surface on a tide of free beer. Out on the street, Valentine's face hurt. He threw the dressing away. It was no way to go into the Mambo. The scratches were swollen. He felt brazen. War scars might ward off aggressors.

He wanted a toot. A line of charlie. A gram of speed. Anything to make it seem right. His mind screamed out for some FX, the real taste of honey. Then if they hit him he would not feel it. Time would jump for him.

A1 was dashing. Valentine's stride was short. He had to keep up. Lanterns hung outside the cheapest Chinese restaurant in the world. Bodies spilled out of the Polar Bear. There were no friendly faces.

A mass of people swarmed by the door of the Mambo. Light spilled out of the doorway. The neon sign shone blue, its lettering indistinct.

There must have been one hundred people outside, a mixed bag of lowlife trying to get in. The clamour was angry. There were Japanese, pale-faced trendies shouting, a gang of black youths arguing the toss. Three black bouncers stood defiant, their tuxedos straining across their chests. No-one would get in without a ticket.

A1 stormed through to the front. Their only hope was catching Ferdi's eye.

Valentine stood straight, a foot behind his partner. The group charged behind him. Drove forward. He was trapped. People around all sides. Once inside he could dodge confrontation but in this sea of faces he was easily recognisable.

He was falling forward. His flesh burned with excitement. Courtney might be in the crowd. Carlo. Christy. Anyone might take a potshot, just for laughs.

Heels crunched on his feet. A hand flew over his right shoulder, lunging towards him. There was no room to move. No way to counter. His hands were wedged by his sides, the scarred knuckles crumpled by his thigh.

Then there was a shout, a scream. The hand tapped his back. He saw who it was.

"Hey, Crazy, it's me." Scally was about a yard behind him. Valentine tried to turn back. He was trapped. The crush had knocked the air from his lungs. There was no way of calling out. He hoped Scally caught his smile.

Valentine was nearer the door. A1 held him up by the collar. There was no release of the pressure, only more struggle. He thought he might suffocate.

A1 called out. Ferdi had to notice him. He brandished his ticket. It was no good. Ferdi only saw who he wanted to see. A1 was nothing. Just another black man.

More arms waving in the flood. Regulars sailed through. The bouncers moved in. Valentine had to do something, otherwise fall. Recognition could save him, nothing else.

He shouted, "Ferdi". The voice was inaudible. Just like the rest.

He shouted again. It was a wail, piercing, pleading. The cry of a desperate man.

Ferdi's face flinched. There was a faint knowing. He looked down at the struggling Valentine.

He smiled. A gold tooth glimmered among the white. He vaguely recalled Valentine. He recognised A1.

He leant a muscular arm forward. There was a dramatic surge. He plucked Valentine and A1 out of the crowd. They steadied themselves in the doorway. Faint traces of a bass drum were audible. The stairwell had changed little in four years.

Ferdi chuckled. At the Mambo he was the law. It was a nice feeling to play God, particularly as they all knew his first name. He bellowed "Tickets only" into the street.

It made no difference. The throng struggled like maniacs. A fight to the death for a free beer. A blood rite over the women.

A1 went first. They stepped up. The wall teemed with murals. Grecian. Roman. Cubist. Strip lights hung from the ceiling. Valentine rebuked his fright. This was home. He knew the rules in this place. The beat went on.

There was everything here. Love. Hate. Destruction. Inverted class snobbery. The players and the played spinning the same disc. His time was now. He had to find Jack.

He stood with A1. They peered through the foyer. Music blasted through the door.

The woman on reception was about nineteen. Her hair was blond, swept back. Her breasts were clad in a cross-over top. She knew A1. He smiled, charming, winning. She tapped two on the till. The LED flicked over.

The final bouncer stepped aside. He was smaller than the others, not so aggressive.

The doorway was narrow. It led from light to dark. Valentine walked through. A1 followed. There was a sense of elation. An electric infusion.

The atmosphere in the main room was sticky. It dripped with sweat. Bodies gyrated, a swirling, weaving mass. The sound system groaned with power. Cigarette smoke hung at head height. Women's perfume. Sodden aftershave. A musky smell of sex.

Oh, how they wanted it. Everyone was there for the taking. Nobody more than Valentine.

He lost A1 in the crowd. It was intentional, a calculated risk. He was motivating. Cruising for a bruising. He wanted a drink. He felt like screwing somebody. Anybody.

His anxiety ebbed. The music carried him away. He was somewhere else. Hairs were plastered to his forehead. He was sweating. It was easy moisture. A natural lubricant. He ran his fingers through his hair.

The bar looked intense. The punters clamoured for the free booze. Men mounted up cans of beer. "Five for my friend."

Everybody was kissing each other. Revellers spilled from the dance floor. Valentine lit a filter, dodging the furore. The upstairs bar might be more laid back. He motored to the spiral staircase, brushing torsos all the way. The lack of air was heady. His steps were short, broken up by the crushing.

A crowd gathered by the swing door. They all wanted to get upstairs. He paused. His body bumped a woman. She was unperturbed. Her eyes caught his. She was pretty. He stepped back. They did not speak. She reached for his mouth. He held his breath.

The filter tip left his mouth. She held it between her fingers. Her lips stretched wide. There was a lull. She blew smoke into his face.

Valentine did not know how to take it. It was a little bold for so early. She dropped her hands to her side. He reached for the back of her head. They drew close. He kissed her. It was a long soft embrace. Her lipstick tasted perfumed. Fresh. She was passionate. Her flesh felt warm. She pulled away. Shook clear. He wanted to say something. The music was too loud.

A bouncer swung the door open. The woman shot through. Valentine was unaware of the swell behind him. He chased after her. Up the spiral. Round and round. The treads were angular.

His legs kicked high. The leather soles slipped from underneath him. He leapt the last three.

The second floor was not as packed. He scanned the crowd. No sign. He wondered who she was. He had to find her. It was a chance too good to miss. Her relative ordinariness made her interesting.

There was no point in looking for her. The Mambo was like a mass. He walked towards the bar. There were other fish to fry.

This room was much brighter. There were monastic chairs, ebony oval tables in the centre. The people were a little older. They were not dancers. It was a mixed bag of minor celebrities. Fading pop idols. Rag trade boys revering Gaultier. Fortunes had been made and lost. Valentine would bask in the reflected glory.

Valentine clambered to the foot rest. Eventually his arm reached the bar. The marble top was cold. Everyone was annoyed with waiting. To differing degrees they were used to better.

Valentine called for three cans of Brew. The bar girl said nothing. She looked like a dwarf Liz Taylor. She grasped the cans with her minute hands. Plucking one from the four pack, she slid the remains. Valentine caught them.

He opened one. The others sat in his pockets. It might be some time before he got served again. He poured the linctus down his throat.

He noticed an admiring glance. This one was more his type. Her glasses were pitch black. A distorted reflection danced on the lens. She might have been a photographer. Maybe a stylist. Her hair was tousled. The jeans clung round her crotch. Sex.

He lowered his eyeline. The cans bulged from his pockets. He felt stupid. There was nothing to lose. He flashed a smile. The woman slunk across. Her voice was husky. She chanced a snarling hello.

Valentine thought of Virginia Nixon. She said Valentine's smile was like Clark Gable's. He blushed, flattered. He felt more like Scarlet O'Hara.

This woman couldn't get served. Her glass was painfully empty. Valentine toted a can in bonhomie. She refused.

Katherine was a commodity broker. This was the killer blow. What a bore. Predictable. Safe. But successful. The gravelly voice was put on, masking a sloaney twang. Virginia had been the same.

It triggered visions of FX. He had to find out.

Katherine asked what he did.

Valentine stared at her crotch. Sex with FX. The best mixture he had ever had. "What about some FX?" he said.

Katherine removed her glasses. There was recognition.

Valentine grew inches.

No. She didn't know FX was the name of a drug. It had sounded to her like a slang word for fucking. She thought Valentine was offering a slice. Sex with this small stranger seemed distasteful. The scars on his face swelled with sweat. His nails were bitten. Probably his dick smelt cheesy. Katherine felt ill.

Valentine touched her hand. It was not yielding. The skin tightened.

"I don't want to FX with you." She must show no fear. "Go screw yourself, pervert." That would throw him.

Valentine jolted. She pushed him out of the way. The anger spilled his drink. There was a hoot of laughter that cut into the hip-hop beat.

A1 Jay was having hysterics, skin wrinkling around his eyes, his glasses almost falling off. A1 was with a well-dressed woman. A tricorn poised on her head. Valentine dared not say anything. Third parties bothered him. Particularly women.

A1 introduced her as Chrissie. Chrissie Gold. The name suited her aquiline nose. She worked for Raye Baxter. They did the PR for the Tower. She was the appointed consultant for the West nights.

Valentine felt incredibly vulnerable. She had seen him perform. It was not impressive. He scratched nervously at his face. Heat irritated the cuts. He tried to be genial.

It was no good. The beer had taken hold.

She had heard a lot about Valentine. All the clubs he had previously done. He was a bit of a star by most accounts. Her words dripped sarcasm. No winner would be dressed like this, picking up drunk women for cheap laughs.

Chrissie Gold was no feminist but Valentine's manner was difficult to stomach for any woman. She asked what he had done recently. He grew reticent, his eyes drawn to the dancers. He wanted a clever answer. The truth hurt.

He stammered that he had run from all this bullshit. He had no friends anymore. Just a long line of coke to keep him warm.

She looked straight through him. They would have to tell the press of a Stateside tour. Valentine had been looking for his roots. That would be the angle. It sounded believable. Nobody wanted broken men, only success stories.

It was unfashionable to look beat. The jeans would have to go. She said he must be more outrageous. That was what the people wanted. Outrage, not debauchery. He could wear theatrical costume, a wild hat. He could be a Love God. Casanova. A funny Valentine. Chrissie could see it.

Valentine did not like it. This was not him. This was some jumped-up joker. He despised the woman with her easy charm, that affected speech impediment. She did not remember the Underground or who Valentine had been. She saw him as a burnt-out sleaze. He looked at A1 for support.

A1 fawned. He was probably taking Chrissie home. Wasn't he the lucky one.

Valentine realised he was envious. Why had he got so little? If the Tower wanted a son of fun that was what they would get. Fun so crazy they would not be laughing for long. A new Underground. Brighter than the Kings Cross fire.

They were in agreement. All the pre-press had to go out. They could have a PR meeting in a few days. It made a weird sense.

Chrissie would create a new Valentine. Palatable. Sharp. To the point. Fuck it.

A man whispered in Chrissie's ear. He was tall, almost handsome. He sneered at Valentine. His skin was tanned, the stubbly beard well kempt. Valentine glared at him over his scars, mildly amused.

The couple engaged playfully. Chrissie would not mix business and pleasure. She fought the brute off with one hand, the other grappled with her chunky black leather bag. She managed to pull out a card. The man's kisses jarred her as she gave the card to Valentine. "Call me if you think of anything."

She had to go. There were other contacts to see. She pulled herself free then left.

A1 looked cut up. He would be going home alone.

Valentine choked on a mouthful of beer, furious. A1 had stitched him up. He was a puppet for the Tower, and he would go the way of all puppets. The way the strings pulled.

A1 winced. "Don't worry."

Valentine wanted to exorcise aggression. He wanted to dance. "All night long." There was nothing else for it.

The music upstairs was hip-hop. House. There were no soulful grooves. The crowd danced predictably. One step wonders. They waded across. Most were smashed. The bar must be dry. Empty cans toppled from the table. One man lolloped like an invalid.

Valentine picked up unfinished glasses of spirit. Some were tainted with ash but he could not taste it anymore. Shirt stuck to his body, he drank as he dashed. He dashed as he drank. One glass after another. The staircase was hazy. He grabbed A1's shoulder. People bashed into them. He scowled back. His head bobbed side to side.

They crashed through the door. The main room swayed. Each plank buckled on the dance floor. His feet started tapping. It felt good. The DJ was spinning Car Wash. This was the platter that mattered.

Valentine dashed into the breach. His hands swung in circles. His hips gyrated. His feet were flying. This was how it had been. This was how it could be. Freedom. The knowledge that you could move. Move in time. Jog with the B.P.M.

The horn section wailed. Clarinets growled. A1 was a good dancer. Valentine was surprised. It was not A1's kind of music, but he rode the groove.

It was good to dance again. Valentine had not forgotten how.

Good went to better. He was dancing with the woman who had kissed him. His eyes were not deceiving him. He was drunk. Not that drunk. She swayed up to him. Her breath smelt of garlic. There was a small tattoo on her bare shoulder. She kissed him again.

Valentine felt lucky. She drew away. Dancing back and forth. There was a crescent-shaped scar on her face. He watched it move. It beckoned like a curled finger. She was dancing further away. Then she was dancing with A1. Valentine still watched the scar. It captured his drunken imagination. It was nakedness. It was sex. Then an F. Then an X. It was FX. The word jumped about.

A1 was grinning. She was with him now. He loosened his tie. Arms flailed in the air. They were working in the car wash. She was holding A1's hand. He was sharking in.

Valentine grooved over. Keep in time. Keep in time. There was a smashing of glass. It was time to move in. Then there was a thud. Valentine looked round.

His head popped. A figure rolled on the floor. He was a tall, heavy man. The voice was recognisable. The stupor was familiar.

Valentine slipped on spilled beer. Shards of glass stuck in his shoes. He stood still, his eyes cloudy. The alcohol threw double images.

The giant staggered to his feet. He flicked the hair from his eyes. Even in the half-light the face was clear. He smiled a gentle smile. It had been a long time. Four years to be exact. He let out a whoop.

"Val, what the fuck...?" His words were slurred. He was elated.

Valentine was happy, too. He had found Big Jack.

But the happiness was short lived. He recognised the shadow behind. The piercing glare was the same, the suit as sharp as ever. This was no ghost. He was real enough. It was Courtney.

CHAPTER THIRTEEN

Valentine's fear pumped. All the skeletons danced out of the cupboard. He owed Courtney a grand. Courtney was not the kind of man to forget.

The fuck-up jumped into frame. The End of the Line had been a disaster. It had sucked everybody down with it. Courtney narrowly avoided bird. Valentine had made off. They were equally to blame but Courtney had taken it. Valentine wanted to apologise. It was too late for that. He perceived anger, hostility, the score to settle.

Courtney shone red. Valentine's head hurt. There was no way out.

He tried to explain. His voice dried up. He wanted to get Courtney a drink. His pockets were empty.

Courtney put his hand on Valentine's shoulder. This was the payoff. He braced himself. He had seen Courtney knife a man. He had seen him relish the pain. Now it was Valentine's turn.

Courtney stared. "I heard you was here," he bawled over the beat. "Let's get a drink."

Valentine walked in front, then Jack, finally Courtney. Jack knew the score. There was nothing he could do, nothing anybody could do but wait.

The bar had run out of beer. All that was left were spirits. Courtney ordered three double scotches. The barman lined them up in plastic cups. Not fitting for a funeral toast.

Courtney explained his position. Valentine had caused him a lot of trouble. The police had beaten him up. His brief had saved him. The money was no longer important. The grief was. He had been caught with the takings from an illegal unlicensed venue. That was for starters.

It was the six grams of coke that were the real problem. They belonged to Valentine and Courtney had been nicked carrying them.

He owed Valentine.

Then he would have killed him. Broken his legs. Cut up his face. But that was then. He giggled. Somebody seemed to have beaten him to it.

Valentine touched his scars. His hand shook. The whiskey was sour. Valentine savoured the taste. It might be his last.

Courtney knocked his back. The gold cufflinks glinted. He asked Valentine to step into the khazi. It was not an offer. It ran like an order.

Valentine set off. He glanced back over his shoulder. Courtney was still there, his eyes bloodshot. He had always been an alcoholic.

The crowd would once have parted for Courtney. He was not that powerful anymore.

The walk seemed long. It was only ten yards.

Valentine gulped. The door was blood red. Men's Room. He stopped.

Courtney pushed him through the door. There was a smell of dope. Amyl nitrate. Stale piss. Into the cubicle. The bolt clanked shut.

Courtney had waited for this moment. "Look at me, Valentine."

Valentine cowered. The lavatory seat dug into his knee. There was a knock on the door. Courtney shouted "Fuck off." He would not allow any interruption.

His hand flew into his pocket. He was reaching for his blade.

Valentine wanted to be brave. There was nowhere to look. He panted. He closed his eyes. There was orange in the blackness. Terror. Shaking. He heard Courtney's voice, rumbling. He could not bear to look.

"You're just the same. A gutless wanker. The same shit clothes, no money. I've moved on. I don't need this. Here's what I owe you."

Valentine threw his arms across his face. He felt a pressure on his stomach. Air shot from his lungs. He had been hit. Chibbed. He crumpled onto the toilet. His head bashed on the wall. He looked down to assess the damage, see the blood. Vomit wedged in his gut. His body convulsed.

There was no wound in his line of view, no knife hole. Courtney had hardly touched him. The impact he left was from a package.

Courtney had foisted a plastic bag on him. The bag contained six others. Each was full of white powder.

The debt. Valentine's six grams of charlie.

Courtney was gone.

Valentine was going to be sick. He collapsed on the floor. Muscles strained. It hurt. He choked. Puke spurted. His head was in the pan. Churning, stifling torrents. Orange and sickly. He wretched again. There was more. A mixture of lager and beer. It smelled rancid. It tasted vile. It was violence. The mixture tainted his lips. It splashed his face.

He clambered to his feet, spent. His flesh felt cold. Damp. His breath was heavy. There was no trace of Courtney. Only the bag left in his hand. The cubicle gaped open. He walked out.

The lights seemed brighter. He pushed the six wraps into his top pocket. There was no sense of victory or defeat. Courtney had been playing with him. He would not finish Valentine so quickly. Not in a public place. He wanted him to stew. Realise there was no running any more.

Valentine glanced into the mirror. His face had no colour. The eyes bulged red raw. Vomit stuck to his cuts. He splashed water on his face. It was cold. Diluted puke dripped into the basin. It stained the porcelain pink. He wiped off the remains.

Back in the club the atmosphere was heavy. The volume slapped his brain. It seemed louder than before, more intrusive. There was no sign of Courtney. A bouncer breezed by and mumbled despairingly. Valentine looked like a wreck. Another drunken casualty. He stumbled towards the bar.

The crowd had thinned out. He was not sure how long he had been away. It might have been minutes. Perhaps half an hour.

The gear must be spiked. That was Courtney's plan. Valentine would go off his head. Maybe top himself. The coke would cut him up much cleaner than a blade, and a lot more painful. It made brutal sense.

Valentine needed a drink. He could still taste the puke. The stench remained on his fingers. His vision was still blurred. He eased through the gap.

Everybody was drunk, though some charged on a higher plain. The new Levis model stood alone, fighting off all admirers.

Jack was slumped by his empty glass. He had been drinking all night and couldn't take much more. His hair wilted. There was a rip in his shirt. The cap of ecstasy was taking its toll. His skin tingled. He was up for anything.

He turned to watch a woman pass. Valentine was shambling towards him. The sweaty face filled his view. A look of pain. A sense of loss. This was all wrong. Everybody should be happy tonight. He asked what was wrong.

Valentine said it was Courtney. There was no escape. Courtney had passed him some bad coke. He wanted revenge. Valentine shivered. The tears welled up in his eyes. Jack passed him a fresh drink.

Valentine guzzled it. He wanted it to finish. The pressure was too much.

Jack put his big arm on Valentine's shoulder and tried to explain. Valentine had the vibe all wrong. Courtney was not out to get him. They were on the same side. He just wanted to give Valentine his coke back. It was all his fault he'd been caught with it four years ago. He was a rich man now, everything legit. He had become a rag trade boy. Courtney Trading. Import and export. Lacoste copies from Thailand. Sportswear. T-shirts.

Valentine did not believe it. "How much is Courtney paying you?"

Jack shook his head.

Where was Courtney waiting?

Jack couldn't handle Valentine's paranoia. He had enough of his own.

Valentine rubbed his face. He was safe as long as he stayed here. He had a hangover. A1 was kissing his woman.

Now he had to convince Jack that he was raising the Underground. The men from the Tower wanted the old team. He wanted Big Jack to DJ.

Jack looked incredulous. The punters wanted new DJs. He hadn't worked for years. All his records were out of date. Valentine was old news. Nobody wanted to know.

Valentine felt gutted. It was the truth. He had to try. The offer of a hundred and fifty quid pacified Jack.

Sure. He could get records with that. He had no belief in himself.

Valentine ranted.

Jack was not listening. He forced his attention on an Italian woman. She ran her hands down his back.

Valentine pleaded in Jack's ear. His voice was strained, thoughts jumbled. Jack had to say yes.

The words beat into the ecstatic head. "Nobody wants to go to the Tower."

Valentine pretended not to understand the slur. Things were going to be different.

Jack knew Valentine was fucking himself. He agreed to DJ. He wanted no more talk. His mouth was too out of control. He managed to garble one last sentence. Valentine could see him at work tomorrow. At the Bridgewater. It was a hotel in Piccadilly. Anytime during the day. That was OK.

Valentine held out his hand. His friend was in no position to shake. Jack staggered to his feet. He tottered. Then with an almighty crash he fell on the woman. She slumped under his weight. They fumbled to kiss each other. She bit his neck.

Valentine finished his drink. Dancers stripped to bare skin. One more lonely night. Ready to return to cold empty houses. He lit his last cigarette. His taxi fare jangled next to the coke. He dare not take any.

It was late. There were plenty of totties but that was not what he wanted. His legs were giving way. He had to sit down.

The dance floor was easy for a drunk to stumble across. Those that still danced were in hyperspace. He slipped on occasional patches of spillage. Nobody really noticed him. He was just another punter.

Tables that were not strewn with people were piled high with debris. He spied a space. A bottle had been knocked over, a broken glass scattered. There was a pool of red wine. This was the place.

He pulled a chair round. The feet scraped along the floor. A glass fell to the ground. His denim was sodden. Red. He did not care. Many nights finished like this one. Solitary. Alone.

He dared not think of what Jack had said. Nobody wanted to get him. Courtney was not angry. Few had even recognised who he was. Maybe he was played out. He blew on the cigarette. Smoke streamed green under the light. The FX had been real. He had to think hard. Gaps in his memory gaped. Perhaps he was going mad.

His brain seemed to whirr. It did not engage. Thoughts would not tumble out. He had to get back into the swing of the party.

The isolation was hard to take. None of these people wanted to listen. He was a hothouse flower. Without attention he wilted.

He banged his fist on the table. The knuckles turned white. Blood dribbled from the cuts. He licked the scars clean. The Tower had to work for him. It was the last lifebelt. He was drowning in his own insincerity. He was full of shit. It didn't matter if he stitched Fly up. Jack was just a tool. Perhaps he was blagging himself. Even the self-deprecation slipped from his grasp.

There were no more cigarettes left. He reached across for the dregs of a can. He shook the crumpled metal. Just enough for one last mouthful.

Anna would listen. She cared about him. Correction. Anna cared about a percussion player. That was different. One more reel of bullshit.

The FX could free him. It was a bullshitter's dream. No reality. Greed could run riot. No second thoughts. No commitment. Anything you wanted. Then walk away unscathed.

But what was the price? There was always a price. Valentine could ill afford anything.

He had to have a cigarette. Then he would get a cab. Work was over. He had found Jack, fronted Courtney. That was enough excitement for one night.

There was a single woman sat on the right, her back turned. Smoke floated above her head. She would have a cigarette. If she blanked Valentine, he could buy some later.

His hand tapped her shoulder. There was no reaction. She slumped further into her drink. Valentine had to get out of there. Even drunks negated his existence. She looked over her shoulder.

Her eyes were dark, wild. They turned angular at the edges. Valentine crashed back into his seat. He was off his head.

The woman raised an eyebrow. He asked her for a cigarette. She held open a packet. The movements were slow. He leant his bloody hand forward. The fingers trembled. The situation seemed simple enough. It was not.

The lighter was brass. Zippo. She flicked the top open. The flint grated. A flame raged, three inches long. It danced on her oriental face. Valentine drew on the flame. He held his breath.

She was going to turn away. It could not end like this. The cigarette smouldered. He watched her red lips. She looked at him. At his face. The scars. Still nothing.

Then she said "Valentine?"

It had to be Miki. The face. The fingernails. Valentine's lighter.

Miki had not forgiven him. He had given her nothing. Except the lighter. She had kept it, not as a treasured memento but a warning. It would never happen again.

He wanted to kiss her. Feel her warmth. His hand brushed on her arm.

She flexed her muscle. It stiffened under his fingers. She was repulsed by the scars on his skin. The veins bulged.

The only thing in her head was revenge. He had said it was forever. He had locked her in the dressing room, the key in his pocket. Then he left. She had been skint, alone. Men had knocked on the door. They were after Valentine alright. She had not been scared, just resentful. He was like a contagious disease. One touch and you were infected. She pulled her arm away.

Valentine tried to explain. Sweat dribbled into his eyes. He could not have taken her with him. There was no time.

He could not help himself. The lust would not evaporate. She was naked in his vision. Another piece of meat. One more arse to haul.

She flicked ash at him.

The dress was threadbare. Not quite the thing. Her face was not beguiling. The grease spots shone. Mascara painted black rings around her eyes. Even in the half light she looked dazed. He wanted to spend the night with her.

He told her about the new venture. The Tower. Rapunzel. Rapunzel, the Tower. Tastes of puke burbled back into his mouth.

She did not care what he was doing, where he had been. He looked repellent. Greasy. The smile was insidious. "More bullshit, Valentine. Tell me another." Her voice grated.

His last feelings for her evaporated.

Lipstick had stained the paper cup red. She tore it into pieces. The petals of plastic fluttered. "It looks like you love me not."

She was about to turn away. That was the last he would see of her, the back of her head. He imagined her on FX. The things she would see. Multiple orgasms. He could almost taste it. He grasped her shoulder.

His fingers hurt. Valentine would not touch her again. Each red talon dug in. The grip tightened. His hand wrenched free. Miki revelled in his distress.

The cigarette sizzled between her fingers, burnt to the filter. Small pressure in the ashtray, then it was out. The music battered her ear drums. She wanted to forget.

The smell made her stomach wrench. There were traces of vomit on her shoulder. She dare not look around. He might still be there. It would have been better to stay in. She closed her eyes. The room pitched like a rollercoaster. Eight double scotches. Maybe twelve. She could not remember.

Something landed on her knee. She flinched. No more spilled beer. Please. Her hands felt for the damp.

There was no beer. Only plastic. She looked down.

Even in the shadows it was clear what it was. A package. Chopped white powder. Crystals. King Sugar. Charlie. There were four wraps, maybe six. The powder sparkled.

None of the bouncers must see it. She grasped it in her palms. There was a hot breath on her neck. The same stench as before.

"This is for us," Valentine whispered. A debt that he wanted to pay.

His face glistened. She held her breath. There was enough to kill an elephant.

It made no difference. She was no prostitute.

The plastic clung to her skin. It was calling her. A relentless rap.

He kissed her cheek. So what? She could fuck Valentine. It would not be the first time. There was no shame. People sold each other every day. He was the one getting ripped off. She might not even remember tomorrow.

"Your place or mine?"

Valentine said he had no place.

CHAPTER FOURTEEN

The walk from Piccadilly was not a long one. Streets were surprisingly empty. It was a funny time, around three. Executives had returned from late lunch. Lowlife was still in bed from the night before.

Valentine was wide awake. He threw the sodden boxer shorts in a dustbin. The smell of sweat lingered.

It was a mild afternoon. No clouds.

He wore a cropped white blouse. There were tucks where the tits should go. The fabric cut into his waist. He had left Miki in bed, stolen the blouse. It was all he could find.

Nerves ticked under his eyeballs. His teeth felt sore. It was familiar. There had been too much coke to handle. Even a few lines for breakfast. There hadn't been any food in the house, only a small packet of prawn salad lifted from Marks and Spencers.

He strode erratically towards the Ritz. It was car thieves' paradise. Rollers. Porsches. Maseratis. All in a neat row. No double parking. Traffic wardens walked in pairs.

Coke-speak embraced each step. Power. Pumping. Pounding. A metronome inside his head.

There was no traffic in Albemarle Street. It had a Victorian serenity. This was a nice place to walk. The buildings had stood for a hundred years. There was a sense of history, the old order that could never change. No beat boys here. The only dark faces were middle eastern. Yashmaks. Kafirs.

He needed a holiday. There was no money left. Nothing until payday. He could sell some of the coke.

The photograph stuck to his palm. The resin was malleable. It was not a token of love. This was the way to remember, fixing the vision in his head.

Pus matted his hair. The wound seeped. There was no time to make himself pretty.

The Bridgewater looked impressive. He imagined Sherlock Holmes stepping out. The sign was authentic, the same for generations. Tourists must have loved it.

The place was worn enough to be expensive. This kind of style costs. Stairs led to a basement restaurant. The hall was lined with mirrors.

He passed by a luggage porter. Gilt dripped from his lapels. Jack had begun in the hotel trade. It was now his last refuge. The uniforms were free.

He ignited a Chesterfield. The repossessed Zippo sat squarely in his palm. One last look at the passport picture. She was alluring. It was an old photograph. He felt cheap. The grinding head-rush could not disguise that. Exorcise the ghost. He put the picture in his back pocket.

The portals of wealth were unnerving. A poor man could not play this game. He tried to catch an eye, break the ice. They would not give in.

The Front of House Manager was young. This vagrant could be dealt with by underlings. His tail coat gaped, a bad fit.

Valentine breezed up to the desk. A glimpse in the mirror frightened. His flesh sagged. Black rings etched deep. The nose was purple, bulbous.

The desk clerk showed immediate disrespect, his manner surly. This was no prospective guest. "How can I help you, sir?" Valentine reeled, demonic. He wanted to shout the fuckpig down. There was enough coke in his pocket to hire the bridal suite. He held himself back.

His drawl was transatlantic. Perhaps he was an artist, a wealthy eccentric. He asked where Mr. Cullen was.

The clerk realised he was looking for staff. That made sense. He extended a white cuffed hand. The finger pointed straight over Valentine's shoulder.

The hall porter's desk. Through the hallway.

The papers crackled under his ballpoint. Urgent invoices. He snorted.

Valentine smelled bad, a mixture of musty denim and women's perfume. He wanted to roll the pen pusher.

He inhaled stray grains. The nasal hair flickered. Last dabs of chas fizzled in the mucus. It seemed alright again. Mendacity on a higher plain. He threw his shoulders back. It was his town. The weak could have no inheritance.

The carpet was soft underfoot. Cartoon Americans stepped out of the way. Glass cases were full of expensive souvenirs. Jewellery. Watches from Switzerland. There were no price tags. Mahogany archways passed overhead.

He stole another glance in a mirror. It was not so bad. Tiredness, that was all. There was just a perception gap.

The restaurant was lavish. Menus pale peach. Onyx stands. Fat waiters. Slobbering saliva. Every face bloated, struggling with an extra portion.

The porter's lodge had a narrow entrance. Openness teemed from the woman's face. She was about thirty. The round-shouldered figure bowed in front of her was familiar. Jack was talking to the hall maid.

He rose from his haunches. The glee flowed freely. Valentine found it difficult to react. The surrounding normality was chilling.

They shook hands heartily. Jack apologised for the night before. He had been off his head. The ecstasy was strong. An Italian girl had given it to him. They had gone home together. The bit in between was hazy.

Jack ran his finger under his collar. It was too tight. There was an uneasy silence.

Valentine mentioned Courtney. Jack had not seen him for months. He was a serious businessman now and didn't mix with riffraff any more.

Valentine's hands grasped maniacally for his hair. He mentioned the Tower.

It wasn't good for Jack to talk here, too many overzealous ears.

He would change out of his uniform. They could go for a cup of tea.

Valentine agreed. Jack pulled off his grey morning coat. He would be a moment. The swing doors flapped behind him. Valentine would wait outside.

Jack unbuttoned his waistcoat. He was pleased to see Valentine but the management disapproved of his friends. Valentine should not have been so wired. His twitches were unnerving, restless. The customers didn't like it.

Valentine hovered in the hallway. Porters whistled by. The Head Waiter snarled. Valentine rocked backwards and forwards, his visage singularly unappealing. The Manager hoped he would move.

Jack put on his jeans. The knees were split.

It was sunny at the entrance. The mirror glass shone. There were fifty Valentines looking at each other. He moved his head back and forth.

A tourist swung through the door. He was a regular. The Manager smiled. Valentine edged round him, flat against the wall. The floor had a horrible tendency to move.

Outside, the breeze was soft. Valentine lit another cigarette. Jack seemed to be taking forever. Standing still was a problem. He paced up and down. The awning made a flapping sound. It was blue.

There was a "Yo" and Jack stood behind him. He wheeled. Eyes flared. He could not be angry. There was no point.

Jack suggested Albie's. It seemed a reasonable enough idea. Valentine would do the business then go. He needed to get his head together. Maybe have another line. That was a bad idea. Things were too fast already. He could not stand still.

They charged up Albemarle Street. Albie's was on the left. It was a brasserie, kitsch of the worst kind, with a painting of a moustachioed German. Asphalt steps, white tables outside.

Jack pulled up a chair and placed his satchel on the ground. Valentine didn't mind sitting outside. He could gauge the surroundings much better.

Cocktails were scribbled on the back of the white menu card. Tea would suffice. "Lemon or milk?" the waitress asked. Her accent was foreign. Maybe Dutch. The lipstick was red, appealing. It could

have been Miki's. Her hair was blonde though. Valentine wished she would go away.

Jack paused long to order espresso. Her thighs bulged through the skirt. He watched her walk back inside.

The door flipped shut. Valentine could speak in secret.

He rambled about West. It could be his new Underground. Fly was already convinced. Jack could DJ. The PR would be spectacular. Photographs. Advertorial. They would be back on top in a month. It was the best of plans. A hundred and fifty quid. That was what he was offering. Cash money. The full monte. Jack had to agree.

Jack paused. He wanted Valentine to stop fucking himself, stop blagging. He could see gear talking. He knew nobody wanted to go to the Tower but there was no explanation that Valentine would hear. He was on another planet.

"OK." Big Jack would DJ. He needed the hundred and fifty.

A crazy man, a junkie and a no-name. What a combination.

The waitress brought the drinks. She bent forward. Jack swooned. She was wearing Opium.

Valentine clammed up in her presence. They were all spies. A fresh filter smouldered in his fingers. The hand shook on the table. Jack stirred his coffee. There was a brief thank you. She was gone.

He asked about Miki.

Valentine shook his head. He had not seen her for years.

His hand slipped inside his pocket. He rustled through the papers. It was still there, crisp and new. He placed the card on the table. Four thousand were going out on Friday. His eyes bulged with self-satisfaction.

Jack picked up the ticket. It was about six inches long. The ink had a veiled lustre. Each name in its proper place.

Your host, Valentine.

The Underground rides again.

On the wheels of steel.

Fly Macari and Jack Cullen.

He flipped it over. The lettering was bold.

West. As large as it could be.

The Tower of Babel.

Every Friday.

Now and Forever.

Jack sighed. "What if I'd said no?"

The answer was obvious. Valentine would have used them anyway. He spilled the remains of his tea. The trembling hand fumbled with a serviette. Liquid stained the table cloth.

Jack saw a sorry failure. It was all bullshit. Valentine wanted it so bad, it was burning him up, boiling his sweat like cabbage water. The cigarette butt singed his index finger.

He hardly noticed. More important things were inside his head. What celebs would arrive on opening night? Who would take the pictures? No outlay was a gamble. They could make it back on the door.

Jack finished his espresso. He licked the spoon. One last try. He owed Valentine that much.

Times had changed. The faces had moved on. Punters wanted a new flavour, not the same old taste. The Tower was a promoter's graveyard. Jack had seen it.

Explanations whistled over Valentine's head. Cells burst with six digit numbers. Next year in Jerusalem.

He had no contact number for Jack. Valentine ripped a corner from the menu. The ballpoint slipped unruly in his hand. Coordination was a battle. There was no fighting the tremor. Jack leaned over. He snapped the top open.

Valentine insisted he was fine. Another toot would straighten him out.

Jack had seen him like this before. The gear did him no good. There were enough marbles already missing. It was a lonely road.

He stared at Jack. What was the problem? Words blustered and angry. He needed a phone number. No eulogies.

"492 6500." The hotel. Split shifts.

Valentine could work it out. The paper and ticket slid back in his pocket. There was nothing else he needed. It was an uphill struggle to convince Jack. There was always nervousness on a new project. He could not stay here. Minutes like hours. They had sat forever. His time raced double. Why was Jack always so slow? A doubter. Valentine did not need him. He was doing the hiring and the firing. A month, then Jack might have to go.

Valentine was the Underground, not these men without vision. Somebody had to pay the bill, straighten debts out. Courtney was nothing. He had lost his bottle. Valentine had enough balls for the three of them. They had lost the taste for it.

The chair scraped backward. Jack leaned across. It was his shout. Only a couple of quid. At least he got regular wages. Though the extra would come in handy. Maybe he would get some new kit. He took a last look at Valentine. This was his friend. An arsehole in most people's books. The same old yarn. The blag. It was his only truth.

"What if it doesn't work?"

Valentine scooped up his lighter. He hated this place, the listlessness. He had to get out of here. Anna's was one idea. He could phone Miki. He shouted to Jack. "I'll give you a call."

Albemarle Street was getting busier. He lurched towards retiring commuters. They were nothing, feet rattling like ants. Shop windows were full of objets d'art. A crowd queued by a cash machine. He thought of money. The lack of it. There was warmth in his groin, stickiness. He remembered the trashed shorts. Anna might have a spare pair.

There had to be a khazi around here. Somewhere to have a line. They would be clean in Green Park. Westminster would make sure. He crossed into Piccadilly. The Ritz was all lit up. The uniforms were certainly better than Jack's.

He mingled with a crowd. They seemed well dressed. Men in suits, too trendy for round here. Maybe they were car salesmen. Too sharp even for that. The sole flapped on his shoe. It was unglued. He tried to keep pace with a pretty woman. She was wearing a cocktail dress, well cut, expensive. He traced a line with his eye up from her ankle, straight to her neck.

The shoe was a problem. It slowed him down. There was a slur on his right foot. He wanted to throw it off.

There was no respite. Rap. Rap. Flap. He tried moving faster. Doorways shot by. Colours blurred. He was almost running.

A hand grabbed his elbow. It jerked taut. He flew back. What the hell?

It was Virginia Nixon.

She stood straight. Elegant. He was not sure where she had come from.

The crowd circled round, their chatter getting louder. Words splurged. Eyes flickered. There was no sense of charm.

Her hair was scrunched into a French plait. The make-up was business-like, subtle in its precision. He asked where she was going.

She took his arm. "Wait and see."

The soles of her boots made no sound. The leather crinkled with newness. She set a leisurely pace. The others looked on, rakish. Nobody else wore denim. No traces of sweat on collars. Hands were manicured. She looked at his battered knuckles. A nice souvenir. He had not smoothed away the memory. She was hard to forget.

The heat added to his unease. Valentine was in tow. Her grip was firm. The coke sat in his pocket. An insurance policy. Enough for two. A dirty weekend.

She was happy to be with Valentine. The unpredictability was exciting. The bevelled glass stretched their frames much taller.

His forearm juddered next to her. His eyes skirted her chest. It was a mystery tour, destination unknown. They would separate soon. He wondered how close the khazi was. There must be one in the Dilly tube station.

Associates filtered into a revolving door. It spun rapidly. They funnelled into a body-jam.

The doorman bowed towards Virginia, his top hat tilting. She genuflected.

Valentine had never been in the Zenith before. The profile was cool, European. He fiddled with his bitten nails. Things were happening too fast. It was difficult to balance the books. Each picture was more crammed than the last. He wanted to walk away. Opaque obelisks stained the glass.

She dragged him through. He was caught. No reason to break away. A small child on a shopping spree. Mother always knew best. This was her favourite shop. A haven for browsers. The capital of FX?

It was a tennis game in his head. They crossed the court together, shaking hands as they went.

The banner stretched across the hallway. It hung from pink pinnacles. Domaine presents. A health drink. A way of life. GLOW. Purity for a nation.

An usher approached. The clip board was steel. He clung to it. Valentine's instinct was to fade into the crowd. Virginia held him fast. This was her world. She was relaxed. Valentine fidgeted. No figure of authority was friendly.

The man stood in front. Servility oozed. Things had to run smoothly. Money assured that. Virginia mentioned her name. He rifled through his list. "Reaction." He was pleased with himself.

The badges were plastic, in the shape of a fountain. "Virginia Nixon" was neatly printed.

She closed the safety pin. The monogram hung from her lapel. Recognition was all important. Valentine craved anonymity.

"And your guest?"

He dared not run. The parquet floor was slippery. No sudden movements or he might flip over. She was his only link with FX. The coke downer was getting worse. No sonic boom. No surging downward flight. The pores were blocked. Nerve ends frayed. He felt breath whistle from his nose.

Virginia explained her associate was incognito. Valentine clawed at his eye socket. Fingers hovered in his glance. The man presented a badge, Valentine handwritten on it.

Valentine had not heard her speak his name. He tottered incoherent, the name tag a cause for alarm.

She wrestled the badge from his hand. Concentration was a black hole. It fell from his grasp. The pin pricked his flesh.

The usher floated backwards. Valentine could not see his feet. There was a draft from the door. They edged forward.

The crowd was deep, variegated, not entirely predictable. There were several black faces. Waitresses swirled in between. Pink uniforms. Short skirts. The trays were silver. Men grabbed for tall glasses. There was a statue of a nude man. He held a huge bottle in his groin. It spurted a white torrent. The liquid was GLOW.

Tastes of stale tea crept up Valentine's tongue. He leant hard on Virginia's shoulder.

She inhaled the rancidness. It was bearable. He would not back out of this dance, not until she stopped the record.

A different refrain rang for Valentine. A weariness. A pain. The record was scratched up. Different samples. Some in reality. Others retro. Stray hellos. Percussive touching. He could not make out what they said.

Virginia's head flashed from side to side. Acknowledgements. "Darling, how are you?"

Media buyers. Health-mag journos. Food trade executives.

Keiran was good-looking. His hands covered her eyes. "Guess who?"

She turned round. There was laughter. The jacket was square-cut, emphasising broad shoulders. Valentine rested against the wall. Men like this had good hair cuts. No sense of tension. He rubbed his neck. Tendons felt knotted. Time was catching up. There was no room for a breather.

He lunged at a waitress. She jolted abruptly. The wine tasted cool. He took another. A glass in each hand. The right shook more than the left. It made no sense to put a full one down. He finished both. Wine spilled onto Miki's blouse. They might notice he was wearing women's clothes. He dared not look.

Keiran stepped over. "Ginny has told me a lot about you."

Valentine tried to place the empties on the floor. One slid away. Crash. It was broken. The cut on his hand. He cowered upright. The man was gloating. The complexion was smooth.

Erotic. The man was attractive. Why was Valentine thinking this? Public school accents. Naked shower scenes.

Virginia's face pressed over Keiran's side, grinning. "Are you alright?"

He was shaking hands with Keiran. A firm manly grip. Hands slapping his back.

"This is Virginia's friend."

Faceless men. Women weighed him up. Not much resale value.

Virginia gave him a lighted cigarette, the butt covered in lipstick, damp with saliva. He took another lug. A voice cut across.

The MC's voice was insistent. It beat in his brain. The hubbub died down. No more frenetic greetings. She tapped his shoulder. "Come on."

He looked at her again. Strange perfection. Affordable lust.

People flooded through the foyer. It was a call to arms. Men got up from their seats. Stubbed out cigarettes. The waitresses picked up the empties. Hotel staff were clad in sombre regalia. The promotion crew stood out, a psychedelic nightmare. Staircases split off on either side. The show was about to begin.

Valentine lurched. Cigarette smoke was choking. He coughed. She told him to put it out. Her voice seemed excessively loud.

This was another world. It ticked with military precision. The right amount of alcohol. The perfect level of persuasion. There was something sexy about it. It was foreplay. Somebody leading you on. With the final blow right on target. The audience, the punters, ready to be sold. Compelled to spread the word.

The armchairs looked inviting. He wanted to sit down. That was out of the question. She urged him on.

Women handed out brochures. Their uniforms were steward-like. Green flashes. Tousled hair.

The doorway bulged. Fighting to the front, they almost lost each other in the crowd. She held his hand tight, fingernails retracted. She did not want to soil the merchandise. Valentine floundered. The loose sole stuck to the carpet. Legs fluttered. He broke free.

They flew forward. She had a brochure in her hand. Valentine crumpled his. It might fall from his fingers. He would not be able to pick it up. His hand might be trampled.

The cover was white. The lettering grandiose.

GLOW. A new kind of health drink. Domaine and Partners. A Taste for the 80s.

He did not know what it meant but it made him thirsty. There were no more drink trays. Virginia was not in view. He got more flustered. The size of the room became apparent.

There were large tables, twelve chairs round each. This was a banqueting suite. There was no smell of food. It was warm. A podium stretched in the distance. He felt very small. It was like a big pool. Sound bounced into the vaulting. He heard his name. "Valentine."

A choir of voices. Distorted choristers. Virginia was still next to him.

They had to sit down. Valentine slumped in Louis Quinze. He placed his palms on the table. The centre piece was made of polished rock. Jagged. Small mountains. It was an adult theme park. Phallic symbols abounded.

She played with his leg under the table. Her hands stroked up and down. None of the others realised. They nodded to each other blankly. He tried to read the name tags. The writing was too small. All too far away. Everything was getting further away. She looked at him. There was no sign of contact on her face. He was not sure if she was touching him. It might be in his head. He felt for her hand. The flesh was cool. It was definitely there. But why was he?

She rubbed her fingers on the cuts. Pain twinged. He wanted to say something. The sensation was too pleasing. Drifting in and out of phase.

This was the Garden of Eden. Full of serpents. The men's tongues flashed in and out. No words. Big bold gestures. Sales and returns. Imagery. Enigmatic. It seemed woozy.

The gear was in his pocket. He licked his finger. One dab. He sucked the powder from the tip. It tasted bitter. Normality ruled. Jitters subsided. Time to play again.

He asked why they were here.

It was plain to see. This was a launch party.

He moved her hand from his thigh. Virginia looked miffed. He showed her the ticket from the Tower. It paled into insignificance beside the GLOW brochure. It was kid's stuff, amateur night for those who know no better. He was churlish.

It was time to leave.

He couldn't go now. The fireworks were just about to start.

He leant forward, about to get to his flailing feet. She held his hand flat on the table.

The lights went down. Valentine was worried by this darkness. Somebody was pulling a plug inside his head. He heard the sound of his heartbeat. Two hundred people breathing. It was like a religious rite. He tried to regain his bearings. All heads were turned to the screen that hovered above the stage. White blankness. She wrenched him back into the seat.

A low music rumbled at the back of the hall. It grew louder, more powerful with every bar. Valentine held his ears. It was too much to take. Nobody else looked disturbed. He told himself it was manageable. The pressure ebbed.

Kettle drums. An orchestral horn section. Building the colossus. The tune was unfamiliar. It sounded like the fall of the Roman Empire.

The screen lit up. A point of light bloomed. Overwhelming. Bright. It flared with serenity. There was a huge face. Suntanned. Taut.

They all seemed to know him. He spoke in transatlantic majesty.

145

"On behalf of Domaine and Partners, welcome."

It was not Big Brother. This was Big Business.

There was appeal in his words. No shred of stage fright. He was a pro. Holographic realness. This was his new campaign. He hoped they would like it. The product was going worldwide. Similar launches were taking place this very day. New York. Paris. Tokyo. When they left they would know the truth. "Ladies and Gentlemen. I give you GLOW."

Valentine felt mystified. The voice had been reasonable, built on logic. But something about it undermined thought. The size. The self assuredness. It was off-world. A nightmare. The smile melted into a grin. Then laughter. He was laughing at the audience. They were swallowing whole. Without a second thought.

The eyes looked uncaring. Cold. Blue. It was corporate deception. The biggest lies of all. Raping sanity. Making black white. Coins. Silver. Gold. Dollars. A river of dollars.

He nudged Virginia. She was mesmerised.

What was he complaining about? None of them could see.

A buzzsaw in his brain. He licked his palm. The flesh sticky and wet. He rummaged in his pocket. Another dab. One more drink, bartender. He rubbed the charlie into his gums. It fizzled. More salt on his wounds. The face was still there. Hands rippled applause. It was self-gratification. Masturbation. They were praising their like-mindedness.

One more fanfare. A sunset of gold. Burning white hot. The face dissolved. Blackness reigned again. The sensory eclipse was embalming.

Voices murmured anticipation. The door to a new order was creeping open. The Delphic Oracle had spoken.

Then the quad sound kicked into action. Rumbling from the rollercoaster ride. Shaking the table. Rippling layers of fat. Clothes hung heavy. His frame felt redundant. He could not move. This was second sight.

The title loomed large. Healthy after GLOW.

The man ran up the mountain track. His frame was athletic. A volcano erupted. It was twilight.

She turned over in bed. Naked enough for seduction. The grey muslin swathed her shoulders. There was no escape. She had not noticed the explosion. Wine dulled her senses. The bottle rocked on the shaking table.

Boots scrunched the screen. His pace quickened. Valleys of lava raged. Molten red. He was breathing heavily. The denim stretched across the groin. It bobbed from his pocket. Protruding. Larger and larger.

Her hair was matted. Sweat dripped from above her eyebrow.

The lava got closer. Further down the mountainside. Houses crumpled in its wake. Faces charred black. Running for freedom. Running for safety.

The man threw his shirt off. The temperature was too high. He was panting.

She turned over again. She was beautiful. Dark skin. Long legs.

His eyes pained. It might be too late. He sprang towards the door.

The lava ran over gas pipes. There was an explosion. It threw debris into the sky.

Her eyes flicked open. Terror. Fear. She screamed.

He burst in. The door splintered.

She held out her arms.

The bottle flew from his pocket. GLOW embossed on the label. He ripped off the lid. Foaming white water gushed over her flesh. Cooling. Cleansing. They embraced tightly. The kiss was passionate. She moaned.

He turned the earthquake film off. The TV screen went blank. He looked at the bottle. "Don't get too hot."

Applause raged round the hall. Hands clapped loudly. A ripple built into a roar.

Valentine was not clapping. The room spun round. He was still on the big wheel. He would not make it over the top. His hand was in a vice. Virginia's hand gripped harder.

He was unsteady on his feet. She was pulling him along. They were sneaking out. Now was the best time. Nobody would notice.

He fumbled in the dark. It all looked the same. Feet tripped over chair legs. Shadows swung imaginary punches. He had to get out. The blind leading the blind.

His pulse hammered. Her hand was strong. All he could see were silhouettes. She pushed an usher out of the way. Valentine crashed into him.

There was a chink of light. Fresh air wafted in. The door handle clinked. This was freedom.

CHAPTER FIFTEEN

The car swung into an underground car park. There was a screech. Admission by special pass. Computerised bar code.

She flicked the credit card onto the dashboard. The veneer had been newly cleaned. Lights flew by overhead. A blur of yellow.

Concrete struts shot up from the floor, each one painted with numbers. She raced the engine. Braking was sudden. His stomach skipped. The contents spun like a washing machine. She eased the gearshift. They were reversing. She was a good driver when sober.

A glance in the rearview. Plenty of room. The car edged against its marking. She tossed her head backwards. Wheels wrenched into the gap. A little further. Chrome brushed the wall. The engine roared. She relaxed the ignition. They were dead still.

Crosstown traffic had been hectic. It had been exhilarating with the top down but Valentine was glad to be out of it. His companion had said nothing. The strain showed on her face. The prim make-up had faded. He had constantly watched her. The movement on the pedals.

She checked her face in the mirror. Beige lipstick had smudged. She wiped away the remains with a virgin tissue. The hair grips were irritating, pressure on her temples. She unlaced the restraints. Hair fell limply. Her fingers teased stray strands out of her eyes.

She opened the car door. Her boots crunched cracked tarmac. The door slammed. Noise bounced off the walls.

Valentine sat facing concrete. His body showed signs of distress. The air was dank. Why had she picked him up? The face of the ad man stuck in his brain. That distasteful laughter hung as a refrain.

He clawed his chest under the blouse. The unlit filter bobbed from his lips. A No Smoking sign filled his view.

"I'm not moving until you explain."

She leant towards him, about to say something. There was a glimmer. Then nothing. "Stay then."

She blew smoke against the sign. Her strides were clipped. She segued into the half light.

Valentine had to go after her.

He chased her shadow. Fumbling, lighting the filter. She did not look back. Her hips jogged from side to side. The ankles were thin. Phlegm crept up his throat. He swallowed it back. His lungs tightened. Following the dream.

There was no problem in catching up. He wondered if it was worth it. The price was high.

Light streamed in front of him. The incline was steep. His body angled. He could see her outline ten yards ahead. He kept close to the wall.

She was gone. The rectangle of twilight was blank.

The walk broke into a jog. He was unfit. Sudden movement racked him. There was pain in his ankles.

Light to dark was instantaneous. He could feel the evening air on his face.

Several people passed in front. Topo Gigio was opposite. He hovered in the portico glancing up and down the street. There was no trace. Bodies milled about. Acid heads gleamed in dayglo shorts.

Virginia was waiting. Her black glasses shielded the face. Her legs arched against a bollard. A dispatcher zoomed close by.

Valentine crossed the road. He tried to act nonchalant. The sole flapped again.

The van was on target. He jerked out of the way. Thoughts rattled. The mindfuck oscillated. Danger phased him. He had not looked. A minor loss of face, there was no disguising it.

She tittered. Off down the street again without a second glance. He was hard to take seriously. She did not mind that. It was part of the deal.

Still in motion, she removed her jacket. Her back was bare, the halter neck obscured by her mane. The shoulder blades looked pert, toned.

The comic mart was bright. Old film posters crowded in the window. Jewelled fantasies of Bogart, Audie Murphy. The Day of the Jackal. Walking several paces behind, he pawed at his stubble. He needed a shave.

She cut a fine dash. His movement stuttered, slowing down with the right, speeding up with the left. Peep shows garish. Bright perspex nameplates. Small pieces of paper. Young model on the first floor. The arrows pointed upward. Pussy galore.

The pavement was stacked with scaffolding leaving only room for one person. He stepped into the road. He staggered. Thighs lolloping. Crippled. Back on the sidewalk.

The tart with the Spanish mantilla looked old, impatient, not interested. This was a weird little pervert. No money in his pockets.

Virginia looked over her shoulder. He was still there.

The sound system pulsed from Hitman Records. A house track from Chicago. Machine gun samples cut into the road. He dodged the shattering blast. Feet, don't fail me now.

She turned into an alleyway.

The pork butcher's axe hit the joint. There was a smell of blood. Crackling spun on the rotisserie. Juices dripped. He must not lose her in the crowd.

Flagstones buckled. He avoided the dog shit. Into the alleyway. Up the mews cobbles.

There were no cars parked here. The walls were white. The path sagged in the middle. Valentine trod the centre. He scanned the doorways. There was a green glass awning.

Company motifs wrestled against each other. A defunct animation lab up for sale. Showbiz solicitors. Bold as brass. She had to have gone in somewhere.

There it was: "Reaction."

The sign was etched in wrought iron. He ran his fingers along the twisted length. The edges were smooth, beaten into conformity. He looked up the spiral staircase. Quirky enough. Shafts of light bounced through open treads.

The metal rattled as he progressed upwards. The hand glided on the balustrade. He felt quite pleased. He had just about stayed the course. One more step, then the landing.

He looked across the courtyard. The wheels of creativity had ground to a halt. A trumpet riff slashed. The recording studio was still operational. Musos did not keep regular hours.

A door swung in the breeze, wide open. A disembodied voice insisted. "Come in." Last call for the 'Gentleman's Excuse Me'.

Valentine poked his head round. There was no sign of life. The secretaries had gone early. Art Directors were in the pub.

He stepped onto bare boards varnished new. The terrain was uncluttered. Drawing boards row after row, sectioned off by partition walls. Telephones bold in colour had rung themselves out.

He crossed by a rubber plant. The leaves brushed his face. Nothing could stabilise the vibe. He was on his own.

He looked through the facing door. She stood by her desk, impatient for him to come in. Sound was swallowed by the rug. She double clicked the answerphone.

There was a large picture of Tokyo above her head. The Geisha relaxed inscrutable, her hands clutching a MaiTai.

Virginia gestured toward the chaise longue. He sat down.

The desk was unusually oval. Papers piled askew across the intray. Her hands riffled through letterheads. Nothing very important. She snatched up a square package. Smiling and relieved, she tossed it into the desk drawer. Then she filed the rest of her mail under S for Shit. They fell into the dustbin.

Valentine felt forlorn, the next piece of filing to be done.

She padded across the room. He had not recognised the stealth before. She locked the door. Nobody must come in.

The sponge in the chair was soft. It sucked up the remains of his energy. She tossed her jacket by his side.

His eyelids were heavy. The room strobed on and off. She rested one boot on the table. Her hands moved swiftly. The lace was undone. He prayed to avoid a sexy scene. He was fucked already.

The boot flopped on the floor. She wriggled her toes. "Hello, Valentine."

She had picked him up off the street. Off his head. None of her friends liked him. Why was he still in tow?

She winked. What could they do now? She was hungry. He sank lower in the seat. It was obvious they could eat each other. But any such reply would be too predictable.

He rummaged through his pocket. Half a pack of cigarettes. The remains of his loose coppers. It had to be there. He produced the plastic bag. The contents shook to the bottom. It was damp now. Saliva had stuck the particles together but it was still usable. Enough for two. An hors d'oeuvres. The main course could be flesh.

Only enough energy to undress her mentally. She undid her other boot.

He threw the bag onto the table. Services rendered. The only card he had.

The package landed on the desk diary. Virginia held it up to the light. She licked her bleached lips. She did not approve of drugs.

153

The contents of the bag poured neatly onto her palm. The air was sickly. He rubbed his forehead.

Cocaine. Commonus vulgaris. Cheap shit. Not the thing for adults. "Do you not think so?" She puffed out her cheeks. She could blow it all over the office.

She was too wacko for Valentine. He had to admire her.

A grain dropped from her hand. Then five. She was pouring it onto the diary. She blew him a kiss. The charlie scattered.

He jerked to his feet. Something had to be done. Blind with rage. Spinning round with no direction home. A complete unknown.

She laughed.

The floor bristled with cocaine. It could not be picked up. The Persian rug was dotted with breadcrumbs. He could fall to his knees. Master and servant normally turned him on. Not this time. She slid the drawer open.

Valentine sat back in position. There was incredible clarity now.

Virginia fluttered her eyelashes. She began to open the square package that had come with her mail. Inside was a bag. Its contents were green. Unmistakable. The Taste of the 80s. It was begging to be tooted.

She laid the photo frame flat. It caught the light. This was the field of honour. A green hill cascaded into view. She was pouring out more than before. There was no correct dose. One over the eight might be quite nice.

The pile stood three inches high. There was plenty more in the bag. No sense in being greedy. Her fingernail swirled through the crystals. Valentine had a raging hard-on. It was nothing to be ashamed of. Blood filled every crevice. They were locked sexually.

The room gaped between them. Space and time had no power. Her chest rose and fell. They were coming. This was a different orgasm.

She slowly tore off a notelet. Valentine's chest tightened. The paper was pale green, cool to the touch. The glued edge made a fine seal for the tube. She placed it by the frame. Now for the best part. She wielded the letter opener. Drawing like a scalpel. Four fine incisions. Crisscrossing the bass line. The job was nearly done.

Featherlike lines extended along the photo frame. Hearts beat faster. Four bars of latitude. Green. Iridescent. Glossy with purity.

A last deep breath of normality.

She raised the tube to her nostril. The paper rammed home. It was wedged among the hair. A long inhalation. Annihilating inch by inch. The first line was gone. The second like all flesh. Melting into the bloodstream.

Valentine was on his feet. He reached the desk in two steps. The tube contained blood from her nose. The paper was damp. Sticky. He did not think of it.

The conduit reached as far as it could. The edge bashed on a nerve. He did not care. FX lay below. His back arched like a cat. Each disc popped with tension. He buried his head in oblivion.

The first line was orbital. Swirling through nasal passages. The second cleansed. Disinfectant. A new bleach.

He stood straight. Snot burned. Molten jelly.

She said they could go to dinner now. The bag was back in the drawer. She threw her coat over bare shoulders. The door rattled open. Virginia was in the outer office.

Valentine had to try. Reparations. He was a desperate man. He slid the drawer open. There was no lock. He transferred the bag into his pocket. The FX was snug against the dirty fabric. Virginia called. She must have seen him. "Don't you want to eat? It'll be fun. Trust me."

She hadn't noticed. He slid the drawer shut. A home run.

Valentine walked into the outer office. Past the empty typewriters. By the silent phones. All remained still.

He joined her above the stairs. She stepped back inside. Her hand reached for the alarm. The orange light blinked on. They were safe. From burglars at least. She locked the door behind her.

Valentine rattled off down the stairs. The sun was just setting. He commented that it was a nice evening. She smiled wickedly. He could not imagine what they would see tonight.

Long shadows striped Poulteney Mews. The cobbles seemed softer than before.

Valentine reached down for his shoe. The stick-on sole would flap no more. He tore it free. The black rubber flew over his shoulder. The remaining leather was strong enough for a short walk.

Virginia stood over him. He noticed her change of attire. The Weejuns were oxblood. Collegiate. Her arms were folded. Their eyes met once again. He rose up, hydraulic. This would be the best meal of all.

They strolled through the archway, out into the alley. A skateboarder careered by. Reflections darted in the window. There was no sign of change yet.

The chef was paring off kebab meat. Fat trickled from marinated waste. Salad dishes looked forlorn. He turned the gas jets higher.

Valentine had no time to preen his mirror image. Virginia's doppelganger passed in front. The sky was turning black.

The moon was still there. Water splashed on the dog shit. His sock was already damp. It was not certain where they were going. The Greek diner was out. She was a vegetarian.

Turning the comer, Valentine felt the rush. He reached for her hand. Bang. He walked into a scaffold post. The metal glanced his forehead.

Brain cells clanged like bells. He was angry. A fist ploughed into the metal.

She stood laughing. The show of strength was fruitless. What a macho man.

He flexed his fingers. His hand was turning black. Pictures of Audie Murphy. Then the pain was gone. Her eyelashes were curling into feathers. The eyes were blue. Then green.

She took his hand. It was a claw. The ring on her finger was a silver skull. It needed polishing. Instinctively he licked it clean.

She pulled him between parked cars. Placed his hand in her back pocket, out of harm's way. They stopped in front of the Japanese restaurant. Her face pressed against the glass. Steam drew a circle round her mouth.

The raw fish was made of plastic. The lobster tail sprouted armour. Then tentacles. It was an alien knight at the round table. The platter spun, a windmill. Time was welded to the spot.

She slid her lips across the glass. They met Valentine. Flesh licked from the bone.

He was eating an elver. It slithered across his tongue. The grey skin tasted oceanic. Saliva gushed like sea water.

He was drowning in his own juices. She pushed him away.

The waiter was impertinent. Globules of spit rested on his white lapels. A kamikaze headband strapped his brow. Brains splattered as he hit the deck. His leather jacket burst into flames.

She could feel the heat. Inches away, it charred her flesh. They ate dogs' heads in this country. It was not right. They had eaten her pet. A mongrel hobbled with one leg.

They couldn't eat here. The menu was too expensive.

The prostitute crossed from the sunny side of the street. She ran her hand along a brittle hip bone. The red warpaint looked like a scar.

A rag trade rail poked from the sherpa. It was a rifle barrel. Charles De Gaulle had to be saved. Valentine was running. The troops stood in ranks. Brass buttons popped at the seams. He pushed towards the General. His boots cut into his tendons. He had to be strong. Stop them before a mind snap.

The crowd were shouting all along the Champs Elysees. Vive la

France. Vive la France. He reached his objective.

A car backfired. The shot sped towards the parade. Melons split in half.

He crushed onto her chest. The last kiss for the dying leader. He smothered his face against hers. The blood smeared on his cheek. She was fighting to the death. The angel of destruction. Tottering. Hands punching his balls. The Jackal fled on crutches.

The dress rail gouged his shoulder. The rag trade boy looked aghast.

Soldiers threw him off. Policemen with blue tits on their head. A common drunk groping a prostitute. His loving wife saved him from their clutches. "Leave him alone. He's pissed off his head. This is our wedding day."

The law stared into his face. A hanging judge. The black cap sat on his wig. Virginia was pleading for sanity. "Forgive him. He knows not what he does."

The officer looked uncaring. Arresting this lunatic meant trouble. The sacred black books went back into pockets.

"We must be on our way." Another Metropolis to save. The blue capes unfurled. Valentine saw the Superman symbol on the police shirts which flew into painted sheets of celluloid, jumbled and cartoon-like. Final credits rolled.

Virginia held his hand. England would be green again now the Virgin Queen had crushed the Armada.

The leper's hands felt swollen. Plague had cut him to the bone. She dare not look at his face. The sores were sticky, rotten to the touch. Clothes could cover the naked shame. A tailor must be found. Her eyes were drawn like a magnet. She dare not. Such terror. The face of an outcast, bulbous with growths. And she had slept with him.

Valentine stopped in his tracks. He stared into a shop window. It was the wall of a perspex prison cell. The models moved balletically. A strobe light flashed on a catwalk fashion show. The beam penetrated.

He was back in the Mambo. Percussion players were bashing each others' heads. Clubs were drawing blood. Veins burst spurting. Goblets overflowed. Wine, wine.

They were drinking each others' blood.

Virginia was fastening her coat. The buttons crumbled to dust. The jacket blew off in the wind. Bra straps snapped with age. She was dragging him nearer. He pressed his hand to the naked shoulder.

Francis was a transsexual. She was not surprised. The hand was still mannish. It was only natural to want to discover which bits remained. The shirt was feminine. Embroidered cotton. It was slimy, almost rubberised. Breasts sagged on the once flat chest. She clawed for a nipple. It had been surgically removed.

She looked at the groin. The dick throbbed. He. She. Her hand was a scalpel. Slashing. Tearing. Cutting off a prime hunk. That was not enough. Digging deeper. Creating a huge red gash.

They were all the same underneath the skin. God was a woman.

A baby was crying. It was her child. She could not let them take it. Suffocation was the only hope. Better no life. Virginia ran to it. The disinfected floor slid beneath her feet. A news seller waited on the corner. "Evening Standard, Evening Standard."

The thief was running away from Valentine. The money was gone. Cocaine scattered on the bonfire. Burn the witch. Singe any remains of the drug.

The street swarmed with New York cops. The guns were drawn from holsters. There could be no escape. He had to chase the gear. The empty syringe was in his pocket. They wanted to shoot him. He wanted to shoot up. The Spanish kid got further away.

A car broke in front of him. The driver waved his fist. Valentine wanted major league gang rape. He was sprinting for the line.

Her clothes were in tatters, ripped by his flailing hands. He grabbed the molten stump. Miki's hand? She had saved him. He touched her face to make it real. There was no sign of aging. He said her name in disbelief. "Miki?"

Virginia heard. "Bitch."

Topo Gigio was the best Italian restaurant. But the place was full of gangsters. She urged the bald matriarch on. They must step into the shower. The Roman pillars hung with barbed wire.

Lebensraum Block was square. The people sat in rows. Hunger etched on the skin. Everything was grey. The SS officer's tunic was brand new. He smiled that they might step inside. There was nothing to fear. The experience would cleanse.

She was a nice enough girl. Despite her shaved head. There were other ways to serve the state.

Virginia held the old Jewish man tight. Her husband.

A pizza flew into the air. CS gas poured from steel pans. It was a fragrant perfume, the smell of napalm on the trees.

Broken men and crushed dreams. The surgeon guided them into the theatre. The corpse lay in front. Her nurse's uniform was checked. The priest laid a wreath on the face. She sat beside her father for comfort.

He pushed the wheelchair under her limbs.

Waiters pushed chairs in for Valentine and Virginia.

Valentine was pleased to ride on the tram. He sat opposite the driver, watching the newscaster put on dark glasses. Masking the truth. They could not hide from him.

All the crew were watching. The camera slid by. It was an electron microscope. His hands were pincers.

The insects clattered their jaws. The table was a hundred foot across. The vase, a tower.

Virginia toyed with the knife, a carpet cutter ready to slash throats. The light danced on the blade. A mirrorball from a ballroom. Spinning. She had danced awfully well. They must come here more often.

His fingers were knotted with arthritis. He tried to grip her hand. He was a hundred years old. She was the youth he had lost. A bracelet hung from her wrist. He could make out the writing. This was the mark of an AIDS victim. A chain for death. She clicked the handcuff shut. He could not leave her. She was the carrier. Every fuck closer to death.

He looked into the cloakroom. Body bags all stapled together. The glass frosted over. They were in a morgue. He tried to wriggle free.

A waiter stepped over for the game show. Large checks on the sports coat, his tie made of human hair woven into pound signs. There were a handful of molten credit cards.

He asked what they would like. "What prizes can you take home?"

Virginia glanced down the pale menu. Everyone clapped. The wah-wah horn snarled. This was a strange strip club. The symphony orchestra dressed in black. They banged tin trays. Bashing them on Valentine's head. Metronomic. Automated.

He was a choirboy. Organ pipes bellowed behind the presiding Las Vegas minister. It was a lesbian wedding. Their names were not on the call sheet. Virginia Nixon to marry Virginia Nixon. Her clone looked better than she did. The breasts were fuller. Silicon implants.

The waiter recommended the al forno.

She was ugly. The reflections in the spoon could not lie. She pouted. Just say cheese. The teeth were all broken. Ripe blue veins in the stilton.

"Do you take this woman to be your lawful wedded husband?" She mouthed "I do."

The waiter took this as yes. He scribbled on his pad. "For you, sir?"

The German barber asked if he would like anything for the weekend. He pointed to his daughter, the bra and pants torn into shreds. A blow job for starters. He only wanted to talk. She spat her tongue out. A guttural grunt. Unable to speak his name.

They all had no tongues. Stale flesh on clean plates. Eating their own communication.

Valentine tried to speak. The words bounced around. More mucus. Silent regurgitated saliva. A world of silence.

The waiter asked again.

Disembodied human voices. The bay, pretty as a picture. His mother sat opposite. He looked at the bill of sale, a trim fifty deutschmarks.

The shapeless fraulein tried to kiss him. Bite out his tongue. He was vomiting. All his innards spilled out. Gold coins. He was spewing loose change. Shit money splashing through the letterbox.

He could only speak in German. "I'll have a piece."

The waiter wrote two of the same. Tagliatelle al forno.

A plate of worms arrived in front of her, churning black in crude oil. The mechanic nodded. He placed a carafe of cold water on the table. A cloudy sample. The bottle could be used in bed.

Jackboots clicked on the floor. The Italians whooped. Hats flung into the air. Mussolini charged forward whacking the peasants' heads clean off. A body wriggled undead.

The chef dished out whitebait from a steaming pot.

Valentine saw a bowl of steamy used condoms.

Virginia saw sperm-stained sex manuals.

The plate in the centre of the table. It was Valentine's head. The eyes oozed with maggots. She stuck a fork in. One soggy mouthful. Crunching like cornflakes. It was still warm. Chewing her own flesh.

His jaws wrestled with the pasta. Prison food at its worst. He mashed it into a sticky goo. The beautiful assassin in front of him. They had ripped out his fingernails. Broken his spirit.

Food slobbering. It was a hundred people fighting in his jaws. Bones snapped as kindling. Shards stuck between his teeth. The fork was a slim vibrator buzzing uncontrollably.

Pouring the goblet full of Christ's blood, sweeter than grape. The medicine flowed down his throat. Fumes rose from the stifling rat poison. Bubbling acid coursing down drains.

He offered his mistress a jewelled tankard. Jewels were eyes, watching. Staring. The President accepted the bomb. She shook the detonator.

Floors ruptured. Tossing up mangled children. Plague victims. Withered deformity.

They were stitching the big red button. Grafting it onto his heart.

The chef forced vegetables onto skewers. Fixing the implant taut. He tore his guts free. A handful of cheesy spaghetti. The entire world deflated like a balloon. England's glory, soiled with dried cheese.

She lunged for the last bottle of wine. The old wino was jeering. Her chin sprouted grey hair. Purple effluence made him blind.

She depressed the plunger. White light imploded, sucking everything into nothingness. Fallout ripped through skin. Organs on show in the open plan kitchen. Seething with flies. Hung out to dry.

A scream hit out. The little girl was wailing. A sledge hammer was crushing all her toys. Blood spurted.

Red wine spilled on the tablecloth. She touched it.

The psychiatrist's face was kindly. Peter Rabbit's fur was worn. She clung tightly to him. Other kids in the ward taunted. "Ginny is a crazy girl."

The doctor would not revoke the commitment papers. They had locked her away for safekeeping. Hands tied behind her back. The straps were taut. She rocked backwards. Stabbing father with the scissors. A neat gash in his neck. He had tried to hurt her baby.

Virginia rammed the knife and fork upright in the bread roll.

Dad sat there, repeatedly stabbing himself with scissors. One wound. Then ten. No virgin flesh left. So many open mouths. It was a male voice choir. The words got louder, more offensive. They were chanting. "Fuck. Fuck. Fuck." Storming towards her, chasing down the alley.

She hit the brick wall. Her head beat harder on the table. She had to break through, dash into the masonry. The fabric flew back. It was a pair of boxer shorts. The lion's mouth opened. She was burying her head inside. The hot breath fused hair together, sealed strands across her face.

The warder was wiping the dirt away. A rag made of cotton wool. She felt its force. Blocking her throat. It was a used tampon. Old and worn. They were suffocating her.

Valentine wiped the sleep from the angel's eyes. She was pretty. It was wrong that he had strangled her. So many people he had killed. That was part of the job. Being God. No friends to talk to. A trail of humanity clawing his robes.

Walking through playgrounds. Snatching lives. The mothers crying. They were crying still. Soldiers' broken bodies. Heads splattered in car accidents. He was completely in control. It was part of the deal to say whose life would end. The higher plain.

Nobody could see him. The forgotten lord. Wishing people would save themselves. Nobody believed anymore. Not even himself. It was a nightmare in his brain. He wanted to be loving. They had even taken that.

It was a waking nightmare. The rambling of insanity. So what if they tortured each other? He did not care anymore. Peace was for the dead. Hell reigned on earth. God said "Fuck them." Let them be fucked.

God wore a trilby hat. Allah. Jehovah. He jangled greed in their heads. Commanded Heaven's host of relentless industry. The false idol was power.

The waiter fawned in front of him. Slimy as human dirt. He could crush this man. Into the void. Silence. Fire and brimstone tasted too good. Kiss her forehead. She was the devil. The fallen angel. Let her do the work.

He guided her hand above the button. A game called Global Holocaust. The fusion reactor was inside his chest. It was His decision.

He forced her hand onto the button.

The chain reaction all over the world. Babies cried. Energy burned bodies to dust. Limbs fell in acid rain. Silent mouths.

All was dead. Even the devil was dead. Age evaporated from her face. She was a young woman. Newborn in his arms. He held her tight. She did not cry.

God was completely alone. He could hear nothing any more. The land was barren. The word did not remain. One last still-born child.

He tried to cry. No one could hear. No one would ever hear. His pulse dropped to a single bleep. Brain dead. Watching a nothingness in space.

The man in the white coat spoke. He told her the rooms were ready. She was in a straitjacket. Slumped in the wheelchair. She gazed at her brother. He was also in restraint.

They injected him with morphine. His neck jerked. The body was still.

The syringe pierced her skin. Rage ebbed into euphoria. Men wheeled them down the corridor. Human nodding dogs looked on. In the bowels of the asylum everything was colourless.

The door slammed shut. They were still together. He smiled. Their sentence: "euphoric blankness."

A lifetime. Forever. She pulled her eyes closed. The lights went out. He kissed her goodnight.

Then they walked out of the restaurant.

CHAPTER SIXTEEN

Blood ran onto the blotter. Valentine watched for Domaine's breath. The jacket shoulders rose. It might be the breeze. The gun slipped from his hand and bounced on the carpet. He slammed the window shut.

There was a chill in the air. His feet felt cold. He prayed it was over. There ought to be police sirens. Plain clothes men flying through the door. The cameras could stop rolling. Cut to the epilogue.

There was little he could do. Someone else was directing the scene. He was outside his body. Feet crept across the deep pile, softness drawing down. Slippery as a swamp. Hands trembled.

The body was a dead weight pulling on his forearms. He swung it from the desk. Domaine flopped into his chair. The skin was pallid. A large cut etched into the nostril. Blood smears, garish like lipstick.

Valentine cowered. Guilt ridden, he shook uncontrollably. A wet patch appeared on his trousers. He had pissed himself.

They would never believe his story. Steel doors slammed in his brain. Instinct told him to run. Fear welded him stiff.

The lights flickered. That moment recurred in vision. Valentine hit him. Valentine hit. Valentine hit him. The gun was swiping in slow motion.

He fell back into the chair crying like a baby. Tears dripped, cutting trails in the black rings. The last sight he would see. A corpse. The smell of death. He was going to be sick.

Domaine's lips stretched a smile.

Valentine had finally gone mad. Illusion seemed so real. He was hallucinating. The last FX trip had never landed.

Domaine opened his eyes. He was breathing alright. Valentine tried to turn away, scared what the face would become next. He knew he could not hide. Sight was in his head, not through his eyes.

But Domaine did not metamorphose. He scraped the blood from his lips. There was pain in his eyes. The hurt would not bother him. He had learned to think through it.

He took a filter from the box. A click of the lighter. Domaine smoked from the right hand side, the untarnished profile. "Poor little Valentine. Can't think straight anymore." The words rasped from his gut. The voice was not so lilting now.

Valentine curled up in the chair. He wanted the cold leather to swallow him up. This trip was out of control. No godly vision came over him. He blinked and blinked. Each time he looked again. The song remained the same. This is not real, he kept telling himself.

His crotch was warm and damp. Mental faculty in shreds. Unconnected.

Domaine stood up. He was walking. A limp stuttered his leg. No shadow image left in the chair. The corpse haunting the murderer.

Valentine needed help. Alone with the terror of madness, there was no one to save him. He called out. Anna? She thought he was mad. Virginia? The highlife was over for her. Miki? She rotted in a grave. The headstone was blank.

"You think I am dead," Domaine whispered.

He crouched over Valentine's shoulder. The filter tip singed. Domaine drew it across the sweaty cheek. It carved a purple burn. Valentine was screaming, unsure if he could feel it.

"You really don't know." Domaine was laughing. Valentine was his human ashtray. He stubbed the butt deep into the palm. Valentine reeled from side to side. The pain passed through him. It had to be a nightmare. All a conjuring trick. He willed the burning to stop. It would not. The smell of charred flesh filled his nostrils.

He was running away, seeking refuge in the subconscious. His mind was blank. All the passion had been erased. Gaping chasms of memory. He was not even sure where he was.

The man bearing down on him was familiar. The recurring word was death. The man was spinning in his chair round and round. The room whirled. All the colours blending black. It felt like a fairground ride. There was no thrill, only swathes of disorientation.

Stomach muscles were steering against each other. The emptiness sent forth a belch. The chair stopped moving. Motion continued in his throat, sphincters pressured to bursting. A spasm enveloped his chest.

Stale beer and corned beef sandwiches erupted from his mouth. Then a second wave. Pieces of undigested food spattered his legs. Yellow with bile. The scent of effluence rose. The ripe taste clung in his mouth.

He was trying to catch his breath. Rub the sourness away. There were no words left, no pictures. He spat the remains into a charred palm. He sat in his own debris, the leather throne rank with piss and vomit. All the shit of a lifetime piled thickly. Gluing him stationary.

Two unblemished shoes rested in front. They belonged to Richard Domaine.

Valentine scanned up the figure. The crease was sharp in the trousers. The jacket button at eye level. A hand outstretched toward him. He felt it grip the back of his neck. The man bent his head into view. The nostrils flared. Each cold eyeball had black pinpricks for pupils.

He smiled a knowing smile. There was sanity written there, not disgust. Logic, not fear. The face loomed inches away. Domaine brought his lips to bear. He kissed Valentine's forehead.

"You are my best subject. We must talk." A last fleeting glimpse, then Domaine's arm swung the chair back to face the desk. Valentine lolled immobile.

Domaine installed himself in his chair. He rocked back. The brogues rested on the table. The soles were unmarked. He dabbed his lips dry. The handkerchief was silk. "Now."

He stared at the wretched figure. It was better than he had hoped for. The physical addiction had taken hold.

He felt for his inside pocket. Gripped the silver key between thumb and forefinger. It was only two inches long. With surgical precision he wielded it. A slinky fit in the lock. One turn anticlockwise. Dual plungers dropped.

The high-pitch creak hurt Valentine's ears. He was dazed, unconscious of Domaine's purpose. There was no more hate left. He wanted the end to be swift. This insanity was unbearable. Not exciting like a trip. A mind snap. He felt no oxygen was getting to his brain. Somebody was pulling out the wires. He could not fight it anymore.

Domaine waved the cold metal. "Here is the key." He tossed it into Valentine's lap. It landed amidst carnage. Held fast by vomit.

The drawer was open. It was not very deep. Secret. A burglar might think it was a solid slat. Domaine placed a file on the desk. It was grey plastic, embossed with a large seal. *Clearance: Unclassified. Board level only.* He flipped the cover open.

Valentine did not understand. The answer had to lie in pounds or dollars. Not this drab file.

Domaine placed several large photographs in a row. Unfolded a crisp computer readout. He coughed. The words of explanation were sullen, the statistics mind-numbing. Whole strata of existence had been reduced to a list of numbers. Everybody had a classification, income bracket, way of living.

Domaine sold lifestyles. He had to know. This was his largest piece of market research, faultless in detail.

Left-wing or right? He did not care which way the wind blew. This was real power. The truth behind the smile.

Everybody trusted a smile. Hitler smiled at the German people. They followed. The Ripper smiled at his victims. They could not suspect. The women on the commercials smiled. Domaine flexed a row of immaculate crowns.

Valentine's head fell.

Domaine pointed to a number. It crackled at his touch. *Valentine.*

Nothing was secret. People had loose jaws. They always returned questionnaires. News of Valentine's exploits had filtered back through Virginia's associates. Well, it was part of business. Corporate communication. Valentine was new on the scene, not a big splash. Others were High Spend, so merited much more attention.

Valentine was crucified by the thought of his anonymity. He had gone completely mad yet hadn't even been famous for his fifteen minutes. Valentine had wanted so much. His sense of loss festered.

There might be one last chance. Valentine looked at the pistol, still on the floor. One shot could have finished it. But the gun was useless. Domaine's empire was unshakable. If it wasn't him it would be somebody else. There were hundreds waiting to take his place.

Valentine was scared, really scared. The tears began to stream again. The burns on his face and palm ached. His clothes stank. He was unsure what was worse. The shit on his lapels? Or the bullshit inside his head?

Suicide still remained an option. But that took guts and his guts had spilled out moments earlier. A last cigarette might make it easier. Just like in the films. That moment before the firing squad took aim. Any last requests?

His voice quavered. "Can I have a cigarette?"

"Help yourself," Domaine said graciously.

The box was still open. Valentine's hand shook as he took one. He struck a flame from the table lighter. The filter tasted minty. Domaine had been smoking menthol.

The minty flavour reminded him of green. He should never have taken the first line of FX. Green was an evil colour. It was the colour of greed. He had stolen the package. Involved his friends with Virginia Nixon. They might have still been alive. It was all his fault.

Valentine looked at the gun for salvation. Domaine noticed. Both eyelines rested on the pistol.

Domaine stood up. Then walked over silently. He picked up the gun, turned to face Valentine. The facts were in front of him. Cold metal rested against his palm.

Domaine felt for his lip. The cut protruded slightly. He padded back to the desk. The gun clunked as he placed it between them. He reclined back into his chair.

Domaine turned pages of the printout. "You want to know why I give it away."

Valentine relived Courtney giving him the coke. Then Virginia giving him a line of FX. Then Miki snorting half of his stash. He had taken it all. Given nothing in return. Favours had exchanged hands. Someone always had to pay. He was paying now. The price was sanity itself. And he had no more to give.

The blag from the Tower had run riot. He couldn't talk his way out any more. It took his entire concentration to lift the cigarette. The smoke dried up his last drops of saliva.

Domaine promised it was going to be alright. He had the answer. He held up a large bag of FX, could be half a pound. It was darker than the rest. Opaque emerald in colour. This bag was one hundred percent pure. It was straight from the source. One line might be lethal. "Try it and see," Domaine urged.

Valentine tried to concentrate. One line would finish it. He could see God again. His mind would be cleansed. Then life would be over, snuffed out like the flame of a candle. There would be no more comedowns. No more flashbacks.

He felt very lonely.

His arm stretched taut. The bag was just out of reach. His pain was intense. Domaine needed to understand Valentine's anguish. It would fill the missing gaps on the questionnaire. His research had to be completed. Only then could he close the file.

"Don't you want any answers?" Domaine was losing patience.

Valentine shook his head. There was no room for any more. His mind was rammed, the seams of logic fit to burst.

Domaine looked perfectly normal. He was the Housewives' Choice, not the Prince of Darkness. That frightened Valentine. Nobody wanted the truth any more. The commercial breaks had become reality, not the programmes. People fucked each other over a Renault 5. Worlds turned for a can of Shake 'n' Vac. All the potatoes wanted to be Smith's Crisps.

Greed made it work. Joe Public needed men like Domaine. He told them how to live. He showed them how to think. He was the oil in the wheels of industry. Without him they had nothing.

Valentine swiped at the FX.

Domaine dodged and pushed him back in the chair. "Not until I tell you." His anger subsided. This was business. No need to waste emotion on it.

He took more photographs from the file. Then began his presentation.

Valentine squirmed.

Domaine spoke in deep tones. His gestures were broad. It was just like his media launch. "We are both promoters, Valentine."

His multinational was so large they didn't just deal in advertising. They owned factories. A Building Society. Even a small airline. "Here is our newest product."

He held up a black and white photograph. It had an opaque lustre. The picture showed a plastic bottle of GLOW. The Taste of the 80s. "Let me fill you in."

GLOW was distilled in a major European city. The spring rose high in the mountains. It bubbled deep from the black soil. Mixed with rain water, it washed through this ancient spa town. It washed past rubbish dumps, by chemical plants, gathering soluble fertilizer, assorted biodegradable animal tranquilizers, even human effluence. Few people knew. Even less cared. It was a closely guarded secret.

Domaine's lips curled into a grin. This was the clincher.

Land subsidence had prevented them from building in the mountains. It was unsafe to construct a bottling plant there. So they built the factory on the low ground.

For generations invalids had travelled to this place. They wanted to drink from the spa. It was supposed to have health giving properties. That was then. The world was a different place now. Human pollution had corrupted the water. It no longer tasted sweet. But the time was right. The location was right. The sums made sense.

The people of the world wanted a new spring water.

Domaine had backed the construction of the plant. They filtered out the impurities and the 'boys in the lab' had come up with GLOW. It was perfect. There was only one problem.

The refining process had come up with a by-product, a mutant insoluble filtrate. All the waste from a thriving community in compound form. It was a green dust that outstripped classification.

He toyed with the bag. They had mountains of it.

It had proved useless as a fertilizer. But when introduced into test animals' blood streams it had a strange effect, first producing tranquillity, then frenetic activity. It was a powerful stimulant. But in small doses it might give a 'kick' to soft drinks, to GLOW itself.

They had to test it somehow.

It was never intended as a hallucinogen. Let alone a street drug. They had hoped it could be a 'happy' compound. If it proved harmless they could use it as a food additive. Domaine had revelled in that notion. Profit from debris. It made good business sense.

The lab animals had revealed little. A monkey could not say how it felt. Only human beings could tell whether there was too much salt on the burger.

Here was Domaine's quandary. He could not sell a potentially dangerous product. Yet he could not do his public market research. The press picked up on such things. "Look at the Thalidomide scandal."

Domaine paused. He unfolded more of the printout.

GLOW was a lifestyle product. The research had to embody that lifestyle. Who better as guinea pigs than the image makers? The ad women, the media men, executives, young directors, maybe the odd diplomat. High Spend at its best.

Valentine could not accept it. His brain jangled. He wanted the truth.

This was the truth, documented and recorded with precision. It was a marketing scam. There was no conspiracy. Just the crushing tide of hard sell.

He was drowning in this sea of bullshit. Perhaps no one had really died. Perhaps he was not really crazy.

Then he noticed one of the other photographs, the ones from his file. He leant out and touched it. The resin felt real enough. The picture was of a dead girl. Her body was horribly mutilated. She only had half a face. It might be Miki. But he could not be sure.

Pain was the only certainty. The burn on his palm was purple. He screamed.

Domaine raised his eyebrows. He took a pen from his pocket. "It's finished, Valentine." He crossed Valentine off the list.

Domaine had tied him up like a Christmas turkey. Who would believe Valentine if he told them? A wealthy businessman giving away drugs for market research? The quantities sounded too large. The entire thing seemed absurd.

Domaine dabbed his cuts. He would tell the Board he bumped into a door. It was a question of values. All the others involved were successful, rich. A little loss of sanity didn't bother them. They had businesses to run, scams to churn out. Who would notice? Zany was a popular lifestyle in the 80s.

Then there was Valentine. He still stared at the full bag on the edge of the desk. He was of the wrong social class. He had not filled in a questionnaire. Unlike the others, he just would not walk away. He cared too much.

Valentine blinked his swollen eyes. The green dust filled his vision. It was free. It had to be safe. He was tired of thinking.

Domaine lit another cigarette. He gestured to the file. "Now I have to bury the results." The silver key was in his hand.

Valentine felt disorientated. He couldn't remember returning it. He was shaking again.

The table was a huge mincer. Domaine's hands were being munched by the desk drawer. The words echoed in Valentine's head. *I have to bury it. I have to bury you.*

The huge windows were video screens. Images of Valentine's life flashed fast forward.

Domaine was reading the eulogy at Valentine's funeral. Miki was a sullen angel. Virginia tossed in some scorched earth. It oozed toxic green.

Jack smiled. He was wearing his uniform. He opened the door of the Bridgewater and it was the door to the Tower of Babel.

"Nobody wants to come."

But the crowd still danced there. They were housewives, young couples, all first time buyers.

Designer Stubble. Designer Violence. Designer Drugs.

Valentine had pumped Fly full of heroin. The body jerked. The room jerked. Valentine was jerking. He was falling to earth. Faster and faster.

They were all dead. Fly's body had crumpled on the ground. Miki's body was cold as steel.

This was the truth. Valentine had seen his own death. The last thing he would see was this room. The puke that spattered his suit. One piece of carrot on his lapel. That was the last thing he would see.

He felt cold. He felt lonely. Why had it all been so insignificant?

Insanity was his only freedom. He snatched up the gun and pointed it at Domaine's head. His voice screamed shrill. "Give me that bag of FX."

His thumb clicked the safety catch.

CHAPTER SEVENTEEN

A1 Jay tapped the space bar. The LED flicked over, a long list of names on the screen. Studio producers. Young soap stars. A rake of photographers. Each one had a code number, graded by degree of influence. Blue pass holders were marked by an asterisk that meant permanent free admission. These people attracted the high spenders.

High spend. That was what it was all about. The men with little taste but wallets full of fifties. Happy as long as there were Page 3 girls to ogle.

Valentine did not like it. These were the wrong type. They could break a club before the first night was over. These one-step wonders couldn't even dance.

No money left in his pocket. He had been out every night. He took one of A1's Chesterfields. They always tasted stale.

The Scene was different. Nobody believed anymore. Valentine had posed outside the Mambo. Assorted trendies palmed the complimentaries, not interested in his chat, jostling for cabs. The second-hand suit was full of stains. It was not the outrageous costume Chrissie Gold had wanted. He had sprayed the three-day shirt with aftershave. At least the armpits smelled nice.

The tickets were scattered along Oxford Street, four thousand strong. Westenders marched them underfoot. Muddy with stale beer. Clustered in club doorways.

He wriggled on the chair. The Tower office felt uncomfortable. The ceiling was too high. Pale pink walls crowded close. The plaster was full of cracks. He slumped on the table top.

A1 passed over the clipboard. The guest list was neatly typed. He recognised few of the names. Feelings were always predictable on an opening night. His throat was dry. A brain full of maybes.

The ballpoint rattled in his grip. He was tired. The letters shook spidery. He copied the names over. Guests that were drunken memories, girls that had said yes. Underlining Miki. Closing Scally with brackets. Virginia would not show. It was worth a try. He dotted the three i's.

The pen was back in the tower-shaped pot. Every sheet of paper bore the phallic emblem. Embossed.

A1 was quiet. He looked at the bulletin board, with weeks split into nights. The word West spanned the Friday slot. He was unsure of success. Valentine was difficult to trust. His heartfelt promises had not materialised. Fly was uncontactable. Jack had not rung in. There might be no DJs for the night.

He switched off the hard disk. The screen went dead.

Valentine never used a mailing list. The thought of thousands of people stored in plastic was frightening. Someone could erase the whole thing, rub out West like a waning hangover. He asked A1 to say something.

A1 told him not to worry. It was opening night blues.

They were both thinking the same thing. Nobody might turn up. All the work to get to this point, then nothing.

Valentine had viewed the days of the Underground with rose-tinted glasses. He clung to old memories. Embroidered. Embellished. Lies. It had not been so good. Loss usually outweighed profit. The flat was always cold. Good fortune was always around the comer. He was a compulsive liar.

The last chance was here and he had no stomach for it. The bullshit had gone too far and now was meeting itself on the way back. A riff of Chinese whispers. Even Miki had swallowed it.

Love was buying everyone with gear. The problem was it worked.

The tape was A1's favourite. Cool jazz. Valentine had never heard of the artist. Music rode the shiftless atmosphere. A1 pushed his ear close to the speaker. It was his last refuge, constant, above the vagaries of fashion. It soothed him.

Valentine had no such solace. Something was wrong in his head. He could not remember if he had read the listings. The magazines were open in front of him. Pages looked thumbed. He fingered the glossy corner. There was his photograph. He was not sure how he had got there.

Jumps in logic were recurring. He was treading a fine line.

Words were coming out jumbled. One magazine had called him a 'Funny Kind of Valentine'. The other said 'The Underground surfaces again. Hopefully it will not drag too many people under.' This was not what he wanted to see.

His hand scrambled through the newsprint. They had quoted him in the Standard. *"It was THE but Valentine not shockable York New the ago four years."* This was not English. Sweat appeared on his forehead though the room was still cool. His hand was twitching.

The pink was getting darker. A1's face was changing.

He rummaged through his inside pocket. The FX wrap landed on the table.

He was shouting at A1. The coverage was all wrong. The PR people had fucked him. This would turn off the punters, if there were any left. The tape was shit. What time were they opening the doors? He was on his feet. He was sitting down. The clock had stopped. The wrap torn open. Grains of green. Sharp to the touch.

Then it stopped. The sweat was gone. A1 was bemused. They had had this conversation half an hour ago.

"What's in the wrap?"

The words ceased echoing. "That's my problem." The wrap was back in his pocket. He started to read the paper again. The notices were still bad.

He was not sure what was happening in his head. The sensations were alien, terrifying. Not predictable like the paranoia. They passed in uncontrollable waves. One last cigarette.

The phone rang. Three high pitched beeps. A1 winced, startled. He raised the receiver, snug against his right ear.

The clock face was white. It read ten thirty. It was time.

A1 said "OK". He replaced the receiver. There was silence. They looked at each other. Neither wanted to move. It was safe in here. But they had to go.

Valentine scrubbed his hands through his hair. "It's showtime, folks." He rose to his feet. The jacket button flicked shut.

A1 walked into the outer office. The redhead said good luck. There was an empty smile.

Valentine hovered on the landing. The walls were dark blue, cold as midnight. His hand gripped the balustrade. He was trotting down the steps, breathing heavily.

They passed beyond the cocktail bar, ninety degrees off the landing. A tall, thin figure blocked the doorway. He did not look like a bouncer. His face was tanned. The row of perfect teeth sparkled. The plastic visage was grinning at Valentine. More like a game show host. He nodded at A1 and pulled the crimson rope out of the way. They passed through velvet curtains.

It looked better than during the day. The lights painted everything cleaner. No sign of grime. Damage hidden in shadows. Valentine licked his lips. They could never take away the odour of drunken rancid bodies that hung in his nostrils as a memory.

The ceiling was high, vaulted. Chandeliers dripped from the pinnacle. The walls bounced a bronze caste. This was Tara for

Mizz Magnolia. The Star's home on Sunset Boulevard. A mausoleum for Liberace. No blonde was too brassy to pose here.

Valentine kept telling himself it was alright. A fuck was a fuck on a Friday night.

The head doorman shouted from ground level, his voice sucked into the dome. Valentine turned to A1. He was supposed to have carte blanche, no monkey-suited brain-dead to call his tune. A1 was gone. The voice rang out again.

He would have to sort it out himself. Tell the guy where to get off. He needed to be strong. His confidence faltered. The man looked so big, even at this distance. He bounded down the stairs trying to look relaxed. The treads were wide. Nonchalance gave way to tension. His stride stuttered.

He was at the bottom of the stairs. The leviathan towered over him. His shoulders were broad. A gilt chain clung round his neck.

"You Valentine?" He blew smoke downwards.

Valentine wanted to lash out. Ray was a first degree arsehole. His suit was a bad excuse for trendiness. Muscles bulged the fabric. There was no reasoning with this kind of man. Say black, he would say coon.

Valentine had once broken men like this. Not any more. He managed a cheap jibe.

"I work here, you know. You can call me Val."

Ray passed a poor excuse for a sneer and ushered him to the door. They stopped at reception. The till was ready. The display shone *6.00*.

He had met Nicola before. The make-up was heavy, the grin dirty. There was no time to wonder what she would be like. The game was afoot.

He looked along the marble top. Ray was talking to the fat bouncer, the two men equally as large. Tasteless flared tuxedos. Hair cropped short at the back.

Nicola's voice purred. "Nervous tonight?"

Valentine's mind was elsewhere. He had a lot to prove. Anyone might crawl out of the woodwork. He needed a cigarette. Nicola would have one. He fawned politely. She opened the packet. His hand struggled.

Her perfume smelt expensive. She obviously worked here as a hobby. He struck the Tower bookmatch.

"You're a funny man, Val." Her voice was posh.

He inhaled the smoke. "Come here often?" She blew out the match.

One of the doormen snapped the bolt, about to open up. Valentine began to panic. There was no music. There were still no DJs.

He was treading water. Thoughts jostled for space. Was there anyone outside? Jack wouldn't let him down. He had the gear for Fly in his pocket, a credit deal with Bryce. The foyer rang with his footsteps.

There was a knock on the door. "Where's your fucking music?"

Ray spun round. Nicola shrugged her shoulders. The knock came harder.

The fat bouncer was angry. "We're not open yet."

The main room was quiet. Lights blinked on and off. A laser cut over the stage. The video screen was masked by slide projections. The word Underground floated on the London tube station emblem.

Valentine tossed his cigarette butt to the floor. Shoe leather slipped on polished boards. A barman glanced at the solitary figure. Valentine was watching the ceiling. The stillness felt ecclesiastic. There was no God, not even good fortune anymore. He had run away once too often. He heard men shouting in the foyer. The voices were angry. They wanted him.

The stage was empty. Silent decks rested on trestle tables. Strobe beams danced instead of people. There was nobody to cry to. He had bought all the warmth he could afford. The bag of FX was his only friend. Even that was turning nasty. A pocket full of hope suffocated by the plastic. Green with envy. Devoid of any humanity.

It was funny, he did not care anymore. The whole world was up for sale. A sticky pile of shit that was not worth owning.

He asked the barman for a beer. The liquid flopped against the glass. It tasted cool. The head plastered his top lip. He wiped off the excess. It was not strong enough. No medicine was powerful enough to stem the paranoia that lurched inside his body, shapeless and unrelenting.

Maybe it was the FX. Maybe he had been wacko to begin with.

He would have to face the music. He placed the empty glass on the bar. The walk to the door would be the longest he had ever taken.

There were now other footsteps in the room. His feet had not moved yet.

He had only left the foyer minutes ago. It seemed like forever. Ray must be out for blood. The tall figure was in the shadow. A voice shouted across the blackness.

They would throw him out for sure. Nobody liked fuck-ups. A musicless club on a Friday night. That was monumental. Even for Valentine.

The figure was swaying.

Fired before he started. He held his breath. There was nowhere to hide.

The man was calling out his name. It rattled into the rafters, powerful like the voice of God.

A purple light hit Valentine's face. Blinded by the flare. Unable to decode the shape.

The beam arced round. Shadows fled. This was no bouncer. The familiar round shoulders. His arms stretched by record cases. A glow painted his profile.

Clawed from the jaws of failure. A smile stretched his face. It was going to be alright. Big Jack was walking towards him.

There was no time for explanation. He had a club to run.

His hand prised a case from Jack's grip. It was heavy. Sinews pulled across his shoulder.

He slung the box onto the stage. It bumped dead as a stone. Jack was staggering. He hoiked his unresponsive frame upwards. His jeans were full of holes. The naked flesh looked varicose under the strobe. They both staggered in slow motion.

Jack leaned forward. The smell of strong beer floated in his breath. He said he was sorry, his face sad with regret. The drunkenness fried him. "Look, Valentine, I -". He closed his eyes.

Valentine knew. Jack had almost sailed them down the river. False sentiment would be meaningless, apologies hollow. The blag could not flow. The pieces shattered on the floor.

"They've finished us, Jack. They've finished us."

Big Jack could not look at the truth. The alcohol steered him elsewhere. He clicked open the larger box. Twelve inches rifled through his fingers. He pulled out a slab of vinyl.

The disc would not sit easy on the pinion. It fought against penetration, then rested flat. A shaky hand positioned the stylus. The fader slid upwards. Funk to begin with. The powerdrive kicked into action. *Superstition* ripped through the bass bin. A clavinet roar. "I know you'll understand. Superstition everywhere."

All was sane in the big house. There were lights, there was action. Valentine felt reassured. One more time. He walked towards the foyer. His pace was rapid, purposeful. He would not let them rile him.

The hair dressing stuck strands to his forehead. Dax, short and neat. The belt was too tight. His stomach bulged under trouser buttons. This suit had a few moth holes. Nobody would notice in the darkness.

Ray was bearing down on A1, his voice booming threat. A1 floundered in the verbal barrage. He was the paymaster but at the door all things were different. Valentine smiled at Nicola, calculating how far he could push his luck. A bouncer was screaming "Where the fuck is he?"

Ray spun round, his anger now directed at Valentine. He used to work a club in Tottenham. Westenders were either ponces or wankers, always late, never able to handle their drugs. He despised their acquired knowledge, their faggoty mannerisms.

Valentine stood the shaking ground. The insults fell, dull cannonballs rippling the water way off-target. He summoned a last flare of energy. His hands clawed his head. "Just open the fucking door."

A1 looked away. The bouncers stepped back. A hand came to rest on Valentine's shoulder. Ray stretched to his full height. "I don't like to be kept waiting." His eyes pierced. Valentine gulped. The lull before the storm, then "You're alright." Ray's broad chest erupted into giggles.

He nodded over his left shoulder. A large hand felt for the bolts. They clunked free from steel loops. Tony and Richard peeled back the arched panels.

Fresh air rushed through the gap. They switched on their walkie-talkies. A brief crackle.

Open for business.

CHAPTER EIGHTEEN

The crowd swayed on the pavement, twenty or thirty deep. Maybe two hundred people, bodies trailing off at every angle. More coming round the corners. Joining the snaking queue. All the bad press, the forgotten names. But clubsters still turned out in force.

Valentine scanned the faces. He did not know any of them. Miss Selfridge mixed with Versace. Young girls with blonde streaks. Faceless office workers, pissed, arriving too early from the pub. Bouncing ripe breasts. Out on the pull. None of the Underground regulars.

He had visualised it much trendier. Now he knew it would never be. The pull of the Tower was strong, but with an axis tipped different from his, characterless in its urbanity. Just as Jack had promised.

He picked out the prettiest woman he could see. Ushered her closer. Blonde, she waddled on cuban heels, the cowboy boots unstable. "Good evening. How many?"

She wanted four. He slipped the chord from the hook. The crowd surged forward. Bouncers shouted, "No pushing. Plenty of room inside." She crossed into the inner sanctum where he tendered four complimentaries. "You are guests of Valentine tonight."

She smiled winningly. He watched the cut of her jeans. Flesh poked through holey denim. The bike jacket was raunchy. Her friends were Hampstead girls on a weekend pass, three of the few reasonable punters he could see. Pairs of feet clattered up the stairs. A1 watched through the doorway. Four clicks on Ray's hand counter.

"Have a nice evening." Valentine had not entirely lost his touch. Bravado bobbed its head above nerves. Riding the blag again. His hands were still shaky. The shoulders hunched with tension.

Figures crammed through the door. Pound signs spun in A1's head, large multiples of six.

Camera-clicking Japanese, all Michiko and Doctor Martens, voyeurs of the wrong kind. Black funksters, each one victimised by flares, shook Valentine's hand readily. He was the affable white man trying to be street-cred.

More free tickets. Nicola collected them hand over fist.

It was all wrong. The wrong crowd. Guaranteed to spread dissension. He was letting in the totties. Normally he would have turned them away. These people would bury him. Half did not know a good night from a bad one.

He had raised the Underground alright. Passed it into the palms of wankers. The ink rubbed off West tickets, staining everything it touched, making white black. He needed to fill the place. Any street sense criteria passed into oblivion.

The bouncers turned away men with dirty shoes, but they loved the fat wideboys. Yuppie credit cards embossing addresses on slips. Bulging wallets. Loadsamoney. Leering cockney soap stars were ticked off the guest list. Ray greeted them with pride.

Valentine was losing control. The strong wind was chilling. He forgot who he had let in. The bouncers kept stepping in to stem his chat, making him look foolish. It gave them a sense of power.

A woman shouted out.

He turned from the clamour of casuals. Even Valentine would not let *them* in. Ray was asking where they got the tickets from.

There she was. He had not expected her to show.

Miki's hair was swept back under a hat. He gripped her hand across the barrier. He wanted so much to love her. The photograph was in his pocket. There were no feelings left. He checked his obvious thought. She had a bed to share tonight. He said he was glad to see her.

She flashed a stolen bottle of vodka from her bag. The bouncers did not see. Her face was happy. She wished he was more together, like before. It was obvious the night was fucked. When Valentine got serious it was all over.

He reached for her wrist and began to pull her through the crowd.

She had no money. A freebie would be the better part of valour. Valentine ticked her name off the list. Ray was shouting. She passed inside. One last look. Valentine said he would see her later. His voice quavered.

A motorcycle roared up the street. The newly replenished crowd was still rumbling. The bodies Valentine welcomed were becoming a blur. Ray was constantly breathing down his neck. A local wino was taunting them, his words deranged, features melted by alcohol.

Some blustering teenagers stood next to an aging Turk. His skin was tanned. This man would be buying all the drinks tonight. He had picked them up in Stringfellows, split skirts, plump thighs. There was a leer in his every word. He might have been a record company man.

Valentine wanted to blow him out. Send him home to his wife. One girl licked his ear. Her giggle was charmless. She would have done Page 3, spread them wide if the money was good enough.

Valentine said it was a private party. She was far too young.

The man unfolded a wad of notes. "How much?" The girl's hands were all over his body. Egging him on. Bringing him off.

Valentine wavered. Of course he wanted the money. Any gift they could bestow. He knew how cheap he was.

A twenty quid note wafted into view. This was just for starters.

A black hand slipped the barrier. The money was re-sheathed. A1 Jay ticked a name off the list. "Have a good one," he bid the old Turk.

A1 tried to explain. This man was a regular, fresh from a cable channel. The girls were getting younger as his wallet got fatter. This was High Spend. Nobody could shirk it. Not even Valentine. It was the jam on all their bread.

Valentine needed to say something. He was the butcher at the meat-market, hacking off slabs ready for consumption. Cash was the only proviso. A1 did not want to listen. He followed a tall black model inside. Her legs stopped just below the neck. The boots were laced high.

Valentine unbuttoned his shirt collar. The crowd was parting. Somebody was pushing through. The stripped-down Harley raced back in the opposite direction.

Ray was arguing. "I don't give a fuck who you are. Not in that gear." The beat-boy looked as if he had seen a ghost. Nobody stood in his way. His stance was mechanical, held in place by an invisible bolt.

Valentine waded by the doorway. Three bouncers blocked his way. He unhooked the rope and pulled Fly inside.

Ray muttered threats. Fly was notorious, a dodgy junky. He had broken too many glasses. But this was one point where Ray had no veto. The music could not stop tonight, regardless of who he hated.

Valentine grabbed Fly's arm and walked him up the stairs. Fly struggled with his case. His arm was cold to the touch, clad in black leather. Even in the gilt-edged haze his face looked white. But it was alright. The three were back together again.

They skirted the queue by the till. Nicola looked disapprovingly at Fly. She had once caught him cranking up in the women's toilet.

The foyer was packed. Bodies absorbing sound. Coats being slung into the cloakroom. Assorted VIPs floundering in the stairwell. The vibe was not good. But people looked happy. Drunk.

Fly's bike boots rattled against the floor. The buckles splayed open. He asked about the gear. Valentine felt in his pocket. It was still there, resting in a sweaty plastic skin. But Fly had not performed yet. He looked too relaxed to be straight. There was no shake in his movements. Pilot glasses hid his eyes. Valentine was worried. His DJ might be totalled already.

They stepped through the partition door. The bass rumble was shaking feet. The dance floor was full. Tracys and Sharons dancing to Public Enemy. The projections blurring heads with light. Video screens clicking over. Worn out excerpts from Easy Rider, the picture speckled with drop-outs. A seething mass of bodies flickering under the strobe.

The stage looked green, with people dancing on the edge. It bounced up and down. The record jumped. Jack looked up from his headphones. Valentine and Fly stood in front of him.

This was no tearful reunion. Cynicism had cut deep on all sides.

Jack mouthed words. The music was too loud, communication barely possible. Nothing really linked them anymore. They inhabited different worlds.

Fly leapt onto the stage and pulled up his case. The handle jerked against his wrist. This was the record collection. One box. Ninety five minutes of sound. He had busked it together. The brown sugar had made him unsure what the case contained.

Sensation was internalised. He was unconcerned about the crowd. He crouched, clicking the locks open. Light bounced off his glasses, the lenses too dark for him to see through. He slipped them down his nose. Fingers ran through the cardboard sleeves. Similar tracks to before, with a little acid thrown in for currency. This stint would be a nice rest. The end justified the means. Enough of the chinaman to rub out the weekend.

Jack flicked the crossfader. A fresh mix stuttered in. He glanced at Fly. This was not his pal. The old Fly Macari had burnt himself out. A shadow remained. The V.U. meters pulsed, peaking red out of green. The floor was rammed. A twelve inch static in his hand, Jack aimed to blank Fly. Hammer home his displeasure.

Fly hovered by his side. He could wait. He owed Valentine nothing. Jack even less. They could not push him. Valentine must know that the crowd was shit. Yet there was no affirmation on Valentine's face. He stood in front of the moving masses, a cigarette hanging from his lip, several handbags by his feet. There was a strange look of pleasure.

Fly tapped Jack on the shoulder and lifted the headset clear. Jack did not say anything. They were like strangers. Rival jockeys vying for power.

Fly tilted the white label into the light. It was an acid track, the title shakily written. *Phuture* by Phuture.

The right-hand turntable was spinning. Jack removed the motionless disc from the left. The spent platter slid into its sleeve. Three seconds. There was a fresh disc in his hand.

Fly took the pause as an invitation. Jack must be bowing out. He felt flattered, eased the white label onto the pin. His hand shook slightly. The needle sat in the groove.

Jack was now on his feet. The junkie had skanked in. He did not like it. Fly was wrecked. That was clear even to Jack's drunken eyes. Fly's fingers were gnarled like twigs. One rested above the start/stop button.

Fly looked into the crowd. The gyration was hypnotic, knocking his brain into dream-sleep.

Jack noticed the track marks trailing up an expanse of blue veined neck. Fly had run out of arteries on his limbs. Now he made do with his jugular. A shaking hand held the stylus.

Fly's thoughts were elsewhere. He punched start/stop on the deck. No sound in his cans. He was confused. The house track still cracked its way into the crowd. No sign of his white label. The disc was spinning. He did not understand. In desperation he zipped the crossfade. The V.U. lights stopped kicking. There was absolutely no sound. The crowd stood still. Faces turned towards the stage. People were booing. Fly heard a wail. Valentine stepped onto the stage.

Jack dropped the needle back in place. Ray raced through the door. There was a loud oscillation. A space age sequence popped rhythmically. Valentine was saved. The crowd was moving again.

The three stood together once more. Ray marched up to them, cutting a swathe through the crowd. Jack tapped Fly out of the way. He was furious. This was what happened with junkies. They could never be trusted. Jack was not malicious. It was a question of professionalism.

Valentine stepped to greet Ray. "Just a loose connection." He was more relaxed. A part of him had stepped back in time.

Ray was not convinced, but Valentine wouldn't say any more. Something had changed. They still didn't give a shit about each other but the three had created the old triangle, covering each other's back. That was comforting.

Jack positioned a twelve inch ready for a mix. Fly flipped the vinyl over. "The B-side is sharper."

Jack was surprised at the clarity of the voice. He had underestimated Fly. There might be something still inside. An old memory the gear could not erase.

Fly smiled. He could twist Jack around his finger. The strong metal zip crackled. His bike jacket fell open. It was getting warmer.

The dancers were swaying their arms. Manic, with invisible football scarves. Aeroplane landing signals.

Fly eased in the new track. It was simple to pick out good acid house. He was off his head often enough. That was why he understood.

Jack was tapping along to the track. He felt for the cap of ecstasy in his pocket. Save it for later. The plastic skin was still dry. He brushed the hair from his eyes. Fly wanted to take the gear from Valentine. Then he could leave. Neither could move.

Big Jack wrestled a promo release free. He wished he was more pissed. Money was the only thing that could make everything right. The hundred and fifty notes. Jack still had old debts. Barclaycard interest heavier than a millstone. Why was Fly such a wanker? Jack's throat was dry. He had mislaid his free drinks ticket. There was a hole in his waistcoat pocket. Valentine could get them more free beer.

"Want another beer." Jack slumped on Fly's shoulder. He saw how blemished the skin was. Fly's gaunt head scanned the crowd for Valentine. Beads of sweat were dripping. He wanted a dragon.

The lights made it difficult to make out. A black guy landed in the splits. A buxom blonde swaggered to the music, cowboy boots unstable as before. It was the blue pinstripe suit moving next to her. The bulk was unmistakable. It was definitely Valentine.

Jack chopped in the next tune. It was not as harsh as the others. *Superfly Guy*. Cleopatra Jones strobed onto the video screens.

More people were dancing to this track, but Valentine didn't like it. He whispered in the girl's ear.

The boys on the stage watched powerless as the two pairs of feet slid off the dance floor. Fly was dying for a hit. Jack was dropping into painful sobriety. Their confidence walked out of the door. Valentine felt cooler in the foyer. The woman's manner was flattering. She wanted a drink. Well, there were thirty free drink tokens in his pocket. He dared not look at her too long. His eyes always rested in the same place. He walked the woman through the throng. He wanted to make her feel special.

Faces were all happy. It was that point in the evening. Men were throwing good money after bad. Sickly cocktails dribbling down dehydrated throats. Psychedelic umbrellas upturned in empty glasses.

Valentine was chomping at the bit. It registered now in the calmer light that the girl was very young. They tottered down the stairs. The murals looked harsher than before. He gloated in the mirror glass mosaic. Large cartoon-like faces. Huddled stickmen. Childish brush strokes. A splash of the sun.

A tall man waited by the toilet door. His girlfriend was shouting. Her face snarled. Tight leather trousers fringed, distressed in western styling. She grabbed his lapels. The contention was unclear. He shouted to Valentine. "Yeah." A hand flew out. She winced. He slapped her. She was crying.

Valentine felt helpless. His blonde shied away. The tortured girl wailed. There was blood on her face. Large hands came from nowhere. The bouncer grabbed the man's throat. Three fast punches in the face. The denim jacket was awash with blood, his nose crushed like a walnut shell.

His palm fell open. A dozen shrink-wrapped microdots fluttered. They drifted onto the floor. The bouncer scooped the tabs into his pocket, tossed the freak up the stairs. There was a dull thud. The body bounced like a rubber ball. Blood smeared the marble steps.

The bouncer was pleased with himself. He liked the action.

The girl raced after him. Her voice was educated London. She wrestled with his free arm, biting his wrist. He grunted, dragged her upwards by the hair.

It happened very fast. Valentine spotted a yellow speck. He was scared to reach for it. His body seized up. The bouncer threw one fleeting glance that burned Valentine's cheek. Then he was gone.

Screams still drifted downward. The blonde held his hand. He looked at the yellow. The microdots were still falling. The punches etched in his brain. He was shaking.

It happened again and again. Virginia's nails were shearing his face. The cuts opened up. He was back in the restaurant.

The waiter bowed. Mussolini. General de Gaulle. Police officers kicking him. He held the prostitute's hand. It grew old and wrinkled. He looked at the face. The microdot. Everything was floating into green madness. The blonde hair fell to the floor. He was strangling her. Vocal chords snapped, gutted with piano wire. She fell into a bath of vomit. She was drowning, pulling him under. He could not breath. All the punters had died. They were dying still.

They were walking down the stairs again. Nothing had happened. The fight was a memory. He was not sure if it had been real.

On the level again. It was darker down there. He gripped her hand tightly. The palm was sweaty. Her name was Sidonie. Her lipstick was very red. He did not want to know.

The doors were painted with Pullman livery. Wide maroon stripes. They slid open like a high tech railway carriage. Fan lights merged inside.

They were talking about acid house. Deaths were bound to happen. The first one might be here, might be tonight. His hand was shaking again. He dared not ask what had happened. The answer may be too frightening.

Couples groped in the dark, sat on benches made from railway sleepers. He put on his mirrored glasses. The bar loomed large. It was steamy in here. She wanted a coke. He needed a beer. The barman wore a porter's cap.

They were busy tonight. Young men jostled at the bar, rubbing elbows shiny on the spillage. Several recognised him. He blossomed in their recognition. The glass clunked on the marble.

He pulled the ring tab from a chilled Red Stripe. The barman scooped the drink tickets clear. There was plenty more where that came from. She sipped the soft, sweet mixture. Next to Valentine she seemed viceless. There was so much she wanted to know. He had no answers. But the lies came easily. Shallow waters. There he could be sure of sanity.

Her eyes flickered with youthful sparkle, the one thing he could never own again. She wanted him to have a motorbike. He said he had a stripped-down Harley. Police shocks. An engine block virgin of catalytic converters.

They could go cruising. She liked the sound of that. Straight down Kings Road, hair blowing in the wind. Why wouldn't she just strip off now? They could cut through all the small talk. Burn brightly for an instant. That was what Virginia would say.

He never wanted to see her again. She had fried his brain.

He moved in for the kill. He watched her breasts. They pulsed in time with the music. She moved closer. It was dark enough to mask his tension. The bulging eyes were in shadow. Her hand slid up his leg. He flinched.

"I like you a lot." He had often said that at the Underground. Time leapt backwards. They were all there again. The faces. Valentine the strangest face of all.

He kissed her. The lips tasted fresh, sweet as ever before. He closed his eyes.

There was a dig in his ribs. It was sharp, painful. He looked up.

The glass tipped over. A full Bloody Mary flowed over his head. The tomato juice dribbled down his face. Ice careered to the floor. His shirt was stained. Sticky. The glass was empty.

Miki blazed. "You wanker."

Sidonie slid the stool away. She did not want a cat fight. Several people were laughing. He had blown it. Sidonie marched off, rattling on the Cuban heels.

Then Miki walked away. She had been watching all the time. There was no reason to look anymore.

He shook his head. Excess vodka and juice spattered. His hands felt glutinous. He wiped his face with a paper serviette. Humiliating.

He never remembered Miki being possessive. The can of lager rested in his grip. He gulped it dry. Nobody would ever own

Valentine. He was too fast for that. Maybe she cared more than he imagined. This thought hurt him.

He took the picture from his damp pocket. She was younger then. Time had not been kind. He had promised her it would be different. They were all floundering in the mire. The faces had stopped laughing. Back to the order of serious drinking.

One was laughing still. "Another Bloody Mary?" A1 Jay's glittering row of white teeth were shining just when Valentine wanted darkness. "Don't flip out on me now." The door take had been good. He handed over more drink tickets and placed a spreadsheet in front of them. Seven hundred and eighty people, lots of paying customers. They could hatch big plans between them.

Valentine was no longer interested. A1 was speaking a foreign tongue in the Tower of Babel. The sums were adding up but it was not what Valentine wanted. He noticed his reflection in the mirror. The eyes were narrow. No trace of humanity left.

A1 raised his eyebrows. The promo rights would be huge. Something for everybody.

The rhetoric sounded logical. Valentine had always spoken in these terms. But the ground beneath his feet was moving. Pins in his brain snapped. The night was bad. The worst kind of crowd, tasting shit and wanting more. Has-been DJs.

Valentine was not even a has-been. Just a never-was. He realised how little time he had left. He rubbed his face. The sweat would not go. No matter how much beer he drank his throat would still be dry.

He placed the two bags on the table. One was green crystals. The other brown dirt.

A1 stopped in mid-sentence. "Put it away. No one has to know." A1's voice was uncertain. He had the feeling they all knew already.

He pushed the plastic back towards Valentine. The bags slid

over slops. There was no way of knowing how far Valentine had gone. All users were junkies. There could be no dividing line.

He uncrumpled the spreadsheet. The plan would still work. Valentine only had to say the word. The first night of many. A floating Underground. Different one-offs every week.

Valentine rubbed his finger over the scrawled numbers. The verbal barrage jolted him. Pound signs knelt like crippled pharaohs.

It made no difference to A1 if Valentine was hooked. "Drink your beer." He pushed back his muslim hat. "Don't worry." There were always plenty more blondes. This was the first night. They were bound to have teething troubles.

Valentine's breathing was hard. He tried to see the sense of it. People milled about. Just as he suspected. The crowd was duff. Philistines in Eden.

"No more bullshit." He straightened himself. A last sip of beer. Sure it would work. Victory was very close. So what if it was on their terms? A smile appeared on his face. Everybody always seemed to smile. Or nod their heads. That was what he was doing. The normal thing. Social graces that greased the day. "I have to find her." Apologise.

A1 was smiling, too. This was the Valentine he knew. Nervousness was only natural. The stained suit did not matter.

Valentine grasped the sticky drinks tickets. He showed A1 Miki's photograph.

"She's nice." A1 straightened his glasses. The manner was reassuring.

Valentine took one step back.

"Going so soon?"

Valentine was unaware of time. It might have been ten minutes. Maybe ten years. He strangled his emotions. "Excuse me." A cockney maiden stepped towards the bar. Valentine was the stranger on the train accused of a crime he did not commit. A1 had convinced him. He was not sure of the fear. Things repeated inside him. He checked everything to ensure its reality. Everything was safe in his pocket. The gear. The picture. The tickets. He turned tail and ran.

The siding flashed by him. His steps were shaky. Come on, Valentine. Come on. The crowd did not notice his madness. Perhaps it didn't exist. He bumped into a cocktail waitress. She spoke in an Australian accent. It was alright. Only the hired help. Their bodies had brushed, smearing sundried tomato juice on her apron. The doors slid open.

A group of tourists stepped with him. The towel boy was mopping the floor. Muddy water sloshed. It was the smell of bleach mixed with puke. There was no sign of blood on the stairs. The microdot was gone. Just another harmless daydream. Nobody had really got hurt.

His frame was distorted in the mirror. His steps got larger, two at a time. He hoped she had not gone. Speed was of the essence. He never wore a watch.

The toilets seemed very busy. A lot of people doing lines. Probably less menacing than that. He ran his hand over the mural. The surface was uneven. Cracking gloss paint stuck under his fingernails.

He was at the top of the stairs. Lack of air stifled reason. He could not remember why he was running. The momentary gap would not fade.

Three girls hovered by the landing. Dutch. All dressed in black. Striped tights clinging to long legs. They were watching puzzled as his head flicked from side to side. The oldest one tugged his sleeve. He recoiled.

Valentine looked straight into her eyes. They were pale blue. There was an air of cleanliness about her. She asked if he remembered. The voice was loud. Cutting over the throbbing, unintelligible music. Her accent sung. She was pushing him, moving closer, an orange coloured drink in her hand.

Back in time. The red juice spilling over his head. The alcoholic rain. He could not stop it.

"Don't you remember? Brigitte." She was pointing to herself. A long well-turned finger. They had met at HQ.

He was waving his arms. Talk spilled. Loose change. The gear was safe in his pocket. They could not understand what he saw. Drowning was too difficult to explain.

Why was he here? What was he running from? Always the same questions. She was real enough. He touched her arm. She flinched. The face was more edgy than his.

Her friends stepped over, country cousins. They were not as tall. His hand scrambled in his pocket. Their eyes lit up. He foisted complimentaries in their hands. The bouncers always let them in for free. This was not the same man they had met. It was different on Camden Lock.

He pushed by them. They huddled back together. The English men never talked much.

Valentine was anonymous in the crowd. The bustle pushed him back. He craned his neck. A suited man burped in his face, oblivious.

Miki was leaning against the wall. She saw him. Her eyes were all screwed up. The duffle bag pulled on her shoulder.

Valentine bulldozed towards her. Indignant faces. Elbows clashed. He halted in the small gap. There were three yards between them. She looked straight through. There were no regrets, just anger. She felt betrayed.

The glass hovered by her lips. She gulped. Coughed a little. Then rested the empty vessel on the edge.

He touched her arm. She shook free. The action seemed repetitive. Not deja vu. It was stronger than that. He had been here before. So many times. So many times with her. Tears welled up in his eyes. The words would not come out. He wanted to feel something. The moment was empty.

She could not bear to look anymore. The suit was full of moth holes. His face was bloated. A real turn-off. She had never liked fat men.

"We could have a wild scene." He pulled her closer.

"No." She wanted to slam the door, walk off into the sunset. There were too many people. Airing dirty linen in public, that was too seedy. Even for Miki.

"It's your big night. Enjoy yourself." Miki broke free.

She was immediately swallowed up by the crowd.

CHAPTER NINETEEN

Guarding the Star Bar door, Terry licked his lips. The plastic face showed no signs of tension. The management liked him. Calm flowed under his control. He lifted the barrier. Valentine dashed inside.

The piped music was sultry. Images from the monitors flashed onto Valentine's face. He looked for an empty chair, but there was no rest for the weary. He leant on the bar. Women pushed him closer to the ice bucket.

It was nice to rub shoulders with the rich. Their air was heady like valium. Essence of debauchery. Destruction.

Nervously he shouted for a beer. The bargirl said it would cost. He told her "I work here" and tendered a drinks ticket. He rotated on his heels, looked to the far wall. It was a two-way mirror. You could see the dance floor below.

He approached the glass. It was like being God, peering down from the viewing gallery. Everything looked distorted. His face was crooked in the dark reflection. He watched Fly and Jack on the stage, arguing. It was like a silent film. Arms swung back and forth. They were very small. A1 was with them. His flesh shone black. Fly towered above him. Papers were tended. The friction stopped. It was some kind of payoff.

Valentine was not sure what was going on. Control was slipping away. He was helpless, a voyeur. Fly stepped from the stage.

It couldn't be any gear. Valentine reached for his pocket. He might have dropped it. It was still all there. His hand touched the glass. Dancers' arms swung stiff. Robotic. Signalling. The strobe was playing tricks on his eyes. His throat tightened. He flopped onto the edge of a table.

Beer cans fell away behind. Cocktail glasses smashed on the floor. He said he was sorry. The snogging couple did not care. The man rescued a fresh can and jabbed the base with a key. "Shotgun." The beer shot into his mouth.

Valentine gauged his reflection self-consciously. The red-stained shirt bragged of a fight. The beer made him burp. He swayed as he stood. Back to the bar.

He was about to order another drink when Fly walked in. He tried to scramble out of the way. Peanuts slipped through his fingers, itchy with salt. Valentine could not bear the thought of parting with the gear in his pocket. Bryce hadn't made him pay. He could still sell it. So what if he skanked Macari? It was saving them both in the long run.

Fly was pulling Miki behind him. Her hair was wet. The damp jersey clung.

He squeezed into the gap. Valentine was an animal. He couldn't see her as a person anymore. Fly thought he'd be back on the door. That was his job. The DJs were performing adequately. Why wasn't Valentine? They would all get blown out. It was that simple. "I heard about your shower."

Valentine was kissing the girl. They were by the fireplace, his suit stripped from naked flesh. He was watching the dancers. Fly brandished tickets. "Two large vodkas." The maid responded, facile in distortion. Miki brushed closer. He could just about keep it together. The flashback was as sharp as the crystals. Fly asked for his wages. Valentine closed his eyes. Black, then normal.

Miki tapped his arm and reached for the drink. The look was glazed, blanking Valentine. She kissed his cheek.

Fly was chuckling. He had walked her out of the rain.

"What have you given her?"

Fly raised an eyebrow. He feigned puzzlement.

Miki marvelled at the wave of togetherness. That was all she'd wanted. Valentine was arguing about her. They both thought they had her. But she had them. The tab made her playful. Mascara ran down her face.

Valentine took a step back. Any sign of pressure zipped his brain elsewhere. She was a whore selling herself for a fresh hit. Fly was exactly the same. They had been swapping secrets. He covered his ears. The words stopped.

It was like a plague. She was apologising. Fly was apologising. Valentine could only hear the drugs speaking. They were off their heads. Fly was carrying her duffle bag. They made a strange couple. Perhaps she was screwing him on the side.

She kissed Valentine's hand. He was unable to break free. The junkie may have given her AIDS. The fear was irrational but strong. He wiped the saliva across his sleeve. Thousands of demons he could never see. He set off. Fly did not turn round. He was content with Miki's presence. Anyway, Valentine would not bow out. He had received no wages either.

Terry slipped the hook. He was not surprised at Valentine's pace. Jilted front men often ran. "Have a nice trip."

Valentine blocked out sound. The stairs were a blur. There were always the same faces in the foyer. People who did not know how to have a good time. The air from the door smelled damp. He jumped the final three steps.

Nicola hated him. He was always asking for cigarettes. She pretended not to hear. The bouncer lurched him away from the till. He stood his ground. This was the one who had punched the thin guy. But he could not be sure.

Nicola totted up the spreadsheet. The pen was chrome, fluid in her grip. Six pounds, hundreds of times. The air was stifling.

Got to escape. He tottered through the portico.

Ray was hiding under an umbrella emblazoned with a black tower. The rain spattered on Valentine's face. The cold wetness was real. He could be sure of it. The elements had raged forever. And would do long after he was gone. The wool suit soaked up the rain.

"You must be mad." Ray angled the umbrella to protect him. A hot dog man had positioned his cart. The steel was steaming, wafting smoke. Pink sausages with yellow mustard. The greasy smell of ripe meat.

Valentine picked up Ray's clipboard. The guest list was no longer sheltered from the rain. The ink ran. Most of the names had been crossed off. One of the bouncers showed him a clicker. The figures read white on black. Eight-eight-nine. Valentine faked pleasure, disorientated. The run had knocked the wind out of him.

Beer belched up through his guts. He could not fight it anymore. Enjoyment had slipped into anarchy. A fingernail lodged between his teeth. He bit hard. Pain receptors were sending the wrong signals.

People were leaving early. "Good night." The cab drivers stared. Fat black men stood by Japanese cars. Toyota. Nissan. He pulled back the guy-rope. "What happened to the rappers?" A1 must have told this woman about rappers. Valentine didn't know. He didn't care.

He put his hands in his pockets to keep them out of the rain. The wraps were still there. One small line would straighten him out. A large one would make his cold warm.

He looked at the trickle of punters. They had not even noticed. Perhaps his behaviour had not been that strained. They had obviously enjoyed themselves. "See you next week." He gave a few comps to Sidonie's friend. The faces were all familiar. His memory had not totally gone.

The toilet beckoned, his bladder fit to burst. He had not thought about that before. A nice safe place to do a line.

The sound of clattering high heels rattled across the road. A black cab sailed off. There was tingling in his limbs. The big leaps in perception always started like this.

He clawed his face. The liquid was pouring over his head again. Miki stood watching him. His face in the frame.

He looked at the shadow. Large and looming. A black convex dome. It was only the umbrella. He must snap out of it.

Then there was a voice. Cold and icy. It was Virginia's voice. She was not on the guest list. He was not sure if he had put her there. He flicked through the list again. Dotting the three i's. He remembered. His teeth hurt. The sodden blue ink ran onto his fingers. He looked up. Vision was unclear. Rain dribbled across his eyeballs. He blinked. There she was. The face had changed but it was her. He grabbed her arm to make sure.

She was shivering in the rain. "Hello, Valentine." Virginia was not afraid of the rain. It pitter pattered off the leather jacket. Her real hair was scrunched under a wig. The monofibre was black, chopped angular across her forehead. Oriental in precision. The pale eyes were coloured dark by brown contact lenses.

Valentine was unsure. This masquerade seemed strange. She was good at being herself. It made no sense to playact. The colouring reminded him of Miki. She could not know that.

Valentine crossed a name off the list. It was a man's name. It did not matter. He had no time. The metal hook chilled his palm. He pulled the rope back. "I didn't think that -"

She cut him off in mid sentence. "It's very dangerous to think." Even the dialect seemed more clipped.

She walked through the gap. He saw the high heels, tacky and charmless. She had never worn them before. She did not speak again, just passed straight inside. He left the rope dangling. It bounced on the floor. He followed her. Passive like a slave.

Nicola was surprised. This was the third woman she had seen Valentine with. He passed over a complimentary and she placed it in the till. One more figure on the clicker.

Men leered at the long legs. She knew how to turn heads. Part of Valentine registered pride.

Virginia unzipped her jacket. Her movement was feline. She gauged the surroundings with precision. Lowlife fascinated her. Faceless people she would loathe to meet. The music was calling. Street culture from the colour supplements. A violent film where she was the star. "Let's dance." She jeered Valentine forward.

His eyes flickered. Roles reversed. He yawned. It was play-time. A line. A trip. A fuck. He could take it.

The music got louder. Metronomic light flashed on her face. They broached the edge of the dance floor. Neither of them wanted a relationship. She had not returned his calls. He had left no number. There was never anyone at home, only the answerphone.

Passive voyeurism excited him. He had watched her leave work, safe from a distance. It was better this way. Tracking her like a detective. Skulking in her local boozer. She always drank vodka. The clothes changed chameleon-like. She had never sensed he had been there.

Her feet moved in time with the riff.

Jack watched Valentine closely. The Cameo Dub slid in. "She's strange." He had a commanding view from the stage. Valentine's arms were folded. His head bobbed irregularly.

The woman danced wildly. A gap was emerging around her. Young soul rebels edged further away. The spiralling arms were unavoidable. She was not a dancer. Her steps were permanently out of sync. Each handclap broke the beat. Jack curled his lip.

Valentine concentrated on the movement. Her street knowledge was a veil. Virginia's skirt rode up. Her dance steps were arcane. Taut muscles rippled on her thighs.

He could not face the ungainliness. It must be in his imagination. His beautiful vixen was nothing short of a fraud. The cracks gaped.

Hours spent in northern soul all-nighters had paid off. He started with his feet. Kicking back and forth. His right leg feigning a slide. The arm movement was easy. Rolling backward into a snap. The adrenalin pounded. He felt free as a bird. The sweat poured. Valentine enjoyed the sense of power. He swayed faster.

She could not keep in time. The well-toned body was wasted below the shoulder. He did not want her anymore. Virginia had no soul, the only thing that had separated her from the rest.

A couple of diehards were smirking. He attempted a back drop. His feet landed off-balance. The overpadded body was staggering. Fat and sweaty. Unable to cut it anymore. The steps slobbered out of control.

Being a good dancer did not matter to Virginia. Pleasure came so easy. She rotated her fists like Travolta. Giving him the come on.

It was a big turn off. She was magnificent under the covers. But not here. This was all he had, the floor. To disgrace it was sacrilegious. She was ripping apart his world. Pissing on it.

The gear might be to blame. He lowered his standards. It was no good. He noticed the expression on Jack's face. They were laughing at Valentine. His feet stopped dead. He could not look at her, scared of what he might see. Miki danced so well.

He wanted another drink. Another line. He turned his back. Drunk debutantes filled his floor space. There was a huge chasm. Virginia seemed light years away. He did not care anymore. They had screwed each other, that was all. It was the FX that had trapped him. He had thought he wanted her. His real goal was the mailing list, priceless like a jewel. He could trip with anyone, the Sidonies of this world. Even Fly would suffice. He walked away.

The music was endless. He must have a last line. Get up and out of it. He took off his jacket. The stained fabric rested on his shoulder. He was swaggering a bit. It looked stupid. So what? The whole world was stupid. Angry for death. Life was so cheap.

The throng was humming. A swarm of bees. He exorcised extraneous thoughts. People were very small. Arguing. Buying each other for the price of a pint. He had the antidote. They did not.

He approached yet another flight of stairs. Virginia stood there. She had circled behind him. "I thought you wanted to dance."

Valentine's stained shirt was clearly in view. Her clothes exuded cleanliness, a kind of sanctity. "I want it to stop." He had bitten off too much.

She shook her head. Took his jacket. He was powerless. They walked towards the Pullman. "I know what you've stolen from my desk drawer."

The door snapped open. Memories rested in the mirror. He had traversed this maze already this evening. There was no way out. It was unclear what she wanted. Her words were riddles. The makeup was heavier than before. Sordid like a vamp.

He pressed his guts against the bar. She remarked how the decor had changed. It was different every month. Last time, cold and monastic. The splashes of purple were "elegant".

"What do you want?"

She pointed towards the vodka, her hands masked by driving gloves.

"Two Bloody Marys."

The glass pouring over his head. Again. Again. They were in the barman's hands. Straining against the optics. He poured with a flourish. The red juice cascaded. Safe in the vessels. He placed them square in front of her. They lifted the glasses. She said cheers. Her voice was softer. More real. Her lips pouted against the glass. She downed it in one.

He stacked the drink tickets on the table. "Three more doubles." The barman was quick to respond. Valentine put his arm around her. "What do you want?"

It was a difficult question. She paused. Virginia wanted more. She had seen the world. Her career was successful. She just wanted more excitement. Palaces could never be big enough. Cars never fast enough. Valentine certainly wasn't a good fuck. His karma was more special than that. He was crazy. She basked in his fear. The energy it gave off was destructive, powerful. She wanted to watch the wreck burn. That racetrack kind of lust. "Let's swim in hell. Nobody cares either way."

Valentine bit his lip. It was a sales pitch for addiction, holding craziness as the only hope. It was the gear talking. Valentine imagined the headrush. He downed another double. She gave him her lighted cigarette. The filter was damp. He watched her eyes. There was no trace of lying. She really did admire his hate.

Miki loathed his flights of insanity. Virginia thrived on it.

He watched the punters. They groped each other under the table.

Virginia had shown him a world where anything was possible. The FX had even made him good in bed. He never wanted it to stop.

Virginia finished her last two vodkas, arranged the empty glasses in a row. She took a tissue out of her bag. Blotted the lipstick. The screwed up paper rested in an ashtray. "You don't have to answer."

The voice was coming from miles away. Echoing inside his head. He pulled the stool closer. The leather squeaked as he slid aboard.

She looked up at the tall man. His bike jacket was similar to hers. She offered an explanation. This was not her regular attire. 'King Sugar' were throwing a party at the Medici. They had played the Academy that night. This look would fit in better later. Her sigh was flirtatious.

Valentine did not look round. He buried his face in his palm.

Fly leant against her. His mouth inches from Valentine's ear. "I want my gear."

Valentine was startled. He almost fell off his chair. There was no room behind him. Miki blocked his rear.

Fly would never get violent. That was not a problem.

He glanced about for his jacket. It rested on Virginia's shoulder.

He braced himself on the marble slab. The sensation was that of falling forward. He slid to his feet. Miki's face was at eye level. A stupid grin stretched across her face. He hated what Fly had done. He hated his own impotence.

Virginia reached into the coat pocket. She felt for the second wrap.

Valentine struggled for words. He stuttered. Very quiet against the piped music. Fly stepped closer. Valentine was pinned to the bar. Everything slipped into slow motion.

Miki smeared the make-up across her face. She was giggling like a child.

Virginia lifted the two wraps clear. One green. One brown. She pushed the green one into his trouser pocket. Her fingernails scratched his groin. There was no pain. The touch was soft.

Fly raised his palm into the air. It was heading straight for Valentine's face. He craned his neck backwards. There was a snap of sinew. The palm moved closer and closer. Miki's head bobbed from side to side.

An inch away, Virginia stopped it. Her palm met Fly's. The brown powder pressed along protruding veins. "I think this is yours." Virginia's voice emanated command, control.

Fly felt content. He clicked the press stud shut. His hand tapped his pocket. Justice had been done. It was business. No moralisms. No lecture.

Valentine wanted to cry. He had actually done it. The grave was dug. Virginia had thrown in the first handful of dirt. Valentine had watched.

He wriggled steadily. Glasses fell away behind him. He touched the FX in his trouser pocket. Maybe it was not so bad. Fly did ask for it. "Not such a bad night."

Punters eased to the bar, unaware. This train was not going anywhere.

Miki kissed Valentine. She rubbed black mascara from her eyes. It stained the finger tip black. She dotted a beauty spot on Valentine's cheek. He shied away.

Virginia clawed Miki's shoulder. She spun her round, then planted a sloppy kiss on her lips. The lipstick smudged from mouth to mouth. Fly raised his eyebrow. He was not really shocked.

They moved apart. Valentine gloated. Lust bubbled to the surface. Four figures were facing each other.

Virginia felt she was pulling all the strings. Valentine said nothing. He was only half dressed. The pinstripe jacket tottered in her grasp. Her movement was calculating. She shrouded his shoulders. The sleeves dangled free.

Virginia was wading in headlong. She took Valentine's dark glasses. The metal hooks clipped over her ears. The reflection was clear. Valentine saw himself. Miki saw a distorted Fly. They each saw one another.

There was a long pause. Valentine was not certain of the action. She might just walk away.

Fly offered around his cigarette packet. There were only four left, ample supply. They each took one. The brass Zippo flashed a large flame. This was the pipe of peace. Valentine noticed the nicotine stain. His middle finger was buff brown. He realised how many he had smoked. There was a tight lump in his throat.

Virginia's voice was callous. She did not like it here. The crowd was lowlife. She expected better from Valentine.

There was no defence from Fly. He was going back upstairs. The night was not over yet. His records were under dubious control. Jack was still up there. He put his arm round Miki. His elation was unshakable. The trip had miles to run. Fingers locked into his, she wanted him to look after her. They might do a dragon in the toilet. This was the first order of business.

Valentine felt deserted. Another biker marvelled at Fly's boots.

There was a shout. Fly thought it might be Valentine. "There is somewhere better to go." The voice was indistinct. Desperate. Fly's head creaked backwards. Valentine's lips had not moved. His eyes were closed. He was flicking the cigarette tip.

It was impossible to locate the sound. Fly was intrigued. He backtracked. Miki floated alone, oblivious to the proposed departure.

Valentine flicked the butt to the floor. It was clear Virginia was plotting. He pushed Fly away. His arms were weak. The more he moved the heavier the fabric pulled.

Virginia hitched up her collar. The leather stood to attention. "Let's go." She need not ask Fly twice.

They paraded to the centre of the room. Virginia took Miki's right hand. Fly took the left. The progression was rapid. Rattling boot straps. High heels throwing the weight forward. Weight hung in the middle. Suspended by cantilevers. Miki's heels dragging. Towed on the lead.

Two made company. Three an orgy.

Valentine watched. The best deal was not to go. Fly had already stolen Miki. Miki had dropped the tab. Virginia was keel-hauling them both. She had passed the skag. Written Valentine off.

He reached into his pocket. He would not display the FX in the light. There was enough for total destruction.

The three paused. A pulse of electricity. The door was sliding open. Pullman split into Pull man. They were going. No more sex. No more women. No more gear. The portal was sliding shut.

Others were approaching the bar. His view was blocked. He ran forward. Bodies appearing from nowhere. Nobody tried to retard him. Nobody cared. He lunged. His arms were boxing the atmosphere. There was no way of judging the distance. Large heads swayed drunk. Narrow hips butted in denim. The model girls were so tall. They were not his. His possessions had got up and stepped outside.

He staggered through the half-slid door. Video cameras panned at his movement. The security system was unobtrusive. Only the motorwind gave it away. He felt caged. Somebody had been watching. Now. Always. The murals bashed garish. It was like a carousel. He was spinning round and round.

Up the stairs. Into the lobby. The others were well past the reception desk. Virginia was spouting toxic words. She took Fly's handful of tickets. They scattered across the marble. Nicola's arms scooped them together. Colours blended, the pink and blue. Nicola muttered "Fuck off'. Nobody heard.

Miki was shouting at the top of her voice. Incoherent babble. The bouncers backed out of the way. The DJ and the tart were throwing this drunk out. Miki threw her arms across her face. More comps fell on the floor. Vodka from the open bottle. Spillage from the rucksack.

Virginia charmed Ray's anxiety. It was alright. They were taking their friend home. The car was outside.

Valentine yelped "Wait".

Ray did not hear. He was flattered by the brunette's interest. She stroked his thigh.

Miki licked the rain from her lips. It tasted different. Manna from heaven.

There was a police siren. Not for them. Virginia winked. Fly thought he knew what that meant. His records would wait until later. The corner seemed full of people. Irishmen were arguing over cabs. The rain got heavier. They had lost Valentine in the hustle.

"Don't worry. It's not far."

Virginia knew exactly how far they would go. Two new friends to play with. The leather garb was tight, strong enough to stop anything falling out.

Valentine panted. His arms hit the reception table. "Wages?" Nicola sprung the till open. She had no veto. He grabbed her wrist. "Wages." A bouncer waded in. She shook her head. "It's alright."

Two brown envelopes, *F. J. Macari and Valentine*. Everything was in order. He told her to leave the third for Jack.

"Nice friends you've got."

Valentine bit his lip. "Tell A1 not to worry." He had to go.

She said nothing. He was like all the rest. Off his head.

The envelopes were already moist in his palm. The view into the street was blank. Somebody pulled him back.

Scally was angry. Valentine had changed nothing. The Tower was as shit as ever. The reputation of the Underground was lost. Valentine could not get away. Scally was chanting in his ear. The same brown zoot suit. "Get me into the Star Bar." Scally's words were stained with tequila. He spat as he sounded the 'S'. A full glass undulated in his fingers. "I am your friend." He hugged Valentine. Everyone knew what leeches Jack and Fly were. They were sucking Valentine dry. Why couldn't he see? "They're screwing you, man. They're screwing you."

Scally glugged more tequila. He couldn't say what he really wanted. "Don't."

That was the last Valentine heard. They must not get away.

He cowered outside in the rain. Tears mixed with rainwater. It all tasted salty. He looked up towards the roof of the Tower. The flags still waved. Pink neon frizzled in the damp. The hurdy-gurdy of the sound system hee-hawed.

It was a fairground attraction. A freak show where the freaks paid to get in.

Ray snorted. "Get your burger then."

The street was empty to the right. No human traffic. They must have gone left.

What about Jack? What about A1? Let them live to fight another day. He was running.

His guts churned. Every step nearer the end of the road. No more Tower. No more Valentine.

Another corner to turn. The yellow cashpoint threw light in his path. A bagman curled up on old boxes. The streets were paved with kebab wrappers. Red Kentucky boxes. Enough chili sauce to sterilise a wound.

He kicked through the garbage. The rain washed dregs down the drain. A night bus screeched at the lights. He coughed. How he coughed. He pushed his head into his chest. The stay-press shirt soaked the rain from his neck. He swallowed the nicotine phlegm. And pulled up his collar.

Then he shouted after them. One voice echoing towards Oxford Street.

CHAPTER TWENTY

A street lamp frizzled orange, flashing on and off. Soho streets were quite empty.

Virginia's foot landed in a black puddle. Dirty water splashed her leg. She felt cold. Fly would not hurry up. His gait was awkward. Miki pulled hard between them. Water dribbled rivers of make-up. She needed a piss.

The Medici Club had a revolving door. It stood astride two Italian restaurants. The canopy was royal blue. A large white Cadillac parked alongside. The driver curled up, asleep.

A man stood under the canopy. The large felt hat hooded his eyes. Virginia dragged the others out of the rain. She snorted, shook her head. The wig did not come off. Steam rose from damp denim.

Virginia took an invitation from her bag. The card had simple black lettering. There was a bold record company motif. She flashed it towards the man.

A couple spilled out from the door. The leggy blonde had excessive facial hair. She placed an empty bottle on the pavement. It tottered over. Her companion was tall. His zip was undone. He patted the girl on the back. She staggered forward. Pearls of rain shone on his greasy hair.

The man with the hat ignored Virginia. He waved at the limo. The engine raced. Exhaust fumes bellowed from the tailgate. The couple cavorted into the backseat. Then the car pulled away, naked legs flailing from the open window. A flash of chrome and metal. The engine was a whisper.

Virginia foisted the ticket in his hand. "Plus two." Her voice was insistent. Still calm. The man took his hat off.

There was a splash of feet across the road. "Plus three."

Valentine was breathing heavily. He had run all the way. The wool gabardine had shrunk around his form. He pushed the ratty hair from his face. His shoes squelched.

The man looked at the ticket. There was a glimmer of recognition in his eyes. "Reaction Agency plus party?"

Miki caught her laughter in the handkerchief. Virginia glared.

"Don't you recognise me without the beard?" He bared his teeth.

"Tony?" Virginia grasped his wrists. Her attitude changed. She could ride the storm again.

He smeared his body against hers and whispered some transatlantic flattery. "Go inside." Tony hitched up his peg tops.

She slid away from the two-tone correspondents, nudged Miki in front of her. Fly was already inside the revolving compartment.

Valentine dragged his heels.

"Wipe your feet, bud." Tony's Americanism was demeaning. Valentine could not fight it. He rubbed the thin soles on the rubber mat. Virginia beckoned coyly. The door swung rapidly. It catapulted him out of the cold.

Inside the weather was fine. The entrance hall was panelled with oak. Impressionistic paintings hung in spatial expanse. No expense spared. Even the receptionist was beautiful. There was an air of cleanliness. These people never got wet.

He saw the signature in the guest book. *V. Nix. plus.*

The girl looked worried by his incoherence. Water dripped from his sleeves. He put on his best smile. Voices screamed inside his head.

"That way." She closed the big red book, safe from autograph hunters and journos. Strange odours emanated from his

218

dampness. There was no way of telling who he was. Only that he was in desperate need of a towel. The feet plodded away.

There was only one chucker-out. They expected no trouble. Roadie-turned-minder-turned-bouncer. The flesh protruding from his collar was adorned with tattoos. He leered at Valentine, disgusted.

Everyone was looking at him. He tried to fake disinterest. The last part of the corridor swam with heat. The music got more virulent. He sashayed through the carpeted interface. Good sense met gold. A room opened out in front of him.

It was all too loud. Forty or fifty tables ranged on three levels. The small dance floor writhing flesh. He walked by a long bar. Record company execs fondled secretaries. Four young black guys wore matching jackets. The DJ was hidden in the corner.

He scanned the tables. Hands fought over tiny bags of green dust. One man seemed to be filling in a form.

Fly reeled in his chair. His head bobbed like a footballer. Virginia wielded the green bottle. A cork popped. Foam shot over her front. Miki opened her mouth. The liquid poured uncontrolled, splashing onto their already wet clothes. They pleaded like seals. She thought it was funny.

They gorged on what was free anyway. The record company was footing the extensive tab. Virginia cracked open another bottle.

A middle-aged man brushed past. He felt for her tits. With her free arm she grabbed his crotch. There was a lot of laughter. He slobbered a greasy kiss on her cheek. Faint traces of garlic bread stuck on his hair. She groped him closer. He slipped. The overweight frame crashed onto another table. Fag ash mottled his shirt. "Thank you." His beard dipped into the punch.

Virginia raised the open bottle over Miki's head. She tilted it forward. Drips transformed into a flood. Miki giggled with delight.

Valentine wrenched the bottle free. He raised it into the air. How he wanted to smash it on her head. Nobody would care.

Beat her brains in. Steal the gear. Stop it all.

They were all in outer space. Movements ran in slow-mo.

"Do it." Virginia was vehement.

"Come on." Fly wanted it.

He could. His hand was shaking. Champagne spilled everywhere. Onto his shoes. He raised the bottle to his lips. He drank. There was no air left. Some more. And more. The bottle was empty. It slipped to the floor. He turned to get away.

Virginia dragged him onto her knee, a ventriloquist's dummy. Then he was on his own chair. He was still Valentine.

Fly asked if the vibe was safe. He had never been here before, just seen pictures in the Sunday papers.

The crowd seemed friendly enough. Perhaps friendly was the wrong word. A woman was baring her breasts on the dance floor. The other flashes were more rapid. A newly installed strobe flickered. Two microphones stood on the stage. The bass guitar was in the shape of a bazooka.

Virginia quaffed the dregs of a bottle. In a world of fools insanity was king. She looked at Valentine.

He was still licking his wounds. The smell of dope flayed his nostrils. There were no social policemen here. Reserve had taken a holiday. The record company had even paid for that. Valentine recognised Bryce only three tables away. He recurred like bad curry.

Virginia urged Fly on. He unclipped his pocket. Took out the wrap. It fell stone dead on the table. Still out of Valentine's reach. Miki fingered it.

Fly unfolded the piece rapidly. Virginia grabbed his hand. Grabbed the foil. It shone above the white linen. Inside the Medici Club. Valentine could not stop it.

A gangling hippy approached. His cowboy boots were authentic. He stopped next to the table. Virginia folded the cloth to cover the druggy trappings.

The man swaggered confidently. His hair was tied back. He

leant on Miki's shoulder. She swam in his blue eyes. The accent was fake cockney. "Can you sing?"

Valentine thought 'old bill'. Fly slid his chair back.

The man bragged about the Chart Show. He had a twenty-four track. Always on the lookout for BVs. "Backing vocalists." Miki giggled.

"I produce these guys." He dropped a calling card on the table. It looked expensive.

Virginia picked up the card. "Damon – Something unpronounceable." She held it in the candlelight. The edge caught. Curls of flame ripped up the centre. Smuts fluttered into the ashtray. It rested there, consumed.

The man looked unperturbed. Plenty more fish to blag. He poked his half-smoked joint in Miki's mouth. "Compliments of Mr. Bryce." He shrugged his shoulders and lurched away.

Miki gagged on the smoke. She spat the weed out. It extinguished itself in a glob of spit.

Fly raced for the cloth. He tossed it back. The silver tube emerged from under the table. No cause for alarm. Bryce's jokes were never funny.

He was about to meter out a chinaman. Virginia stopped him. Valentine knew.

She said there was something better. She would give him a taste. Fly looked interested. He could always bow out.

Virginia produced an orange Rizla packet. She split the back with her nail. Six folded paper squares fell out. Fly asked what was in it.

She pushed two into her pocket. The zip rasped shut. There was a pause.

He rested on his haunches. "What *is* that?"

"That is everything."

For a second he was unsure. Probably a dab of coke. There could be no danger. Virginia seemed fine.

She arranged the white papers in a row. "Have one."

Valentine cut in. "That is FX."

Fly scrunched up his face. He thought Valentine had said "X", another tab of Ecstasy maybe?

Valentine's eyes were flickering. He knew Virginia was trying to get his friends involved. She had already sucked him in. It was too late.

"I don't want to do it on my own," she whined. Her eyes looked lonely.

Fly understood the feeling.

Valentine tried to warn them. It was all a big game to her. Miki and Fly hadn't tried it. They were still safe. It would be best for them to walk away. The FX was sending him permanently off his head. He needed another line just to stay sane.

Fly wouldn't listen.

"Leave now," Valentine begged. He started crying. The tears were selfish. Not for them. He was crying for himself. There seemed no way out. He needed some more from Virginia.

Fly could see no possible addiction from one hit. He had nothing to lose. What was worse? Another dragon or this tiny white wrap? At least the Rizla tab would be less obvious.

Valentine made a grab for the four white wraps but Virginia whacked him in the chest. He jerked back into the chair. Wind rushed from his lungs. He tried to speak. The words came out hoarse, only a whisper. "Tell him the truth."

Virginia gestured towards the rest of the room. "Everyone is taking it."

The words rang loud and clear. They bounced inside Valentine's head. He gazed into the crowd. What if it were true?

Thoughts and vision suddenly connected. Everyone seemed to be passing bags. They were chopping out green lines behind the DJ console. Fat executives swooned on the edge of trips. These were the right people. These were the successful people. They were all doing FX. They were mad for it. This was their summer

222

craze, not smiley t-shirts or bandanas.

Valentine pointed his finger at the wraps. "This is just one bad trip."

Fly felt the buzz in the atmosphere. The greed was electric. This stuff seemed very precious. Perhaps Valentine wanted to keep it for himself. He stretched out his arm.

Miki had been laughing all the time. Now she swiped one of the tabs. Then chewed heartily. It tasted bitter. She swallowed.

Fly's hand reached the second tab. He put it in his mouth, swallowing it whole.

There was nowhere for Valentine to look. The last-but-one tab balanced on Virginia's fingertip. Strobing light hit it. The white square danced. Then she swallowed it.

The last one was for Valentine. It was the last rich chocolate in the box, the one that really made you feel sick.

Miki's gawky eyes snapped shut. Her whole body fell forward. The head banged on the table. Then bounced.

Here were all the things Valentine wanted. He was rubbing shoulders with 'the rich and famous'. He was in the world renowned Medici Club. He was involved in one of London's great highs.

His entire life, all his striving suddenly seemed worthless. There was nothing else. And that scared him. He shook. The chill cut to the bone. But it seemed to make no difference.

Nobody really cared.

Valentine picked up the tightly folded Rizla paper. The others watched intently. As usual, it looked harmless enough. They were waiting.

He put it on his tongue. And then Valentine swallowed.

He made one final gesture. "Fuck you all," he snarled.

Virginia was manipulating the whole situation. The drug was manipulating them. They were manipulating each other. And the drug was manipulating her. It was one big circle. There was no way of stopping it now. The party went on.

Bryce was trying to find out what everyone was taking but Steven would not tell. He slugged another sherry. Sherry chopped out a line for a rock star. The rock star gave some to his manager. And the manager began to trip looking at Bryce. Bryce was definitely lowlife. They would never admit him into the exclusive FX club.

Virginia took off her high heels, ready to dance. The music was Latin.

Ecstasy still seared Miki's perception. Fly lifted her face from the table.

Valentine saw her dress tear open. Was he tripping already?

Fly said the whole thing was bollocks. He could feel no change. Nothing was happening.

The stilettos rested upturned on the table.

Valentine had to prove he was right. He had to show them how FX made crazymen. He positioned his palm above the stiletto heel. There was a guttural groan from his throat. He rammed his hand on the point. Then twisted it around. Blood oozed down the patent shank.

He pushed harder. The trip ground deeper. There was a lot of blood. His arm was shaking. Then his whole body was shaking. He held the wound up for display. The sign of the cross, red for the blood of the martyrs.

Fly grabbed his hand. He wound a napkin tight as a tourniquet.

Valentine made a fist. The flow was partially stemmed. There was no pain.

Fly didn't understand. He looked down at his bag of skag. They were pushing a needle into his vein. They were holding him down. Pumping his body full. He had to stop them. The millstone pulled on his neck. He opened the bag and emptied its contents into a glass of champagne. The liquid frothed.

It was his morning Alka-Seltzer. But this was not his bathroom. It was a long corridor full of women. He was in a public toilet. His foot lurched involuntarily. He was kicking open all the doors. Wood snapped soft as balsa. The table leg splintered.

A champagne bottle tipped over. Golden liquid spilled onto the table.

They were squirting glasses of piss over the porcelain. Women seemed oblivious to his presence. Golden showers splattered off his restrictive leathers. He had only paid ten pence to get in. Cheap for such action.

Miki was filling his mouth with champagne. The liquid brimmed out. It tasted foul. He tore at her hair. Hands ripped at the black chasm. Strands came out in his fingers. There was no blood from the scalp. Fresh locks sprouted. Then he was in the barber's shop. The chaise steel was brazen. Silver turned into gold. It made a deep incision in his eyeball. This was his surrealist film. He was cutting it up with a razor blade. The mirrored walls were all shining black now.

Virginia placed the black glasses on her nose. She snapped the sleeping blindfold tight. It pinched at Fly's temples. She tried to spin him round. They were playing 'blind man's buff'. His arms looked deformed. The hands were joined at the shoulder. They were a woman's hands.

On the stage a girl played congas. The beat was meant to augment the records.

Virginia only saw the drum. Its skin was human skin. Her face had become a rubber mask. She tried to pull it off. Then it wasn't her face anymore. Somebody else's face had been grafted in its place. It was stapled under the hairline. It was ugly. The flesh was rancid. Yet it still pulled tighter and tighter. Her teeth had been wired together. The mouth was all stitched up.

She had the fork from the table in her mouth. She tried to speak. Nothing would come out. A man in a flight jacket walked past, a fighter pilot. He was an oriental model. His eyes stretched like slits.

They were rolling about on the table. Her head hit the metal ashtray. She tried to retreat from the man's steel arm. But the scar gaped. The bottle was tall as a tower, the Eiffel Tower. The flight to Paris had been quick but they never seemed to land.

She clung to the edge of the table. It was a long wing, a huge wang. The Parisians were crunching squeeze boxes. Hands were clapping. She looked at the dance floor. Gelled naked bodies writhed next to each other. Limbs were wrenched from their sockets.

She lifted the candle from the table. The massive flame of the Olympic torch burned brightly. Molten wax scorched her skin. She was a human sacrifice. He was raping her on the altar. The noose pulled tighter.

Valentine gripped her wrist. He was trying to stop her falling over.

The blue suited policeman was dragging her away. Her wrist snapped. Blood sprang from the wound. It looked like her flesh had been gored. Then there was no more flesh, only cancerous grey bone. There was no way to spit out its foul taste.

He tried to pick her up from the floor. Each fingernail was torn from its socket. She was sliding into the inferno.

Valentine tried to soothe her. He placed her thrashing body on the table top. Nobody reacted alarmed. How far were they all really gone?

Virginia was manacled on the stone slab. She raised her legs into hospital stirrups. A masked doctor poised above her spread legs with a coat hanger. Dr. Valentine was unconcerned with her screams.

He walked onto the stage. Then brandished the microphone above his head. He was The King. This was Viva Las Vegas. The young fan had kissed him. Yet the lipstick smudge looked like track marks. The syringe had gouged his cheek. Chemicals oozed from his nose. There were mouldy white stains on his shoes. The Colonel must have had a wank.

A woman clawed at Valentine's leg. He kicked her. The boot seared the chest open. The unborn spilled out. Record executives watched her cavorting. Was it some alternative comedy? A few even clapped. They were Romans in the amphitheatre. He held up his damaged palm. This was a sign from God. Then he told a joke. "Take my wife?" The audience of angry Yorkshire miners, deposed and dispossessed, started throwing glasses. Somebody pulled the plug. There was a loud fizzle. He could smell burning flesh.

Fly had turned off the amplifier. He saw molten plastic drip from Miki's face. She was screaming. Virginia tripped backward off the stage. Vomit spurted from her mouth. Fly tried to catch her. He was the catcher in Trapeze. She was the Ripper's last victim, butchered. People held their breath. She was still falling. He still tried to catch her. There was no safety net.

Tony caught Virginia. He dragged her twitching body across the stage. "Get a fucking cab."

Virginia tried to escape. Stars flashed in the sky. There was no voice, only wailing sirens. He was taking her down an alleyway. Wedged up against the wall. Her knees were trembling. The bricks scraped her back. Fingers cupped her elbows.

She kissed her godfather. Wires were plucked from his pacemaker. It ticked no more. Metal plates fell from his hip. Her heel tripped him up. The small boy broke his legs. Six inch nails plummeted through bone. The clothes tore. His body was hairless.

Tony fell into the floor. Virginia was free.

She looked across the field. A plane was dusting droplets of poison. Acid rain melted tables, stripped layers from the surface. Rotting carcasses. The pilot stood astride. He reached to throw a blanket over her. Forcing a pillow on her face. Suffocating. Floods jutted from sunken darkness. The ship was sinking. Tear-veiled captains crouched angular, like icebergs. Waving the torch as a signal.

Fly was waving a burning table cloth.

The glimmer from Valentine's lighter had ignited the fabric. Tatters of charred linen plummeted. Smoke had set off the sprinkler system. Brisk jets of water doused the crowd. Some fled. Others danced. Hot bodies cooled off rapidly.

Fly tasted the morning dew. There was a perverse freshness. Water cannon bounced off cell walls. Battle-torn flags dripped dirt. They were cleaning the world. He rubbed his forearms. Junkydom would not wash off. Buttons burst into sores. Washing in spit. Fivers slid down the walls. Disintegrating into dust. Brown dust knee deep on the floor. A glut of skag. One hundred cadavers jerking. Cranking each other up.

The shakes took over. There was an earthquake. Poppy fields springing, ramming forth from scorched earth. They were coming closer. Two naked women begging for more. Sanatorium nurses. National Health morgue attendants. Scooping the poison from his veins. He dived off the balcony. There was no gravity to pull him down. Floating. Strapped to the wing of a glider. The bonds broke. His head snapped. All the frame broken.

The tattooed minder punched Fly in the chest. He collapsed on the boards. The room was emptying fast. Tony dragged Miki and Virginia towards the door. The bouncer made a grab for Valentine.

Valentine watched the Contra shoot a newsreader. A headless body pulsed on the gatepost. The sleepy village was littered with corpses, dead bystanders. Uniformed men tossed off into the atmosphere. It was raining blood. It was an operating theatre. It was a courtroom. It was the MGM Grand. The act was dying. Lenny Bruce on his last night. There was no outrage anymore. He was singing 'My Way'. Trying to screw the Queen. The executioner grabbed his throat. He felt a lethal dose puncture his skin. He was impotent. Castrated. God pushed him in the hole. The big fella. Shouted. Arabic Hebrew. The father, son and holy ghost. A benediction. The gravestone. He was in a double grave. Fly nuzzled next to him.

The chucker-out manhandled them outside. The bodies were dead weight. It was raining inside and out. Tony pushed Virginia into a cab. The driver haggled.

Miki paddled in a puddle, her tattered body stung with bruises. She cried like a baby.

The night was at its darkest.

Fly staggered to his feet. His hand was tarred. The petrol burn singed a layer of skin. They had wreaked havoc.

Taunted idols dashed into the rain. Drunks searched for company cars. Some had enjoyed the 'floorshow'. Secretaries vied for a place to stay. There were no buses to Sanderstead.

Fly whacked the bouncer.

Madison Square Garden was in his head. The crowd were black men. A thousand Mr. Ts. He threw the punch. The replay in his head. *Rocky! Rocky! Rocky!* The head hit the pavement. He felled a tall tree. It was a copper. The uniform full of bullet holes.

Miki crawled on top.

He had killed his father. The head cracked like an egg. It was the unknown soldier. Damp as a tomb. A child presented flowers. The dress was figured with ethnic motifs. A single flame for the world. The streets were barren. No movement in the ghost town. Completely alone. She was his spirit. The last flicker of humanity. He grasped the hand. The spectre was cold.

God was holding her hand. The big house was safe. No more prostitution. Freedom. Everything was free. The audience clamoured. She had won the lifetime supply. The Host's smiles turned into a leer. Plastic happiness at the end of a rainbow. Sanitised. Ready for consumption. She loved this man. She had loved him forever. One kiss. It could be hers. She was kissing a woman. She was kissing a man. This was the grip of life. A cup of oblivion. The pain was dull, then still.

Tony watched. Miki and Fly disappeared onto Oxford Street.

Valentine cradled the man's head in his arms. The gash seeped. His sleeves were bloody. The hat rested in the rain. Water filled the upturned crown. The pop band stood angled, silent like pall-bearers, crouching over the carnage.

The taxi engine rattled. The door still open.

"Get a fucking ambulance." Screams punched into Valentine's head. It was a huge film set. The actors had played it for real. A director was still shouting. Dancing street gangs drew switch-blades. They stabbed each other. It was his turn. The lynch mob was approaching. He was a child pomographer. They were all kids. Rapists roaming the streets. Sewers of effluence bubbling to the surface. It was all around him. The stench of his own death. A hell of insane barbarism. A gameshow. Death was the prize. The plane shot for the sun.

The cab pulled away.

Virginia thought she would choke. The anesthetist blew gas inward.

Valentine kissed the faceless head, the mad woman. The expression had been surgically removed. There were no lips. He was breathing life into his death, saving his soul.

They laughed. Neither knew where it came from. Thoughts fluttered in transparent heads.

The cabby turned on the radio. It was a flutter of white noise. The engine raced. The radio programme stopped.

Three beeps of a time check.

No more pulse. Nothing.

C H A P T E R   T W E N T Y - O N E

Water dripped onto Valentine's face. There was a click track in his head, drumming constantly.

He woke up. Even his teeth hurt.

The shower was still dripping. He was in the foetal position. Curled up in the pan. The fibre glass was unyielding. Bright orange. He slipped the frosted glass door. His legs creaked out into the bathroom. Feet felt for the parquet floor.

The bright sunlight was chopped by the louvres. Golden strands.

He rose slowly. The sun hurt his eyes. There was a full length mirror. It was a shambling testament. The right leg twitched uncontrollably. His shorts were wet. He was dying for a piss. The toilet seemed a long way. The bones quaked along, raddled like an old man.

There was a terrible smell. He lifted the seat. The bowl was full of puke. Stuffed high with toilet roll. Not a second too soon. His brain had wrung itself dry.

Where was he?

There was blood on his hand. He shuddered. A round hole was gouged in the palm. The more he looked, the more it hurt. He bound it with toilet paper.

Gotta get some air. Find the clues.

He was worried. Something, someone had gored him. He trod on cloth. Clothing strung beneath his feet. It felt silken. He picked it up. Smelled the folds. There was perfume. Traces of sweat. Blood. *His* blood? There was no way of knowing. The gaps were haunting. He could have done anything. Maybe killed someone. He turned around. His breath was a little faster. Sensation was returning to his extremities.

The bathroom was scattered with debris. Smashed wine glasses. Cosmetics smeared across the tiles.

A message was written on the mirror. Lipstick. Pink. It was unintelligible.

He followed the trail of clothes. A pair of torn knickers, stockings tied in a knot, a suspender belt. Each garment brought him closer to earth. It was like a mystery movie, always a dead body at the end of the trail.

His pulse raced. He was no killer. Drops of blood drew a wavy line. It hurt inside. The wall clock read seventeen thirty. Most of the day had vanished. Lost forever.

He walked through the door. The phone was ringing. Piercing. Shrill. A Trimphone. He lifted the receiver. There was not enough energy to talk. He put it down.

The room seemed longer than ever. "Hello. Hello?" They had hung up.

Devastation cut him down. He fell to his knees. Objets d'art were smashed beyond recognition. The oriental screens splayed open. Rice paper burnt full of holes. He crawled along the floor.

There was the bike jacket. A sleeve ripped off. No sign of the dress. No sign of a body. He skirted round the glass table. It lay on its side.

The floor swam. A cocktail of spilt spirits. He felt sick. The futon was slashed. A huge kitchen knife jutted upwards, wedged in raw cotton. The innards had been tossed to the four winds. There was a smell of burnt coffee. The filter maker still fizzed. Gaping cracks in the jug.

A trail of fresh vomit. Spread along. Ending at his shoes. One loafer rested on an upturned chair. The grey chintz was spattered with blood. He shot up. Ran over.

Somebody had written a message. Two letters. *V+V.*

He touched the fabric. The blood was dry. He half remembered the woman. Virginia.

They were playing with a knife. A stiletto. The tip had cut flesh. It was his flesh. It was hers. Deepening the groove, sealing a blood pact.

She may be dead. His head rushed. He scrambled over the chair.

Other things toppled behind him. Revolving, stabbing motion. A stifled scream. He saw her. His heart was in his mouth. Dizziness swooped. Muscles wrenched against each other.

She was half covered by a duvet. Her naked top poked free. His blue suit was scattered around her. There was a red *V* cut in her shoulder, four inches across. The blood was smeared. He inched closer. Stretched out his arm.

The body was face down. Still. He touched the hand. It was cold. The nails were broken.

She was dead. Tears ran down his cheeks. Not for her, but for him. He could not remember. Nobody would believe that. There was so much guilt. He could not look anymore. The Venetian blinds were drawn. Too dark to see clearly. Must think.

He walked to the window. No air, no time, nothing. He pulled the cord. The flaps sprung horizontal. Evening poured in. The old docks were still. A distant city going home from the shops. The real world. Not like here.

There was a shaky voice. "The aspirins are in the cupboard." He turned back. She was looking at him, eyes narrowed in the light. Her face was drawn. White. Greasy patches on the forehead. Singularly unappealing. He walked over, shivering.

"Make some coffee."

Nobody was dead.

Relief became fear again. He put on his jacket.

She rubbed her eyes, wearily scanned his frame. The turmoil became more apparent. The beautiful collection lay in ruins. She groaned. There was intense pain. Her shoulder blade was sliced through. "What happened?"

He said nothing. The machine frizzled. It seared the void, growling like a buzz saw. Soft footsteps echoed in her head.

"There's no coffee left." His voice was a monotone. Beans had been scattered across the kitchen. Cold air poured from the open fridge. He picked up the milk. It tasted sour. A cheesy moustache etched around his lips. He slammed the door. "Black tea?"

One bag in each cup. Somebody had broken the handle. Water cascaded into the kettle. The plug slipped into the socket.

"What happened?" She was sobbing. Tremors under the covers.

He looked again. All this wealth. Lots of nice things. Nothing left.

He shook his head. "I don't remember. I don't remember." He was angry. Every bit that makes up a man had been sucked out. Empty like the coffee pot, burnt dry.

He tried to comfort her. The words spilled out in emptiness. It was babble. Padding. Insincere. Incongruous. He crouched next to her. The shiny boards skinned his knee. He folded the quilting.

"Help me." Her cry was childlike.

He held her. There was no feeling. That was gone too. She did not want him. His eyes bulged maniacally. The jacket sleeves stunk. There was no strength in his grasp. He held no answers.

She steadied herself. Broke free of his arms.

Valentine's mind was elsewhere. Virginia tottered to her feet. The duvet fell to the ground. She was naked. There was no titillation in her movement. The cowboy boots were next to the chair. She gritted her teeth. Pulled them on. The heels clattered towards the bathroom.

He breathed heavily. Closed his eyes. There was a faint sound. Piss spattered on the fibreglass. He opened his eyes. The damage was no less.

She flushed the toilet. Stale puke burbled down the drain. The effluence did not scare her.

Valentine wrestled in his pocket. There were no cigarettes. His throat stung. The taste was salty.

She appeared again wearing a pale blue robe. It rasped her shoulder. She winced. There was no regret in her eyes. Strands of knotted hair dangled. She forced it back. Fixed the locks with a grip. She licked her lips. "Tea?"

Steam shot from the spout. The kettle was boiling. Valentine felt unnerved. Perhaps she had done it all. His arm could not reach his shoulder.

Her boots clattered, assured in purpose. She switched off the kettle. Steam ebbed. The cupboard door snapped open. Silver paper shards were in her hand. She popped out two tablets, small blue capsules. "Fancy a valium?"

Valentine rested his head on the floor.

She balked, gagged a little. The pills slid down her throat. Valentine grasped his aching palm. "What about all this?" He gazed at the ticket. The photograph. Last night's wasteland.

She paused. Hot water splattered on the tea bag. She brushed flakes of sleep from her eye. Hot liquid scorched her lip. She would toss out the smashed furniture. Mop up the vomit. Then go back to bed. Valentine was chattel. She might throw him out, too. "Your tea." She held up the other cup. He was slow to react.

The ticket was torn. It had his name on it. *West*? It rang a vague chord. The photo was of Miki. A drinks ticket. Free beer. Logic did not fit. Pieces were missing.

He staggered to Virginia. She coughed. Her breasts poked from the robe. A trace of blood seeped through the fabric. He remembered kicking her. Maybe she would ask him back to bed.

He pretended it was alright. Then time jumped. She was sprawled across the bed. A lit cigarette bobbed in her mouth.

He turned on the cold tap. The wound chilled in the water. It still festered. There were coffee grounds in the sink. Damp brown powder? Skag?

Bryce? He felt for the inside pocket. No wrap.

He had given it to Fly. Virginia had given it to Fly.

Trying to think. The Tower. It was all a stupid game.

She asked if he was alright. The eyes shot disdain. They were contact lenses. The real eyes were green.

Virginia stroked the raw cotton. It felt different. Sensory lapses did not bother her.

Valentine pulled his pants on. The fly buttons were difficult. Virginia's form was inviting. The mood was not. He was drowning, no memorable landmark in sight. He tucked in the tail. There was lipstick down the front. "Is this yours?" His voice was still weak.

She shrugged her shoulders. Flicked the half smoked cigarette. It landed in the mug.

He could not understand her candour. His mind jumped to conclusions. Hers just coiled, poised.

She sat up on the futon. "Make some coffee."

He stood silent. She did not remember. The scattered grounds. The cracked jug. Time was a big circle. They were riding round and round. He had to find some answers, fast. "What if you never remember?"

Virginia pulled her robe tighter. She extended her legs. Eight paces. Then much closer. She stood next to him. The boots made her tower above. He was still barefoot.

She must say something. Anything? Her silence was cold. She cared nothing for Valentine. Even less for the line of chat. Twilight lit her face. It painted pockmarks yellow.

She picked up a broken record. Glided her finger across the

label. It was Roxy Music. She had never liked Bryan Ferry. Not even on the cornflake commercial. Words poured out of Valentine's mouth but she was not listening. The expanse of the city was transforming. It looked like a children's playground.

A small boy was shouting. Then it was a girl. Then it was Valentine. She put a finger to her lips. Her robe became a uniform. Then there was just the debris. There was something restful about the carnage. A battlefield. All the soldiers were dead. The last post fluttered into silence. She straightened her back. There was that pain again. The cut had torn a nerve.

Valentine was still asking. She had no recollection. She tried to explain. There was no blame to be levelled. None of the damage mattered. The gaps in Valentine's memory were his problem. She could offer no solace.

It was part of the game. The agony and the ecstasy. She giggled.

He was going crazy. She was laughing. The rich could afford to forget. Not Valentine. Memories were all he had left.

She pointed across the vista. Her hand was shaking. "It still goes on. If you remember or not."

Maybe he had slept through the whole of Friday. Maybe a hundred other people were blank. He felt powerless.

She took out a cigarette packet. It was bloodstained. No sight made Virginia recoil. She shook the packet. Offered him one. He took it ungraciously. A filter hovered in her lips. Both remained unlit.

He fumbled in the trouser pocket. The brass was smooth. A flame leapt from the Zippo. He lit hers, then his. The flame danced. He had felt something else in his pocket.

She pulled the slats apart. The view was a pleasant distraction.

Valentine shook out the contents. There were two envelopes. One had his name on it. The other said Macari. Both were greasy. There was a kernel of memory. A plastic wrap in his palm.

The bag of FX was almost empty.

He tapped her on the injured shoulder. She grunted. Their eyes met.

Valentine had been at the Tower. Here were his wages. The drug was sapping his sanity. He could still fight it. Fly had been there. He would know.

She blew smoke in his face. Valentine cowered back. He stared at the bag. It had been the beginning. The end. And here it was again. He pulled socks from his pocket. They were sticky.

Virginia despised his rage.

The socks could wait until later. He searched for his shoes. The swollen feet eased inside.

"Keep the FX for a rainy day." Her tone was mocking. It already poured.

Valentine was oblivious. Words sailed over his head. The last of the cigarette singed. He tore open the wage packet. Ten pound notes bristled, a sheath of brown. He peeled off ten. One hundred pounds. "For the damage."

She refused. A hundred would not even pay for one partition. He could buy nothing, not even a cup of coffee. Valentine remembered that much. He was a cheap little man. The world was full of his kind. He stumbled towards the door. Over the chairs. Crunching on the broken glass.

Virginia threw him the jacket. It landed clear of the screen. He wrestled it on. The buttons dug into his wounds. He dropped the catch.

She shouted "Wait".

Valentine looked around. He hoped for answers. Had she remembered? Was there some compassion? There had to be.

She told him to look inside the earthenware jug. It rested cracked on the floor. A placebo? Maybe an antidote. At least a Bandaid. He felt inside. Pulled out the papers. There were three twenty pound notes. Crisp. Fresh.

"Take some cab fare." Her voice echoed in the blackness.

Take. Take. Take. He looked at her again. She was proud. She could never admit defeat. This was an adult's game. No prisoners. No bottle merchants.

He picked up one twenty pound note. Services rendered. They had sold him, just like a worn-out Cortina. He shut the door behind him.

Virginia looked out of the window. Water spattered in the dock basin. Her shoulder muscle ached. Maybe another line of FX?

Who wanted to remember Valentine anyway?

CHAPTER TWENTY-TWO

The Grove was still busy. It was getting dark. Rotten fruit crushed under the wheels of his black cab. His stomach churned. They were surging downhill. He checked the address again. The old black book came in useful. Illuminated handwriting littered the page. Red ink, blue ink, green ink. The bag of FX sat in his palm.

He had bandaged the wound. Pain throbbed through the grey handkerchief. His trousers stuck to the seat. It was too warm. He eased the window open. New air rushed in. He saw the driver reversed in the mirror. The meter ticked over. Time was money. Valentine lolled back. He closed his eyes.

It had been so perverse, injuring each other and getting off on the pain. Lack of explanation wrinkled his forehead. The money would not last long, he knew that. The skag for Fly had gone. Hope for West drowned.

If he could only remember, there might be a way out. He could make amends, start fresh on Monday, build up a new crowd. The Underground could work again. It was a small setback. Bryce could fix Fly every week. Jack still needed the money. Valentine wasn't crazy. Stupid, not crazy.

The FX would have to go. He held the bag at the window. All that trouble over this. It cascaded from his grasp. Blew away in the wind.

It was almost over. He took out the twenty.

The cabby halted at the lights. People crossed in front. Pubs were open. He could do with a drink.

The floor shook his feet. His ankles were cold. He wedged the stale socks down the side of the seat. A railway bridge flew overhead. It stole the remaining light. Shadows crawled. Moving black fingers.

Valentine was afraid.

They shot out the other side. The road had always been his friend. Safe to run. New places to hide. It should be no different now.

He watched the concrete. Tall buildings became Christmas trees. Street lamps were watching with slanted orange eyes. The engine was a back beat. Thudding like a bass drum.

His hands were feminine. The bitten cuticles stretched long. Painted red fingernails? Valentine was inside Virginia's body. She had eaten him. Only the thoughts were his. The notes were covered in puke. Blood spurted from his back. A hand carved a *V* deep into the skin. Burning.

The cab pulled up. His body slammed forward. Glass wrapped the forehead.

"This far enough, mate?" The cabby leaned over. His fare must be pissed. He looked on the floor. Valentine was curled into a ball. His eyes were twitching. The cabby turned on the light. It painted the black golden.

Valentine opened the door. He pitched out into the gutter.

The driver was unconcerned. This one would not run away. He swung out, a cigar butt edging from his lips. Beer had melted his features. Grey hair poked above his shirt.

Valentine slipped along the black coachwork. Muscles sagged like old rope. Saliva dribbled from his mouth. The driver spoke but Valentine did not understand. His ears just fizzed. Senility gripped his mind. The fright was worse. He could barely control his body. His lungs wheezed. Numbers on the note were hazy. He passed over the twenty.

The driver counted out change, twenty pieces of silver in his palm. "Fifty makes eight. Two pound coins. A tenner. Twenty pound." He squeezed Valentine's hand shut. The money crunched inside. There was no malice in the action.

He jerked into reverse. The cab jolted back. A rush of air. Tyres whined further away.

It was very quiet. A muffled jukebox was the only sound. The pub was shaped like a pillbox. Fluorescence lit the slits.

He walked forward, trying to move quickly. Vision exploded like landmines. Regulated council houses as uniform as cell blocks. An endless street of electric blue Escorts. The world was changing. Tearing his psyche with it. The blind man was seeing for the first time.

His legs were stiff. What if there was nothing to remember? What if no one was at home? What if distortion would never stop? The roadways dragged by. Unintelligible. No subtitles. He had been here before. It had been more regular then. The tower blocks looked smaller.

He turned up the jacket collar. Damp fabric attracted the cold. Hedges rustled. The rolling was on snare drums. He was stepping up to the guillotine. He wanted it to stop. He wanted to see clearly.

Cigarette packets. Government health warnings. He started to read car number plates. Count the number of garages. Feet lumbered avoiding the cracks. Treading in globs of dogshit. Stumbling over broken flags.

Feeling was returning. His head hurt. The ground was not moving. Council notices had refreshing graffiti. He climbed up the steps. Parking spaces were deserted. His footsteps echoed. No more eerie samples, only clean crisp sound.

He fumbled for the money. It was still there. Number forty-two lodged in his head. That was his destination. He took the cigarettes from his pocket. Put one in his mouth. The block drew closer. It was too windy to light up.

He was dashing. His ankle ached. One foot after the other. Wind on his face felt fresh. It was Saturday night. He and Fly might go up west. That was a joke. West. He still didn't know. It might work.

He kicked the empty pizza boxes. They blew out of the way. His shoulder knocked the door. There was still no glass in it. He was safe. The fluorescent tube still flickered.

Valentine paused in the foyer. He took out his lighter. It reminded him of Miki. A blob of mascara on his nose. Strange thing to think of? He struck the flame. It bobbed low, almost out of petrol. The filter tip glowed.

Why do high-rises always smell of piss? Telephone directories were strewn across the floor. Shrink-wrapped in polythene. *London: Western District.*

Valentine lugged on the filter. It tasted smooth, almost a new experience. Now to unfathom Friday. He stepped over the books.

The even number lift was on the left. Steel doors had been freshly sprayed. Aerosol yellow dripped down. He pressed the call button. Nothing lit up. The exposed bulb was intact. He stepped out of the pool of paint. His feet planted tracks.

The noxious fumes tore into Valentine's nostrils, propellant mixed with cigarette smoke. He coughed up phlegm. There was a sign at his feet. *Out of order.* The graffiti artist had torn it off. He spat. A green glob landed on the board.

He felt apprehensive. Fly might be off his head. A junkie would never remember. He pressed the other lift call. The arrow lit up. Valentine would get off below, do the rest on foot. He tried to wipe the paint off his sole. The stain would not shift. Paint ran all over his hands. Yellow gloss.

The bathwater rumbled down the plug hole. Hairs twisted on the chrome. She looked in the mirror. It hung from the medicine cabinet. Her face was pale. Rings round the eyes were red. Hairline rivulets rested on the eyeball. She ran the cold tap.

The basin was full of shave foam. Bic razors snapped like straw. She splashed water on her face. It did not feel refreshing. Just cold.

The bathroom was grimy. Cracked tiling peeled from the wall. Smells seeped from the S-bend. She coughed. Her frame shivered. There was no heating in here. She tugged the jumper lower. The wool was itchy. It barely covered her thighs.

She walked into the hallway. The mess was stifling. Useless collections, the things everyone else had thrown away. Old bicycle wheels. A disconnected cooker.

She peered through the darkness. Clear vision was hardly possible. Splinters stuck in her feet. It felt worse than a hangover. Bells were sounding in her brain. Ordinary things took on weird dimensions.

The hit had been good, a fantasy adventure thought-bound. Bits were missing. It was like all the best drugs. If you wanted to play you had to pay. She was paying now. Miki's body shook. She was not sure if it was just the cold. It was odd to wake up here. Odd to be with him.

She padded forward. The door was open. There was no sense of time. No watches. No clocks. It was warmer inside. The electric fire was on. Three strips of glowing orange. She crouched beside it. She would get her things and go. No reason to stay.

The room was dark. Blankets spread across the window. The atmosphere was sticky, acrid. She looked around for her things. They were tossed across the floor. Sodden garments that were once clothes. Her glance reached the chair.

There he was. His flesh was ashen. The knuckles devoid of blood. Fingers quivered. He grasped the foam harder. Bones were visible below the chest cavity. Not enough flesh. Total emaciation. This was the ghostly shadow of a man.

Numbers lit up. The lift came closer. Valentine made himself ready to react.

Miki tried to speak. Her words were incongruous. There was nothing to say. Neither wanted an explanation. She was ready to move on. She noticed the track marks that peppered his arms. Small skin bumps above the tattoos. The ink stretched green.

He jolted forward. The naked torso followed behind. Fly rummaged across the table. Broken records fell on the floor. He could not find it. His mind turned in on itself. Two different people were squabbling. One said go to sleep. The other fought for oblivion.

It was there somewhere. It had to be.

He was getting more annoyed. Deeper into mental debt. She had taken it. No, she had given him it. That was Virginia. But Miki was with him now. Who had brought her?

He had fucked her. The thought bemused him.

Under the chip wrapper? He tossed the greasy debris away. There was a large wrap, foil and a lighter. It was alright. He placed the equipment on his lap. This would salve the nightmare and stop the flashbacks.

Rapid movement left trace images.

She fluttered her eyes. Miki was having problems. Fly was in the chair. Then he was not. Then he was. It was not Fly at all. It was a stranger. This would not be the first time.

She had screwed him. It was repellent. Not the sex. Not even the partial madness. It must be the gear. She felt unclean. Truly soiled for the first time.

She grabbed the underwear. Pulled on her knickers. He was not interested. She pushed her thighs together. The fire was getting too hot. Her cheeks turned red.

Fly believed he was in control. Hallucinations splurged. He tossed the hammer from the table. His boots seemed alive. Not a moment to lose. The bag was full. Valentine had been generous. He poured out a spoonful. Brown powder shook on the silver. The tremor engulfed the whole room. Pictures spun.

The tube tasted metallic. It rested in his lips. He struck the lighter. Warmth projected from his hand. The flame hit the paper. There was ignition. Lift off. Smoke curled off the silver. A coiling serpent in his brain. The skag ran. Darting around. Fizzing. He sucked harder.

There was no oxygen left. He was floating on thin air. He crumbled backwards. The paper slipped from his grip. His eyes were shut. The room kept spinning. Then there was absolute clarity. Sight beyond sight. He was hardly moving.

Miki was scared. He had really done it this time. There was a black scar on the paper. The accusations would fly. She shouted. There was no answer. A lonely voice. A lonely room. She smelt death.

The chair became a coffin. The room was a tomb. Flesh fell away. The bones were clean. Tattoos munched like maggots. Stripping him bare. They were in bed together. She kissed him. Now he was dead. It was strangely real.

She rubbed her face. Make-up smeared her hands. She was drowning in the bath water. She was not asleep. Her legs stiffened. She crawled to the table. Scrambled for her clothes. The jacket moved further away. It was on a wire. She picked up her handbag. It was open. A tampax fell out. Loose change bounced off shards of broken albums. Then she saw it.

The two wraps were made of Rizla paper, white and crisp. One was split. Green grains fell out. This was where they were.

FX. Rivers of FX. This would be the best kind of hangover cure. Her fingers edged over.

Fly opened his eyes.

Valentine was travelling slowly. The lift motor hummed. He watched the numbers. Not far now. Only one more floor. He edged forward to get free from the stench.

The dragon did not take its normal course. Fly was seeing double. Her hand moved closer. She must be after the skag. The package fell from his lap. Powders sprinkled in a line.

Miki held the white packages. One would be enough. Ditch the big guy. Get out of there. Her shoes were by the chair. There was no way of getting them.

Fly blocked the retreat. He wanted his gear back. He was crying like a child. It was all gone.

"No more," she said. "No more."

They were in different worlds. Different spaces of consciousness.

He leapt onto the floor. Glass cracked under his knees. Talons clawed his flesh. He was beating back locusts. The teeth made a buzzing noise. It grew into a howl. Hungry wolves biting at the heels.

Miki drew back. Her arms rested against the electric bars. The fire guard was missing. Black mohair scorched. The yarn fused with her flesh. Trails of smoke fluttered.

She did not feel the pain at first. The burns got deeper. Tanned skin wrinkled. Sticky liquid. Molten plastic. Hurt tore through nerves.

She screamed.

A chilling cry. Raising the hairs on his neck.

Tears streamed. Energy passed through the fire. Sucking her dry like a conduit. She wriggled.

There was no movement left. Her battered body dropped. Pink fingers grasped the rug. She bit her tongue. The scream still flowed. Blood trickled from her mouth. The limbs curled around her head.

Fly retched by the human barbecue. None of these things belonged. The shoes were alien. He was wearing other clothes. There was no gear. The lighter was an aerosol. *Hello from Marbella* read as hieroglyphics. The smoke came from a pyre. They were burning old tyres. It was bonfire night. Steel handcuffs grew from charred silver foil. It was all the same.

Then he heard the scream again. Somebody was laughing. Giggling in his head. A comedy show called *Junkie*. He was the star guest. The audience passed the parcel. One player to the other. It was a deal of skag. A bag of FX. He could not tell. It moved too fast.

The hostess sat in front of him. Her face was obscured. The black dress sparkled. *Come on down.* Truth was only a scream. He had to stop it. Make them listen. He grabbed her wrist. The red coral bracelet was warm.

Fly's fingers spanned her burns. The friction increased the pain. It was a rope noose. They pulled it tighter.

She would not let go. The package was too valuable. A sedative. The last grains of sanity. Sweat poured from her flesh. Hidden strength erupted. She bent forward.

Miki opened her mouth. He saw a row of razor blades. A rack of needles.

She bit hard. Teeth sank behind the knuckles. Veins split. Blood spurted. He let out a wail and then meaningless tirades of anger.

She heard music. They were opening the gate. "Set my people free." All the bonds were breaking.

Fly was powerless. He had been bitten by a shark. His hand would not move. Rows of razor sharp teeth sliced deeper and deeper.

The lift door slid open. Valentine stepped out. He was a floor down. The walls were thin. He heard screams. Something wrong.

Fangs sank deeper still. Closer to the bone. The treasure was almost lost. He must get the gear. Fly felt for a heavy object. Slap the nose. Hit the bouncer. It would do no harm, just warn it off.

Miki could hardly move. Her jaws were locked tight. She still had hope right in her hand. They would never take that.

Fly touched the hammer head. It was cold steel like the end of a microphone. He raised it above his head.

She saw a silver star shining in the heavens. Shooting down to earth.

He was waving the paint brush. Bringing it down faster. Faster. Red paint splattered. It hit the wall.

She felt intense pain. Someone had flicked off the lights. No more craziness. "Good night". Nobody heard.

Fly was hitting the bouncer again and again. The skull was crushed.

Red paint flowed from the canvas. The stretchers splintered. The champ kept falling to the floor.

A blur of silver. A blur of red.

Rocky. Rocky. Rocky.

The screams got closer. Valentine charged upstairs. Louder. Shouting. Wailing. It was coming from behind George Clinton. The painted door swayed on the latch. He kicked it open.

The figures were lit by the fire.

An arm bashed up and down. Relentless. Inhuman. He looked to the floor. Blood drenched the rug. Limbs splayed left and right. The head had half a face.

The teeth broke free. The stained wraps fell. He screamed.

Fly's hand stopped in mid air. He looked at Valentine. He recognised little. His arm was damp. A deep red stain.

The hammer fell from his grasp. He picked up the packets. They were doused with sweat and blood. He'd got the gear back.

Valentine stood motionless. His stomach wrenched. It was Miki. The game was over.

Fly tapped the body. It twitched a little. There was no breath. He hoped they would stop the cameras.

There were no cameras. It was not make-up. He tried to cry. There was no feeling left. There could be no sorrow.

He saw Valentine's blue suit. A uniform. They would not stop him this time. He rose to his feet.

Valentine fell to his knees. Vomit spurted from his mouth. It splashed the floor. Spattered towards the body.

Fly pulled down the blankets. Moonlight streamed in a bright light. A pure light. He felt cleansed. There was no more anger left. No more reason. No more logic. She was dead. He was dead. But the spirit was still free. It floated over the city.

Nothing had changed. He looked at Valentine. No colour in his face. Their eyes met. Fly smiled. A peaceful grin. Blank like a corpse. The humanity sucked dry.

Valentine winced.

Fly launched himself through the window. The glass shattered. There was no scream. Only Valentine's cry twelve floors up.

The air was cool. Silver foil blew across the floor. Two white wraps.

Valentine drowned in hallucinations. A body in heaven. A body in hell. Oozing green flakes. Lines of FX. Tabloid mastheads exploded. *Blood Bath Riddle. Drug Death DJ.* One bloody Valentine. The walls were closing in. Nobody would believe it. The wind whispered guilty.

Miki had no face.

He could have stopped it. This was the last nail in his sanity.

The building was stirring. Fingers whizzed in telephone dials.

He ran. Tainted with his own vomit. Blood was on his hands. White noise stuck in his head. Crunching like a bone breaker. Terror tripped down every step. Cold grey slipped into black. He motored down a thousand stairs.

The night was bitter. He stumbled. It was in black and white. Like a dream.

Red soaked into the rug. Emptiness seeped from Fly's cracked skull.

The city opened paved arms. Valentine was swallowed whole. The thousand wailing seconds would never stop.

CHAPTER TWENTY-THREE

Valentine thrust harder. Deeper. More sweat on his naked back. She was clawing his arse. Wriggling like a stuck pig. He was ramming home. Holding his breath. It was not taking long. It never did. Bang. Bang. Bang. A hammer splintering bone. Her muscles spasmed. Sucking him deeper. She was shouting. "Yes. Yes. Yes." He never liked women that shouted. The momentary tension exploded. He was shooting his load. He wanted to hurt her. Nothing between them. The condom was full. There was no pleasure.

She groaned. Her head flopped on the pillow, energy spent. He pulled out his sticky dick. Rolled over. It was not that sordid. Maybe it was. Boxer shorts clung to his ankles. There were no sheets on the bed. Buttons poked from the mattress and dug into his spine.

She lit up a Marlboro. It was a bad cliche. The tape faded out. A stop button clicked off. "You have placed a chill in my heart." No, it had stopped minutes before.

Valentine stepped outside himself. It was weeks before. His breath still tasted of tequila. He sat up. The clock beamed red. The time. The day. The date. Thursday. Pieces were missing. Wiped clean. He had gone mad.

He looked at the woman next to him. It was Virginia. The hair was tied back. She turned to face him. Oriental eyes. It was Miki. The surroundings were all wrong. Music was playing louder.

Strangled samples. He touched her face. The skull caved in. Bashed by his fingers. He clambered back along the mattress. Blood oozed between her legs. Her body writhed. He closed his eyes.

The thigh felt warm. It quivered against his cheek. Then it stopped. She sighed. Valentine opened his eyes. She had come. The naked body extended in front. He glanced along the leg, past the breast. She was smiling. Satisfied. He half recognised the face. She lit a Marlboro. It was the woman from the coach. Anna. He was not sure why.

Hair plastered on his forehead. A coarse strand stuck to his lip. He spat it out. She kissed his lips.

Valentine watched the clock. It was 11 a.m. Sunday. She sat up. She coughed. The weekend was total oblivion. Memory stopped on Thursday. Somebody had erased it. Maybe him. He felt strangely guilty.

The cigarette sat in the ashtray. Anna had disappeared through the door. The curtains shrouded the light.

He padded across the carpet. Out into the hallway. His steps tapped a muffled sound. The pounding was in his head. Maybe just a hangover. It was too violent for that.

Anna stood in the kitchen. She switched on the radio. The Kensington drawl was familiar. "Hello, pop pickers." She smiled to herself. The pots were unwashed. A pan half filled with pasta. She rinsed out two cups.

Valentine leant in the doorway. She turned around. Her body was still naked. There was plenty of time. A day spent in bed. He could take that. His dick started to get hard. Her flesh was very pale. She shut off the tap. Spurts slowed to a trickle.

His glare was piercing. The dark eyes looked empty. Anna was a little scared. All men could be savages. Even this wrecked specimen.

"Are you alright?" Valentine shrugged his shoulders. He did not care what she thought. He hobbled to the chair. The polished wood chilled his arse. He pushed away the Sunday papers. There was never any real news. Valentine started to worry. He saw his jacket.

It was a duet for one. Anna spoke. Valentine was miles away.

He glared at the sleeve. It was stained red-brown. The marks looked like blood. Too much to spill and survive. The tea cup rested beside him. "Herbal. I make it myself." He was still not listening. The china was hot. It burnt his hand. He sipped gently then put it down. The motif was middle eastern. Jade from Persia. He fingered his palm. The scar did not hurt. A large yellow scab had formed.

"Do you want a bandage?" Anna was concerned. Not for the wound. But for its cause. It was too round for a blade. His explanation had been crazy. She sat opposite him.

Her crotch hovered above the chair. She placed the tea towel under her groin. The thigh muscles sagged. She rested firmly.

Steam swirled from both cups. Valentine seemed delirious. His manner grew more anxious. Something was wrong. Anna followed his eyeline. It rested on the jacket.

She leant over. Her breasts bobbed forward. Their lips brushed. It was like kissing stone. Valentine's gaze was fixed.

She forgot about the tea. The chair slid forward. It made a grinding noise. She groped under the table. Her tongue traced a line. Along the flat of his leg. Hairs stuck between her teeth. Anna moved closer. Midway to his groin. His dick was limp. Lifeless. She took it between her lips. It was like he was dead.

Valentine could only see the red. Pictures unfolded in his mind.

She sucked harder. Nothing was happening. The tongue moved back and forth. Still nothing. Her hand spanned his ankle. Tight for support.

The pressure increased. Valentine felt trapped. They were restraining him. Preventing any reaction. Locks of hair brushed his legs.

He suddenly felt it. A vice in his groin. The head rasping upward. He could not control it. His neck snapped. He was looking down. Her head was in his lap. Surging. Slurping. She pulled him further down. The legs were giving way. Closer to the abyss. His feet slipped on the lino.

It was happening. She had pulled out all the stops. His muscles tensed. The arm flicked across the table. It hit the cup. There was a clank of china. A running river. Hot infusion. It spilled over the formica. Hips jerked forward. The hammer driving home. Tea splashed onto her back. It scalded. The first shot. Splashing down Anna's throat. A silver bullet. She swallowed amid the heat. Her body recoiled. His tool slipped free. She bounced on the floor. Valentine saw the corpse. Miki smashed beyond recognition. He yelped. Threw his arms around his head.

Anna struggled on her haunches. She wiped sticky white. It glided from her face. Valentine was sobbing. Her palms reached the table. She pulled herself up. "All that talk about murder. What are you on?"

She tried to piece it together. The bloodstained jacket. All the scars. Valentine had arrived screaming. Why here? Why after so long? He kept repeating a name. "Mickey."

She chose her words carefully. It might get violent. Billy had been the same. The slight scald tingled. "What happened to Mickey?"

Valentine felt himself surfacing. He shook his head. Communications floundered. There were so many things in his head, unjoined incidents. It would not flow. She had sucked him clean. Fists banged on the table.

Anna recoiled. It was getting colder. She unhooked the jacket. The fabric smelled strange. One sleeve was very stiff. She ran her fingers down the stripe. It looked like a bloodstain. She had hardly noticed it before. The thought genuinely scared her. What if somebody had really been murdered? What if Valentine was the murderer?

He might have been tripping. A pub brawl. Beating up his girlfriend. She did not want to find out.

She edged away. Distance between them was the answer. The door creaked on its hinges. Valentine turned round. No, mate. Not this time. Her hand touched the Chubb key. It slipped free. Lock him in. Then what?

There was no time to finish the puzzle. Valentine was shambling towards her. She froze against the door. He lashed out.

The fists were flailing. Valentine was on the floor. His head bashed up and down. Glancing off the lino. Thud. Thud. Thud. He wanted it out of his mind. Visions of death. The hammer cracking the skull.

She wanted to kick him. One for all the beaten wives. Payment for the lies. She had discovered that the percussion player from Sonido D 'Espresso was in the States. This man was a fraud.

It made no difference last night. She wanted it then. Not anymore. The foot made contact. His belly shook. Force sprang through her body. Valentine heaved. He rolled onto his back. Anna towered above. Her anger had evaporated. "Who the hell are you?"

Valentine looked up at the ceiling. Hairline cracks in the plaster. The naked thigh. Connected to a body. Miki's body. An arm raised above her head. Hammer in hand. Silver. Dashing. Up and down. Fly's hand. There was death here. Fly had killed her. Open wraps. Fly had killed her. Vomit spilling from mouths. Open wounds. Fly had killed her. The naked thigh. Fly was gone. Cracks in the ceiling.

Anna raised her leg again. He held his gut. She looked at his face. Glazed eyes pleaded pathetically. His sweaty face lolled. "I am Valentine. No murderer."

She held back. The chubby figure looked ridiculous. She no longer felt threatened. Her foot rested by his head.

Valentine slid upwards, balanced on his elbows. Even his own name sounded strange. It was like a nightmare fading in and out. He asked for her help.

Anna walked away. She had no stomach for it, not in daylight. She opened the fridge. Marks & Spencer's packets. Half eaten chicken tandoori. She reached for a can of lager. Snap. Icy liquid soothed her frayed nerves. She felt like a dupe, always falling for the dick at the end.

She looked across. Valentine was on his feet, quaking like a pensioner. It was strange what she had done. With him? His legs looked blotchy. They had used a condom. She had swallowed the rest. STDs. The clap. Maybe AIDS. It was a high risk practice. She paused between gulps. "Put some clothes on." Valentine was slow to react. "Cover yourself up."

Her voice spattered his brain. The trousers were slung over the pedal bin. Valentine tugged the braces. Mud stained his turn-ups. He stepped into the legs. Fabric creased around the crotch. The buttons were no easier this time. Stray threads scratched his arse.

There was a sense of falling. Shattering glass. Out into the night. Air rushed past his face. Hard on ground zero. Hitting the chair. He sat down.

Anna flicked through the morning papers. *The Observer. News of the Screws.* Fact and fiction.

Valentine begged again. "Please help me."

"You need a doctor. Not a journalist."

Sunlight dazzled off the colour supplement. The pages were stuck together. Gloss tacky like glue. She slit the corner. Her fingernail flicked. Frank Sinatra's neck tore. She opened the centre pages. A bright splash of colour. Two large heads. Bloated. Chopped from the neck down.

"A murder. A suicide. W9."

His voice was surprisingly clear. Anna looked up. She moved the colour magazine aside. The heavy breathing was noticeable, a glimmer in his eye. She held her breath. Valentine made a grab for the papers.

His eyes roamed across expanses of print. The rag paper was damp but the ink had not run. *The Observer.* It would be in the stop press. He chased top to bottom. *Holiday Deaths. Rock Arrests.* Teen Addict dies in hospital. *The Weather.* It was not there. Nothing on the front page. Lawson. Poison. The party. It was not there. He pulled across the tabloid. The colour pictures were blurred. *Her Royal Shyness* Fat Princess Margaret. *Secret of Cheating Killer.* That was it. No W9. No suicide. No murder. Valentine thought he was going crazy.

Anna folded her arms. Swirling newsprint in the tea. She wanted him to go. The can was empty. She rattled the ring pull. A fanfare sprang from the radio. The pips. Burbling in the background.

Valentine lurched to his feet. She watched him run. His hand twisted the knob. The volume was too loud. Booming voices in the kitchen.

Valentine held his breath. The headlines. Forty six die in air-show horror. IRA revenge. Three more die. Hysterical mourners at Zia's funeral. Die. Die. Die. No mention. Scattered showers. Generally fine. Nothing. Valentine slid down the cupboard. He crumpled in a heap. It was in his head. Not for real.

Anna switched off the radio. All was quiet. The wall clock still ticked. Cars drove by outside. Sunday. This was more than she bargained for. She buttoned up the jacket.

A half smoked cigarette sat amid dimps. She picked it up. A matchbox. "England's Glory". The smoke tasted stale.

Valentine lifted his head. He had been out of it last night. All weekend. Off his head. His new club had opened on Friday. He could not remember the outcome. Fly. That was one of his partners. He went round. A council flat. It was a mess. Well. It was worse than that. The door was open. Tears ran down his cheeks. There it was. Fly was bashing Miki's head in. His girlfriend.

Ex-girlfriend. He might have been earlier. He might have stopped it. Then it was too late. Fly crashed through the window. Nothing left. There was no front page story. No news flash. It was a game in his head. He felt cold. Very cold. Time to go.

Anna sat down slowly. He was lying before. Why not now? She pulled on the filter. Burnt to the butt. She stood it upright. A brown tower on the table. Bullshit. She looked at Valentine. "Why?"

It stabbed in his brain. Why? That was the worst part. It still made no sense. He stumbled to his feet. He could still walk away. He asked for his jacket. The voice shook. She unhooked the buttons. The sleeve grazed free. Blood. Real blood. Not from the wound on his hand. Why?

The sun broke from the cloud. Rivulets of light on the table. It might be a nice day. The jacket hung in his grip. It was like a portal where dream meets reality.

He sighed. Rubbed the sleeve. The stain would not budge. He walked to the sink and turned on the tap. The scrub pad was already wet. Water dripped on the fabric. Pale pink discharge ran away. It seeped from the elbow.

Anna startled him. She stood by his shoulder. Bad breath on his neck. A boozy odour. Valentine turned off the tap. He was sure of what he had seen. It dripped in front of him.

She was breathing down his neck. Too close for comfort. He sidestepped. There was no point in running. His feet were still bare.

He said he was sorry. Even that was not real. But normal people said it. That made it alright.

A painty sweatshirt sat on the sill. She reached over, took it. Her body was pale.

Valentine looked elsewhere. He picked the rubbish from his pocket. All covered in crumbs. Stray strands of tobacco.

The shirt dropped below her waist. The crotch was hidden.

He felt used. Worse than that. He felt wasted. Ten minutes. Then back on the street. He placed the old tickets on the table. His shoes must be in the hall. Maybe the bedroom.

The hallway smelt musty. A heap of clothes by the stairs. Female debris. A torn denim jacket. Bras ready for ditching. One trusty loafer. He fished it out.

Anna swept up the garbage. The ticket was creased. Black. Complimentary stamped across. It rested in her palm. She scanned the writing. West. Raising the Underground. The Tower of Babel. She had been there. It was shit. Valentine. So it was his real name. Or at least real pseudonym.

Valentine was shouting. "Where's the other shoe?"

It had started in the living room. "Try the living room." Her tone was detached.

There was another name she recognised. Fly Macari. Valentine said he was dead. A dead DJ. That was a good one. The ticket was dated Friday. She shook her head. The time scale was right. No. No murders. No news story. Bullshit. She walked towards the pedal bin.

Valentine was in the bedroom. He buttoned up his shirt. The stench lingered. He needed a bath. Not here. Jack might be in. Maybe Miki. He blocked out her face. There might be a nightmare again. He picked up Anna's cigarettes. The packet slipped into his pocket. Theft was easy. He had no conscience.

The pedal bin flicked open. Something was sticking to her finger. It was wet. Three sheets of cardboard peeled away. She looked closer. Unclear in her own shadow. Cigarette papers.

She sat down. The light hit it. Gripped against the moisture. Anna shook it onto the table. Two folded cigarette papers. One was torn.

Both stained brown. Green crystals fell out. Stuck together. It looked like sherbert. Coke dyed green.

She dipped her finger in the mixture. Wondered how it would

taste. It looked inviting. She brought her finger closer. Up to her mouth. An inch away.

Valentine grabbed her wrist. "No." She stopped. He sat down.

This was the real 'why'. No bullshit. A drug called FX. Free. It sent people wacko. Made them forget. Hallucinations so real, you couldn't tell. Valentine couldn't tell. Blood on the wrap. Fly must have fought for it. Miki, too. Losing control. Feeling no pain. You could fly on FX. Really fly. Landing in Concorde. He heard Fly hit the ground. Then he was back in the kitchen.

Anna was incredulous. A free drug? Somebody must be paying for it. Pulling the strings. It didn't even make the news. More bullshit. Valentine's giant conspiracy theory.

"You can write about it," Valentine pleaded. Tell them all. Exclusive.

She was no Woodward or Bernstein. He scooped up the wraps. Nobody would believe it. Valentine only half believed it.

There was no more emotion to waste. A crappy music journo. This grubby flat in Camden. A blow-job in the kitchen. There were no answers here.

CHAPTER TWENTY-FOUR

Courtney walked down the stone steps. His house was early Victorian, formerly a retreat for Franciscan monks.

He pulled on the cord. The neon tubing flickered and then came to rest. The light seemed purple. He puffed on his joint. "You can come down now," he shouted over his shoulder.

But there was no reply. Courtney turned round. He tracked a shadow along the balustrade. The figure at the top was shaking. His sleeves fluttered beneath the light. There were a lot of bloodstains. At least it looked like blood.

Then there was the look on the face. He had seen it before. The eyes looked cold, as if they didn't want to see anymore. He wondered what Valentine had seen, why he was so incoherent. He said he wanted to kill himself.

Courtney stretched out his hand. He offered Valentine a blow. Still the figure wouldn't venture into the cellar. "Come down the stairs, for fuck's sake." Courtney didn't want his wife to hear.

Shakily, Valentine ventured down. He looked around as he stepped.

The cellar was quite large. Every available piece of space was rammed tight with packing cases. One table was piled high with Thai-copied Rolex watches. There were bags with fake Vuitton and Armani motifs.

Valentine hovered in front of Courtney. He looked for compassion and understanding. But there was none.

Courtney grinned, then stubbed out his joint. Fifty quid was not a good offer, but there was to be a big laugh at the end of this deal. He opened the blue tool box and lifted out the top compartment. Screwdrivers and hammers were now put aside. His fingers deftly removed the oily rag. And there it was. Flat in the bottom of the tool box. A large black pistol.

He held it up to the light. "This is a Luger 33 calibre automatic," he said proudly. Then undid the clip.

Valentine had never seen a real gun before. Brass-cased bullets glinted in the magazine. He was mesmerised. This was real power. The power over life and death.

Courtney clicked the magazine into place. "Why do you want to top yourself?"

Valentine knew the real answer. But he could not say. His mind jumped and repeated like a scratched record. He took five ten pound notes and wafted them at Courtney.

For some reason Courtney was not interested in the money. He looked distant. "Maybe a bullet wouldn't be such a quick death." He watched Valentine squirm.

Valentine couldn't stop shaking. Courtney grappled the money from his hand and slid the gun into Valentine's jacket pocket. Perhaps their old rivalry was not yet over.

"I hope there are enough bullets." Courtney was smiling.

Could there ever be enough?

Valentine got ready to walk away. It was going to be a long walk.

CHAPTER TWENTY-FIVE

The wine bottle was green translucent glass. She pulled it out of the fridge. It was pleasantly chilled. She walked towards the table. Placed it in the centre. Everything matched. Set out neatly. Three different forks. She had spared no trouble. Satay was piled high. Crisp salad lay in black bowls.

She glanced at her reflection. There were no traces of make-up. The hair was tied back. She felt clean. Not for long. She loosened her blouse.

Keiran was a rising star of the ad world. They often enjoyed dinner and uncomplicated sex. She could drive him to work tomorrow.

The phone rang. A high pitched trill. She picked up the receiver. "Hello?" Her voice was controlled. The mouthpiece smelt of somebody else's spit.

"Ginny? It's Keiran. I tried to call before."

Virginia half listened. The knife was by the phone. The blade was untarnished. She had forgotten to put it away. Fingers fondled the hilt.

"I called you yesterday," he said. Somebody had hung up. He was sorry. He was filling in for a friend.

Virginia did not like to lose. The knife slid from her grip. She blew him a kiss. It was over. "See you some other time." No glimmer of regret. She slammed the phone down. It did not bother her.

Of course it did. She stormed over to the kitchen. The plastic bags slipped through her fingers. Food scuttled off the plates. An expensive cocktail mushed together in the bin liner. She didn't like satay. Peanut sauce looked like puke. All into the bag. She tossed it across the room. It zipped past the bin, thwacked against the barbecue.

She peeled the breath-freshening gum from her teeth. It stuck to her fingers, grey and pasty. She smeared it down the wine glass.

Virginia hated being alone. It was boring. She picked up the remote control and pressed the button. The CD skipped a track. Then the music started. Bill Withers' remastered greatest hits. She couldn't remember the name of the song.

The corkscrew tore deeper. She plucked the cork free. Sweet wine? It lapped as she poured. She finished one glass, then another. The finest Sainsbury's could sell. Visions of the Last Supper. A man awaiting trial. It might scare others, not Virginia. She flushed her mind dry. There was tomorrow. A fresh week.

She slumped into a dining chair. Rested bare feet on the table. She barely remembered what Keiran looked like. The mental lapses did not bother her. The forgotten bits? They were probably as shit as the rest?

She positioned the cigarette case square on the table. Her hand shook. The motif was enamel. A Swiss mountain scene. From Brick Lane. She could lose herself. Not much fun on your own, but better than nothing. The catch was stiff.

There was a knock on the door. Four stuttered taps. Keiran was a practical joker. He had a radiophone. This was not a new one. He once blew her out then turned up minutes later. She let him wait.

Virginia closed the box. Only a few seconds had elapsed. There was no second knock.

Valentine felt for the gun. His head spun with blinding pain. Cold turkey.

Virginia loosened her belt. She sashayed across empty space.

Valentine gulped.

Her hand slipped the latch. The door swung smoothly. She looked outside. Something was wrong.

The engine raced. Smoke poured from the exhaust. Keiran did not look round. He twitched the gear shift.

Virginia called out. The roar was too loud. His window was shut. She stepped onto the concrete. Ran in bare feet.

He pulled away. The BMW surged out of the gate. She had gone out. He didn't care.

Virginia felt cheated. Why did he leave so quick? Her perception was skew. The 'few seconds' had taken several minutes. The dark chill cut into her feet. He had really gone this time. She would not call back.

It was very dark. Only house lights cut into shadow. She dashed back inside, closed the door. Must keep calm. Nobody walked out on her. She took several deep breaths. Something was pulling her under. It was anger. That was all. She would not admit anything else. Her feet etched black stains on the rug.

A black shadow loomed by the window. The tentacles grew longer. A mantis crunching her brain, eating the detritus, killing the husband. Crane-like arms swooping across her face.

It was only the clock shining. She sat down. It was late.

"More wine?" The voice came from nowhere. Rhetoric in her head. The bottle was half empty. She swigged from the neck. It stank like piss. Golden showers raced down her throat. She replaced the bottle. It was wine again.

The CD was scanning back to the beginning. There was no music. She saw something outside the window. A formless black shape. Virginia stood up.

Darkness masked his face. Valentine was sure the car would not come back. All the times he had watched. He could move in. The footsteps echoed. Nobody could stop him. It was too late for that. She must have some answers.

The gun weighed down his trousers. Each sinew tightened. He shook with fear. Afraid of his own shadow. Inches from hard facts. He could feel her presence inside. He moved slowly.

The shadow engulfed the balcony. It lurched forward.

She heard a crash. Broken glass shattered on the floor. Breaking through, it lunged from a great height. Chopped flesh skewered on the glass. Evening spilled through the gap. It had finally arrived. A ghost from the past.

The figure moved closer and closer. It had a human face. The chair fell behind her. She gripped tighter. A writhing mass stood up. It was a woman. It was *her* face, wrinkled, ragged with age. The Spirit of Christmas Future. There was a scream.She closed her eyes. The wailing continued. It was banging in her head.

The wail seared through Valentine. He waited. It sounded real. He knocked again.

Virginia opened her eyes. She looked down. The broken wine glass rested on the table. The window pane was intact. Minor cuts crisscrossed her palm. Tiny red scratches. Her reflection stared from the glass. Wailing blurted from the CD.

She waved at her reflection. It waved back. The unmarked face was gilded by the panorama behind. North pier illuminations hung across the bridge. Someone was knocking at the door. Keiran had arrived. Perhaps he had never gone.

Her steps were unsteady. She walked towards the door. Cold feet rested in reality. The dinner could be microwaved. Her jeans seemed a little tighter. She no longer felt clean. Sweat dripped onto the door handle. The Yale clicked free. Virginia put on her best smile. Swung the door open.

The look rapidly turned to disgust. Valentine hovered in the fanlight. He was unshaven. Shadow distorted his face. His loafer wedged against the door frame.

Virginia looked down. "No need." Her tone was mocking. She walked away. "Shut the door. It's not a doss-house."

266

Valentine was not listening. He stood goggle-eyed. There was no trace of damage. No slashed bed. No upturned furniture. The burnt oriental screens were gone. Just a huge expanse of clean space. Virginia sat by a glass dining table.

He walked in and closed the door. Each step eroded his conviction. She held up the wine bottle. "Want a glass?" Valentine shook his head. He crumpled into the chair, flesh taut in shrunk fabric. He mentioned the scream.

She cut him short. Somebody else was expected. Valentine would have to go. The dinner was in the garbage. This was the last bottle of wine. She drained the dregs. Excess liquid dripped from her lips. Bony fingers dabbed them dry. "What do you want?"

Valentine glanced round the room feverishly. No clues. He saw the cigarette case. His arm stretched out.

Virginia grabbed the box. The contents were precious. She told him it was empty.

He floundered. He asked about the room. There was no damage. No evidence of a fight. Chromium Cadillacs were straight from Japan. A sunrise was bent from neon tubing. The Sabitier rack was fixed on tiles.

She was reticent. It was as it had always been. Her home.

Valentine wanted to cry. He had no stomach for it anymore.

He laid down the tarnished wrap. It sat between them. Central on a dining plate. His hands were face down. Flush against the surface. Extraneous movement had stopped. He looked at her. Visual signs were confusing. The vampish make-up had been wiped clean. Her usual calm teetered. He began.

Words ran jagged, scratched like a record. The gear had liquidised his brain. He opened the wrap. The crystals had turned grey-green. Dampness had sapped the lustre. Valentine needed answers. What was it? Where had it come from?

Virginia laughed. She shrugged her shoulders.

Valentine panted. It was as if he had run all the way.

Her chair slipped back. She stood up, way beyond arm's length. She padded across bare boards. Cold breath steamed onto the window. She could not take him seriously. "Go home."

She glanced over her shoulder. He was still there.

His teeth ground a machine gun burst of words. There had been six wraps. Only one was left. At the Medici Valentine had one, Virginia had one, Fly and Miki.

She had vague recollections. A man and a woman. He had been very tall. She gazed at the City. The Heart of the Matter.

Valentine beat harder. Pouring as rain. The sweat ran down his nose. He choked on the words. Fly and Miki had fought. He wasn't sure. They wanted more. Another hit. Clinging for grim death. Tearing at each other. Fly bashed her with a hammer. Crushed the skull. Then he jumped twelve stories.

The music stopped. Virginia turned round. She swallowed.

There was a sheath of newspapers in the rack. She had seen no mention. No murder. Her spirit grew stronger. He had really gone crazy. This situation was dangerous. Tears were running down his cheeks. She had to get rid of him, check any violent notion.

She unclipped the hair grip. Locks fell down her back. Virginia smiled warmly and took a step closer. The score was simple. She whispered a more logical vision of the truth. Four trips, still one missing? Valentine had taken the fifth. Dreamt up the whole scam. It was not real. Just a trip. She took another step closer.

Valentine lifted up his sleeve. It was stiff. The bloody mark would not wash away. She leant against the table. Her breasts bobbed. The hand felt gentle. She turned over his palm, the source of pain. His heavy breathing subsided.

Virginia felt safe again. She kissed his forehead. The lips brushed free. It was like defusing a bomb. Sensation stepped lively again. She could throw him out now. Maybe do another line.

Valentine rubbed his palm. It was best to believe her. Truth had shaken free after the first line. She turned away. The scar peeked under the strap, an etched pink 'V'.

She put down the cigarette case out of harm's way. She no longer listened. Keiran was expected.

She felt him stand up. Air rushed against her back. She heard a click. It was not the door. She looked down. The cigarette case was still shut. She slowly wheeled. Heard the voice. "What if you took the fifth trip?"

The safety catch was off. Valentine stood two yards away. His head swam. He had the Luger in his hand. His finger coiled around the trigger. The gun metal was grey. She gasped for air.

He screamed. He still wanted answers.

"Don't make me do it." Valentine sounded like an old gangster film. *Ridiculous in Pinstripe*. He wanted revenge. Not for his friends but for sanity's sake. She had blown his brains out. It was his turn.

He only wanted to scare her.

Her voice ripped into Valentine. The bare feet edged forward. What was real? The furniture she had thrown away? The scar on her back? Or murder? She gestured towards the window. Everybody was screaming. Trying to get ahead. Killing each other. Greasing the wheels with booze. With coke.

FX was no worse. It was a reward. Every closed deal they sent a fresh bag. So it warped the brain a little. So there were bad flashbacks. It rated you. It said you were good. It proved you were a winner. There was no conspiracy. No craziness. Only crazy people.

Valentine waved the pistol. "Who are they?" His voice was shrill. He couldn't do it.

The gun pointed straight at her. There was no room to manoeuvre.

"Give me the names," Valentine shouted.

The hairs were standing up on the back of her neck. Her palms began to sweat. She reached over to the table slowly. Her thumb and forefinger clasped the cigarette case. She tossed it over. One last hit.

The thin metal box bounced off the floor and landed at Valentine's feet. He crouched down. His stare still fixed on her body.

She spat venom. "There are no *real* answers. Can't you see that?"

Valentine clicked the case open. The contents were unalarming. There was a small bag of FX, several sheets of folded white paper and a small yellow card. He unfolded the paper.

He alternated his glance between the 'evidence' and Virginia. She carried on shouting. He tried to concentrate on the written words.

The white A4 sheets had a PO Box number printed at the top. It would be difficult to trace. He was confused. There was no mention of FX. He read the title back to himself. The words were underlined twice.

PHYSICAL EFFECTS SURVEY. (All answers strictly confidential.) Please type, or print in black ink.

His arm fell to his side. The gun pointed towards the floor. *Physical effects. Effects: FX.* These papers were a questionnaire on the drug's effect. There were multiple choice questions with boxes to tick.

Any loss of breath? None. Some. A lot.

Any visual distortion? None. Some. A lot. And so on.

Valentine was not threatening anymore. There was a vision in his head. All across town the 'right people' were snorting fat green lines. Ticking off the boxes as they went. All going crazy.

Somewhere there was a mail room. Bald, bespectacled men were adding up the figures, collating the data.

All the trips, all the pain were just one big probability curve.

There were no compromising photographs. No Watergate-style tapes. No kingpin drug barons. Madness had been given away free, like trial-size muesli.

It was all a big marketing scam. A spiralling commercial for mass self-destruction. The questionnaire fell from his grip.

Maybe nobody had died. Maybe nobody was crazy.

The corporate logo on the yellow security pass was bold. *Domaine and Partners.* Valentine thought back. He had seen it before. These people had run the GLOW launch.

"That's the last bag," Virginia said. They were sending no more. She didn't seem angry anymore.

Every deal she closed they had sent a fresh bag. Domaine's communication network infested every sector of business life. He had no spies. Only computers. Huge data banks crammed full. His secret society.

Everyone knew where it came from. Nobody could tell the truth. They all had too much to lose. Besides, he was giving it away. It had to be safe.

Valentine put the yellow pass in his pocket. His head was spinning. There was no way to stop it. His madness had gone too far. One thought was paramount. Revenge.

Domaine's FX had killed Fly and Miki sure as a bullet through the head. His world had been shattered. Virginia could walk away. She still had all this. He looked around the room.

"What are you going to do?" Virginia asked.

Valentine had finally stopped shaking. A single tear ran from his eye. It drew a bloody line down his cheek. No moment had ever seemed this cold or worthless. He wanted her to comfort him. But he knew she would not.

He paused for what seemed an eternity. Then the answer burbled out. "I'm going to kill him."

Virginia harnessed her fear. She must not let him stop it. She tried to come up with alternatives.

Valentine didn't want to hear.

Her voice was growing louder. Valentine could threaten Domaine. They could get more FX that way. Maybe they could kidnap him. The ransom could be paid in FX. Her voice still grew louder. Domaine would never tell the police. There was too much at stake. They would make a good team. Like Bonnie and Clyde.

Valentine covered his ears. He wanted to leave. He had to think. Work out how to kill Domaine. The passion of his death wish seemed the only reality left.

Virginia was walking towards him. She got closer and closer.

Valentine told her to stop. He still had the gun.

Virginia carried on walking. She couldn't let him leave. Not with the gun. She needed FX like she craved money or sex. She was a winner.

Valentine raised the gun.

She took no notice. Her hand stretched out. She clasped the gun barrel. "You're safe now," she whispered. Her lips pouted.

Valentine thought she wanted to kiss him. His eyes were swollen. He could barely see.

Then her knee jerked into his groin. Pain flashed through his body. She grappled for the pistol. He tried to shake her free. Fingernails gored his skin.

He tried to move his finger off the trigger. But she crushed it nearer. His flesh slipped on the grip.

He was drowning.

There was an explosion. One single shot.

Valentine could feel his finger on the trigger. He was still alive.

CHAPTER TWENTY-SIX

Valentine surfaced above the flashback. He tensed his index finger. It fluttered on the trigger. He braced himself. The desk dug into his groin.

Domaine hesitated. Still holding the bag. He could not envisage his own end. The evidence. The barrel of the gun. It made no difference. He could always close the file. Stop it. Dead. He tossed the bag across. It skimmed the desk.

Valentine glanced down. A flash of green. His fingers closed. Pincer-like movement. All the gear he needed. A line to make it right. This time it was not enough. He held the bag open.

Three photographs remained upturned. Difficult to decipher. Domaine clung to his control. He moved slowly. There would be no accident. He bared two of the glossy sheets. Both were pictures of death certificates. The handwriting spidery. A smudged signature. Macari. Male... Cause of death... suicide. The other was identical. Only one difference. Cause of death... Misadventure (Motor Vehicle Collision).

Subverting reality was easy. Domaine dealt in dreams. Any unfortunate crossover could be 'rescripted'.

Beads of sweat on his forehead. Sallow taste in his mouth. Domaine's repose was cracking. Valentine seemed unmoved.

Valentine's tension flowed through the Luger. There was no look of terror. No secret admiration. Veils of humanity peeled away. He was laughing. Laughing at Domaine. This reaction was unpredictable.

Domaine felt uneasy. He expected compassion. Regret. Fear of corporate muscle.

Valentine would not have the last laugh. There was too much at stake. Domaine turned over the last picture. Head card in the tarot. Predictions for the future. He breathed deeply. "It has all been ditched. Four thousand tons."

Valentine could taste vomit. The picture was of a steel container. No indication of size. No corporate logo. No destination marked. The letters were stencilled. Red. *Toxic Waste*. Tossed into the ocean. Buried in a pit. Out of sight. Out of mind. The where was unimportant. Power lay in the knowledge that it was gone.

Domaine rustled the photographs. Folded the printout. He held open the file. One last look. He snapped it shut. He had allowed Valentine entry to prove it was over. Any resistance was futile. He folded his arms, pressed his weight onto the file.

The onyx clock read twelve thirty. Time for lunch. There was only one loose end. Valentine.

Valentine opened the bag. He tipped it upside down. Crystals cascaded. The pile got larger and larger. A mountain of green.

Domaine raised an eyebrow. Whatever next? He tried to explain. So what if a few Ad men went crazy? It made the commercials more creative, more appealing. He never intended anyone to die. That was certainly regrettable. But there was no connection with him. He pressed harder on the file. FX had never caused death. Only pleasant delusion. Violence dwelled in everybody's head. Alcohol was an equally murderous catalyst.

Valentine placed the gun to Domaine's head. He blocked out the voice. "Public confidence is at stake."

He told Valentine to put the gun down. Walk away. It had gone too far.

Valentine was not listening. Revenge was not enough. His motives were entirely selfish. He spoke calmly. Words almost a whisper. Birdsong became machine gun fire, tap water blood. He did not care about the madness, 'saving the world'. It was not worth saving. There was one link Domaine had missed. He blustered, violent. "There is a dead girl. Jamaica Road."

Domaine shied from the barrel.

Valentine pushed closer. Virginia Nixon, shot through the head. The bag of FX in her hand.

It was twelve thirty. The police would be arriving. A phone call.

Running up Fleet Street. Crunching through the Isle of Dogs. She still had the questionnaire. The corporate logo. The police might not fry Domaine but the competition would.

It was still not enough. Valentine felt for the trigger. "You will never know."

Domaine always conquered fear. He could not lose. He picked up the telephone receiver. It was not too late. He would call Virginia up. Call security. Call the editor. But there was a shred of belief. What if Valentine *was* a murderer?

Valentine depressed the hook. No more dial tone. Dead. Domaine breathed heavily. He jerked off assurances. There would be no charges. A payoff. An antidote. Valentine could take the bag. A lifetime supply. Domaine squirmed. Repeating the mantra. He could not lose. He would not lose. All his power. Master over all. Show no fear.

Valentine grinned. He felt pleased. In a way, Domaine had won. Valentine was insane, destroyed. But there was no sadness. He saw fear in Domaine's eyes. Confronted with death, few are brave.

Domaine had a choice. Only one. "Why not do a line or two? *Or ten.*" Valentine cocked the gun.

Domaine shook his head. He restrapped his nerves. Grasped the table. White knuckled.

Valentine lowered the pistol. He could hear his heart. Thud. Thud. Thud.

Domaine tensed. Dark eyes met.

Valentine lunged. The free hand shot forward. He grabbed Domaine's hair. The head rammed into the desk. Face in the pile. Green crystals everywhere. In the atmosphere. Fluttering like dust. Domaine's arms grappled with the air. He would not inhale. His neck turned purple. Valentine drove harder. It was no use. He let go. Sucked for oxygen.

Domaine flew back into his chair. His eyes bulged. The flesh was dusty. Peppered green.

Valentine raised the Luger.

FX. The sweetener. The turkey at Christmas. The best. Like death.

Domaine yelped. Cornered like a rat.

Valentine squeezed the trigger. A shot rang out. Exploding. "You'll never know."

Domaine snapped back. His head jerked. Then still. The room was quiet.

A bell went off in Valentine's head. The whole world hummed with an intense vibration.

A blue car sailed down Praed Street. Passers-by hardly noticed. It was lunchtime. Bodies spilling out of doorways. Cheap sandwich bars. Office girls rustling luncheon vouchers. Slurping espresso machines.

Cruising at 65. Then a foot on the break. The car did not screech. It snarled. Opposite the black building. The engine was still running. Twelve thirty-five. Only minutes late. The driver looked across. Figures scattered through the foyer. Running. Marching.

An office junior had hit the alarm bell. What if he had been wrong about a gunshot. A car backfiring? The bespectacled manager shook him. He winced. An act of terrorism. It had to be.

People jammed for the corridor. Panic had set in. Clambering into lifts. There was no room. Steel doors snagged arms. Two fat security men blocked the main door, checking passes. Ex-police officers.

Three other uniformed men tore up the stairs. No one had called the police. It was against company policy.

Domaine's eyes were still open. Valentine dropped the pistol. It bounced on the carpet. He did not panic. He glanced at the body. The FX. The table. He felt no remorse. Maybe this was just another flashback.

The alarm bell rang in his ears. It was all real. He had to get out. Twelve thirty-seven. Maybe too late. He did not care anymore.

Valentine picked up the file. It was heavy. The weight of a lifetime.

He sucked in air. His cheeks puffed out. He blew as hard as he could. The jet of breath hit the desk top. Smashed the remains of the pile. A thousand crystals. Swirling in the air. Twitching to the floor. Speckling Domaine's clothing. His hands. His face. Green.

Valentine turned and ran. It was a childish gesture. Worthless for what it achieved. Valentine chuckled. The child was now free.

The driver raced the engine. People jostled from the glass door. Instinct said drive away. The foot hovered on the clutch. Dry in the throat. Five more minutes. That was all Valentine deserved.

Guards checked more passes. No sign of an assailant. No sign of a body. The foyer was full. "Bert?" "Harry?" The guards took no notice. "An orderly line. Please don't push." Cockney accents. "There is no need for alarm."

Valentine careered down the fire escape stairs. A spring in his step. He paused at the fire door. Pulled an envelope from the file. It was crumpled.

He opened the flap. Thinking on the run. The FX file slid inside. Photographs, too. He licked the gum. It tasted salty. The envelope was now sealed. Nobody would see the contents.

He shook his trousers. Sticky pieces of food fell away. This was no time for vanity. He bustled through the door, onto the main landing. Valentine charged for the lift. He pressed the button.

The lift was taking forever. His nervousness soared. What if they caught him?

He looked behind. A corridor of doors. All gaped open. No workers were left. Half-drunk cups of coffee. Telephones off the hook. It was a ghost town. A teleprinter still clicked. Where the fuck was the lift? "Come on, come on." He banged the shutter. He pressed his ear against the metal. There was a low rumble. The lift was coming.

Three security men burst into Domaine's office. He was slumped in his chair. A guard picked up the gun. "Mr. Domaine?"

One ran his finger along the table. Green dust?

Domaine's eyes were open. There was no blood. The three stood still.

Domaine slipped down. His lips moved. "A blank?"

The lift door slid open. Valentine marched out. He clutched the package. The crowd parted. His smell was bad.

He pushed himself forward. Angry Seniors ranted. They knew their position. They knew their rights. A steady stream of people. The door opening and closing. Then it was Valentine's turn. He held his breath. Somebody stopped the alarm.

Domaine was furious. "All he had were fucking blanks." He picked up the phone.

The receiver buzzed at Reception. Valentine stood still. The other guard wanted to answer it. People pushed him back. They wanted out. The phone still buzzed. The guard in front of Valentine floundered. "Wait a minute. Just wait a minute."

Outside, the driver heard the alarm stop. Still no sign. Hands gripped the wheel tighter. He must have been caught. When will they drag him out?

The guard stared at Valentine. Unshaven. Smelly. The burglar? The terrorist? The phone still buzzed. Thirty seconds. A minute. Valentine waved his yellow pass. Held up the package. He sensed the guard's mistrust. He had blown it.

Valentine spoke forcefully. "Look, I dropped off a message to Mr. Domaine. Picked up this package. It's urgent. That's probably Mr. Domaine now." He looked towards the phone. "It makes no difference to me. But Mr. Domaine likes things done yesterday. You pick up the phone. Tell him you stopped me. He can't fire a private contractor. What about you?"

The crowd was pushing harder. Valentine stood his ground. The other security man shouted. "Answer the phone, Harry."

Harry looked at the phone. Valentine. The security pass. The package. He thought about Domaine. He did not like him. Dispatch riders were invariably greasy. And he had a pass. Company regulation.

Harry shouted. "Wait a minute. No cause for alarm."

Valentine held his breath. He wanted to piss.

The crowd clamoured. "Let him through," Harry stuttered. He opened the door.

Valentine felt as light as air. He walked into the cool afternoon.

Domaine snarled. A man answered the phone. It was too late.

The car was waiting. Valentine tore down the steps. She flung the door open. Valentine jumped inside. Her foot slipped off the clutch. He tossed the file onto the back seat. It bounced onto the floor. The Karmann Ghia shot away.

Valentine was laughing. He looked at her. "Blanks." Virginia's laughter seemed feigned. She had heard the joke before. Courtney had screwed them all.

They were going faster. Along the Westway. Fifty. Gear shift. Sixty.

Virginia snarled. "What about the gear? The FX? Is it in the envelope?" She slowed down. Heading into Little Venice.

Valentine licked his lips. "The gear? There's no FX left."

Virginia pulled over, alongside the muddy moorings. She switched off the engine. "The FX. You promised. It was our deal." She picked up the envelope. Whining words. A scream. "Is it in here?"

Valentine sat silent.

"What is in here?" She fumbled with the flap.

Valentine opened the door. He stepped out. Looked along the water. The bobbing boats became huge steamers. Bodies torn in the paddle. Churning. Crunching. Blood. The sun beat down. Natives. Grass skirts. Swimming. Drowning. Going crazy.

A drum washed up on the beach. A steel container. The writing was stencilled. Red. *Toxic Waste.*

There was a rupture. An explosion. Green crystals spilled out. The water ran green. The whole world ran green.